WIN A LUXURY

DANONE
Being better every day

G000094967

Begin your New Year with the right resolution!

0% Fat

DANONE
Vitalinea

✂ -

Win a luxury weekend trip for 2 to The Lodge & Spa on Inchydoney Island, Co. Cork.
Relax in comfort whilst experiencing a range of health treatments. To be in with a chance
to win simply cut and post this to: Danone Promotion, FREEPOST, P.O. Box 8663, Dublin 2.

Lodge & Spa

at

Inchydoney Island

Your Name: _____

Your Address: _____

_____

_____

Telephone: _____ Mobile: _____

Email: _____

Competition Terms & Conditions: 1. The promotion is open to people over the age of 18, excluding Danone employees, their families,
agents or any other person connected with the promotion. 2. Entry into the draw is automatic on receipt of a completed entry form
from this promotion and other DANONE promotions linked to this draw. 3. Only fully completed applications on the original
application form will be accepted. 4. The prize is a voucher, which will entitle the winner to a weekend break for two people at The
Lodge & Spa on Inchydoney Island, Co. Cork. This voucher includes two nights Bed & Breakfast, one evening meal and six treatments.
Transportation to the Spa is not included. 5. No alternative prize will be given. No cash will be given in place of the prize.
6. Completed competition entries must be received by 30.07.2003. 7. Winner will be notified by post no later than the 31.08.2003.
8. The promoters reserve the right to alter the specification of the prize should that specified be unavailable for reasons beyond their
control. The alternative prize will be of equal value. 9. Defaced entries or illegible entries will not be accepted. Danone accepts no
responsibility for forms lost in the post. 10. All competition entries to Danone Promotion, FREEPOST, P.O. Box 8663, Dublin 2.

Class Act

Alison Norrington

POOLBEG

Published 2003
by Poolbeg Press Ltd
123 Grange Hill, Baldoyle
Dublin 13, Ireland
E-mail: poolbeg@poolbeg.com

© Alison Norrington 2003

The moral right of the author has been asserted.

Typesetting, layout, design © Poolbeg Group Services Ltd.

13 5 7 9 10 8 6 4 2

A catalogue record for this book is available from the British Library.

ISBN 1-84223-086-7

Cover Design by Slatter-Anderson
Photography © Powerstock
Typeset by Patricia Hope in Palatino 10/14
Printed by
Cox & Wyman
Reading, Berkshire

www.poolbeg.com

About the Author

Alison grew up in Brentwood, Essex and has spent the last two years living in Cullenstown, County Wexford, with her two young sons.

She is perpetually 31 and will continue to be so for as long as she can get away with it.

She has taken many evening classes and so is a qualified beauty therapist, an amateur linguist and a half-hearted pianist and gave up evening classes when she realised that she enjoyed the social aspects of "student life" much more than the academic.

Class Act is her first novel. She is currently working on her second.

Acknowledgements

This is, undoubtedly, harder to write than the whole book, so I'll keep it simple – (I hope!).

1998, the year this book was written, was one of those that passed by in a blur! Since then I have had an excellent support network as *Dirty Gertie's Thirty* matured into *Class Act*.

This wouldn't have been written without you, Mum. Thanks for your overwhelming, endless support, for reading when your eyes were already out on stalks and for innocently providing cracking one-liners. Your passion for broadening our horizons will always be with us – a priceless gift! And don't forget the tramp who helped you with the camcorder in Elephant & Castle!!

Thanks to my brother Ian for your vision, strength and encouragement (and some blinding London slang!). I admire your refusal to be pigeonholed and the way you are forever pushing the boundaries.

To Ryan & Conor – for enduring (or enjoying!) *every* episode of *Tom & Jerry*. Thanks for your humour, and love. For keeping me on my toes & for just being . . .

Thanks to my special friends – Martine, Allie, Sara,

Leigh, Lou, Kirsty, Belinda, Anita, Jeanette and Steve for your support, quotes, misdemeanours and for confiding your hideous moments – you know who you are!!

A special thanks has to go to Maite Miguel who, from Valencia, answered question after question at a time when she was extremely busy doing her "proper" job! I *will* get to see you soon.

Thank you to the unnamed lady who let me in on her piano evening class. It really was an amazing experience – and I'm sorry – I really *didn't* mean to laugh!

I was once told by one of the top UK literary agents that Poolbeg was an excellent place for nurturing the debut novelist – he was completely right. Thank you to Paula, Sarah and Georgina for your guidance, confidence and for believing in *Dirty Gertie*. Thank you to Anne for your advice and helping me to prepare for those awkward moments. And thank you to Gaye – your ability to retain humour during extremely busy and stressful times reminds us of our priorities in life.

Geraldine Nichol, my agent, is a delight to work with. Your enthusiasm and commitment, both to your work and to your family, are exemplary. You have made the fun times better and the hard times bearable. Your consistent guidance and ideas, enthusiasm and support have boosted me more times than you probably know. To my very own "Geri" – thank you.

Thanks to Ned for the overwhelming, unconditional support. And also for the constant flow of coffee, hot chocolate and toast! It hasn't been easy getting to *really* know me whilst I've been locked away writing for hours on end – but you've stuck by me through a very sad and hideous year. I reckon you're right – as usual – it can only get better, eh?

And lastly, but by no means least, thank you to Dad. Despite the thirteen years gone by, you still continue to inspire us and we are eternally grateful for your wit, sense of humour, mischief-mindedness and balance. xx

Love is a word
that cannot be heard
by those who are graced to have it.
Love is a word
that sings like a bird
for those who know they want it.
They say love
can be cruel and
love can be kind
but that's a whole
world away
when it's love you can't find.

IAN NORRINGTON

Chapter One

Fact: *I was an **unofficial** Geri before the arrival of any other famous Geris, official or otherwise, and the handle, Geri, was not attained overnight. No sooner had they slapped the life into my wrinkly blue arse and severed all umbilical attachment than I was landed with the name Geraldine Cumbers. I consequently endured years of cruel taunts and jibes at school, where I was dubbed everything from Gelatine to Germolene, Gerald to Raldy, Deanie to Eenie – heck, you know what kids are like.*

Fact: *This Geri is the miserable owner of heavy thighs, a 32B chest, and a new strain of body-fat that I have entitled PPF. Or Post-Pregnancy-Fat to those yet to procreate. Unlike the father of my two delightful but very small children, this PPF has stuck rigidly and limpet-like to Me.*

1

Fiction: *I've confidently mapped the rest of my life, am more than content with my lifestyle and sweaty with excitement for the future.*

Fiction: *I brim with confidence that I can successfully raise my two sons, given my new single-mum status. And then, of course, there's the plan to return to a career with ridiculously high pay.*

Fact: *I'm thirty in a week's time, and "head-in-the-sand" and "in denial" are expressions in the forefront of my mind, as I feel increasingly like "Incontinent-Pad-Queen" and "Meals-On-Wheels-Breath" . . .*

I stand gawking and gaping at my hideous reflection: post-pregnancy triangular flaps that once housed fine firm breasts, now hanging their heads in shame, nipples staring at the floor like reprimanded schoolboys. I reassure myself by insisting they're suffering from Post-Traumatic-Breasts-Disorder having been subjected to the trauma of breast-feeding my two sons. A loose cushion seems to have taken permanent residence on my tummy, clearly oblivious to the fact that the extra insulation is no longer needed as I have, in fact, given birth months ago and it should be long gone by now. Did you hear me? I said months ago! Begone, damn you!

Still, they say tenants have rights too, even if they're not paying rent.

* * *

Class Act

The year had begun with two disturbing and enlightening experiences: one concerning my reflection in the bedroom mirror and the other involving a "Dear John"— at best, Kevin's inadequate list of reasons for infidelity, left cowardly on the kitchen table. It seems he couldn't cope with my refusal to become his full-time servant. I did my best but I simply couldn't fill the role of his mother. The awarding of his own pint glass at The Horse & Groom had delighted him, but disgusted me. And I'd only infuriated him by calling the revered place The Gruesome Horse. This had since been revealed as a place with more than innocent refreshment experiences. It seems this is where he met her. Despite our history together: the joint purchase of an iron, nursing each other through illnesses (he'd had "Cupid's Itch" when I'd met him – hell, why hadn't that put me off?) and even the subsequent birth of two beautiful sons. We'd even discussed him visiting a Dick Doctor and having the snip so as to free-up our future sexual selves and start swinging from the rafters again. And now? And now she was the recipient of his sexual repertoire.

I suppose that alone should make me sympathetic . . .

"The only pounds you'll ever lose long-term are pounds, shillings and pence. I've told you that before, love." Cynthia's cocky tone instantly raised the hairs on the back of Geri's neck. The cracking of eggs frying in the thickly oiled pan did little to help her new-found willpower. Watching her mother hum tunelessly to the sounds of Melody FM, Geri picked up Reece's Thomas the Tank and began to wheel him along the worktop, unthinking.

"Hey, don't go scratching me Formica! I won't be replacing that before I pop me clogs so keep it nice, eh?"

"Sorry, Mum." Geri felt instantly eleven years old.

As Cynthia balanced the dripping fried eggs on the spatula and slapped them onto Geri's plate, she continued, "New Year, New Me. Didn't you say that last year too?"

Grimacing at the sight of the breakfast in front of her, Geri whispered,

"Probably, yeah."

"It won't bring Kevin back, you know."

"Why'd you have to say that? You know how badly this has affected me. It took me at least two months to even reach for my toothbrush."

"I know. Sorry, love."

"Look, Mum, the promise has been made, so I'm gonna try and stick to it."

"But when do you get the time these days for the design and production of a 'New Me'? It's not like them pre-pregnancy days, you know."

Geri knew she was right. Pre-children her life had held a safety net when it came to "sorting herself out once and for all" and "getting back on her feet". Treatments with a distinct feel-good-factor were always handled first, bringing out the hedonist in her. "To get my mind right," "to get in tune with my body" had been the justifications. Algae scrubs, massages, flotation-tank therapies, days at The Sanctuary and even the indulgence of weekends away at Hydro Springs had kicked off the new regimes.

Cynthia spoke again, her mouth swimming with greasy egg and brown sauce.

"If you ask me it's the last thing you should be thinking of. You've got two kiddies to raise. Surely finding a job's the first priority?"

Geri felt once again irritated by her irrational mother. Pushing the sloppy mess aimlessly around her plate she realised that now, with a severe lack of disposable income and with maternal commitments, she was faced with the nitty-gritty of beauty on a budget alongside a future heavy with single parenthood.

* * *

"Shit!" she cursed as she flicked the remote control to a less disturbing channel not involving fashion pundits, supermodels and masses of tanned sleek skin. Before she was pregnant everything had seemed fine. The little black dress was having its heyday, the feet of an entire nation were revelling in the open-toed comfort of the revival of mules, those yellowed toenails communally breathing for the first summer in years. And now? Now "they" were announcing that mules would be out this year and the stiletto back in. The bloody stiletto!

"No chance of breaking you back into the swing of things gently, is there?" she spat at the telly, bitter at how after months of sweat-free, flat-footed freedom she was expected, at the mere drop of a titfer, to squeeze her swollen size eights into the pointed ridiculousness of stilettos.

"Have you ever tried walking in those things after

years in flatties?" she challenged the clipboarded presenters.

At the time, each nine months of pregnancy had seemed like an eternity, with the tent-like dresses and kaftans which hung proudly from her milk-filled mammaries shielding from sight all bumps and lumps.

She hauled herself from the sofa and made for the kitchen, grabbing the last unopened packet of Chocolate HobNobs. She loved that there was no-one to glance sideways at her with that irritating one-eyebrow-raised expression. Re-entering the room, she noticed the twinkle of toddler mischief in Cameron's eyes as he noticed the biscuits.

"Beescits!" he squeaked, delighted.

"Wait till I sit down. God, nothing's sacred any more, is it?"

Oblivious to her possessiveness of the biscuits he grabbed the last two, leaving her with the ripped packaging and crumby remains in the bottom. As she flopped onto the sofa she glanced back at the ever-grinning, plastic TV presenter. As he gurned toward the camera he patronisingly confided that – well, you know how brown was the new black? And remember how, in the name of fashion, you had bought enough brown to put you seriously off chocolate for life? Well, hold onto your seats! Now "they" have taken it upon themselves, probably at some indulgent Perrier-and-ciabatta'd luncheon, to declare that pink is the new brown (that *was* the new black). Sometimes Geri yearned for the easy monotonous cloning of her school uniform.

Navy blue and white, week in, week out, for five years. It had felt like regimented hell at the time, what with Duran Duran, Spandau Ballet and Adam Ant screaming black eyeliner, and new-romantic frills, ruffles and pleats at you from every magazine page, but now she wished there was some kind of "uniform" she could fall back on. And *not* the new-mumsy-flouncy-cover-ups that she'd hidden herself in more recently. With her attention now distracted, she lay back, gazing at the ceiling, watching the shards of buttercup sunlight forming streaks on the white paint, and wondered,

How will I ever regain some kind of identity beyond motherhood?

Will I ever regain some kind of identity beyond motherhood?

Is there ever some kind of identity beyond motherhood?

Agnes b had been her favourite designer, pre-pregnancy (her life now being sectioned into two parts, every other landmark falling to the wayside). Feeling frumpy and bulky, Geri definitely felt more Evans than Agnes at the moment.

"Hey, you know, Cameron?" He looked up at her momentarily, his face coated with the melted chocolate and the HobNobby part left in tatters on the floor. "I'm actually sick of maternity clothes and the safety of soft comfy shoes."

He licked and sucked at the saturated biscuit base hoping to find more chocolate, totally uninterested in his twittering mother.

She continued regardless, "The pain of being a woman is very difficult to take on. The high chunky boots, Wonderbras, thigh-shapers and coloured contact lens were all born just after you were. And it seems I missed out on their arrival. Until now."

He didn't know and he didn't care. He played with his soft Winnie the Pooh, coating the bear's yellow fur in chocolate.

"Alongside the Internet and www-dots everywhere. You know, in my maternal state I'm nothing more than a corporate dinosaur."

Her complaining was disturbed as little Reece woke from his mid-morning sleep. She lurched to a standing position in her grey, over-washed holey leggings, one of Kevin's large denim shirts and her battered but hanging-on-in-there beachy mules that wouldn't recognise a grain of sand if it jumped up in front of them and danced the hula. She kicked them off in the hallway and skittered up the stairs to find that she'd arrived in time to simply re-plug Reece's dummy.

"Go in," she whispered as she tried to wiggle it back between his clenched lips. "Go in, will you!" As he finally resigned to the disturbance he opened his rosebud mouth, sparrow-fashion, and Geri slid his dummy back between his pinky gums.

"There. Best invention yet," she whispered into the half-lit room. This is enough to make him smile sleepily in his innocent slumber.

Cameron met her at the top of the stairs, having crawled his way to the top. She crouched to face him, then cradled him in her arms, carrying him back down the stairs with her.

"You know," she whispered close to his soft neck, "I do feel a bit guilty about the dummy thing. Especially in the shadow of mega-mums who boast how none of their lot would even *recognise* one. You'll both probably hate me in years to come as you despair at your pubescent appearance. I mean, isn't teenage acne, and boxer shorts livelier than a bag of kittens bad enough without buck-teeth knuckling in on the act too?"

Worse still, they might even adopt some awful, incurable sucking fetish.

Placing Cameron in front of the *Postman Pat* video once again, she padded down the hallway, pulling the bathroom door gently closed behind her, hearing it swish on the carpet as she did so. These days she was reduced to sitting on the loo for just a few minutes' "me" time. She stared down at her baggy, pink maternity knickers, the label screaming "Motherhood – Size 16/18" faded to near anonymity, her cellulite-sprinkled thighs starkly reflecting the white of the light bulb, with dazzling effect.

"Here I am, days from my 30th birthday. A bloody-sore-sight for bloody-sore-eyes . . ." On hearing her talking, Cameron appeared at the bathroom door and watched her, intrigued. "My post-pregnancy figure disappointingly samey," she shook her tummy in her hands and laughed as she told him, "making me the unfortunate owner of a shell-shocked birth canal and an extra three and a half stone."

Without warning he burst into tears and ran to her.

Still seated on the loo, she pulled him up onto her bare lap and cooed,

"Oh, yes, and two most gorgeous sons, but both of you under three!" She felt like a statistic – a sucker to the system, despite her passionate hopes and dreams.

Now, even worse, a rejected single parent.

An economically abused sucker to the system.

Something had to be done.

And fast.

* * *

Sinead couldn't hang on much longer. Her back arched beneath her as his sweaty white body thrust down on her.

She gasped, *"Ohmigod! Ah, ahhh, ahhh, oooh!"* her voice a loud rasp.

Encouraged by her noisy praise he upped the tempo to more of a fox-trot (not that she knew what speed a fox-trot was danced at – but she'd never seen a slow one). Mindlessly he bounced his hipbones off hers in an almost space-hopper fashion. She nearly giggled as she likened herself to one of the gross orange rubber bouncers that she'd jack-hammered her parents' lawn with twenty-five years ago. Coming back to reality, she started to get bored now. And she'd played this game for long enough. As any self-respecting girl would tell you. Enough really is enough. Time to put an end to this, and fast. Triggered by the boredom, she began acting out the finale. She screwed her eyes tight and clenched every possible muscle in the cheeks of her bum. She thought he'd notice that, being as his hands were buried somewhere beneath them.

10

"Oh Jesus! Neil, Neil, Neil! *Aaah, oooh, ooooh, oooooh . . .!*"

She tightened her body and stretched her back into another convincing arch, then relaxed, feigning exhaustion, beneath him. All was still and quiet in the clammy room. Then, as she peered at her watch, to her utter disgust and severe disappointment he continued with the hip-bouncing and panting. No! she thought to herself. She'd hoped that her faked orgasm would have been enough to end this fiasco. This travesty which had been bestowed upon her. Literally. This excuse for horizontal aerobics, walloping the mattress, bouncy-bouncy — although only the latter of these titles seemed even mildly appropriate for this encounter. Twenty minutes later she was congratulating herself, as she sat on her wicker chair smoking a Marlboro Light, on diplomatically getting rid of him with expressions of mock exhaustion and praise for his technique. In reality, "Is it in yet?" was an expression that insisted on leaping to mind as she had writhed and wiggled beneath his severely *lacking* technique. Stubbing out the cigarette she went for a shower, feeling unsatisfied and edgy. She felt a slight pang of guilt as she remembered the articles she'd read in women's magazines preaching how young women of today shouldn't need to fake orgasms. How "girl-power" and the likes had brought women into the twenty-first century riding on the wave of a huge and natural "O". Hell, hadn't everyone faked it at some time?

She was soon stepping out of the cool shower into

the stuffy room, her wet feet making slapping sounds on the smooth terracotta tiles. Irritated at the heat in the room, she cursed the air conditioning for failing again. These company apartments weren't quite what she'd expected them to be. She roughly dried herself and scrunched the bath-towel, dropping it on the floor of the archway between her kitchen and balcony. She was determined to put him out of her mind.

"Remember," she reminded herself aloud, "the best way to get over a bad lay is to get under a good one." As she rooted amongst the pigsty that served as her bedroom, she threw various items of light clothing across the room. They were her weekend clothes – this was a Monday morning and the gawdy red LCD numbers were flashing 8:28 at her. She was going to be late again!

Sinead was the very epitome of the clichéd success story. Already very financially comfortable before she'd reached thirty, she had found her platform on the career ladder and was working her way higher – driven furiously by the dreaded prospect of inheriting her father's bathroom and shower business. On this unusually stormy Monday morning in Buñol, she was unprepared for wet weather. As if trying to dodge the raindrops she ran out onto the cobbled street to her gleaming Mercedes SLK, thankful that she'd put the roof up last night. As a high-flyer in Finance her international assignment had been organised for an initial three years, and had recently been extended by another two. Her Spanish was now excellent and she enjoyed many benefits as an expatriate. As she sat in the driver's seat, the windscreen and interior mirror both steamed up immediately as if deliberately slowing her getaway. Settling herself in the seat, she threw her briefcase and bag onto the floor. An optimistic swipe with her sleeve temporarily and patchily cleared the steamed windows, so she started the car and turned the fan on full. It blew out cold on her legs and face, but she didn't care. She was too late for it to matter. The streets of Buñol were no strangers to her, and she steered confidently through the small villages that led her to her place of work in Valencia.

As she breezed in, assured and poised, through the air-conditioned offices, she noticed the empty desk of Eamon, her one colleague *and* friend.

Sinead's first encounter with Eamon had been an intensely embarrassing one, but had culminated in a fun, firm friendship. Sinead had only been resident in Valencia for a week when she'd been instructed to contact one of her colleagues in the Finance Department. The extension number she'd needed to ring was 2063. So she'd dialled. He'd replied,

"Two oh seeks tree; I'm on lernch."

"Christ!" she'd thought on his response. And put the phone down. Checking her watch she noticed that it was 11.42. He's at lunch? Already? With her confidence still a little shaky in her new surroundings, she'd decided to let the famished Spaniard have his lunch. She'd call him back later. However, she had always got the same reply: 3.35pm, 4.00pm, 10.23am, even 9.03am, the phone would ring a couple of times and then she'd hear, "Two oh seeks tree; I'm on lernch."

Initially Sinead had felt amazed that he was getting away with it. "And why answer his bloody phone if he's eating his lunch!" she'd say. This new-found joke had caused her much hilarity and, if nothing else, had succeeded in seeing her through her first few weeks. It had made her feel good to think she had a private joke that nobody else knew about. Almost as if it set her aside from the others and gave her back her identity in a faceless office. How *did* he get away with it though? Surely other people, even managers, must have rung him and heard this reply. And what about the other people in his office? Didn't they say anything to him about this? Sinead's bubble had been painfully and cringingly burst, however, a couple of weeks later. The dialling of 2063 had now become a habit just to confirm that he was still performing true to form, and she had totally forgotten the original reason for ringing him. She had dialled, ready for the speech: 2-0-6-3 . . .

"*Hola!* Eamon Lynch's phon."

Sinead was stopped in her tracks. Totally put off by this unexpected voice, accent and message, she was dumbstruck.

"*Hola?*"

"Er – um. – hello?" she'd managed at last.

"Hello! Oooo ees speaking, pleease?"

"Um. Hello. Erm. *Whose* phone did you say this was?"

"Haa! You not know who you reeenging?"

"Yes, I do – just checking. Who did you say?"

"Eamon Lynch. He on 'olidays theese week. Can I 'elp?"

"Em – er – no. Thanks."

Eamon-bloody-Lynch!! I'm on lernch! I'm on lernch, Eamon Lynch, I'm on lernch, Eamon Lynch! What a damned fool she'd been making of herself. He wasn't bloody Spanish; he was Irish! An expat like herself! She'd felt so sick that afternoon that she'd left early and had returned to her apartment, embarrassed at her pathetic misconception. But that had been years ago . . .

* * *

What had begun, this morning, as a humid stormy day soon dissolved into the typical scorcher that Sinead had got to expect. Having worked an extra hour today, in a futile attempt to drive away any gossip that Neil may have spread, she was now pleased to be back at her apartment. She lay languorously in her bath amid huge cloud-like bubbles, each one filling the scented warm bathroom with exotic aromas. Feeling more detached from the morning's debauchery now, she thought back to how she'd faked the experience with Neil, resenting herself for being so shallow and hating herself for inviting a work colleague back to her apartment. She didn't want to start getting a name for herself at work and vowed to be more selective in the future. The men were bitchier than the women.

The truth was she was bored with the nine-to-five and the groomed professionalism that her high-powered, high-paid job demanded. She'd many times decided to resign and had spent numerous hours (paid, of course) scribing her resignation letter, incriminating all the right people. She wondered what it was about writing your resignation letter that immediately transformed everyone you'd despised for the last six months into instant soul mates, a total metamorphosis beyond the wildest capabilities of even Mother Nature herself. She'd dreamt of how she'd make sure old Clarkey's name was down as a vegetarian for the next official Finance Seminar in Madrid, given his distaste for vegetables, and so humiliating him amongst his peers both in Spain and London.

However, the humour always dispersed and the smile slid off her face when she thought of home. Her two homes. Her birthplace, Kilkenny, and her sister, her friends, her parents. And her adopted home, Elephant & Castle, London, and her school-friends, her college friends, her workmates. Her cat. The shops! Here in Valencia she had a handful of girlfriends from other offices, mainly girls who had re-located to Valencia with the company, and also a few local girls; but few friends in her office. Apart from Eamon. A good Irish name too, just like her own. She felt an allegiance to Eamon as they'd discussed colcannon, Guinness and St. Stephen's Green in great detail. She had to admit though, she missed her loyal friend Gertie, in Elephant & Castle, most of all. Even a hundred Eamons couldn't make up for her!

Chapter Two

Reece and Cameron were, remarkably and unusually, thought Geri, sleeping and *EastEnders* had *only just* ended! Amazed at her good fortune, she stretched out onto the sofa, leafing through a back issue of *Marie Claire*, trying to ignore the niggle that the washing was still sitting in the oily, cold water in the sink.

"Here I am now, only two days away from the milestone 30, and nothing has changed except my point of view," she sighed into the empty room, the buzzing still in her ears from the shenanigans of pre-bedtime play. Just after tucking them into their beds, she'd tiptoed into her now overly large bedroom to get into her comforting thermal pyjamas and was now stuffing her face with raisins. The raisins had become a habit she found difficult to break, her fetish for them starting over two years ago, all in the name of Rosemary Conley, who was now long forgotten, unlike the raisins. As she flicked the pages idly, her cheeks dimpled with the strain of a mouthful, she pondered over the state of her reflection as she'd undressed. She distressed herself wondering if buxom Page 3 girls had thick red welty bra-marks around their boobs when they took off their bras, just like she had. She subconsciously ran her hand over her beanbag of a stomach feeling it move with her, contemplating the humiliation of any future sexual relations. Could *any* woman stand confident in front of a mirror, naked, free from all red tell-tale marks, she mused. Would a stranger be able to tell what she'd been wearing from the red rivet and pocket-marks around her stomach and hips from too-tight jeans? Criss-cross patterns under and over boobs from digging-in bras? Her disgust and self-loathing were rudely interrupted by the telephone ringing, threatening to disturb her evening of self-deprecation. She silenced it with a grab.

"Hello?" she whispered, fearful of sounds of life from upstairs.

"Geri? Don't tell me they're asleep already?"

Geri smiled at her success. "Yep! The two of them. Reece went up at seven, and Cameron at twenty-past."

"God, that's got to be a first. Well done, love! What are you doing?"

Unwilling to bear the brunt of any remarks her mother might make about her indulgence in the raisin-department, she chose only to explain her idle magazine-leafing. Wriggling to make herself more comfortable, for what she hoped could be a lengthy chat, she propped

18

the hand-piece between her chin and shoulder as she snuggled into position.

"Guess what I bought today?" Cynthia asked, excitedly.

Geri's mum was always buying *something*. She was unashamedly into gadgets, as if the twentieth century had just caught up with her, and she revelled in reading up and researching all the latest quirks. Geri had started to become a little disturbed at her mother's infatuation with gadgetry; finding a chunky pile of mini-catalogues wedged in one of her kitchen drawers last week had been only the tip of the iceberg. While Cynthia had played grandmotherly with Reece and Cameron, Geri had flicked through them, interested. Amateurish photographs and captions advertised a large sheepskin slipper that you put *both* feet into, an electronic potato peeler, a battery-operated nose-hair trimmer, glasses whose lenses folded down one at a time, enabling you to apply your eye make-up whilst still recognising yourself. It wasn't until she reached the order form that Geri's heart missed a beat – half of it was missing, implying that her mum had actually *made* an order.

She had called out, "Mum! These catalogues – what've you ordered from them?"

Cynthia had entered the kitchen, her set hair askew and her face ruddy, but smiling excitedly.

"Oh, Geri. I meant to show you!" And grabbing the catalogue, she'd begun to flick the pages knowingly. "Look! Page three – the shoehorn; page seven – the earmuffs; page fifteen – the massager, page –"

Geri grabbed the catalogue and flicked back to page fifteen, staring incredulously at the "massager".

"Massager! Massager! Mum, that's not a massager!"

"Course it is, look, that lady there's rubbing it on her shoulders, and read it, it says – battery-operated massager, supplied with long handle for those difficult-to-reach places."

"Mum. Look, I'm sorry to say this, but – but, Mum. *That's a vibrator!*"

"A what?"

She handed the catalogue back to her mum. "A vibrator."

Cynthia began to laugh, "Oh Geri, don't be so daft. Course it's not! It *says* it's a massager." She tucked the catalogue back into the drawer safely, turning to Geri as the kettle clicked off, buffeting steam across the kitchen, "Anyway," she smirked, "what would *you* know about such things, young lady?"

Geri reddened, eleven again, then skulked out of the kitchen. There was just no telling her mum.

So here was Cynthia on the telephone now, waiting to enlighten Geri as to her most recent purchase.

"Well, see if you can guess! I bought it from The Power Store and it was just under two hundred pounds."

"Two hundred quid!" Geri sprayed raisins. "Where'd you get that kind of money?"

"Never mind, dear. Just guess."

"Dunno," Geri shrugged to herself, making the phone slip from its precarious balance under her chin onto the carpet.

As she reached over to pick it from the floor her mother was still rambling, "The ones with the cylindrical drum and all that technology attached. Can you guess?"

"What? No. Mum, what is it?"

"One of those Dyson vacuum thingies!"

"Oh great." Geri felt despondent that her mum seemed determined to draw her into the lifestyle of a housewife, forcing it to be even more boring than it already was.

Cynthia continued, regardless, "It's really great, you know, Geri – they're calling it the hoover that doesn't use a bag!"

Geri's face lit up wickedly, her mind working overtime, as she responded with great mirth and pride at her wittiness, "Oh great, Mum! So you *could* say that you've gone from a Bag That Doesn't Use A Hoover, to a Hoover That Doesn't Use A Bag!"

At that point the conversation was swiftly ended in a disgruntled and offended tone and, only seconds later, Geri replaced the receiver knowing that it'd probably take her loads of chocolate and visits with the kiddies to even start to win her mum round again.

She flopped back onto the settee, shaking her head despairingly.

"I didn't *mean* to imply that she kept a dirty house!" she sighed, once again, into the uncomfortable silence as she squirmed to find her comfortable position on the sofa. She pushed her hand down the side of the cushion, inadvertently pulling at a slip of paper that may have been wedged down there for years. Seeing its dog-eared and crumb-and-chocolate coated exterior, she sat upright, feeling depressed as she realised that it was a diary that she'd started writing to herself when she'd noticed the first signals that her marriage with Kevin was heading for disaster.

> I've decided to do my own thing with my life. He's not bothered about us and never asks how our day's been. Talking to him is like pulling teeth, but more painful.
>
> What's worse, it hasn't made a difference! I've realised that all I've been fighting for, is only what *I* want! It's like waking up and cleaning the house from top to bottom for years. Then one day you're so exhausted by it, that you don't do it. And the next, and the next, and the next. And nobody notices. Or cares. It's then you realise you've only been doing it for yourself and your children. And I thought this was supposed to be a partnership! . . .

So much for an evening to herself. Now heavy with depression and burdened with memories of her unsuccessful marriage, Geri resigned herself to bed.

It's strange you know. I'm angry at Kevin for being so neglectful of me – of us. I'm hurt and humiliated that he had the affair, but whilst I'm feeling let down I also miss him. I was a 'lifer' with Kevin – in it for life – for the duration. Now there's a big piece missing and I'm left feeling inadequate. I mean, am I really equipped to raise two children alone? Do I have what it takes to be a single mum? I'm not sure I have the required strength and courage to go it alone. But hey, what bloody choice do I have?

* * *

She awoke the next morning with a renewed spring in her step, a good night's sleep paying dividends, with the additional bonus that the boys had slept right through until 5.30am, an achievement by any standards. As she brushed her teeth, the insides of her head rattling to the beat of her electric toothbrush, she made a decision. Nodding at herself in the mirror, white foam escaping from the corners of her mouth, she smiled as she planned how she would re-invent herself and get out there, and meet a new man. Not just a 'new man' as in comparison to the old ones she'd met, but an official 'New Man' as in the species that cook, clean, sew for you and bring in your Tampax on a velvet cushion. Her mind buzzed with the anticipation of it.

And don't we bloody deserve it? Everyone deserves happiness! The boys deserve a decent male role model and I refuse to sit and mope over that bastard Kevin.

Certainly it meant she'd have to give serious consideration to a diet of some description and it would mean calling on Mum to baby-sit for her occasionally, but this morning nothing was a hurdle to Geri Cumbers. Charging around the lounge floor on all fours at 9.45, Cameron riding on her back, pony-style, she had one ear cocked listening to an American chatshow. She listened as a man preached to the rowdy audience how he'd bought a car thinking it the most gorgeous thing he'd had. "I nurtured it and enjoyed driving it for the first year, then over the period of the next year I'd started to get bored with it. It wasn't the car I'd expected it to be. So I sold it and moved on to what I really wanted. This is the same with partners . . ." The audience began to stir noisily in disagreement. Then an over-made-up woman piped up. Geri strained her neck to watch her, whilst being jarred and nudged.

"That's all well and good, my love, but if you were buying a house, instead of that car of yours, you'd spend a lot of time and money on researching mortgage lenders and getting surveyors to look at properties to value and recommend on them. We don't do this with partners. A mortgage is a 25-year commitment, a partnership supposedly for a lifetime, but we don't spend the same concerted effort over partnership matching. Right?"

As the host struggled to calm his audience Geri struggled to her feet and went into the kitchen, leaving Cameron to play.

That's it then. Letting hearts rule heads should have been abolished along with line dancing.

As she ran hot water into the sink she suddenly realised that every man she'd ever been in a relationship with she'd met in pubs or clubs.

"Surely it stands to reason then," she explained to herself excitedly, "that I need to meet my next one somewhere different." As she thought aloud it became obvious. "The music in the clubs is *so* loud it's virtually impossible to understand what they're saying to you unless you're brilliant at lip-reading, the lighting so dim and coloured with rainbow-flashes of neon that the word complexion doesn't even spring to mind, and considerable amounts of alcohol blur your common sense." These cigarette-smoke-ravaged clubs were the places she'd found herself in her hunt for Mr OK-But-Not-Perfect, But-Who-Wants-Perfect-Anyway! No surprise then, in hindsight, at her sheer horror, disgust and amazement in the inadequate months that followed to find her conquests totally annoying with ant-sized personalities, or unbearably unhygienic.

As she gathered mountains of dirty T-shirts, bibs, joggers and vests for the wash, she made a mental note to try and find some information on places to go to meet suitable male counterparts, reminding herself to call into the Library and pick up some leaflets on social events and stuff and look in the local paper.

* * *

Two days later and it was *the* dreaded day. Geri woke at 4am to a quiet house. No fanfare or early-morning cuddles, although her sex-life had for a long time been her ex-life and she was even more worried to admit, she didn't even *miss* it any more. With the boys still sound asleep, she tiptoed downstairs to the rapping of the rain on the front door.

Yeah, only the rain raps on the door with any enthusiasm these days.

In her melancholy, feel-sorry-for-me mood she switched off the outside light, and padded through to the lounge, for the Opening of the Curtains ceremony. It seemed so pointless now with Kevin gone. Wake up, open the curtains in the lounge, the dining-room, the kitchen, two bedrooms and bathroom – then at the end of the same day, go around and close them all.

For God's sake, pull yourself together. Isn't turning thirty bad enough without all this bullshit too?

Shortly after, the post plopped onto the doormat. Immediately she could tell by the writing on the envelopes who they were from. One from Mum, a couple from aunts, five from friends,

Not bad, they nearly all forgot last year, must be the "thirty" thing. And then she saw it. She knew immediately who it was from by both the writing and the name: *To Gertie Cumbers*. There was only one person in the world who called her Gertie: Sinead. As she flipped the envelope over, stroking its smoothness with affection, she noted what Sinead had written on the back: *"Dirty Gertie's Thirty!!"* As if it was something to be proud of and, shit, now even the postman knew! Her mind awash with wistfulness for their friendship and a longing for Sinead's company, she recalled the fun they'd had.

She smiled as she remembered the time, after much brazenness and alcohol, they'd managed to gatecrash a party only to find it was a Wedding Party. They were hysterical at the fact that everybody probably thought that *somebody* knew who they were. It was then that their old favourite song of "Ooops Up Side Your Head" came on. Full of effervescence, and fuelled by Tia

Maria, they'd screamed, *"Yeahhh, come on, everyone! Oh Gert, I just love this one!"*

"Iwannabeatthefrooooont!!!"

Slumping clumsily into the required splayed-legs position they shouted commands to the trail of "rowers" behind them.

"Totheside, clap, totheside, clap, goround, goround, goround, woah!! Row, clap, row, clap, noweverybody!!! Front, clap, back, clap, front, clap, back, clap, totheside, clap, totheside, clap, row, clap, row, clap, oops up side your head, row, clap! Isaaaaaiiid, oops up side your head, front, clap, front, clap!"

Their faces red and hideously distorted with excitement, it was at that point Sinead had turned to Geri in drunken camaraderie and her expression froze, the commands hanging in the air.

"Whassup? Sinead?" Geri had screamed, her internal organs hopping to the loud beat.

Startled by the sudden change Geri had looked behind *her* to see that they were the only two idiots "dancing" and that the wedding guests were staring at their alien behaviour in amazement. To add insult to pretty painful injury they then realised, as they'd sheepishly struggled to stand, that they'd sat in a huge puddle of lager which had soaked through Geri's white jeans leaving an inappropriate stain.

Geri grinned, remembering. Her depressed birthday mood lifted as she recalled the fun they'd had together. Time after time they'd been outrageous and got away with it. They'd taken stink bombs into discos and dropped them from balconies during the "erection-section" of slow dances; they'd sneaked bottles of wine into bars when they'd been skint but desperate for a night out, hiding them in the cistern and frequenting the loos repeatedly for top-ups; and had caused a riot in more than a few places all in the name of fun.

They once developed a sicko type of game Sinead had entitled "Wawayerb", due to its initials WWYRB, where they verbally backed each other into a corner, demanding, "What Would You Rather Be?" forcing the other to choose between two potentially revolting experiences. They'd go along the lines of: "What Would You Rather Be? A small piece of rotting food stuck between two of Shane McGowan's few black teeth . . . OR . . . a fly buzzing round and settling right on a cow's bum-hole?" Or "What Would You Rather Be? A bum-hair lodged between the odorous cheeks of Eddie Royle, of *The Royle Family* fame . . . OR . . . a piece of toe-jam stuck under the yellow nail of Forrest Gump?" Sometimes they changed the subject matter a little, diversifying with WWYRD, which consisted of "What Would You Rather Do?" and examples would be "WWYRD? Lick a blanket of splattered flies off of a hot car bonnet . . . OR . . . kiss Barry Humphries, tongues and all, for at least five minutes?" Cries of disgust and *'aaargh, yeeuch, nooooo!'* would not be accepted, so a decision would be cajoled and coerced out of each other as they were forced to choose one obnoxious experience over the other. They'd sat up all night on many occasions and cried together, confiding in each other on the most personal of subjects; they'd stood on the box at Speakers' Corner in Hyde Park and tried to put the world to rights. They'd laughed until they cried when the Headmaster of their school had called them up in front of the school in its entirety to reproach them for tying Mr White's shoelaces together, resulting in him falling and breaking his arm. The humour of the experience itself was hard enough to contain but was deemed impossible when the Head(-Ache), mid-flow of the tongue-lashing, misread Geri's name as *Gertie*. Hence, the name Gertie had stuck with her, at least as far as Sinead was concerned.

Now, tearing at the well-travelled envelope, Geri agitated the stiff cardboard and pulled the card out.

The inscription read:

> *To GERTIE,*
> *Hope you enjoy your 30th with*
> *passion, attitude and alcohol.*
>
>
> *Lots of love, hasta luego, mi amiga!"*
>
>
> *Sinead*
> *xxx*   *PS: I'll ring you . . .*

This was the birthday card to change everything.
Those three words.

So inconspicuous and innocent-looking and none of them over nine letters long. But the impact they made on Geri's day was huge and irreversible.

Passion.   *Attitude.*   *Alcohol.*

Three things that used to inhabit her personality

daily. No security passes or ID required. They were known, well-known, accepted and appreciated. They were popular and desirable, without being pushy. They epitomised Geri. *Geri*. Geri-the-fun-one, Geri-who-always-knew-where-to-go, Geri-the-hostess, Geri-the-artist, Geri-the-one-with-an-opinion-on-everything! Translations of these words included zeal, emotion, enthusiasm, animation, ideas, thoughts, and opinion. Words that had personified her. But, she sighed, a "Geri" that she only recognised now in old dog-eared and yellowing photographs. A Geri that she'd long forgotten and suddenly realised that she missed terribly. Nostalgia overwhelmed her as she sat reminiscing dolefully. Suddenly an emptiness that she couldn't explain engulfed her. The 'before' and 'after' shots crystal-clear now, signifying the Pre-Pregnancy Geri versus the Post-Pregnancy one, the happily married Geri versus the abandoned and inadequate one. Sinead had remembered her birthday, as usual, but her words were still clanging with a resonance that Geri was finding hard to accept. She was overwhelmed with the feeling that she wanted to restart her life from *now*. The recognition that nothing could be done to rewrite the past, more importantly the last four years, dawned and whilst she felt fulfilled and refreshed in a different way with the children, she knew she just *had* to map out a blueprint of her life from today.

Just give me a bit of time to think about it.

* * *

"There, now smile please." Sinead spoke to her reflection as she stood at the bathroom sink putting the final touches to her make-up. The refined, relaxed image looking back at her was no match for the insecure loneliness that lurked dully inside. She felt ashamedly lonely. Successful, well-off, independent, professional even, but very lonely. Sweeping her shoulder-length hair up into a swirl, she grabbed her comb and secured it loosely, with a hand of experience and familiarity. She grabbed her bag (forgetting how she had pondered over the very same only a few weeks ago and had spent nearly an hour wondering who ruled that the smaller the bag the higher the price) and rummaged for her car keys.

The master of getting in and out of cars without flashing her lacy lingerie, she paused, seated in the leather seat. With renewed vigour she pulled the half-empty Marlboro packet from the otherwise empty glove compartment, before starting the ignition. She pulled rebelliously on a cigarette, enjoying the warm feeling as her lungs filled with the nicotine.

"Hell," she said, "what harm will it do? I'd never drink and drive, and drugs don't appeal to me." The prospect of becoming dependent on them had been enough to put her off that one. Wasn't that why she'd never had a real, long-lasting relationship, for the fear of dependency? Enough of that at the end of a long day, she scolded herself. She straightened her suit, pushed the gear-stick into position, and roared onto the main road from Buñol to Valencia. As she drove, listening to the Red Hot Chilli Peppers her thoughts turned to Gertie. Smiling as she drove, she recalled fun-filled memories of their respective first sexual encounters and catalogue of scandals, one significant enough to enhance her friend from being just Gertie to *Dirty* Gertie. She delighted in the reminiscence of their closeness, a friendship where *nothing* was a secret. Zooming into the present she wondered where Kevin would be taking Geri for her thirtieth, and how they'd be celebrating as a family. She felt a pang of jealousy at Gertie's world. She had a beautiful family, a supportive partner, a lovely home. She wondered what else Geri could possibly want in life. OK, so they weren't exactly rolling in the readies, but what price love? What price security? Recently it seemed to Sinead that her friends were settling down in monogamous (monotonous) relationships and, God forbid, even having children. She wanted to know so much, like "Is it really like shitting a football?" and "Does breastfeeding de-sensitise your nipples?", and even "Are you really left with two empty beanbags for tits?" She'd posted the birthday card earlier in the week and had made a mental note to call Gertie tomorrow evening, to find out where they'd gone to celebrate tonight and maybe for some answers to those awkward questions.

By the time she arrived at the restaurant it was packed. The Mediterranean odour of garlic cooking blanketed the air and people sat excitedly waiting for their meals, sipping on their wine and contributing to the soft chatter of polite conversation. Sinead sat alone, waiting for Xavier to arrive. As she sipped on her red wine she gazed around the restaurant watching the diners, lovers, colleagues enjoying their evening. She was momentarily distracted by a large oil painting of a Gloucester Old Spot and Middle White tucking in, most vigorously, to a deep trough of what she imagined to be pigswill, although she wasn't sure quite what it was. As she thought how inappropriate the picture was in the restaurant her glance dropped to the portly gentleman sitting at the table beneath the picture, his mouth agape and stretched ready for the forthcoming fork, laden with pork chops in sauce. The inhumanity of it made her shudder. Xavier interrupted her thoughts as he scraped his chair on the terracotta tiles to seat himself. His dark brown, almost black, eyes glinted, competing with his white Colgate smile. Instantly all thoughts of pigs and paintings were melted into oblivion, as Sinead pulled her chair in closer. She checked her watch, wondering just how long she'd be able to wait until she got him back to her place, her bed, but Xavier took this as a hint at his untimeliness.

"I am late?" he asked, his voice husky and apologetic.

"Ah, sure, just a few minutes. No matter." She felt entranced at his handsomeness and was finding it difficult to continue conducting herself with any degree of normality.

Her idiotic expression made Xavier feel uncomfortable, putting him instantly on the defensive, "You 'ave problem with me being late?"

"No!" she replied, attempting to pull herself together.

33

However, the cocktail of Sinead's hypnotic state and Xavier's overwhelming insecurity resulted in one of those heady evenings doomed to be a disaster from the start. He ordered *arroz negro*, a rice dish cooked with squid, complete with its ink which gave the dish its colour, and had gone on to dribble it down his chin, making Sinead feel desperately sick. After only forty minutes of stilted conversation they'd finished their meal, wiped their chins, split the bill down the middle (bastard!) and were returning home. In separate ways. Alone.

"Sod him!" She reassured herself that he was probably lousy in bed anyway, and reminded herself how she'd felt after the Neil experience. She picked up her mobile and dialled the numbers of some work colleagues to invite them around to her apartment for a girls' night in.

"Bring a few bottles and *tapas* and stuff. Come on," she'd persuaded. "Let's have some fun tonight!" And "Don't forget to bring your lace camisole that you said you'd let me borrow!" to Isabella.

* * *

As birthdays go, it hadn't been the best. It wasn't even up there with the top twenty. Still, the new rug felt fluffy and soft against her face despite its rubbery new smell and the fact its woollen fibres were itching her cheek a little. She lay unashamedly on it – it was the only present she'd got and she was making the most of it. It had taken her two hours of intense persuasion to get Cynthia to buy it for her in the first place.

Kevin would have hated this. All those bright colours and swirly shapes wouldn't have fitted in with his regimented ideas at all. Makes me love it even more.

She'd finally got the children to bed amidst three hours of crying, screaming, and tantrums (and that was only Geri) and as she relaxed, lying on her new rug with a drink, she toasted her birthday. Not quite what she was used to on her birthdays of the past, but a bittersweet acceptance washed over her about her 30 milestone. She was discontented at the day she'd had and reflected on the term, 'many happy returns'.

What does that mean anyway? And that crap about life beginning at thirty, and all kind of other over-used clichés that we've heard a million times before?

Three glasses of Jacob's Creek and half a packet of Dutch-crackers-drenched-in-Nutella later, she was vegetating in a slumped state, in front of the television. She was jolted back into reality as she realised what she'd just started to watch: *Crimewatch UK*. She hated herself for being scared of watching *Crimewatch*. It interfered in a disturbing way with her level-headedness, urging her to switch the telly off and go up to bed, but she always found herself rooted to the settee afraid of running into their bedroom in the dark. She always found that the black and white computer photo-fits seemed, through squinted eyes, to resemble either Ann Widdicombe or Tony Blair – a thought that was even more disturbing than the programme itself. She wasn't long into her transfixed state before the phone started to ring. Grateful for the release from the gaudy photo-

gits, she picked it up immediately and was deafened by the raucous laughter being transmitted down the line.

"Hello?"

"Gertie, me old darling! Happy Birthday! Come on, girls, sing it now! *Happy Birthday to you, Happy Birthday to you, Happy Birthday, dear Gertie, Happy Birthday to you!!* Thirty today, Gertie! Old Dirty Gertie! I love you, Gertie! Happy Birthday! How's your day been? Surprised you're not all out celebrating. Was going to ring you tomorrow night but couldn't resist speaking to you on the actual day!"

Recognising the slurring voice and screeching tones, she realised immediately that Sinead was drunk. Momentarily she was a little confused, until it occurred to her that Sinead knew *nothing* of Kevin leaving and her sorry state of abandonment.

God, do we have a lot to catch up on!

"Gertie? You still there?"

"Yeah. Yeah. I'm still here. Thanks for your card." In that split-second Geri knew she couldn't shatter Sinead's hazy illusion of the perfect marital dream and, as her stomach churned with the deception, she decided to lie outright.

"Is that all you can say, thanks for the bloody card! You don't sound very birthday-ish. Are you just out the door or what?"

"Oh no. We're not going out tonight – no, Mum's taking the boys for the weekend so we can have some *real* good celebrations."

"Good on ya! Still keeping that randy git under control, I hope – don't want another godson in nine months' time, you know! Ha, ha, might be twins next time!"

Geri realised that this was going to be harder than she'd thought and, feeling the bubbly stirrings of her emotional volcano about to erupt, took a deep breath and closed her eyes. "Don't you know I can't keep him off me! It's killing me what with trying to look after Reece and Cameron *and* Kevin's needs, if you know what I mean!" A heavy tear came to her eye and the first she knew of it was when it splashed onto her cheek, bringing with it a long line of others.

Sinead cackled. "Told you he was a randy git! He was the same at college. God, you must be knackered."

"Yeah."

"You know, you wanna hand the boys over to your mam for a week and come out here. A bit of sun would do you good, relax you."

Geri mentally jumped at the idea of a week alone, until Sinead continued,

"Mind you, you know how the sun turns fellas into dogs on heat. He'd probably keep you in the apartment for the week!"

Geri decided that she'd just brave it out rather than depress Sinead with her ramblings. "You're having such a laugh there, aren't you? I'm dead jealous, you know. All that sunshine and culture and Mediterranean food and drink. I'd love to be there with you drinking and mucking about."

Sinead was on the verge of explaining how an evening with her workmates wasn't all it was cracked up to be, and had only come about because of yet another disastrous date. But something inside her couldn't quite break Geri's watercoloured picture of perfection.

"Yeah, it's great. And the fellas are just gorgeous. All-over suntans – I can't even ask to see their white bits!"

"Why? You normally do."

"Geri babe, they don't *have* any!"

"Get off!"

"Really. All-over tans. And I mean – all over. You know, it's a shame you can't get over here without Kevin. I'd love to take you round and show you the local talent. It's an eye-opener."

Geri's enthusiasm began to return. "Well, I suppose I could get away for a week. You know how easy-going he is – I'm sure he wouldn't mind."

"Oh no, now don't be so mean. If you're coming, bring Kevin with you. As much of a pain-in-the-arse as he is, you know how I love annoying him."

"Oh, yeah. Right." Feeling the tears stinging her eyes and realising how wet her cheeks were from them, Geri realised it was time to cut the conversation short.

"Look, Sinead, thanks for ringing. It's great to hear from you, and great to hear you're so happy."

"Yeah," Sinead's voice sank a little, "dead happy."

Geri knew she had to get off the phone, before her voice began to crack. Both of them were so busy trying to keep the lid on their own emotions, each failed to notice how the other had gone rather quiet and distant.

"Look," said Geri, "I'll ring you next weekend."

Coming back to life a little, Sinead kicked the vibrancy back into her voice, "Great, and I'll talk to ya then."

"Thanks. Hey, love ya!"

"Love you too."

Before Geri had even replaced the handset, a sob caught in her throat. She gave in to it and forgot the old saying about crying on your birthday and crying all year round. Crying, she returned to the loneliness of her kitchen where discontentment and guilt gnawed away at her. She plunged her hands into the bubbles and, grabbing the nylon brush, scrubbed angrily at Reece's milk bottles and teats in the warm soapy water, realising that she hated herself. She felt terrible for lying to Sinead. Her bestest best friend in the world and she'd had to lie. She knew she should have come clean there and then – it's always so much harder afterwards.

You know, this putting on the brave face isn't all it's cracked up to be.

As she tried to console herself she spat, bitter and tearful, "So, when is a lie not a lie? When it's only a *mild* distortion of the truth? When it's said to spare someone's feelings? I know Sinead would feel terrible for bringing up the subject and putting her hooves into it." *Am I the only one with a double entendre of consciences when it came to lying?* "The truth of it is that when your conscience has taken a weekend-break, and when the cat's away . . . it's actually quite *fun* to lie – I'm embarrassed to admit!" she scolded the baby's bottles viciously.

She had found it sometimes refreshing, even self-indulgent, to slightly change the truth of her suburban marital life. It was almost therapeutic to alter the outcome of events, albeit only verbally. She remembered recalling a particularly uneventful girls' night out to Kevin and how she'd lied. It had felt so much better to explain how Cindy was drunk after only two Slow-Screws-Against-The-Wall and how Sinead and Emma met two really nice guys who just wouldn't leave them alone all night, much to their annoyance. The reality was that Cindy had tried to get drunk with an enthusiasm that was admirable, but the myriad of cocktails that she'd downed all night seemed to have little effect – except to slide her into a sleep full of depressed mumbling. Sinead and Emma *did* meet two really nice guys but their ardour had been more than a little exaggerated. "Oh," she'd decided to exclaim if she was ever unfortunate enough to be caught out in her lies, "is that what I said? Ha, ha! *No.* I didn't mean that, it was the other way round, you know . . ."

But lying for fun was something totally different to what she'd just done with Sinead. She'd deliberately misled her, from hundreds of miles away, with the pretence of saving *her* face, when really, she knew, she was saving her own.

* * *

Sinead's flat stank. Listening to the flamenco music

drifting from the street café below her apartment and in through her open patio doors, she faced a mountain of ashtrays and forlorn, discarded empty wine bottles. Her stomach heaved at the prospect of cleaning up. These "girls'-nights-in" were beginning to prove more rowdy than "girls'-nights-out". She enjoyed the company of her work colleagues and they had very appropriately named themselves "The Witches of East Wing", based primarily on their wicked sense of humour, and secondly on their geographical location in the monstrous building in which they were employed. The work? What about the work? Did anyone ever enjoy "the work"? She doubted it, for she certainly didn't. The acquaintances made at work were the only plus points for even turning up in the mornings. Suddenly the repulsiveness of the task in hand proved a little too much, and she ran, head leading the way by at least two feet, toward the bathroom; more specifically, to the bathroom sink. Where the hell were the sodding Alka Seltzers when she needed them?

* * *

At exactly the same time as Sinead's second portion of paella mixed with San Miguel and tequila were hitting the back of the toilet bowl, Geri was elbow-deep in tepid bathwater and screaming kids. She had a mental image of herself like Hilda Ogden with the three rollers in the front of her hair, headscarf tightly wrapped around the whole package, and a fag hanging droopily from her mouth. Today was going to be the day . . .

Two hours later Reece and Cameron were settled down with a *Winnie the Pooh and Tigger* video and she was reaching for comfort food in the shape of Toblerone. Positioning herself comfortably on the settee, note-pad and pen in one hand and mug of tea in the other, she pondered,

"Right, I'm going to list everything that I've ever been interested in or fancied doing."

She'd woken this morning determined to re-invent herself, annoyed at the lack of structure to her "new" life, it seeming a continuous cycle where night and day merged together without definition. The things that had punctuated her marital lifestyle had been the departure and arrival of Kevin as he left for work and then came home again, demanding his dinner at six o'clock on the dot, his bath at seven, *Coronation Street* at half-past (he'd hated *EastEnders* – bastard), and then *Top Gear* at half-eight. With this behind her she was eager to flick through the Sunday magazines, searching for a blueprint for her new image, excited at her decision to re-invent herself. She struggled with the first two or three subjects, but once her juices were flowing, there was no stopping her. An hour later her list read:

> Music – learn Piano, Guitar, Violin
>
> Languages – learn Spanish, French, Russian – Greek in case of holiday
>
> Appearance – lose 2? stone before Christmas, get more highlights put in hair, have hair cut v.short (Sharon Stone? But only when lost huge and significant amounts of weight)

Yoga, Squash, Tennis

~~Anal Art - what the hell's that about? Oh no,~~
~~Art cross off~~

'A' Level courses – English Literature, Art
General Interest – Architecture, Bookkeeping,
Counselling and Internet Skills
Wear leather trousers (with a short top)
Find out about Jimmy Choo shoes.

She felt quite enthusiastic about these interests that
she'd had for many years and it suddenly dawned on
her that all of her relationships had been with men
sharing *none* of these interests with her. And they'd
never lasted. If that wasn't writing on the wall, then
nothing was. She could hear her mother's voice in her
head chanting: "Learn from this one, Geraldine. It's
commonplace to make a mistake, but it takes a fool not
to learn from it." She could visualise Cynthia's expression.
Geri suspected that her mother felt Shakespearean
when she recited this as she spoke with a righteous and
knowing tone in her voice which fooled nobody but
herself. It went hand-in-hand with her register of
"usable quotes". Geri had often said to Sinead, "Give
Mum a quandary and Quick-Draw-McGraw can give
you a quote. Need motivation? No problem, Quick-
Draw'll remind you, 'Show me a good loser, and I'll
show you a failure'. Want to borrow a tenner? Quick-
Draw'll prompt, 'Poverty makes you sad as well as
wise'. Unfortunately for Quick-Draw, her favourite is
'It's better to be quotable than to be honest' which
reveals her lack of memory, because I'm always

reminding her, 'You need a good memory to be a liar!'"

So, armed with her new list of interests she decided that she'd enrol for three classes and set herself the challenge of finding herself a 'New Job', 'New Me' and a 'New Man' (hopefully one who will enjoy the real Geri, as opposed to the dried-up, sex-starved-and-forgotten-how-anyway matronly one). She was about to embark on Mission(*ary position*) Impossible.

Chapter Three

"Geri? Geri?"

Mum's voice is instantly recognisable, although somewhat diluted, by the sounds of riotous lunch-time diners. I look up to see her vacant moon-like face searching through the lunch-time sea of heads.

"Over here!" I stand up, waving my arms in an excellent impression of somebody drowning, whilst simultaneously trying to rock the double buggy with my foot as I try to keep the boys asleep despite this commotion. As I begin to lose my balance, flopping back down into the chair, at the already cramped table, I shudder with embarrassment as I feel the doughy excuse for my chest shake wildly with the impact. I'm hoping nobody noticed. Scanning the crowd, I wonder whether my path would be destined to cross with any of them again under the vast umbrella of Adult Education. Could any of these be my New Man? As Mum approaches the table, weaving clumsily through the banqueting throngs, balancing *the tray precariously above their heads, I shuffle my chair round, creating a space for an extra chair. My actions are horrifically disturbed by Mum's voice, booming and loud, as she asks with extraordinary politeness, completely unbefitting to the question,* "Excuse me, young man. But would you mind giving me a few inches?"

Oh God! She's at it again!

Momentarily, the uproar settled as inquisitive burger-munchers craned their heads to see who was asking for dessert as well as lunch on a Friday afternoon.

"What, love?" her victim questioned in disbelief.

Geri stared in amazement at her mum as she stood, poised with tray in hand, waiting for him to pull his chair in. She only wanted to sit down. Many pairs of eyes flicked excitedly from Cynthia, smiling innocently, to her prey who was puzzled, confused and yes, more than a little embarrassed.

"I haven't enough room to sit down here, love. Could you move in a bit, please? Just a few inches would do."

Relief swept the room as, en masse, shoulders relaxed, lungs were emptied and within mere milliseconds normality was resumed.

Mr I-Can't-Believe-She-Just-Said-That tucked his chair in noisily as Cynthia sat down, puffing with relief.

"Well?" Geri questioned, continuing to rock the buggy.

"Well, what, love?" Cynthia smiled vacantly, having organised the warm tissue-paper packages and polystyrene boxes that contained their meals.

"How did you get on at the hairdresser's? Did you

manage to get me booked in for this afternoon or not?" Geri was absolutely desperate for some highlights. Despite the long pockets and extremely short arms that she'd acquired since her lifestyle change it was still essential that she maintain her highlights. An honorary member of the fan club that paid homage to the relationship between a woman and her hair, even in the absence of mirrors just the *feel* of her hair in its arrangement on her head had the potential to devastate or animate her day.

Cynthia pulled the face that she used when she'd just humiliated herself, a well-used expression. "Guess what I said, Geri? You won't believe what an idiot I just made of myself!"

"Yeah. I would. Wasn't I just sitting here seconds ago with the other three million listening to you?"

"No! Not that! Not then! Just now in the hairdresser's!"

Geri could feel herself squinting as she gulped from the polystyrene cup, the diet-coke bubbles popping on her cheeks. "What, Mum? What have you done?" She drank down the fizz.

"Well," Cynthia began, settling into her seat, a strange aura of sick enjoyment washing across her face, "I only went in there and asked to see Toni or Guy! Well, you know; I thought that being called Toni *and* Guy, that they'd be the two managers, or owners, or whatever they call themselves these days. Anyway," she tipped her hand poofy-like as an indication that there was more, "what d'you think that they said?"

Geri just didn't dare imagine.

Cynthia continued, unaware of Geri's disdain. "She was quite disgusted at me, I think. She said that Toni was in their salon in Chicago and Guy was at the salon in San Francisco, I think . . . and could Roland, their top stylist, help me?"

Things definitely weren't going to plan . . .

* * *

It took fourteen days for Geri's embarrassment to fade. Shuffling, armed with the local Adult Education Centre Prospectus and a purse bursting with pound coins, she was on her way to be "done" elsewhere. The diluted afternoon sun broke through, shining damply onto the High Street, and Geri felt anonymous amongst the busy shoppers and the damp whooshing of passing buses. Cynthia had been maneouvred into position as baby-sitter for the afternoon, and Geri was now anticipating pure and unadulterated luxury for at *least* three hours. She was disappointed at having to wear her shabby loafers to the trendy hairdresser's, having skulked past at least twice a day for a fortnight to examine the dress-code. She had planned to wear the spike-heeled boots that Cynthia had eventually treated her to, but after proudly wearing them home from the shops, clonking and striding self-assuredly, she'd realised she looked more a throwback from the Funky Chicken craze than a Millennium babe. Days later and her feet were still blistered, the balls of her feet feeling wrinkly and squashed. She inwardly cursed herself for being so impatient. Cynthia had told her to wear them "indoors to break them in first", but Geri just couldn't bear the amateurism of the idea. So now she'd been forced to opt for the more comfortable option.

So, there she was, standing at the reception desk feeling conspicuous. Breathing in the stuffy air, laden with a rancid permy stink, she stood, awestruck at the staff – her mind, not so much wandering as running blindly in panic as she asked herself if they all got in early to do each other's hair every day?

"Bloody hell," she whispered to herself, hypnotised by the larger-than-life catwalk images, "*London Electricity* must make a fortune out of this place – it's absolutely brimming with power-cuts! They all seem too perfect-looking and it's not fair. Especially in a place where people come to make themselves feel good!"

It made her feel nervous and inadequate.

"You awite there, luv?"

Geri jumped – she'd been unaware that there had been someone standing behind her. "Oh, yeah, fine thanks."

"Oh," she tittered, "fought you was talkin' to yerself there fer a minnite. D'ya wanna come over to this workstation? Here, give us yer jacket and we'll gown you up."

Wrapping the silky black gown around her, the velcro strips digging into the sides of her neck, Geri was hustled over to the "station" and was then unfortunate enough to have to endure a good twenty minutes of comparing her own pallid reflection with those of the beautiful people that were going to "do" her hair. The harsh spotlighting reflected off the abundance of chrome fittings, making her eyes shine and glisten. As one of "them" drifted past in a waft of CKOne, she ignored Geri's pink-tinged cheeks and nervous grin. Geri wondered at their aloofness.

How long does it take to acquire the skill? Is it a pre-requisite for the job? Is it difficult for them to maintain the façade?

Geri couldn't decide whether she preferred the aloofers who showed a small trace of humanity by occasionally smiling (although the emotion never seemed to reach their eyes, purely a melting flash of dental perfection) or those who showed none at all and wouldn't break down the invisible barrier, showing no other reaction than haughty discontent at the bother and indiscretion of their untrendy clients.

Her thoughts were disturbed as she heard one of them squeal, "Ooooh, what a gorgeous baby!" A collective mutation seemed to occur as Geri watched them shedding their cloned identity and become strangely human. She watched in the mirror as, clucking hen-like around the pushchair, they cooed and giggled over a sleeping child.

"Look at 'ees 'air! All fluffy and soft."

"Bit like yours, Kaz."

"Get outtof it."

"E's lovely. E's got your eyes, Shell."

"Yeah."

'Ha,' Geri thought, '*I've* got one of *those* if that's

what you're all interested in!' She suddenly felt superior to them, convincing herself that despite their flawlessness they were all sadly lacking in their emotional lives. Slightly more confident, she smirked to herself in the mirror as she imagined them all leaving work at the end of an immaculate day, arriving home lonely, and discarding, almost snake-like, the image. Off came the clothes, the Wonderbras, tummy-flatteners, bottom-shapers and thigh-slimmers; their smelly aching feet exposed for the first time all day and pungently appreciating the opportunity. Off came the make-up, (all three layers), and out came the coloured contact lenses as they plainly sat in front of their tellies.

"Ha," she entertained herself, killing the time as she did so, "they probably look worse than *me* in the buff!"

Her perverse enjoyment was brought crashing and screamingly to a halt as "Jasmine" strode up behind her, the angelic superbness of her appearance mesmerising. If the moment could have been encapsulated on film Geri felt it would have demanded soft-focus lens, caressing breezes sending her shimmering hair dancing around her face in wispy whirls, and dreamy, floaty music.

"Hi," she whispered, the luminosity of her complexion nearly blinding. "What are we doing today then?"

Completely spellbound Geri almost began to explain to her the enthralment of Adult Education classes. To her credit though, she realised, as Jasmine flicked and tugged at her thatch, that she was referring to, and most definitely only interested in, any aspirations regarding hair. The next two hours were spent being moved from one station "for consultation", to another "for washing and conditioning", to yet another "for highlighting". The intermittent music blasting from their sound system only added to the farce, rendering the experience a close second to musical chairs. Staring at her dishevelled appearance under the harsh scrutiny of their carefully positioned spotlights for nearly half an hour, Jasmine returned with her scissors and comb, gushing her opinion regarding Geri's long-term-resident double chin, lank hair and side-burns, suggesting that she adopt a feathered-onto-the-face look. Geri fought back a strong urge to justify her thinning top as a result of pregnancy, but felt the excuse unworthy. An intense verbal struggle then took place as she was forced to remind "Jazz" that she *was only* interested in highlights.

Jasmine busied herself with various potent-smelling mixes and Geri, finally, began to relax, confident that she'd stated her demands clearly enough for "Jazz" to understand and act upon. So opening the pages of her prospectus with more than a little trepidation, she lost herself in pages promising enlightenment, education and enchantment. How things had changed since she left school fourteen years ago. Fourteen *years* ago! She felt her shoulders slump with the realisation of her seniority. But, not to be led astray, she continued flicking through the pages, whispering to herself as she did so.

"Saturday workshops, Decoupage – or as Mum calls

it – De-Cooper-idge, Genealogy, Archaeology. Is it still impressive to have an 'ology', or is that all old-hat now too?" Her mind awash with possibilities ranging from Painting to Pottery, History to Health and Bonsai to Bookkeeping.

"The question is, which courses will the 'New Men' be enrolling on? Adult Improvers section's a certain no-go; Forrest Gump-a-likes need not apply! The choice is mind-blowing."

She closed the book, deciding to pull Cynthia on board the mission, unaware of the clan of giggling hairdressers clustered around the washing station, pointing at the new customer who talked to herself.

* * *

She emerged from the salon two hours older and three shades lighter, coiffed and styled, confident and contented.

And confused.

This Adult Education malarky just isn't going to be as easy as I'd first anticipated. There are just so many courses to choose from! I'm puzzling between the romance of Astrology and the practicality of Counselling.

As she sat on the bus heading back to Cynthia's, her enjoyment of the journey was broken by the sounds of young children bickering. She looked toward the front to see a struggling mother ushering three young children toward the rear of the bus. Geri smiled at her, appreciating the difficulty. The bedraggled young woman settled her three into the long sideways seat and plonked herself next to Geri.

"Hard, innit?" she said to Geri.

"Yeah," Geri whispered, as she began to mentally prepare herself for the cruel and perturbing return to motherhood and all that goes with it: that deflated, guilt-ridden anti-climax that cancels out the fun you had at the shops or the pool or the hairdresser's, when faced with a red-faced, screaming baby and a moaning toddler fighting to be heard over the TV, all else is forgotten. It had happened before – like that time when she couldn't see the carpet for toys and Nana was nowhere to be seen. Slightly panic-stricken she had wondered where she could be, and then had found her nonchalantly scraping the mud off mini Wellington boots with a screwdriver!

"You know," Geri spoke to the harassed mum beside her, "life really is full of decisions, but there are few as tough as those regarding your children."

"Too bloody right."

"You're brave anyway, bringing them all on a bus. That's a ratio of one to three."

"A what?

"One adult to three kids. I've got two at home and one's not even a year yet."

"Yeah, but you have to get used to it. Does the kids good too, that bit of discipline in the outside world."

"Suppose."

Feeling cowardly for never attempting to travel on a bus with Cameron and Reece, her mind wandered back to the boys. As she tried to relax and enjoy her last half-hour of freedom she noticed the elderly man sitting diagonally to her. Finding herself hypnotised by him, she noticed how the young mum next to her was also suppressing a smile. She whispered in Geri's ear, "Why do ageing men seem to suddenly sprout hair from the most disgusting places?"

"Pardon?"

"Their nostrils, ears and even the bridge of their nose."

It was at this point Geri noticed the B.O. of this balding Teletubby – the awful pungent type that smells like onions and paints yellow/greeny tidemarks, rather like corn-circles, but much less intriguing, on the armpits of shirts. Feeling more than slightly bilious, she decided to walk the last five minutes to Cynthia's house.

Bidding her goodbyes to the travelling family, she road-tested her hairdo in the 'real world'. She anticipated further repeated screenings of *Tots TV*. She contemplated the future with the two boys: months of bed-wetting, verruccas, black eyes and worms. Years of fighting, biting, kicking, punching and pinching, and all before breakfast. The guilt she hauled around with her for the absence of a father figure in their lives had shifted her perspective on many subjects. Where she used to be easy-going, she now found herself regimented; where there was complacency now there was discontentment.

As she rang the familiar bell on Cynthia's front door she heard two little voices shouting and laughing inside and she instantly mellowed as recollections of cuddles and playtimes jumped to the front of the queue in her mind, pushing all those negatives out of the picture. Her newly coloured hair was, if the reaction of her family was considered, a success, although she was already worrying about the continuing expense of touching up her roots.

As she slid off her jacket, flicking her lightened locks appreciatively in the hall mirror, she said to her enthralled reflection, "Probably the only thing I *will* be touching up till the *next* millennium."

She entered the kitchen only to see Cynthia plying Cameron with forbidden lemonade. Opening her mouth to complain at her choice of drink for the child, she stopped herself, scolding herself quietly for actually *thinking* like a mum.

"Sitting down for a cuppa, love, before you go?"

Plonking down into the seat she watched her mum pour the tea.

Cynthia digressed. "I'm not going down to Azid Hazzanazzra's again. He was there, ignoring me, and pushing the lemonade under the counter, pushing it, pushing it, and then he picked it up with his small hands and a big poo-scooper of a nail, you should have seen it! Should be on Record Breakers or something!"

Geri just couldn't face any further explanation of corner-shop antics, least of all regarding the moody owner whose name alone was worth a thousand points in Scrabble, so she chose instead to politely nod and smile in mock agreement, just for a quiet life . . .

* * *

Ben Robbins lay sweating, concentrating and

contemplating his next move. A perspiration moustache balanced heavily on his perfect Cupid's bow, obviously reluctant to move from the superbness of its structure. His bronzed muscled body, tuned as an exemplary sculpture, lay anticipating the moment. Without warning he pumped hard at the cold metal, lifting the weights with rhythm and determination.

At thirty-three Ben was an unlikely bachelor in the world of theatre. He was the showy front-of-house with the discreet modesty of the stage door, the rich velvet curtain with the sawdust humbleness of the dressing-room. Ben knew he was good-looking but never dwelled on it, preferring the queues of women to get into his mind before they got into his lifestyle. As an Aquarian, Ben revelled in the obscure, liking the astrologer's prediction of eccentricity. He likened himself to a lottery ticket that had yet to be scratched. Eye-catching and colourful on the outside, but just rub lightly on the surface and see what surprises may reveal themselves! As newly appointed Assistant Artistic Director at the Shaftesbury Theatre, he delighted in working round the clock to get the job done properly. So he made sure that every day he took time out for a workout, believing the old adage that a healthy mind is a healthy body. In the eyes of the many adoring females, Ben had everything. Except them. What they couldn't grasp was . . . he didn't want *them*.

* * *

Cynthia turned the pages of evening classes over noisily, only irritating Geri further.

"What about Counselling? You might be good at that now, what with Kevin going and that."

"What the hell's *that* supposed to mean?"

"You know," she at least had the manners to be a little coy, "helping people in a similar situation to yourself. You might understand how they're feeling."

"Mum! I'm trying evening classes to boost my confidence and help me try and re-invent myself. Not make me painfully aware of what a disaster I've made of things!"

"Daft thing. And look, now you've spilt your tea." Cynthia tended to talk down to Geri when she didn't know what to say. She'd rarely admit herself wrong or ever apologise.

Resting her elbows on the cold Formica table, Geri felt the start of a headache. Not unusual when in Cynthia's company, especially when her levels of excitement far outweighed Geri's.

"What about that Peng Shooeee thing?"

"What?"

"Oh, I dunno what it's called. Peng Shooee, is it?"

"Feng Shui."

"Something like that. What do you think?"

"No, Mum, I don't think I could handle the fact that my whole life may have been different, better even, if I'd only taken down that mirror in the kitchen and moved the yucca plant to the hallway."

"Oh gawd, yeah. That'd be awful."

They finally decided on the classes, making choices to maximise her limited budget. Intent on casting the male-catching net widely, Geri left Cynthia's with a conclusive list:

Monday 5.00 – 6.15pm	Internet Skills	Dave Lomax
Thursday 1.30 – 4.30pm	Beginners' Spanish	Michael Fernandez
Saturday 10.00 – 11.30am	Beginners' Piano	Tim Heffernan
~~Tuesday 6.00 – 8.30pm~~	~~Local Architecture~~	~~Maurice Gormley~~
Every Tuesday night	Gym Gimineez in Cedar Road	

By the end of the evening, once Reece and Cameron had exhausted her playing hide-and-seek she had a second list prepared, and was reading it as she sat on the loo:

1. Ask Mum to mind the boys for me. I'll only be an hour at the gym.

"I will be only an hour, won't I?" she asked the toilet-roll holder, catching a distorted glimpse of her reflection in the chrome plating. "I haven't done anything remotely physical since the conception of Reece, unless running yourself around like a loony for sixteen hours a day is counted. Right, the first thing to do is dig out my gym clothes."

2. Dig out Gym clothes.

"I'm sure they're here somewhere," she ad-libbed as she stuck the Post-it note to the toilet door, standing to pull up her disappointing knickers and bobbly joggers. As she crossed the landing she noticed Cameron jumping energetically on the bed, threatening to put his foot straight through the pine slats supporting the mattress, and wondered where Reece was.

"Reece! Reece! Reece? Where are you? Reece?" she called.

"Goooaaarrr, eeeeegghhhhhhh, caaaarrrrrrooooogghhhaaaa" Reece responded, his face beaming up at her as he crawled from around her bedroom door, her lipstick in his clenched pudgy fist, and painted in a horror-film clown-like smile across his face. Her mind now focused on the hunt for gym clothes, she disregarded Cameron's jumping and Reece's artistry as she pulled bundles of crumpled clothing from a mountainous pile slumped at the bottom of her wardrobe. All pre-pregnancy clothes. The mountainous pile that hadn't existed only weeks ago, prior to Kevin leaving. His very nature, tidy mind, tidy home made it extremely difficult for Geri to get away with slovenly behaviour. She suspected that the rebel in her was fighting its way out, delighted at his departure, and revelling in the opportunity to do anything remotely *un*tidy. Coupled with the fact that she was finding it very difficult to really put her mind to anything with young children in the house. She was finding them, as a single parent, very demanding; wanting to know what she was doing, why, what for, could they help, wanting a wee-wee, needing a jink; so a job that might have taken a ordinary mortal half an hour, could take a 'Mummy' nearly three!

Finally, there amongst the ra-ra skirt, the denim waistcoat and the electric-blue eyeliner they were: the gym attire.

"Mmmm, they look a bit dated. But I'm sure once they've been washed I'll be knocking spots off the rest of them down there."

Geri hadn't been near the inside of a gymnasium since the Jane Fonda Workout days.

* * *

Sinead was a terrible patient. With an entirely non-existent pain threshold, she found it necessary to take two days off work. She was resigned to her bed, sweating (and not a man in sight), and with the telephone off the hook (must be bad). The post, usually retrieved mid-air before even splatting on the mat, in frenzied anticipation of letters from home, was left on the doormat. She had completely and resolutely quarantined herself. As she felt her stomach lurch again in an uncontrollable heave, a disconcerting shift of weight therein, she ran, well practised by now, to the toilet. She'd thought it payback time after the drinking session but, as she'd gotten worse, realised she probably had the Spanish version of Delhi Belly. Much later she emerged, spraying the air-freshener behind her and closing the door. It was only as she shakily placed the canister on the stainless-steel draining-board that she noticed its name: Serenity. Padding across the tiled floor back to her bed, she wondered how in hell anyone could have given it the name "Serenity". Here she was with chronic diarrhoea and she had the nerve to spray air-freshener with the name of "Serenity".

As she lay back in the dishevelled bed, its sheets wrinkled, warm and musty she realised that someone was knocking at her door. Resting her head back into the oppressively warm pillow, she felt goose-pimples as the warm breeze blew in from the open balcony doors. She'd always hated having the shits in England, but to have them here in the heat! With no-one to look after her or bring her presents or sympathy! Despite her attempts to ignore the incessant tapping on the door she found that its rhythm had worked its way into her head, so decided to answer it and be rid of the unwelcome intruder. Passing the mirror on her way she was staggered at her haggard appearance gawping back. Her usually gorgeous hair sat in matted clumps at unusual angles and her make-up-free face seemed sallow though tanned at the same time.

"Ha!" she thought aloud. "This'll soon get rid of 'em – one look at me and they'll think I've been filming *Frankenstein's Bride*." On opening the door though she was speechless to see Charmaine from work standing there, all smiles and no personality. Before Sinead had the chance to get her words out, Charmaine was pushing the door open and striding into her apartment.

"Gawd, it's really lovely in 'ere, innit."

Sinead felt no compulsion to entertain her. As she watched Charmaine strut around and fiddle with her personal belongings, mauling at the photographs on top of the telly and fussing with her CD collection, Sinead couldn't help but feel a pang of jealousy. In spite of her annoying sing-song voice and irritating presence, she had the most beautiful eyes. Sinead hadn't really noticed it before. Come to think of it, Sinead hadn't really noticed *her* before. She was just an insignificant cog in a very big wheel. As she turned towards her

Sinead noticed her unusual lopsided grin and dreadfully acne-scarred skin. Suddenly she understood the nickname the guys from the Finance Department had dubbed the girl with: "Body of *Baywatch*, face of *Crimewatch*."

"Charmaine. Why are you here? I'm not really at my best right now." Her voice was weak and pleading.

"Oh, that's all right, darlin'. Ooh, this is a lovely clock. Did you buy it here or bring it over with you?"

"Brought it over with me. Now, is there anything I can help you with? I'm *really* not feeling too good right now."

"Oh no, we were just wondrin' how you were feeling. You know, it's been a few days now, and nobody really knew what was wrong with you. Thought you might 'ave a bit of sunstroke or something, you know."

Sinead could imagine them all now, deliberating and discussing her absence. Inventing all kinds of convoluted stories, probably involving vibrators, olive oil and Spanish waiters. How she hated their bitchiness and insincerity, and kicked herself for giving them the chance to discuss her *orifice* politics. All horror stories of catty, venomous office women were nothing compared to the nastiness of the brood of short-sleeved white-shirts that she was now working with. And how many of them had room to talk? Many of them leaving their families back in England whilst they enjoyed their European Assignment with more than just the camaraderie of the imported secretaries. Enough really was enough. Time for some straight talking.

"Actually, Charmaine," her tone was extremely cutting, "I've got the shits. I've been on the crapper constantly for the last two days and to make things worse, most of the time I'm not sure whether I need to be sitting on it or leaning over it."

"Oh," with a nervous titter, "oh, right. OK then."

Surprised at her lack of retaliation, Sinead realised the gossip that she'd screwed her way to Valencia must be true – she certainly didn't get there for her personality or her brains.

Disgruntled, but trying to maintain her unconvincing charm, Charmaine retorted, "Well. I'll leave you in peace then." She walked to the door. "We just wondered if you were all right and as I was passing, I offered to call in on ya. When *will* you be coming back?"

"Look, right now I don't know, but I can assure you as soon as I'm confident that I won't need to clench my bum-cheeks together so tight that I'm frightened of knocking my teeth out, I'll be back! Goodbye!"

Slamming the door in Charmaine's face Sinead retreated to her room, smiling as she conjured up what Charmaine would report back to the office.

Then, as the recognition of what she'd just said dawned, she chided herself for, once again, speaking her mind before engaging her brain. If she hadn't felt the immediate urge to rush back into the toilet, she might have cringed with potential embarrassment at the prospect of it.

* * *

Having washed the aforementioned "gym-gear" I can see that perhaps a little assistance is required on the clothing front.

Geri's first stop was the Sports Shop and they bumbled in, all buggy-wheels and carrier-bags, to look for the ladies' wear. As the designer labels screamed at her from brightly coloured and co-ordinating leotards, she realised that they were probably not called that any more. *They all look much too young for me anyway,* she mused.

"God, I'm *thirty!*" She stopped to speak to a rack of unlistening sports wear, feeling the suedette of a lycra top as the realisation hit once again, "I'm virtually middle-aged and need desperate advice on what would be suitable. Maybe I should buy *Woman's Realm* or *The Lady* and see what they mention about keeping fit."

Disgusted at such a vast and confusing choice she decided to take a step back in the direction of the newsagents to buy a Fitness magazine – in the absence of the former two reads.

I'll take that home and read it in bed tonight and scan the pages for some ensemble enlightenment.

* * *

It was three days before she picked up *Fitness* again and, by then, could categorically state, "*You won't catch me in one of those all-in-one things with matching knickers over the top that go right up your bum! I look bad enough in a G-string under my trousers, but over the top? On the outside?*"

Faced with an army of pubescent sinewy babes

wearing skin-tight outfits, seeing gussets disappearing up bum cheeks and more lycra than you could shake a stick at, Geri was beginning to have serious doubts about going to the gym. She *knew* that these were "in", but didn't really think that they were for the "everyday Jo", even less for the thirty-plus bracket. It was OK for Cher and the likes to wear them for *their* exercise videos, but are "normal", "ordinary" women really expected to don them too? 'Back to the drawing board,' she thought, disappointedly.

Maybe I'll skip the gym and just go swimming instead. I used to be able to make a four-second dash from the changing rooms to the poolside, managing to hold a mega-huge towel around my waist until that split second when I jumped into the water . . .

NO! I won't be put off the gym.

She tossed the thoughts around in her head as she tidied up, feeling guilty as she put enough toys to entertain the entirety of the Vietnamese street-kids into plastic stacking boxes. Suspecting that it was probably the wrong move, she sat by the phone and punched in Cynthia's number. She answered after only two rings, puffing heartily, "Hullo."

"Mum, what's wrong?"

"Nothing, love."

"Whaddya mean nothing! Listen to you. What have you been doing?"

"Don't laugh then."

"OK."

"Step Reedback."

"What?"

"A bloody exercise video, Step Reedback."

"Reebok! Step Reebok. What are you doing that for? Have you got a step then?"

"No, I've improvised."

"Go on."

"I'm resting the decorating table on the two stereo speakers."

"Mum, that's much too high! Those steps are only a few inches high, not half a metre!" She began to laugh at the mental image conjured up, "Mum, no wonder you're puffing!"

"Oh, never mind! Why are you ringing me?"

Faced with the heaving Cynthia mid-workout, Geri couldn't bring herself to question the dress-code.

"Oh, I needed to ask you something – it'll have to wait. Reece's just woken. Bye!"

* * *

Well, the gym is now called a Health Spa, the treadmill called a Powerjogger and I'm already fully conversant with the lingo. Lats stretches, abductors and adductors, oblique tighteners, leg curls, bench presses; I'd always been good at languages and this was no exception. Yep, I am going to take to this like a duck to water. Impeded only psychologically by my state of clothes, I've had my induction and despite my inferiority complex linked to my baggy T-shirt, leggings and non-designer trainers, I am raring to go.

Two hours and three gallons of sweat later she has a face that resembles a medicine ball. Clapping her bloodshot eyes on the beefcake before her, she is momentarily distracted from her four-sets-of-ten. Tall, tanned and perfectly formed with the most beautiful mouth she'd ever put her lips to.

Oh . . . no, sorry, I mean, laid my eyes upon.

She feels herself yearning to be in a more attractive position.

Laying face down on a bench with my ankles hooked under an over-inflated shoulder-pad and the full monstrosity of my arse dimpled glaringly under the spotlights! I can honestly say I've met gorgeous men in better positions than this one.

Lying at an incline, her head being lower than her ankles she imagined the puffed-upness of her cheeks (*on my face, my face!!*) and the bulging helplessness in her eyes.

Nobody was more surprised than Geri when he smiled gorgeously at her, and said hello!

Hello! Bloody hello!

She decided that this must mean one of three things:

> *One – he feels sorry for me, obviously aware that I'm new and excessively overweight.*
>
> *Two – My bulging bloodshot orbs are embarrassing him into an acknowledgement.*
>
> *Three – The greeting is an alternative to an intense bout of hysterics as he wickedly enjoys my vulnerability and obvious awkwardness.*

She felt compelled to wait for him to move away from the stepping machine before she could attempt to struggle to her feet. As if it wasn't bad enough him viewing her from this angle, it could be potentially disastrous if she stood up too quickly, hitting her ankles in a jellied shudder, and letting him see her quivering expression.

Fifteen minutes later, he moved away to sculpt his quads and Geri was more than ready to retreat to the "privacy and comfort of the individual, lockable, air-conditioned changing rooms with comfortable seating area and the refreshment and coolness of the showers".

She hadn't anticipated the crowded, airless, hot communal broom-cupboard that she walked in to.

Bare asses everywhere. Full bountiful boobs, small pert ski-slopes. There is no shame! Flesh overload!

As everyone dressed, dried and even applied body lotion from neck to toes, totally oblivious to their audience, she wondered which one of these liberated ladies was her Adonis's partner. Awkwardly she attempted to scan the room, hoping that if she dared raise her gaze for long enough she'd notice surreptitious glances at cellulite, unruly pubic hair of various colours, and nicotine or HRT patches slapped on shamelessly as heads hung in mock rummage through bags.

It seems that they must be a clan of nannies. They all have "Mary Poppins" bags – seemingly and deceptively small on the outside, but their arms go in to armpit level, and pull out all kinds of bottles and lotions, obviously essential after a workout at the city's newest Health Spa.

She skulked around in an attempt to blend in as if she too was thinking about her next move, but secretly horrified at the influx of gemstones in belly buttons.

Obviously the yearning to look like something from a Turkish Delight advert is another trend that has happened since before my pregnancies.

Her forced cockiness did little to dissolve her dread at the impending strip. In mere milliseconds she decided that the showering and grooming experience was all too much for her, especially at such a beginners' level, so she dashed all hopes of refreshment, stuffing her damp belongings into a carrier-bag and making a dash for the car. The chill in the evening air freeze-dried the sweat globules still glowing on her face and neck, making her skin feel taut and her hair feel like cardboard.

"I'll shower at Mum's before I take the boys home," she decided.

On arriving she was relieved to see the boys watching telly peacefully, enabling her to shower, dress and let Cynthia make her some tea . . . and cut her a slice of cake . . . Black Forest Gateau . . .

OK, OK! Two slices of Black Forest Gateau . . .

And a KitKat.

As they sat around the Formica table once again, Cynthia began, "Guess what I did today?" Her voice was filled with remorse.

Again.

Geri just hoped she hadn't been shoplifting.

Again.

"What?" she asked tentatively, not really wanting to know, but desperate to, at the same time.

"Oh God! I'm so embarrassed. You know I've been having problems with my toilet?"

"I thought you'd fixed that. Is the cistern still leaking?"

"No! Not *the* toilet. *My* toilet. Number twos." She was referring to the fact that she'd seen an advert on the telly for irritable-bowel syndrome and had now convinced herself that she'd got it. Tesco's were nearly clean out of stock of prunes and All-Bran as she'd bought enough to feed a small army. "I went to the library today to get a book on it and I only picked up the wrong book. I thought it read *Improve Your Bowels*. You know how it is when you're in a rush and –"

"Mum. What's the problem?"

"Well, I *thought* it said improve your bowels!"

"So? What did it say?"

"Bowls!"

"What?"

"Bowls. Improve your bloody bowls! Short mat bowls. God, I feel so stupid and the man on the counter asked me if I fancied trying something near to the ground, and I thought he was being sarcastic. You wouldn't take the book back for me, would you? I just don't think I can face going in there again for a while."

This was no revelation to Geri.

Cynthia was always getting her words in a mucking fuddle.

Chapter Four

Despite the liberating feelings the workout gave her, Geri's bum felt like it had been kicked; repeatedly. At ten thirty-three on a Tuesday night she'd have rather been sleeping, but the intense ache in her gluteus maximus insisted on waking her. As she lay uncomfortably on top of her duvet, her stripy pyjamas clashing with the colour scheme, she wriggled to find a position a little less painful.

Plus, I just can't get Hot Lips out of my mind. . .

Her cheeks involuntarily flushed as she remembered her arse-cringing bottoms-up pose as he'd walked past her in the gym, then her stomach flipped just at the recollection of his handsome face and cute smile. In a bid to take her mind from the turmoil of these thoughts she reached down beside her bed and grasped the notes from her evening classes, due to start the following weekend.

Losing herself once more in the rules and regulations of the Adult Education campus, she realised that the first class would be the piano lessons, starting on Saturday with Tim Heffernan. Resting the paperwork on her lap and looking at her reflection across the bedroom in the full-length mirror that Kevin had left behind, she whispered, "Mmmm, Tim Heffernan. Tim's quite a sexy name – boyish and fun. But Heffernan?" She began to hum musical notes quietly in practice, "La-la-la-la-la-la-la-la-la. Doh-ray-me-fah-so-lah-tee-doh! Doh! Doh! God, I hope I don't have to sing along or anything!"

Geri remembered how she was always the one in the school choir who was told to mime: "Just mime the words, dear. It'll be so much easier for the others!"

Still, she couldn't wait to tell Sinead about starting the piano lessons. She'd piss herself laughing! She decided, calculatedly, to leave the Spanish and Internet ones a secret though, as she'd love to be able to send Sinead an e-mail *in* Spanish in a few weeks' time. Even if she could only manage something like: "My name is Evangeline. I live and work in Madrid. Two bags please and some oranges." or "Where are the toilets and here is my passport." She wriggled under the covers, chortling at her humour, and was stung with pain by her trapezium in a wicked reminder of over-exertion.

"Oooooh, God," she groaned, as she kneaded her stretched body consolingly, "maybe I should go more than once a week. God!" she squawked as she shifted under the duvet awkwardly in search of a comfortable position. "I don't want to feel like this every week." She stretched painfully to reach for the light and switched it off.

"Mmm," she mumbled into the darkness, "maybe two or three times a week'd be better . . . at least I'd be more used to it . . . it maybe wouldn't hurt so much . . ."

As sleep finally washed over her and her aching body relaxed into the plump mattress her body stiffened, jolting muscular pain down the backs of her legs.

"Maaaaaammmmmeeeeee!!!"

Cameron was awake . . .

* * *

Ben was surprised at seeing her at the gym. He imagined she didn't get much spare time, what with two kids to look after, but it seemed things could be going his way for once. Sick of bimbos and airheads, Ben really liked her – not only the look of her, but she seemed to have got under his skin, and into his inquisitive nature. She seemed mature and responsible, but fun and unpredictable at the same time. Her two small children were always laughing, their happiness probably directly linked to them always being out and about, not like those young mums who loafed around in their dressing-gowns until early afternoon, palming the children off on the neighbours. Ben had seen Geri and the boys at the park when he'd been jogging, at the shops, feeding the ducks on the common and had watched her showing them the trees, explaining leaves and the like. She seemed so full of life and so interesting, and Ben had often wondered what it'd be like to be a fly on the wall in her house. He often wondered about her husband though, as he'd never seen them together. Staring at his reflection in the bathroom mirror, a nineties version of Adam Ant, complete with pore-cleansing strip plastered across his Roman nose, pore-cleansing strip glued to his chiselled chin and, finally, pore-cleansing strip pasted to his tanned forehead, Ben lifted the can of Caffrey's to his lips, attempting to purse his lips around the rim without any wrinkling of the plasters. Feeling their tightness he was relieved that no-one could see him at this exact moment: pore-cleansing strips weren't exactly high on his list of "things to be proud of". Anticipation nagged – he was eager to see quite how much "gunge" these suckers were going to pull out of his unsuspecting pores. Checking, he decided that seven minutes would suffice instead of the recommended ten, and rested the empty can down on the edge of the bath. He peered in closer for the removal, his nose almost touching the steamed patch on the mirror that his breath had misted. The result he found quite disconcerting. To actually see the grime, the mini-stalagmites of crime as they sat in dirty rigid peaks in uniform lines across the sticky plaster. Peeling the other two off, he screwed them up and threw them into the bin. Rubbing at his sticky tight skin, he made his way back into the diffused glint of his stainless-steeled designer kitchen for another beer. Cracking the can open, he slumped down into his antique leather armchair and grasped his sketchbook and pencils. The drawings of David Beckham and Mick Jagger were almost lifelike, as were the mere sketches of Mel B and her daughter Phoenix Chi. But Ben found it more challenging to draw from life as opposed to photographs. He felt he could almost reach into his subjects' souls and capture their presence and personality on his page, something that wasn't possible from polished plastic photographs. Just as he began to map out his portrait of Denise Van Outen his mobile rang, trilling out Beethoven's "Für Elise" into the warm flat. He grabbed the phone without looking up. "Hey?"

"Ben? Mark."

"Yeah . . . what d'you want?"

"Are you busy?"

Ben put down his pencil. Mark was a bit of an old woman on the phone, always wanting to talk for longer than anyone wanted him to. Dubbed "The Lighthouse Keeper" by his workmates due to his skiving off at work, he could always be found gazing out of a window whilst industrial bedlam could be erupting all around him.

"No, you're all right. Just doing a bit of sketching, that's all."

"You should sell some of that work you do, you know. I showed them pictures you did of the Bee Gees to the fellas down the Goose & Duck, and they reckoned they were very good." Ben took this as little flattery, as he doubted the regulars at the Goose & Duck were ever sober enough to see the pictures clearly in the first place, and supposed that their comments of being "very good" pertained more to the Bee Gees themselves than to Ben's pen-work of them.

"Oh thanks."

"No, I'm serious Ben," Mark's voice droned on, "you've been going on for years about starting to go pro with your sketching. You have to bite the bullet some time, you know. Did I ever tell you about my uncle? He enjoyed pottery for years, used to make vases and pots and stuff in his shed and everyone really liked them. But he'd never sell them. Thought they were taking the piss, you see. But they weren't . . . "

Ben had heard this convoluted boring story millions of times – it was Mark's claim-to-fame success story. Ben knew he had the ability to "go pro" but felt that London wasn't quite the place for him to do it. As a young struggling artist he'd taken his job in the theatre, but in more recent years had been contemplating a move to somewhere more creative to encourage his talent, feeling that London didn't really appreciate his efforts. He wanted to live near to the sea and in the country; in a place where, he felt, success would be based on the quality of your work and not on what car you drove and what designer-tag hung on the inside of your boxer shorts. He had been dreaming of a move to a place where he would find the space and tranquillity to be truly creative.

Having turned his neon egg-timer over ten times Ben cut in on Mark, "Hey, someone at the door, mate. Later," and pushed the button to cut him off.

His bare feet shooshed on the elm floor as he made for the long bay window, enshrouded by full ivory muslin faintly tinted orange by the streetlights. Feeling the coldness of the large window as he pulled the muslin back, he glanced up and then down the street, straining his neck to look for any signs of life from number 127. He supposed at this time of night she'd have the kiddies tucked up in bed, and imagined her flaked out, her sassy blonde hair splayed endearingly on her pillow, her sparkling brown eyes closed and resting. As his alarm bleeped to indicate eleven pm, he swung the muslin back lightly, deciding he'd keep his eye out for her tomorrow, wondering how often she'd be going to the gym now she'd started.

* * *

As if returning to work after a bout of the squitters wasn't bad enough, Sinead had returned to work after a bout of the squitters *and* the whole office knowing about it. She'd also realised, on waking, that the pipes in this sanitarily-underdeveloped country were now blocked. She cringed at the thought of asking the gorgeous landlord, the likes of whom would rarely be seen in England, to lend her the drain-rods.

She'd positively *hated* the day at work. Charmaine had giggled and tittered her way through the office and the white-shirts had blown raspberries and guffawed at every given opportunity. Sinead had spent most of the day hiding behind her VDU screen and reminiscing back to the days she worked with Gertie. Their most favourite jobs had been at Smith & Braithwaite working for Ken Matthews, not-so-proud owner of a poorly disguised bald head, his metre-long sideburns confidently swept right up and over the shiny surface, and a predilection for bellowing *"Pronto!"* after giving them even more invoices to process. Sinead's day brightened as she recalled how they'd jointly handed in their notice with a plan to stitch up old Matthews, a devout and proud hygiene freak, who'd been known to drive the fifteen miles home during his lunch-break to merely change his coffee-splattered or baked-bean-adorned tie for a clean one, or to send someone up to Tesco to buy a replacement air-freshener for his office. On the Friday of their last day, unsatisfied with themselves for not making his life more difficult during their employment, they'd left the office together at 5.15 – only a quarter of an hour early! At 7pm they'd both returned to the quiet, empty building, laughing and flirting with the young security guard they'd befriended during their employment. Geri had batted her eyelashes *and* eyelids and persuaded the distracted guard to let her back into the empty office to collect some magazines she'd left behind. He'd soon agreed, with a wink and a pathetic red-faced smile, leaving Sinead to continue their flirty conversation whilst Geri snuck upstairs and tiptoed cautiously into Ken Matthews' empty office. True to form, he'd left his desk drawers unlocked and her heart pounded in her ears as she deftly slid them open as full as they would go. Reaching into her jacket pocket she'd pulled out a small cardboard box, pulling out a small glass vial. Placing one on the metal runners of the top drawer as far back as she could reach she carefully slid the drawer back until it was almost closed, leaving it only slightly ajar. She repeated this on all four drawers on Matthew's desk. She sighed deeply as her task was complete, and it was only as she'd reached the double wooden doors at the exit that she remembered to grab two magazines left on top of the desk entitled *Sue Polyps – Secretary* – funny name for a desk, she'd always thought. Sinead's face had lit up as she saw Geri making her unscathed escape and they bade their farewells to the incompetent security guard and giggled their way up the road to the wine bar.

It was only the raucous telephone call they'd received on the Monday night from Linda Wilkinson – one of their friends from the typing pool – that had confirmed that, true to form, Matthews had, at various junctures *slammed* his desk drawers shut as he always did prior to screaming *"Pronto!"* at some unsuspecting worker. On slamming each of the drawers the fragile glass surrounding the stink-bomb had shattered, spilling the eggy-putrid stench into the desk and office and, Linda had mentioned, on the last slam – squirted the liquid all over his shoes. The office had to be closed for the afternoon as the cleaning staff were called in to air the place, squirting and scrubbing away the offending stink. Oh, how revenge was sweet!

Sinead now missed Gertie dreadfully.

"Sure, she's happily married. A housewife and mother. Her life's totally complete. Unlike mine . . . "

she muttered to her unconcerned keyboard. Determined to ring Geri again that evening, Sinead had left work after an idle day still having to face the landlord about the rods. Relieved at arriving back at her apartment to find his car missing, she reached for the telephone and called Geri. After only one ring she hung up, reasoning that at five o' clock she'd probably be giving the boys and Kevin their dinner, deciding to try again in the early evening.

By now, keen to chat to somebody, she rang her mother in Kilkenny. It seemed every number she dialled from her apartment began "00". "00 44" for England, "00 353" for Ireland. She suddenly realised how few people she rang who lived *in* the country *she* was living in.

Her mother answered the telephone cautiously, her voice a guarded whisper. "Hello?"

"Mam?"

"Sinead! How'ya! What's wrong? Are ya pregnant?" A typical Catholic mother, Mrs Kelly always suspected the worst. Or at least *her* version of it. A car accident, a broken leg, loss of a job, or homelessness would *always* run second to being pregnant outside of wedlock.

"*No!* Mam, no! I'm all right. Just thought I'd ring you, that's all. How's Daddy?"

"Ah sure, you know yourself. Same as ever. Still working all hours God'll give him. He's after signing up for another three years' contract with those big hotel chains, you know. Ah, Sinead! When'll you come back and take over from your father? Give him a break. God knows he's ready to retire. It'll all be yours one day, you know."

Sinead's response was cut off by her mother blurting, "Ah no! The bloody bird's after shittin' on me clean window. And with the whole country *under* him too!"

Typical Mam, Sinead thought, easily distracted. The telephone clanked as the handset was set down abruptly on the wooden table and Sinead listened to the familiar sounds of her mother clattering around the kitchen, turning the taps on with a blast, her mutterings ricocheting off of the painted magnolia walls. She could almost smell the White Linen perfume her Mammy had used for an eternity as she visualised her scrubbing at the splurge on the window. "Why do tomorrow what can be done today?" had always been her motto. Sinead often wondered if this very reasoning stood as the culprit for her seven brothers and four sisters. She'd often imagined her parents snuggled in the rickety iron marital bed, itchy coarse blankets rubbing on her milky skin, and Daddy giving her the nudge and the glad eye, her mother sighing resignedly and declaring, "Ah sure, why do tomorrow what can be done today?"

"Sinead?"

"Mam."

"You still there?" Mrs Kelly enquired down the contraption she held to her ear.

"Yes. Mam, I'm *still* here!"

"So, what's new then? How's Spain? You're not burning too much, are you? You know that skin cancer's an awful thing, and with your fair skin and freckles too, you should be so careful, dear."

"Mam, I work from eight in the morning until half-four in the afternoon – I don't *get* the opportunity to get burnt. More's the bloody shame!"

Mrs Kelly ignored her reassurance, satisfied at the response, and so moving swiftly onward to the most important question, "Well?"

"Well, what?"

"Well, have you a nice boyfriend over there?"

"No! Mam, no! I'm not interested in all that settling down. Most of them working with me are married *and* having affairs all over the place, and those that aren't couldn't if they wanted to!"

"Ah, Sinead! They can't all be that bad! Maybe you're just not giving them a chance!"

"A chance! Mam, last week I went out with a guy who was so skinny I wanted to give him a couple of buckets of water to carry for fear of him blowing away. I'd already planned how I'd explain to his parents, 'Oh, Anthony? Oh, sure, Mrs, the wind just blew and off he went. I think he's up there on the dunes, bustling about with the tumbleweeds. I'm sorry, I *know* I should've given him the pails of water, but I just couldn't bring myself to.' And then, the week before, I went out with José. A great guy, but it'd be quicker to walk over him than around him. It just goes from one extreme to the other. I try to –"

"What was his name?" Mrs Kelly interrupted, the confusion evident in her questioning tone.

"Whose name?" Sinead had lost her flow of thought.

"The tubby one. Hozay? What kind of a name is that?"

"It's Spanish, Mam. J-o-s-é."

"Gawd, it's a girl's name – Josie. Oh love, why can't you come home?

"Mam, I've told you before, I live in England now. When I don't live in Spain. Ireland's not the place for me any more. I've moved on from all that colcannon, ceili and crooning."

"Ah Sinead, it's not like that at all. That Liz Hurley's been looking at places here and that one from the Spices got married here a few years back. It's all after changing, you know. You know, Ireland's economy's positively raging!"

"Mam. I'm very happy where I am. I don't *want* a boyfriend. I love my job." Sinead understood what they meant now about parents and weddings; they just roll it all along in front of you, and all you have to do is turn up! "The only two people in the world I miss desperately are you and Gertie."

"Oh, Gertie! Oh love, how is she? And those two little boys of hers?"

"Cameron and Reece? They're fine. You know she's got a right catch with that Kevin. He treats her like a princess and helps out with the children. Takes her out for meals and he always seems to take every opportunity to work overtime to give them a few extra pound. I'm so pleased for her, but a bit jealous too. Why can't I meet a man like that?" Sinead didn't realise at this point that she'd already met several "men like that". Lying, cheating, deceitful and selfish. Her image of Kevin as the provider, partner and parent was far from the reality that Geri knew.

Womaniser.

Deserter.

And louser.

Chapter Five

Passion, attitude and alcohol. That's what Geri was doing her living best to remember. Passion. The only thing she'd been remotely passionate about lately was getting into size fourteen jeans and Black Forest gateaux. Attitude. She was just *too* tired for this one at the moment. What with running around cooking, cleaning and resolving rows between Pooh and Eeyore, attitude was something low on her list of priorities, assuming Sinead meant sassy, chic attitude and not headmistressy and matronly. Alcohol.

My favourite. Alcohol. A relationship formed in my late teens and never forgotten, although temporarily frozen. The problem I have with alcohol, apart from not being able to get enough of it in large quantities and short time-spans, is the kiddies.

Shortly after the arrival of Cameron, Kevin and she had gone out on a "works do". They were great, those "do's". All expenses paid, free plonk all night long and no work the next day.

Great until I'd wake with a stomach doing queasy somersaults, spinny-rooms in my head, a mouth like sandpaper, an excruciating headache and a baby screaming for milk at 4am. I can still remember sitting, no slumped, against the wall pumping the creamy milk into the baby, watching the rubber teat being squeezed and manipulated by his pink gums. To this day, I'm surprised I wasn't sick all over him. And that was nearly three years ago. I'd probably get drunk on a barmaid's fart now. I imagine that my resistance to the stuff has changed along with the metamorphosis from a spritely lithe twenty-something to a gruesome middle-aged hausfrau whose jeans no longer fit, never mind do up!

A high-pitched squeal from the bathroom forced her to stop this meditation.

"Mummeeee! I'm stuck! Help meeee!" Cameron hollered from the echoey chambers. She ran up the stairs, almost cringing at what she was likely to be faced with.

His left arm was stuck between the concertina folds of the shower screen, while Reece innocently tugged at his right arm, trying to free him from his predicament. She giggled at the sight of the pair of them.

"Wait! Wait a minute. Now keep still, Cameron. Leave him alone, Reece! Now just put your hand here, darling. Come on now, slowly now."

Reece began to giggle at the contorted expression on Cameron's face. Despite her complaining about them, for two young boys they really did have a wicked sense of humour. Almost adult-like. The sides of Geri's mouth quivered as she attempted to conceal her amusement.

"Don't laugh at meeee!" Cameron screeched.

"No, don't laugh, Reece. Come on now, let's help Cameron out of this." In the short space of approximately thirty seconds Reece was in fits of giggles on the fluffy bathroom mat, Cameron lying next to him wriggling and chortling, and Geri standing looking at them both, laughing too.

"Come on, who wants a Milky Bar?" she laughed as she hugged them.

"Meeeeeeeee!" Cameron screamed, as he ran, flat-footed and noisily down the stairs, Reece crawling enthusiastically after him.

God, how will Mum cope with them every Monday evening, Thursday afternoon and Saturday morning? Maybe these education classes aren't such a good idea after all . . .

* * *

Well, Saturday is upon me, me and my excess three stone and ungainly taste in clothes, and I've driven my rusty but trusty Fiesta through the rain, geared up and ready to meet Tim Heffernan and his grand piano. It's not until I arrive that I realise the compulsory and unexpected battle to find a parking space. I meet the same wide-eyed faces at least six times as we all drive around the concrete carousel, ruthlessly hunting a vacant white-painted-rectangle in our attempts at Musical Parking. When the music stops you must find a space; there are half a dozen cars, but only one space. Finally, having reversed into the Kate Moss of parking spaces, it's not until I

stick my foot out that I realise I can only go thigh-deep into
the car park. Stuck, half-cocked, between standing and sitting,
my chunky thigh wedges itself in the gap that my open door
leaves and its battered paintwork bashes brazenly against the
gleaming metallic blue of the BMW parked next to me. I
think I'm smiling coquettishly as intrigued faces gaze at me
in my new dilemma as they pass by, making their way to
various classes.

Christ! I hope none of those smart-arses are learning
piano. Shit! Talk about first impressions lasting! I'll be the
Les Dawson amongst a class of Richard-bloody-Claydermans!

Limping into the class ten minutes late, concealing a
red welt-mark-cum-bruise the size of China on her
thigh, she interrupts the maestro's introduction while a
sea of faces gawk smugly.

"Sorry I'm late," she mutters, her face now as red as
her right thigh.

"Evening," Tim Heffernan smiles. Smiles in an
almost sick, vindictive way that makes her wonder
whether her parking predicament had been recounted
by his many keen-to-make-good-impressions students.
Silence falls as Geri bumps her way to the only available
seat, unfortunately but also typically, next to a middle-
aged tank top with a pasty complexion. As she scrapes
the seat out to accommodate her embarrassed rump,
he smiles revealing a set of yellowing tombstones. A
pungent odour which she could only liken to camel-shit
wafts from his gob as he mouths, as if in slow motion,

"D o n ' t   w o r r y . W e ' v e   o n l y   j u s t   b e g
u n . . ."

"Too bloody right you have," she thinks to herself, "and don't *think* you'll be going any further, sunshine!"

Scanning the room for potential 'new man' candidates she is severely disappointed to see that in a class of seventeen, thirteen are women. Worse still they seem to average an age of sixty-three! Their pompous postures already irritate Geri as they're all excruciatingly polite and chuckly together, the atmosphere choked with airs and graces. The rebel in her, once again rising to the surface, wants to crack a filthy joke and burst into hearty laughter. She daren't. As they all face into the class, a semicircle of musical ignorance, she notices the collection of handbags propped against table legs beneath desks, and already feels agitated by the keen rattling of pencil cases.

Half an hour later and they've gone through that hideous "talk to the person sitting next to you, and be ready to introduce each other in five minutes" scenario. So "tank top's" name was Rupert and he seemed to think he'd be the next Tchaikovsky, revealing his "inner love" for music and dexterity with a keyboard. His mummy bought him a Casio 100 for Christmas two years ago and he could now play "When the Saints Come Marching In" and "Ave Maria" without looking at the keys!

Well, Geri encouraged herself, it'll be entertaining if nothing else. But her real reason for joining piano classes was to find a man. A romantic, musical, artistic man with a temperament to match and passion just oozing from every orifice. With only a handful of men to be considered, her options were instantly limited. Mike of the gold bracelet and electric-tan, tacky but sexy in a Del-Boy kind of way, with wrinkles to match; Tony with the wavy-haired, tousled look, bedecked in Field & Trek clobber and Luke, barely post-pubescent but extremely confident and gregarious. As for Tim Heffernan, Geri is disgusted to find that his flaky skin leaves an exfoliated dusting down the front of his jumper and he walks with such a limp that his whole body sways. Halfway through the class "Tim", as they'd been instructed to call him, announces,

"Right, guys, time for a tea break. You'll find a drinks machine in the foyer and a vending machine for crisps and the like." Checking his watch he continued, "Be back here in ten minutes and then we'll tie it up for this week."

The wet-lipped whisperings began once again as they scraped their chairs back and dragged jackets from the backs of them. Geri took her time to stand, watching the women grappling with their handbags. At the vending machines they hovered sheep-like around, the silver coinage rattling impatiently in their sweaty hands. Sweaty hands that hadn't, as of yet, been remotely near anything ivory, white or black. As the styrofoam cups were dispensed and filled with barely flavoured hot water they sat, hands cupped gratefully around the disgusting drinks, drinks that they would usually bypass with a sneer, although they were now grateful for their warm, wet reprieve.

"I've always wanted to learn to play the piano," one

of the nameless inmates blurted, her voice loud amongst the whispered chatter. None of the unimpressed group seemed to know what to say to her.

In the absence of all other input, Geri piped up. "Have any of you ever tried before?" she hazarded.

"I have." The gross stench of Rupert was accompanied by his nasal twanging voice. Despite the four people opposite him reeling back faint-like, he continued, oblivious, "1967, it was. The last time, that is. The Sixties. The Beatles, Elvis, Dusty Springfield. The musical era of our century."

"None of them played the piano," Geri ventured, superiorly qualified to be irritated by him due to her experiences in-class.

"No, I *know* that, but it was still the musical era. Music is in everybody's soul, you know."

Mike, of the George Hamiltonite suntan jingled his bejewelled hand on the rickety table, wooing her with his surprisingly deep and sexy voice, "The last time I laid my hands on the delicate smoothness of a piano keyboard was when I was a schoolboy."

With that voice, the mere thought of Mike laying his brown shag-piled hand on anything sends shivers down my vertebrae – and, to my surprise, my drawers, which I'd thought were lying dormant due to neglect!

He continued, rendering her awestruck. "The piano is like a woman. To be respected and cherished. Caressed regularly and treated with great affection and love."

That's it! I think I've wet my knickers! Only as I return

to Planet Earth do I notice the hypnotised expression of the other dozen females around the table. I'm half expecting to stand up in a large puddle.

It was Sylvia who broke the precious silence. "I disagree, Mike. I think the piano is like a man. To be thrashed, over-worked, rocked on, worn out, and then the lid be closed down for silence until the woman so wishes."

As Mike reddened awkwardly Sylvia cackled wickedly, prompting laughter from the rest of the "students".

"Sorry, Mike. Only joking with you, mate. Couldn't resist it, that's all." Despite the Mike-Sexual-Expert exterior, Mike was now revealed as a shabby imposter, shielded only by his tacky outdated image. Sylvia, on the other hand, was a surprising character. In an outfit which screamed "No Personality!" she was most definitely a Jack Nicholson in a Nicholas Parsons' clothing.

Making their way back to the class Geri found herself walking next to her, the watery squishing of her rubber-soled shoes providing untimely percussion.

"Hi," she ventured. "Geri. Geri Cumbers."

"Hi. Sylvia. Or Sylvi. Or Sylv. Some of my worst friends call me Saliva, but don't push your luck, girl!"

"Ha! Think yourself lucky. Try and think of the fun you could have with a name like Geraldine!"

"Well," whispers Sylv, "I'm forty-two in a few weeks' time, am twice divorced and still searching for Mr-You'll-Do. Don't look like there's much on offer here though, does it?"

It was as if she was reading Geri's thoughts *and* her intentions!

Just as Geri was about to launch into excuses for joining the piano class Sylv continued, "I've been trying Adult Education classes for the past five years; since my last divorce really. It's surprising the people you meet, and the friendships you make. And I'll tell you something else for nothing. Those Mike-types are everywhere. Sad old bastards. I'll bet you he's divorced, loaded and looking for a twenty-something dolly-bird. Christ knows what he's doing in a piano class! Must be his first year alone. He'll learn."

"Do you mean to tell me that's why you *joined* the class? To meet a man?"

As Sylvia laughed, she spat her spray into the recycled air. Geri suddenly understood her nickname, Saliva.

"Of course that's why I joined the course! Darlin', I'm what you call a serial student! You don't really think I'd want to learn the piano at my age, do you? Ha, girlie, you've got a lot to learn. Especially about men."

Too bloody true. She probably never said a truer word, unbeknown to her. She probably thinks I'm young and commitment-free. She obviously hasn't noticed my post-natal figure.

"Well, you know," confessed Geri, "I even had designs on the tutor. Until I saw him."

Saliva threw her head back in laughter. "Oh, you never knew about Four-foot, Five-foot?"

"What?"

"Heffernan. They call him Four-foot, Five-foot. Cos of his limp?"

"Right."

There's obviously a lot I need to learn.

The classroom had a chilly feel to it as she made her way back to be seated next to the repulsive Rupert. The room now had a strangely familiar aura to it, as though they didn't belong there at all, but they kind of knew their way around it.

"Right, folks!" Heifer-nan bellowed. "Wind it up time! OK, before we leave here tonight, each one of you will spend two minutes tickling the ivories. Remember what I taught you about Middle C and your left and right hands? Now's your chance to prove you were listening to me."

Geri's heart suddenly beat in her ears and neck.

We were supposed to actually be listening to him? God, I thought what with the first lesson and all, the introductions and the coffee break, this was just a kind of warming session. You know, like a pleased-to-meet-you session.

Her mind worked overtime, and she could hear an aged kind of squeaking in her ears as she turned her neck slightly to face the front of the class, realising she was being watched by the repulsive Rupert.

"Right, as with any musical score, rhythm is the key. You will learn over the next 25 weeks how every composer tells us how to play each piece with instructions at the top of the page. The time signature at the beginning will indicate the pace of the piece, and the melody will then structure the tune. It might indicate *adagio* – which means very slowly, but each note is relative to another. Let me demonstrate."

He began to clap his hands slowly and rhythmically, chanting, "One, two, three, four! One, two, three, four!" with each clap. "Join in with me now!"

She felt ridiculous as she clapped along with them, applauding in rhythmic unison. Heifer-nan then led, vocally,

"*DA-da-da-da!*
DA-da-da-da!
DA-da-da-da!

Now try and put mini-rhythm patterns within this basic four beat."

Like a posse of senile sea lions they self-consciously kept to the one-two-three-four as demonstrated.

"Come along now! Try some mini-beats. You won't know till you try!"

It seemed the older ones were either painfully embarrassed or riddled with arthritis holding their hands prisoners as they still maintained the basic four beat. It took Rupert to break the monotony with a flurry of mini-claps in between, then he timidly broke into a Riverdance-like tirade of clapping much to Heffernan's delight. This broke the ice and some of the others tried their hands at faster movements.

It took one of the elder ladies to speak up first. "I can't get the clapping right!" she bellowed, frustrated.

"Keep trying with us, Edith," Heifer-nan encouraged.

Suddenly Edith managed the basic four-beat.

"*Now*, have you got the clap?" Heffernan bellowed.

As Edith nodded proudly, Sylvia screeched into a belly-laugh. "Have you got the clap! You can't say *that*! Wouldn't tell 'im if you did, eh Edith?"

Stirring laughs from Mike, Sylvie had to stop her handy rhythm as she collapsed laughing onto her desk, leaving Edith both confused and red-faced. But still clapping.

"Right!" Heifer thankfully relieved them from this torturous activity, "Geri! You look like a confident young woman. Like to come up here first?"

Not really. 'I'd rather be the only rubber-phobic passenger on the Titanic,' I think, as my body alienates from my mind and I, somehow, find myself grinning inanely as I weave through the desks. The piano stands ominously at the front of the class, unintroduced and looming. It looks much bigger and clumsier than I remembered before the tea-break. Heifernan pulls the threadbare velvet cushioned stool out to accommodate my threadbare fleshy cushion.

"Now," he leaned his chest into her back as she sat poised at the keys.

If the truth be known, a tingle dances through my body, from the top of my head to my toes at the close contact. If only it wasn't Heifer-nan.

He wrapped his arms around her, taking hold of Geri's hands with his, and placed her hands on the keys, the thumb of her right hand placed to the left of two mini black keys. "This is Middle C. Now place the fingers of your right hand on the keys that follow

Middle C, to the right. These are, respectively D, E, F and G. Now, place the thumb of your *left* hand on Middle C also. Place these fingers on the keys to the left respectively, B, A, G, F. Now, keeping your fingers on these keys try, C-D-E-F-G. Right hand."

She managed his instructions quite easily.

"Now left hand, try C-B-A-G-F."

Once again, success.

"OK, Geri, before you finish off, give us a little concerto of right hand going up to your little finger, and then down to Middle C again, C-D-E-F-G-F-E-D-C."

Once again, no problem. She felt she was getting quite good at this and actually began to enjoy her musical success, her dexterity surprising her.

"Now, the same for the left hand and you're done, C-B-A-G-F-G-A-B-C."

She obliged.

"Excellent. Now who's next?"

Having to wait for the others to perform their melodious crescendo was boring and her gaze was averted to the pictures hanging wonkily on the walls, two inches of dust crowning each frame. Wolfgang Amadeus Mozart stared toward the back of the class in monochrome, as if in disgust, his white candy-floss hair tied back into a miniature pigtail, fastened with an ungainly black bow. His lips pursed into a pout, a fleshy tiara topping a lacy ruffle which cascaded down the front of his white shirt. Edvard Grieg, Ludwig van Beethoven and Tchaikovsky all stood to attention, suspended precariously from the fluffy picture-rails.

Why were these men all so god-awfully ugly? What was it about that era that produced such godforsaken phizogs? Mind you, the same era that found the likes of Casanova sexy, complete with pig's gut tied around his dick with a ribbon in the name of contraception!

Her ramblings were rudely awakened by Heifer-nan congratulating everyone on their first attempts at playing the piano and fiddling with the needle of a record player that looked like it belonged to the likes of Rupert, straight out of the sixties.

"Now before we leave, I'd like to get you thinking about next week's lesson. I'd like you to try and list ten famous people known for their pianist skills. They needn't all be classical or operatic composers such as those in our pictures on the wall – remember Kate Bush, Anthony Hopkins and Jools Holland are all known for their piano expertise. I'd like you to be as diverse as possible. But for now, thank you all for your efforts and I'll leave you with this as something to aim for by the end of the course."

As he pulled the arm across over the record and placed the needle onto the first groove, the harmonious tones straight from a cigar advert filled the room. The soothing echoey sound of cello and piano flowed aqueously as he spoke.

"'The Swan', from the *Carnival of the Animals*, by Camille Saint-Saëns. The rich resonant sound of the cello represents the swan, whilst the piano plays a limpid flowing sound representing the water the swan is floating on."

Five minutes later Geri left the class on cloud nine. A definite piano convert. "Never mind finding a man, I want to play *that* song . . ."

* * *

Sinead was slouched on the leather settee, its surface cool against her sticky hot skin. A plate balanced on the arm bore only remnants and crumbs of the eight slices of toast and hazelnut spread she'd devoured in two minutes flat. And all in the name of abstinence. She'd really wanted a king-size chocolate bar, but was trying to diet. What had started out as just a slice of toast to dampen her appetite had snowballed into a mini-feast. And she *still* wanted the chocolate bar. All ten-and-a-half-stone of her slumped in lethargy and disgust as she wiped the chocolate spread from around her over-active mouth. She lazily grabbed the slender plastic remote control for her CD Player. She must have been in reminiscent mood last night for *The Best Irish Ballads of All Time* had been slotted into gap number one. She pressed <PLAY>. The man's voice filled the room with emotion as he began to sing "The Fields of Athenry"; Sinead turned it up to Volume 15.

"By a lonely prison wall, I heard a young voice calling,
'Michael, they have taken you away . . . '"

There was a part of Sinead that loved listening to the songs and ballads that reminded her of home, but another part that wished they'd modernise them a bit. It was all well and good a hundred or so years ago, but what about in a hundred years' *time?* She began to amuse herself with the possible content of modern Irish ballads, with ideas like, "Don't Skid On The Puke By The Chip Shop" and "I Met My Love In Lidl". Cheered a little by her attempts at humour, she pressed the buttons adeptly to track number seven: "Dirty Old Town". As the rhythm blasted into her apartment, almost a musical alien on the humid Spanish evening air, amid the pestering hum of mosquitoes and the heated whoosh of the outside traffic, she was reminded of her cousin's wedding that she'd gone to in Limerick nearly ten years ago . . .

"Mam, Gertie's coming to the wedding with us, is that OK?"

"OK? 'Course it's bloody OK. Don't you know we all love her too. Sure, we'll have a right time."

Geri had always been welcomed like a member of the family. Half-jarred, as would have been expected of them, they had retreated to the toilets sweaty and dishevelled from dancing. They'd giggled and slurred as they'd touched up their make-up, stood in the blast of the air dryers in an attempt to dry their wet fringes and re-arranged their askew clothing. Unbeknown to either of them Geri had stood on a mislaid sanitary towel on her way out of the toilets and it had stuck, unusually firmly, to her shoe. Oblivious to her attachment they'd continued to dance, confident and beaming to their audience of wallflowers. One particular man, with ruddy red cheeks and Aran knit jumper had stood transfixed by Geri and Sinead as they danced.

"Hey, look at your man staring," Sinead had tittered.

"Obviously entranced by our dancing skills."

"And charisma."

"Probably dead jealous he can't shimmy like us."

"'Course! Weren't we the original Dancing Queens?"

The middle-aged man had waited until the music had died down and just a gentle hum buzzed through the hotel ballroom before he made his way over to them, where they stood waiting in anticipation on the dance floor for the next song. As he'd approached, the hum seemed to lull, and he beamed proudly.

"S'cuse me, missus," he said and pointed at the floor markedly, "but I think your thing's after falling!"

Geri and Sinead had looked down, puzzled, only to see this huge white marshmallow stuck brazenly to the bottom of Geri's shoe, illuminated for all its worth by the ultra-violet lights. Geri'd nearly died with embarrassment but had stood her ground, pulled off the offending article, and throwing it off to the side. It wasn't until the wedding party applauded that she realised the total extent of her audience!

It hit Sinead once again how much she missed Gertie, home and the fun they used to have. She loved Spain, especially the clothes and the selection of fantastic leather shoes, but hated the loneliness and isolation that went with it, and was even tiring of the climate.

"Damn it," she shifted on the settee, sitting upright and tucking her legs underneath her, "I'm going to ring Gertie!"

Grabbing the telephone she punched the numbers positively. It rang only three times before she heard Geri's familiar voice.

"Hello?"

"Gertie? Hi! Sinead!"

"Hey, how's things? Great to hear from you!"

"Oh, I just had to ring you. I've been sitting here on my own thinking about that wedding of Veronica's and –"

"And that bloody thing got stuck to my shoe! God, what a laugh we had! Do you still hear from her? What's she doing with herself? Has she got any kids?"

"No! They separated about four years ago. But she's got three children by him."

"Do you think she'll re-marry?"

"She's *still* married. You can't get divorced in Ireland that easily, you know."

"God, yeah . . . I'd forgotten about that. What about the kiddies though?"

"Oh, they're with her. You know the way that the kids *always* stay with the mother, and the father's free to revert to his bachelor days with nil commitment."

Mmm, thought Geri, I know that feeling all too well.

"Not that you'd ever need to worry about that though, eh? That Kevin's a real corker, isn't he?"

Geri felt a pang of guilt at not being straight with Sinead from the start, and pandering to Sinead's perspective of Kevin and their "perfect" lifestyle. Not quite able to lie outright to Sinead, she merely changed the subject.

"Hey, did you ever see any more of Droopy?" she gushed as she remembered another name. "And Huge?"

"Droopy?" Sinead was temporarily puzzled.

"*Droopy!* Droopy Cock."

"Droopy Cock! Gertie, what on earth are you saying to me? Droopy Cock and Huge? I'm lost!"

"Huge Ones!"

"Droopy Cock and Huge Ones! Explain!"

"Oh, you'd better get out of that country quick. The sun's addling your brain? Can't you remember anything? Drew Peacock and Hugh Jones! You remember, the two Welsh guys we met in Tenerife! You gave them your mobile number, remember? And we agreed that we'd meet up with them if they were ever in the area. When you told them you were set for the assignment in Valencia they told you they were headed for Madrid, and they'd ring you!"

Sinead laughed out loud for the first time in nearly a fortnight. Gertie was good for her, and she was missing her desperately. If only she didn't feel so jealous of her domestic security . . . compared to her, Geri had everything.

"No, I never heard from them again. Not too worried about that though."

"No, you're probably not. I bet you're out every night with different guys. You lucky bitch, I bet you're having a great time!"

Now it was Sinead's turn not to disappoint. Guilty as she spoke, she obliged, "Well, as I said before, you know what fellas are like in the heat. A bit of sun on their goolies and they're like wild dogs! And you know what I say, Gertie?"

They both spoke at the same time, repeating their aged motto:

"The best way to get over a man is to get under another!"

As if hearing it for the first time, as usual, they laughed out loud.

Sinead's voice softened, indicating just a hint of insecurity amidst her raucousness. "You know though, Gertie, they're not all what they're cut out to be. There was one guy there a few weeks ago. He had all the right credentials – a nice car, a swollen wallet, two apartments and was in line for the MD's job. But he was a complete physical turn-off! I'd hoped he might've grown on me. He was really reliable and very keen. But still, he just didn't give me the throb!"

Geri laughed, envious at her friend's freedom and confidence.

Two hours later Geri had told Sinead all about her piano classes and the characters she'd met, and Sinead had enlightened Geri on the industrial movement through Spain and her plans for the next year. *And* how she still managed to buy the gorgeous lace *M&S* knickers they both loved from the *M&S* in Valencia.

As the clock struck midnight in Valencia and eleven in England, both women lay – lonely, cold and insecure in their beds – alone with their disturbed and discontented thoughts. Each one more than slightly envious of the other.

Chapter Six

As usual, less than a week since One Parent Family & Child Benefit day, Geri was already quaking at the prospect of visiting the cash dispenser. Using her cash-point card had become a nail-biting, hot-flush-inducing experience. It didn't help that she'd bought a jumper from the market at the weekend in a "long-lasting-quality rather than short-term-cheapo" drive. The guilt involved in spending money on herself, especially now in the shadow cast by Kevin's evaporation was, at times, almost unbearable. She felt selfish and negligent, despite Cynthia's reassurances that spending some on herself was *just* what she needed. With her financial situation worsening she was uncomfortably aware that the time was looming to contact the absent parent and whisper "pounds sterling" into his waxy ear-hole. She was so determined that his responsibility to the boys would be maintained that, for the first time with any degree of seriousness, she was faced with those awful acronyms such as DHSS and CSA. As a total novice she could understand how their true meanings could be misconstrued as Dirty Hairy Shit Stirrers and Can't Stand Aggro. She began to wonder whether the Kevin she so missed and loved (*but kinda hated too*) wasn't quite the 'real' one, that everyone else saw.

Maybe he was boring?

Still, she knew that her bed seemed big and her nightdress long.

As she maneouvered the double buggy through the shuffling OAP's lingering at the bus stop she accidentally caught the thick ankles of Mrs Scittz – mother of the dreaded Ursula.

"*Aarggghh!*" Mrs Scittz hollered – over-dramatically, Geri suspected, solely to attract attention to her clumsiness. As she limped pathetically, pivoting a 360° turn to face her attacker, Geri struggled to contain a wicked grin. It was just great to see her in pain! She looked disappointed when she realised it was only Geri.

"Oh! It's you. Can't you watch where you're going with that bloody contraption? You nearly had me ankles off!"

Disgruntled at Geri's pleasant smile she attempted conversation, unfortunately with the booby question, "How's Kevin these days?"

Alarm bells ring in my head. Does she know? Doesn't she know? Keeping my guard up and my best side out, I opt for the easiest response – the lie. So, like a fish to water, I jump in and lie to Mrs Scittz – I'm a natural, in fact, "Kevin? God, yeah he's fine. Working hard, as usual, you know."

Yeah, working hard at making my life a bloody misery and "her" life fan-bloody-tastic!

"He's still at Sandiford's then?" Then, before Geri had chance to confirm, "He's been there years, hasn't he? Must be in line for promotion soon then. Oh, the boys are gorgeous. Don't they look like him?"

Ten minutes of gritted teeth and false smiles being enough for anybody, Geri was relieved when the key in Mrs Scittz's back finally wound down and she was rendered stationary and silent once again, waiting to be jerked into life by another passing buggy.

Making her way to the library, Geri felt an imaginary black cloud hovering only two feet over the top of her head and following her determinedly.

Once in the library she uncharacteristically parked the buggy in the children's section, leaving Cameron to dog-ear, tear and generally vandalise a great selection of books, whilst she skulked by the psychology shelves, looking for suitable titles which suggested reasons for infidelity and personality assessment. Then suddenly one seemed to stick two fingers in its mouth and *whooooped* her with a loud whistle as if saying, "Hey, over here! Look at me! No! Me on the second shelf down! Yeah, no right a bit. Christ! The one with the blue cover and green letters. Yeah! That's it. Me. Pick me up, you're gonna need me!" Geri's eyes rested on the title, *How to Snare Your Bachelor*. It sounded just

108

what she'd been looking for and, determined to adopt Sinead's approach of getting over one man by getting under another, she plucked it from the shelf.

After reading it, however, she wasn't sure whether she was disgusted or disgusting. The author – it just *had* to be a man – had started with the basics such as "Wear a blouse with buttons to indicate easy access to your breasts", "Wear skirts that loosely outline the body and *appear easy to raise*". He had then moved swiftly onto the secondaries: "Avoid food particles between the teeth", "Are you too fat?" and "Avoid glasses that are too trendy or extreme". For once, feeling proudly old-fashioned, she was amazed as she'd imagined that "Snaring Your Bachelor" meant that you'd want to maintain contact with him for longer than one night! In her wholesome imagination she'd expected this to mean *marry* the bachelor of your choice. She wondered if maybe she was a little out-of-date.

Maybe I am the Delia Smith in the kitchen of Gordon Ramsey; the Jane Fonda in the gymnasium of Pilates. Maybe I should take some tips on board and maybe tonight would provide the perfect opportunity for a drastic, sexy change of image.

Glancing at her watch she realised it was only four hours until she was due at her next evening class: Internet with Dave Lomax.

* * *

With only an hour to go, she strained and squeezed herself into her pre-pregnancy balconette bra, contorting her flabby form beyond belief as she grimaced at her reflection.

"When *is* the best time to make love again?" she asked herself, distracted.

OK, so the breast milk had evaporated months ago, but I'm not sure that my gusset wouldn't yawn uninvitingly at the merest suggestion of amour? I nearly pissed myself just shouting at Cameron the other day. I often regret not doing The Exercises – the crotch-squeezing ones that you can do anywhere, even at the bus stop. But I don't go anywhere on the bloody bus, so what good is that to me? Must be why I never did them.

Remembering what Quick-Draw had always said about first impressions, and how they count and all, she'd decided to go into this Internet class with all guns blazing: a hormonal hurricane let loose. Minutes later, as she stares at the roll of flab straining out from beneath her bra strap it appears she has a bigger bulge *below* her bra, than *in* it!

Sod it! I'll just have to stand up straighter that's all, and push 'em out a bit. Now for the knickers, although as I look down at my forest of pubic hair I see it's so thick and vast that I wonder if I'd be mistaken for wearing a pair of brown furry pants. But still . . . it'd match my fake-fur coat, my fake-fur-trimmed gloves and my fake-fur handbag that I dance around.

She opted for the waisters, the prescription knickers, concluding that she wouldn't be seen in them. Leaving the house wearing clothes unusually tight she felt like a turkey trussed for the oven, the height of discomfort. She hadn't quite bargained on Cynthia's reaction when she dropped the boys off to her for an hour and a half . . .

"Good God! What're ya wearing? Where d'ya think you're going?"

I choose to adopt the thick-skinned approach; easy after years of adolescent practice.

"To the Internet course with Dave Lomax." *I retort smugly, oblivious to her outraged expression as her eyes hop incredulously from my boobs to my short A-line skirt which appeared easy to raise and my blouse with buttons down the front.*

"Oh no! You've got one of those sheepdog bras on."

"Those what?"

"Them ones that rounds 'em up and points 'em in the right direction. Come *in*, will you! I don't want the neighbours seeing you dressed like that!"

Shimmied in over the doorstep and pushed into the hallway, Geri was shaken by the rattle of the front door being banged firmly behind her. The boys had already gone in to ransack their toy boxes.

"Where was I? Oh yeah – in my day a bra was a bra!" Cynthia continued, "Now you've got these bloody uplifters and squeezers. Don't you go forgetting you're a mother to two little chaps!"

"Now, there's a cute name for them!" Geri looked down proudly at her chest. "Kevin used to call them Flopsie and Dropsie, cos you know how the left one always was a bit smaller than the right one."

She's only angered more at my sarcasm.

"You KNOW what I mean!"

Pushing past with her shoulder, determined not to be deterred, Geri checked that the boys were OK before she left. As she did so, Cynthia grabbed her by the bra strap, bungee-ing her back toward her in reverse.

"Christ! That bra's too tight. It's cutting the back off 'o ya! Like a bloody saddle on a horse's back!"

With her confidence now dangerously close to shattering, she said her goodbyes swiftly and promised to be home by seven. Resiliently she got back into her car and made her way to "Internet with *Dave Lomax!*"

* * *

The industrial gutter, known to many Londoners as The Tube, rumbled heavily along its tracks. As they all sat watching their reflections in darkened windows, they were bustled and jiggled in their seats in rhythmic unison. Those unfortunate enough not to be seated were definitively split into two categories – those that did mind being jostled against strangers' bodies and those that didn't! The aromas of various cuisines took on almost United Nations proportions and questionable levels of personal hygiene were obvious as the Tube ground to an unexpected halt in the middle of a tunnel between Chancery Lane and St Paul's. Ben stuck his finger in his ear to scratch it, then, unembarrassed by his audience, sniffed his finger, wincing at the bummy smell: *Hmmmm, I've got poo-ear. Must have a shower when I get home. If I ever get home.* With the train showing little promise of moving this side of next month he grabbed his mini-portfolio, filing through various sheets of paper. He'd sent his sketches off to twenty greeting-card companies and had spent over seventy quid in postage.

You need money before you can even start to get your work seen, he admonished silently as his fingers moved at rapid speed searching for a sheet of white A4. Oblivious to the re-jiggling motion of the train he scanned the page for the address the Director had given him as he'd left work. This could be my lucky break, he mused, fingering the now wrinkled paper, folding the sheet into a small square and nestling it securely in his breast pocket. Before he even had the chance to refasten his portfolio the train screeched to a halt to the commentary of *"Mind the Gap. Stand Clear of The Doors Please"* and he jostled against bodies as they tried to get off of the train. The cold evening air blasted in through the open train doors bringing him out of his quandary and back to earth with a shiver. He grabbed his things and strode off the platform, climbing the old iron stairs three at a time.

Great, he said to himself, still time to get down the gym for a workout. He always felt more human after that.

He rushed through his house quicker than his first orgasm, pausing to sprinkle a few plankton-flavoured flakes into the goldfish bowl. As his eyes darted quickly from one fish to another – he always had to count that all seven were present and correct – he couldn't help but notice how Sneezy and Happy seemed to be bumping into each other and how Doc was swimming almost on his side.

"Mmmm, maybe you're not too well."

A proud pet owner, Ben was desperate for a dog, an Irish Setter, but was making himself wait until he finally made the break from the rat-race of the city – the large community where people are lonely together – to the luxury of the countryside in his pursuit of life as an artist.

He spoke through the glass to his wonky aquatic friend, "I'll have to keep an eye on you. Or are you just desperate and lonely waiting for your Snow-White?" Pulling the drawstring on his soft cream joggers, revealing a glimpse of his downy, tanned six-pack, he asked himself the same question, grabbed his blue sports bag and closed the front door behind him.

* * *

God, did you ever feel like mutton dressed as lamb? I'm horrified and furious with myself, cursing under my breath at my own stupidity. Am I embarrassed! I'm more over-dressed than one of Jamie Oliver's salads, amongst a class of cloned mustard and cress! Dave Lomax is disappointingly aged, the name "Dave" obviously a red-herring to distract you from his real age, and I've got at least ten pairs of male hot-blooded eyes glued to my anatomy in a way that makes me feel like a well-earned hot meal. I've got underwear that's cutting permanent scars into my podgy skin and to make matters worse, we're sitting scrunched into children's chairs at children's desks! The only thing I'm marginally encouraged by is my recollection of office technology.

The only pleasant surprise for Geri as she squeezed

her already compressed form into the small chair was that she was surprisingly familiar with the set up, understanding the office jargon that was being used. Her confidence "on-screen" broadened, only to be shrink-wrapped as the lusty eyes bore into the side of her head, rendering her a trussed-up sack of awkwardness. Now, after only one lesson and already a natural at these evening classes, she had anticipated the tea break with relief, opting to remain seated, primarily for fear of being unable to unfold herself from the confines of the chair. As the others gabbled and gushed their way out of the classroom door, putting into practice their social skills, she – causing much discomfort to her internal organs – took a deep breath. She made a mental note to wear leggings and sweatshirt next week.

If I make it that far . . .

Just as she was panicking, having accidentally found her way into the porn pages of the web, she was aware of an aftershave-scented person hovering behind her right shoulder. She looked up to see a smart navy-blue suit, a classy shirt and yellow tie with a rather attractive, but rugged head perched on the top of it, smiling down at her.

"Interrupting something, am I?" he enquired, smirking at her attempts to spell cunnilingus correctly. She instantly reddened, in her typical fashion, and then, as if her nerve-endings were attached to the outside of her clothes, became aware of her sheepdog bra and revealing blouse, darkening her blush to absolutely crimsonite.

"Mmm. I mean no. No! No. Ha. Ha ha. Just playing, you know."

"Done this before, have you?" He sat, seemingly genuine enough, on the desk next to her, smoothing down the silver paper over a KitKat, sliding his fingernail – short, clean and neat – along each precipice, before breaking each of the four chocolate fingers off, and popping them into his mouth one by one.

"Done what before?" she snapped, the very essence of the term 'attack is the best form of defence'.

"Used the Internet?" he innocently replied.

"Yeah, why, have you?"

"A little bit, just fumbled around at work really. I don't know my way around it properly."

"Where do you work?" Geri was, by now, very keen to shift the weight of interest from herself onto him.

"In insurance. Just a small local company. You've probably never heard of them." With the inmates now making their way noisily back into the room she was glad of the interruption until he whispered quickly, "Would you like a quick drink after this? Nothing heavy, just a quick drink over the road?"

Surely any man worth his weight in PlayStation games wouldn't be interested in a sexual imposter such as me! The clothes alone screamed "clueless". Isn't it obvious I'm post-pregnancy? Doesn't he realise lost identity is sometimes common after such trauma to your body? It can take a year for your hormones to balance out again, you know!! You don't know? Oh . . . as my mind races, I realise he's still looking at me, waiting for an answer.

The easiest option is to nod. This requires no explanation or excuse.

But my bowels have turned to water.

"Great," he places an almost sweaty warm hand on the thin material covering her shoulder, and grins. "Adam. And your name?"

"Geri," she splutters, her voice strangely alien to her.

My concentration is shot to bits! What am I getting myself into? Who is this man? More importantly, will I be able to shake off my maternal guise? Will I spend the evening overpoweringly straightening his tie, dusting his dandruffy shoulders and slicking down his hair with my spittooned fingertips?

The remaining hour flew by in a confusing flurry of search engines and websites. Her mind wandered more than an amnesiac's on the fruitless search for home after a night on the tiles, as she contemplated her impending predicament. Before she knew it, it was time.

"Ready then?" His pearly whites glinted through his perfect mouth. Fumbling with her pen and pad, clumsily, she mumbled, "Right. Yeah. Yeah. Where're we going?"

"The Puking Sailor? I'll drive, then drop you off here after."

"OK. God, am I doing the right thing here or *what?*" she demanded of herself.

"Excuse me?"

"Eh?"

"Did you say something? Sexy bitch."

"Oh, no. Sorry. No."

"Sexy bitch."

She found herself giggling, nervously.

They made their way through the floodlit car park to a gleaming burgundy Audi Quattro.

What is this guy doing on an Internet course?

The perfect gentleman, he opened her door first, watching her as she pulled *down* her skirt in an attempt to cover her knees and pulled *up* her blouse-with-the-buttons-down-the-front to conceal her enhanced valley. The engine purred, the heated seat titillated the backs of her thighs and the dashboard was illuminated with a creamy light. She watched as he deftly stabbed at the buttons to activate the stereo. The dulcet tones of Marvin Gaye washed over her – a little dated, she pondered – in a sensual almost clichéd abduction.

My doubts about Adam begin to diminish. Maybe he is genuinely interested in me. Maybe I am the woman he's been waiting for. He pulls into the car park of the pub, and turns the engine off. I'm just about to open the door and get out when my illusions are shattered. He catches my arm –

"Wait a minute. I'm not ready yet."

He fumbled in his pocket intently. Before you could say "A gram in your hand is worth two up your nose" he'd laid out a neat line of white powder on the back of his right hand, and holding one nostril closed with the other, sniffed it noisily up.

Shock, horror! I'm in the car with a bloody druggie. He probably sells it too – an insurance man couldn't afford this car. I knew something was amiss!

Smacking his lips and smiling wildly, proud of himself, he asked, "Ready now?"

"Ready now? I'm not ready to go anywhere with you. Do you know I've got two children at home waiting for me?"

What in God's name made me say that? I'm not exactly brimming with street-cred, but anyway . . .

"Take me back to the college, please. I want to get my car and go home."

"Oh! You're not one of them, are ya?"

"One of *what*?"

"Those phobics. Look, a little bit now and then doesn't do you any harm. You really should try some. It might loosen you up a bit. Help you lose the paranoia."

"Look, what part don't you understand?"

His eyes switched from pleading to perverted.

Maybe that's the wrong approach.

She attempted to make amends. "Please. Just take me back to the college. I really *don't* want to have a drink with you. I don't know what made me agree in the first place. I'm sorry. Sorry for misleading you and messing you about. Just take me back. Please."

Her cringe-worthy speech seemed to jerk him back to reality and he started the car again, this time heading back to their original location. She was desperate to see the familiar scabs of rust eating into her rear wheel arches and those lovely bald tyres of hers. Finally they were pulling into the car park, and there she was, her snail-mobile of a car. Pre-empting her swift departure, it became evident that Adam had other ideas. Swinging into a darkened parking space beneath a huge tree, he turned off the engine and grabbed Geri around the back of the neck. His sooty breath close to her face, he whispered, hoarsely, "Come on, baby. Just a little kiss. Never mind about the drink. Come on."

His strength was overwhelming, as she was pulled across the slidey leather seat, her knee now jammed painfully onto the gear stick.

"No. Please no. I'm sorry." Panic engulfed her as he forced his tongue into her mouth.

God, it's over a year since I swapped bodily fluids! My mind races, reminding myself of his chemical-dependency, and the erratic behaviour I could possibly be expecting. I decide to go along with the kiss, on the basis that I might get out quicker than if I struggle. Just think of it like going for an interview for a job you don't really want. Participate purely for the practice.

She decided that in this case most definitely, the best form of defence was *attach*. His tongue rotated and swirled in her mouth in a most unappealing fashion. Confused as to how she was supposed to react she found herself kind of swirling too, dribble making its escape down her chin.

Lucky dribble!

Then it happened. The absolute horror amid an already horrific situation. He put his hand on her waist and pulled her blouse out of her skirt. So much for the blouse-with-the-buttons-up-the-front! The author of *that* book hadn't happened upon the likes of Adam!

She could feel his cold, huge hand on her abdominal roll of fat.

Christ! I wasn't expecting this. The sheepdog bra has welded itself to my skin, cutting through the epidermis, now part of my anatomy, it's so tight!

Adam was now grunting and his teeth were clanking against Geri's, almost animal-like. She was both embarrassed and desperate to get out of this new dilemma she was posed with: should she let her abdominal flab remain bulbous OR should she, in the name of pride alone, straighten her back and suck in her stomach in an attempt to flatten it out?

Am I trying to impress him or just maintain my own self-worth?

The quandary intensified as she felt his nimble fingers pinching and twinging on the left side of her abdominal bulge. As if unfulfilled, he then moved to the right side of the aforementioned bulge, almost confused. It was then she realised.

He's looking for my nipples! He thinks it's my bloody tits! He is trying to locate a nipple on the roll of fat that's bulging over the top of my skirt! The Wonderbra's obviously pushing my boobs up too high – he hasn't moved his hand up anywhere near enough! Enough really is enough!

Managing to push his hand away firmly, she strained for breath.

"Come on, baby, let's make love."

"I'm *not* making anything with you! Stop, now please. *Stop!*"

Cut the rolling waves crashing onto the beach.

Screech the needle across the romantic music.

Turn up the lights!

Getting out of his car, leaving him drooling and dishevelled, she crammed her blouse back into the offendingly tight skirt indignantly.

"Bloody library books! These clothes are going in the bin when I get home! Mother Is Always Right! She said I looked ridiculous and she was probably right! God, how can I ever come back to this course again? 'Internet with Dave Lomax', sounded so promising only twenty-four hours ago."

Finally released from custody and back in the surprisingly comfortable chill of her car, she speedily coerced the key into the ignition. The engine rumbled noisily, the cold dampness of the seat making the hairs on the backs of her thighs stand up, and the dashboard illuminated with a sickeningly cold green light. Hitting the button to activate the stereo the crackling inaudibility of Radio Two pebble-dashed the interior of the car.

Thank God for familiar territory.

Driving back to Cynthia's, she wondered if this was what the singles market held for her. Boisterous gropings with definite intent. Gone was the tender courteousness of "going-out-with-someone".

As she indicated to pull into Cynthia's road, she began to feel a depression washing over her.

Maybe evening classes aren't the right place to find a man. Even more, do I still want one?

Ringing the doorbell she felt desperate to see her

boys and be once again anonymous from the outside world, in her own home with the unconditional warm love of her children.

Cynthia opened the door, aware instantly that something was wrong.

"Come in, love. What's up?"

"Put the kettle on, Mum. Can I go up and put on your joggers and borrow a jumper from you?"

"Course you can, pet. You know where they are."

Geri climbed the stairs wearily.

Cynthia made for the kitchen, muttering something about pride coming before a fall . . .

Chapter Seven

Sinead gathered her paperwork on her desk in preparation for the monthly meeting. This was the big one and they'd waited until Friday morning to have it. The one where Head-honchos announced who'd be spending a week back in England to collect more parts and papers. She'd thought that she would be late again when she found the massive cockroach scuttling behind the cistern as she'd brushed her teeth that morning, only to watch it turn back on itself and make for the door. The sickening crunch as she'd pushed the waste bin down on it still crackled in her head. She crossed her fingers discreetly as she folded her arms across the papers and carried them to the meeting room. As she paced her way down the long, carpeted corridor the hum of the air-conditioning was drowned by the screech of Charmaine.

"Nooo, get out of it! Ooh, you are funny, James!"

Sinead turned, purely out of curiosity, to see Charmaine's munchkin proportions shrouded by three handsome six-footers who were smiling down at her inanely.

"Sinead! Hey, Sinead, feeling better now, are ya? You did look rough, I have to say."

Sinead smiled and nodded, unwilling to get into conversation regarding her diarrhoea.

"I was tellin' department RZ 34 about you. About what a lovely-smelling air-freshener you've got." She tittered at her own bitchiness. "How it really did the trick."

"Seems you've been putting yourself about a bit again, Charmaine."

"Don't be like that. I *had* to do the rounds to organise this meeting."

"Seems the whole office has been summoned to this meeting," Sinead quipped without even glancing at her.

Once in the large conference room, chairs were scraped and garbled chatter filled the room as they waited for the MD to arrive. Charmaine continued to titter and flirt, confident in her natural domain – surrounded by men.

"Ooh, I hope it's me," she squawked, giggling as she smoothed her silk skirt firmly down over her ample hips. As possessor of a 32A chest and wide hips, fashion was a constant source of angst to her and she'd been ecstatic at the invention of the silicone chicken fillets that padded out her bra. Checking her chest was maximised sufficiently and her hips concealed, she leant into the table, reached for the jug of iced water, poured herself a glass and then sat down. You could barely see her face over the table now.

"Hope *what's* you?" one of the suits asked, a smile in his voice, a twinkle in his eye and a third leg craning to see over the table at Charmaine.

"I hope it's meee. Going back to England for a week. You know, I'd never flown before coming here. I was so nervous, thought I'd be airsick and everything! But, oooh, it was just lovely! Up there above the clouds, that lovely blue sky. *And* you can have wine too, you know. Mind you," she giggled, giving her best 'Barbara Windsor', "makes me a bit tipsy. Never know what I might do up there!"

Sinead couldn't resist it, and had spoken out before she realised, "Don't go to the loo in them planes though, will you, Charmaine."

The smile slipped from Charmaine's over-made-up face.

"Why?" she questioned, all innocent and cutesy.

"Them pressurised cabins and all. Just sitting on one of those toilets could suck your fallopian tubes straight out, you know."

"No!" Charmaine was totally horrified. "Well, that shouldn't be allowed. How could they allow that?" Then she reddened as she realised the congregation was laughing. "Oh very clever, Sinead. As if I'd believe *that*! Honestly, you're so pathetic. As if!"

"You know, you really put the suck into success, don't you?" Sinead continued.

"Piss off," Charmaine hissed back, reddening.

The disruption was instantly calmed at the appearance of the great revered one – the MD – at the door. They all stood up and waited for him to be seated before they themselves sat down.

"Morning all. Before we begin I'd like to ask Charmaine if she'd mind taking the minutes of this meeting. My secretary is otherwise engaged, and I'd be grateful if you'd do the honours, please."

Charmaine was delighted at the invitation and squeaked, "Oh certainly, Mr Rogers. Now, where do you want me?"

"Next door'd be good," Sinead piped up, causing more mirth and guffawing.

Mr Rogers ignored the interruption, "Just where you are'll be fine, thank you, Charmaine."

She busied herself importantly with her pink-inked fountain pen and began to make notes on her pad, her writing all bubbles-over-i's and loops-under-g's.

The meeting was only fifteen minutes on when a firm knock caused them to look toward the closed wooden door. As it glided open, an unfamiliar face smiled in confidently, introducing himself as Steven Randall and apologising for his lateness. Sinead instantly took a liking to him. Confident yet polite, smart but not over-dressed, good-looking but in an ordinary way.

Mr Rogers explained, "This is Steven Randall. He'll be working alongside you, on the EM411 project."

Sinead worked for one of those companies who

would never reveal exactly *what* they were working on, but gave an alpha numerical code-name for it instead, which usually ended up in *nobody* actually knowing exactly what they were working on!

* * *

The cool basement of the building provided the ideal location for the company bar, next to the in-house gymnasium. Its natural stone walls and dim lighting created an eerie chilliness for the climatic Valencia and provided an ideal place to congregate after these meetings. This ritual, by means of both celebration and commiseration, was the only time Sinead partook in work-related socialising. Her appearance this time was for one of celebration. She'd been selected to return to England in a week's time for four days, and she was delighted. As her gin and tonic was placed on the table she grabbed it eagerly, gulping a copious amount for a first swig. She was in good form, and in a drinking mood. Surrounded by at least ten of her male counterparts, she was able to stand her ground in the drinking department, able for both their verbal abuse and sexist humour. The mood changed as Charmaine entered the bar with Steven Randall and Mr Rogers.

"Oh shit, hope he doesn't come and sit with us," one of her colleagues whispered. "We'll really have to watch our p's and q's. Old Rogers hates swearing."

"And smoking."

"Oh shit. Let's be really boring and maybe he'll make a quick exit."

"Gawd, he'd probably stay all the more then. Boring is his forte."

They were silenced by Mr Rogers' presence, once again introducing Steven Randall to his new colleagues. The conversation flowed as freely as the drink and even Charmaine managed to keep abreast of the current discussion. Sinead attempted to be comradely and offered her a cigarette.

"No thanks, I've got an aversion to cigarette filters – can't stand squeaky cotton wool!" She tittered and jiggled at her own remark. Sinead raised her eyes heavenward in disbelief. Ignoring her, Charmaine bubbled on,

"We were in Vivir Sin Dormir last night, it was brilliant."

"Think that's my motto since moving to Valencia," proffered one of the young English guys who had recently been sent on assignment to the Valencian office. "*Live Without Sleep* somehow coins my lifestyle."

"It took me weeks to find the nightlife," interrupted one of the more established ex-pats. "If you don't know where to go, the city can seem dead at night. It's quite widespread, don't you think?"

"You need to get one of the listings guides. There's three – *Qué y Dónde*, *Carterlera Turio* and what's the highbrow one?"

Sinead was surprised as Steven Randall answered, "*Valencia Semanal*. You can get them from news-kiosks, about one euro twenty cents." He paused. "Or two hundred pesetas." He turned to Sinead and asked,

"Have you been to the *Palau de la Música*?"

She was stumped, having never heard of it, "No? Where's that?"

"On the *Rió Turia*. It's a greenhouse-type glass concert hall. You mean you've not heard of the daily classical and jazz concerts?"

She felt embarrassed that she hadn't. Thankfully her ignorance of the Valencian environs was saved by Mr Rogers, who approached the table mid-conversation. He boomed, "I adore opera! My favourites are Luciano Pavarotti, Placido Domingo & José Carreras. I saw them at Wembley Arena last year. They were truly fantastic." His voice was a boring monotone, endured only because of his seniority rather than his captivating deliverance.

Charmaine had obviously decided that embarrassing herself *once* wasn't enough, so she piped up again, "Ooh, I love the opera too. You just can't beat a bit of culture, can you?"

"Bacteria's the only culture you'll ever have, Charmaine," Sinead interrupted.

Charmaine ignored her purposefully. "Who are they? Luciano Pavarotti, I know him, he's that fat guy with the black hair – looks a bit like Demis Roussos. Who are the other two?"

"Placido Domingo and José Carreras. You must have heard of them," Mr Rogers explained. "The Three Tenors."

Charmaine laughed dismissively as she gulped at her Baileys, "Three Tenors! I'd rather have three tenners in me purse!"

They all cringed and tried to continue with the conversation, despite Charmaine's desperate attempts to join in, and despite her obvious drunkenness which seemed to be accelerating at a ridiculous speed. Steven Randall began to unravel his history to his new colleagues, surprising them with his experience as a horse-trainer. His parents came from Kildare and were big horse-lovers.

"Oh, I love fucking horses!" Charmaine interrupted, resting down her fifth empty glass. Her remark received from the company en masse the one-eyebrow-raised, incredulous expression that only Benny Hill was the true master of. Silence reigned for the first time that evening.

"Excuse me?" Steven asked, ever the gentleman.

"I love fucking horses." she slurred, her face hideously blotchy by now. "Ever since I was a girl. I've just loved 'em."

"Don't you mean you 'fucking love horses'?"

"Yeah! That's what I said, innit?"

"Charmaine?" one of the reps joined in, smirking.

"Yeah?" she smiled, all wobbly and unfocussed.

"If you didn't have any feet would you wear shoes?"

She laughed raucously, over-acting every move, "Course not, you wally! Ha, if I didn't have feet would I wear shoes? Ha, you're mad, you are."

He maintained a straight face as he ventured, "Well, what the hell are you doing wearing a bra then?"

The men all roared with laughter, having taken

about just as much as they could of her fake-smiles and playing dumb. Charmaine, being slow on the uptake, laughed with them until the belated penny dropped and the smile slid from her face.

"You lousy bastards! You're all over me when it suits you. Get stuffed, the lot of ya!" She grabbed her pink fake-fur handbag and staggered fitfully to the door.

Steven Randall leant in toward Sinead and whispered, "Do you think she'll be all right?"

"Course she will. She's always the same. Sad cow."

"You know, they say two-thirds of people have a problem with dependency," Steven informed her, all husky-voiced, deep and meaningful.

"Is that so? Well, do *you* know, they say seven-fifths of all people don't understand fractions?" Sinead replied, tongue-in-cheek.

Steve laughed at her and asked if she'd like another G&T. Sinead accepted instantly. He returned from the bar minutes later with a double for her, and a Jack Daniels for himself.

"Still, Charmaine must be feeling pretty rough," he sympathised.

"Steven. Charmaine really is her own worst enemy. She lurches from one disaster to another, plays herself up as the bimbo and is generally known as 'yo-yo drawers'."

"Mmm, still, I do feel a bit sorry for her. She's such a victim."

"She *chooses* to be! That's the way she likes it!"

"Yeah, but we've all had to navigate a few of our

own crises, haven't we? Maybe Charmaine just needs a helping hand."

"She needs more than a helping hand." Sinead was now tiring of Steven's misguided loyalty to Charmaine, wondering whether he too was snared by her gossamer-thin façade. "Typical," she muttered into her glass, "another willing captive. And he seemed OK too."

* * *

Ashen-faced, Geri'd slept a disturbed sleep. Dreams of snowstorms and men with huge powder-lined nostrils had flashed into her head and she had woken, embarrassed to find herself rotating her tongue, laundromat-style, on her pillow.

"Right, I'm going to put it all behind me," she declared to her damp pillow. "Shit, it's probably just another day in the life of insurance-man Adam; cars, copulation and cocaine. I *won't* let you ruin my week!"

Considering it an advantage that she'd woken so early, and at four fifty-three she still probably had a good hour before the children awoke, she grabbed the thick *Cosmo* that she'd bought a fortnight ago and still hadn't taken the cellophane wrapper, concealing a Liposuction Special, off.

"Time for a bit of an image update," she announced to the mirror, as she glanced up from the glossy pages housing effortless beauty and flawless complexions. She flicked the pages noisily, slumping the magazine down onto the bed, covering her legs.

God, I feel ancient. I feel more like Barbara Cartland than Caprice.

"Of course," she informed the vacant pillow beside her, "it's made harder in the shadow of those bloody Celebrity Moms. The likes of Pammie, Madonna and Posh Spice. And that damn advert with Jane Seymour, with the two dogs, three agents, six fax machines, five kids and a bottle of hair dye!"

The pillow remained silent.

Surprisingly.

"Oh well," she decided, kicking back the warm covers from her legs, "for now I'll console myself with the useless fact that melting an ice cube in your mouth burns 2.3 calories," and made her way to the freezer.

Seeing as breakfast in bed is about as rare as diamonds in my wineglass!

Having frozen her taste buds into minute particles of pain, Geri decided to skip breakfast on the pretext that she wouldn't have been able to taste it anyway, and instead tuned in to the exercises on *Breakfast Telly*. They looked too easy, at least from her armchair. She asked Cameron what he thought of her starting an aerobics class. "Am I too ancient?" she asked his confused and wide-eyed face. So completely innocent! She cupped his milky smooth face and kissed his forehead. "Go on, love, go play with your tractors and trailers."

Still, she told herself, the aerobics classes would be full of young girls, career girls and perfect mums with alice-bands and Executive Husbands. Shifting her wobbly arse from the armchair she lay on the floor, chancing a few quick sit-ups with the breakfast-telly fitness guru before the children began screaming for something or another. Attempting to suck her stomach in and feel her hip bones, she was horrified to find that she couldn't.

Christ! They must be there somewhere! Jesus, my pelvis would cave in without them! Taking the canned advice from the leotard-clad presenter, she tilted her pelvis and, looking at the top of her window, curled her shoulders round to raise her head slightly. As she relaxed her straining neck, her head banged painfully onto the floor and her mind drifted back to the rows she'd had with Kevin under that bloody ceiling. As she digressed she recalled that first holiday they'd had together. They'd only been going out with each other for about ten months and they'd booked an all-inclusive holiday to the Canaries. She recalled, painfully, how they'd lain on the sunbeds on the pebbly beach, the sun absolutely bringing to the boil the contents of her stomach. She had been so hot she remembered thinking that she was going to die.

"Let's go into the sea!" she'd quipped, all fun and enthusiasm, shielding the rivulets of sweat running down the racetrack that constituted her hips and back.

"In a minute." His tone had been final and he'd never even looked at her. His eyes were, she thought, shut behind his sunglasses.

Shit, she'd thought, I can't go in first. I'll just die with him watching my bum swinging and swaying as I walk down into the sea. We *must* go in together. She tried again, "Oh come on. Let's go in and play with the frisbee." The bloody frisbee! God, you'd nearly think she was a German tourist or something. She *hated* frisbees!

His response was unchanged, "No. You go in. I'll be in in a minute."

God! She'd lain back all sweaty, a shining lump of cheese amid a beach full of carrots julienne. She had tormented herself, dreading going in before him. The pebbly terrain had just made it worse. She had imagined how her hips and bum would jiggle at a different speed and rhythm to the rest of her, as her feet attempted to balance her. Close to fainting, she decided there was only one thing for it: go in alone. A surreptitious sideways glance indicated that he'd dozed back to sleep, still shielded by his 1980's style aviators. She had raised herself silently from the sunbed and tiptoed past him, shimmering and quaking her way into the inviting turquoise water, squirming and wobbling over the stony beach. She'd swum, done a small wee, bobbed and swum. Kevin had finally joined her, all smiles and panda'd white eyes. All in all they'd a great day on the beach. The evening transformation from beach-ravaged scarecrow to sun-kissed sojourner had been made and they had steamed their way through the cocktail list in the hotel bar, a mini-collection of paper umbrellas and redundant cocktail sticks sitting in the ashtray.

It was then he had leaned over and said it.

"I've got to say something to you, Geri. I know we've

not been going out that long and everything, but . . .
This isn't going to be easy."

"Go on," she had encouraged, half expecting the
glint of a diamond to catch the moonlight.

"Well, when we get back to England, you know after
this holiday –"

"Yeah?"

She recalled how she'd tried to suppress her
excitement.

"Well, when we get back, I don't want to go out with
you any more. We're finished."

"What do you mean? Why? *What have I done?*" In
total first-love form.

"You haven't done anything. But the sight of your
arse going into the sea today made me feel sick."

But he was so sincere with it too! Like as if she was
supposed to feel sympathy for him because of it!

He had continued, "You're only a young girl and
there's no excuse for it. It's so out of proportion to the
rest of your body. I'm sorry, Geri, but I really felt sick as
I watched you wading into the water. It's almost
unnatural."

Swallowing her tears and embarrassment she'd
managed to whisper, more in shock than anything,
"OK, if that's what you want. Let's just get the holiday
over, eh?"

"Thanks."

Bloody thanks! That was what he'd said. Thanks!

For the first time in six years, bitter resentment and
anger filled her chest, replacing the involuntary tears

that usually welled in her eyes when she recalled this scenario.

I am better off without him. Children or no children. At least the toilet seat'll always be down. Why had I never seen the writing on the wall? They say love is blind. In my case it was deaf and dumb too!

Realising that the exercises had long finished and the news had started, she hopped up from the floor, furtively popping two squares of Galaxy into her mouth. Realising what she'd just done she scolded herself,

"OK, it has been lovely eating for two, twice! *But this must stop! Now!* You're going to that gym tonight, girlie, whether you want to or not!"

Chapter Eight

"You know, Mum, something I never knew about pushing a buggy, is that it makes you invisible to the outside world."

"Whaddya mean now?" Cynthia's tone was impatient, Geri's analysis of life doing nothing but annoying the easy-going Cynthia.

Circumnavigating the High Street with her eyes closed was an attribute she was proud to say she'd learnt since joining the league of parenthood, along with the ability to assess the buildings, kerbs, stairs and ease of access, almost as if she herself were disabled.

"I now have superior knowledge on places to cross – the dips in the kerbs, you see – the shops to avoid due to stairs – no lifts, and just how much shopping you can balance in a stretched-to-transparency-thin supermarket-issue carrier bag on the handles of your buggy before your child kisses the pavement backwards."

Cynthia bustled along beside her, the rattling of her shopping basket on wheels almost blotting out Geri's conversation. She made no attempt to respond and Geri steered them all through a shop doorway.

The glistening spotlights in the chemist's ricocheted off the plastic handles of Reece's buggy and Cameron's snotty moustache. Stopping at the make-up counter amid a menagerie of colours, textures and sleek packaging she caught sight of herself in their mirror. Die-hard facial hairs glinting in the spotlights, she felt despondent, as if she was wearing out too soon, like a bad purchase. A rainbow of colours shone on the shelf beneath her, a bilious buttercup effect reflecting on her double chin as the greens, blues and reds of the nail varnishes made their presence known. Feeling even older now, she fingered the glass bottles, finding it hard to grasp the concept of yellow, green and electric blue on her nails.

"God, Geraldine. Those colours are sick. They just *don't* look right. At your age you should be going for the pearls and pinks. Those dark colours bring out the wrinkles on the back of your hands."

"Thanks! And the pearls and pinks go hand in hand with liver spots. Take your bloody pick!"

Why is it that women get old whilst men get distinguished?

She was distracted somewhat by Cameron cuffing his leaking nose on the leg of her already bobbled joggers. Deciding to rebel against her agedness she picked up a navy-blue nail varnish. Clinking the small glass bottle into her basket, she sought out the Detox diet she was hoping to buy, all in the name of beauty.

She noticed a large figure skulking in the aisle to her left but, paying no attention to it, continued to scan the shelves for the diet drink.

It was then Cameron grabbed her by the arm, shouting, "Look Mummy! What's that man doing, Mummy?"

As she turned to see him-from-the-Gym crouching and rooting through the boxes of Tampax a laugh escaped unexpectedly from her nervous stomach. He looked up at Geri, smiling, his sportsman's bum only inches from the floor, that perfect mouth and gorgeous face obviously familiar with the brand of sanitary protection his girlfriend used, and – here's a 'new man' for you – confident enough to buy them for her! Geri despaired that she'd failed to be as lucky.

"You see, darling," she dismissively explained to Cameron, "the man is *looking* for something. Come on, where's Nana?"

Scurrying away tomato-faced, she felt pleased that she'd seen him again before going to the gym tonight, and thankful for the small mercy that at least her clothes weren't too bad, despite the now-dried snotty trail on her joggers. *Better than the last time he saw me though – arse up and stranded!*

* * *

Doc had made a full and successful recovery, at least according to Ben's diagnosis earlier that morning. Happy, Sneezy and Dopey were butterflying their way around the blue stones at the bottom, whilst Sleepy uncharacteristically chased his rear fin. Their prominent eyes goggled toward the surface as Ben's magnified hand loomed, poised to sprinkle more algae flakes. No sooner had the paper-thin morsels kissed the water, than they were sucked, regurgitated, sucked and regurgitated by the adept Seven Dwarfs. Dismissed without a "thank you", Ben was now redundant until the next day – Cleaning-out Day.

Grateful for the late start, he had reminded himself to stop in at the chemist's on his way to work.

His mobile had rung loudly as he stepped outside.

"Kev, yeah, those bloody auditions last night were a total waste of time. If I have to listen to another wannabe warbling *the sun will come out tomorrow*" I'm leaving the country immediately!"

Pulling his fleecy collar up around his thick neck, he'd breathed an icy cloud out into the hazy morning air as he spotted the blue and white logo for the chemist's. He'd called in to buy some vanity purchases while he had the go-ahead for a flexible start.

Those pore-cleansing strips were quite fun, he remembered, as he picked up two packets and threw them dismissively into his wire basket. Antiperspirant, shaving gel, new blades.

Oh, throw some condoms in for good measure, he'd thought flippantly. Midway to the till he had noticed her, one child holding on to her left hand, and her right hand guiding the buggy through the aisles. Shit! And there he was with condoms and pore-cleansing strips in his basket. Diving between two heavily-laden aisles he caught sight of himself in the mirrored pillar, a hunched bulk of ridiculousness. Peering between the tampons *with* applicators and the tampons without, his nose ominously close to the boxes, he unwittingly produced a profusion of bewildered double-takes from browsing shoppers. His part-filled basket now temporarily forgotten as it had sat patiently at his feet, he crept along the aisle to get a better look. Her cropped blonde hair shone with shards of gold beneath the glowing in-store lighting. As he got lost in his thoughts and day-dreams he was shocked, static in his mid-crouch, to see her standing at the end of his aisle.

"Look, Mummy!" her eldest boy was shouting. "What's that man doing, Mummy?"

Ben had felt himself freeze, still mid-crouch. Her chill-of-the-morning peachy complexion gave her an attractive glow. She'd laughed as she'd looked at Ben, rummaging through the Tampax.

"You see, darling, the man is looking for something. Come on, where's Nana!"

Ben didn't notice her face flush faster than an executive portaloo, on realisation of who "that man" actually was. By the time he had pulled his head out from between the boxes they'd gone.

Feeling like he'd been dragged through a hedge backwards, and looking even more like it, he picked up his basket and made for the till. Unaware that his pomade-sculptured arrangement of hair was jutting out at obscure angles due to reversing his head from between the boxes, he waited in the queue, his mind racing. Would she be at the gym again tonight? Did she recognise me?

"Next please," the assistant mouthed in soporific, almost sedating tones.

Ben unloaded his goods onto the counter. Antiperspirant.

I wonder DID she see me? he'd mused, unloading his basket.

Pore-cleansing strips, Imperial Leather, shaving gel, condoms.

"Condoms!" he'd blurted. Three queues of anxious shoppers looked po-faced, at him.

"Pardon, sir?" the cashier questioned. "Do you *want* these or *not*, sir?"

"Yes. No! No, it was a mistake. I didn't mean to pick them up at all. No, sorry, I don't want them."

As if in slow motion she picked up the offending packet of rubber goods, placing them in full view at the side of her till. Ben rummaged in his jeans pocket for the twenty-pound note he knew was there somewhere, then handed it over to her, anxious to make a swift departure. He looked up to see a middle-aged woman with bleached white hair and black roots, sporting a pierced eyebrow, top lip and nose. He smiled at her, insecure and unsure of her gaze.

"Bloody bare-back riders!" she'd sneered, at a volume for all to hear.

Ben gathered the carrier bag quickly, ignoring her futile smear campaign and strode to the exit.

"Bet you wouldn't be so careless if *you had HIV*!"

Ben coughed into the biting air as if to clear her from his mind and set himself back on track again. The clock outside the station read ten twenty-two; just in time for the ten thirty. Should be in work by eleven, out by five, and in the gym by seven. I just *hope* she's there!!!

* * *

I'm staring at my rosy reflection as I pound the Powerjogger and I'm sure my cheeks used to wobble more than this when I started. The cloning syndrome I'm experiencing at the gym brings with it a sense of belonging. It's as if we are all striving for the same goal. Some of us are considerably closer to it than others but still we're at least showing willing.

Her inflated self-illusion bubble burst messily on the arrival of *him*, paranoia showering over her like a bucket of nails, only more painful. Suddenly feeling fat, forty and frumpy, she reminded herself that, up until now, her idea of a balanced diet had been a quarterpounder in each hand. He noticed her immediately and smiled, although she suspected the escapade in the chemist's had made him uneasy of her. Wishing herself invisible, she discreetly watched him striding the conveyor belt of the PowerJogger, three along from her. The reddened faces of two strangers between them, they caught each other flicking their gaze onto, and then away from each other. His tanned hairy legs, strong and muscly, disappearing into black Nike shorts. God, if she ever wished for x-ray vision! Her mind flashed wickedly, unable to shake off the fantasy. She just loved the look of men in the nude –

145

the swing of their weighted penis as they walked, weighty and heavy, full of anticipation. She would love to see *him* walking in the nude. She imagined his gorgeous sculptured chest, warm and welcoming, and his chunky firm arms wrapped around her.

Maybe I just like him because he's so big and steady; I think he'd make me feel small and helpless. Bring out my feminine side. Anyway, what would he see in me? Overweight, over-tired, and over-the-hill. His girlfriend probably looks just as good as he does, perfection on a bloody plate.

With her sex-life now categorically her ex-life, she knew she'd suffered biological shutdown of all sexual regions, reactions and requirements. Parenting being synonymous with words like bonding, boundaries, responsibility, rewards, punishment and sleepless nights, she knew she was kidding herself.

They moved in muted unison around the gym. As she melted into the exercise bike she noticed him perching his pert derrière on the saddle of another; at the sit-up machines she saw him curling and flexing at the bench nearby. As she sweated for England at the rowing-machine she was aware of him climbing onto the step-machine opposite. If she only didn't look so much like a human radish she *might* think he was tailing her!

An hour later and still too chicken to contemplate the horrors of communal showering, drying and dressing she wriggled her perspiration-damp body into her sweatshirt and made a dash for the car.

The windscreen wiper stuttered arrhythmically

across the screen like a jerking nervous wreck as it jumped and leapt across the semi-wet glass. Her breath cloudy in the cold night, she felt the hairs on the back of her neck spike to attention. Rubbing the windscreen and interior mirror with the sleeve of her sweatshirt, she caught a glimpse of her reflection, rather ruddy and peachy. *Amazing what an hour's exercise can do for you! It's such a shame that my inner thighs and chip-shop arms will think that rigor mortis has set in by the morning!*

As she drove back to her mum's, the road swooshing beneath her at 40mph, she kept stretching to see her ruddy reflection.

The bottom line is, when I check my age in the mirror I see my mum! And I want to see Kylie!

Waiting for too long at the red lights meant a blast of someone's horn shifted her into first gear, and she was off again. It seemed to Geri that her life was dictated by numbers: the clock, the calendar, her bank balance, the candles on her birthday cake, the scales, her dress size!

Little wonder I'm number-phobic.

She felt she represented the desperate cry of a pair of brushed cotton pyjamas (Size 18) who wished they were a silk negligée (Size 10).

If Bernard Manning was the Prince of Ugly Fat Bastards, then surely I must be their new queen!

Pulling into her mum's road, she realised that she couldn't remember the last time she'd got *really* drunk or regretted giving her phone number out.

"Hey," she addressed the windscreen as she parked, "I only gave birth to a child, not my bloody brain."

Tiptoeing through Cynthia's hallway she found the children asleep on the settee, the telly buzzing poltergeist style, a tweed effect of black and grey fuzz, although in silence.

Her mum emerged from the kitchen, her hands covered in chocolate. Wiping them on her apron, she then remembered their coating, taking them to her mouth instead, as she bustled Geri into the kitchen.

"Hey, love, had a good time? God! Look at you! You're drowned!"

"It's sweat, Mum."

"God, you'll catch a death. You should take a hat with you next time. You'll catch a chill driving out in this cold with no hat on!"

"I'm all right, Mum. It's only a few seconds' walk to the car, and then I put the heater on. What're you making anyway?"

"Oh, I'm trying to do some of those cornflaky cake things for the boys. Only I can't remember how much chocolate to put into it. I think I've overdone it a bit!"

Following her into the kitchen Geri viewed the ransacked sink, drainer and worktop and fleetingly wondered who *were* the kids here, as she watched her licking and sucking on the huge wooden spoon, chocolate painted around her open gob liberally. She suddenly felt guilty at landing the boys in on her once again.

"Mum. Do you think I should get a baby-sitter? I mean, do you *mind* looking after them for a few hours a week?"

"Geri, I've told you before, a baby-sitter is a teenager-acting-like-an-adult whilst the adults are out acting like teenagers. Now, is *that* what you're doing when you're out?"

"No, I suppose not. It depends really, what you call acting like teenagers. If you mean struggling to learn from textbooks and dreading handing in your homework, then yes, that's exactly what I'm doing!"

"Tssshk, you know what I mean. Geri, you're a good egg, even though you're slightly cracked and I think it'll do you good to get that no-good Kevin out of your head. You know a farmer learns more from a bad harvest than a good one."

It seems old Quick-Draw McGraw's back on form tonight.

"Thanks, Mum. You know, in a year's time it'll all be so different too. Cameron'll be at nursery school all week. God, they just seem to be suddenly growing up all so quickly!"

She immediately chided herself – she should have known better with the mood her mother was in. "Geri, you know your child has started growing up when he stops asking you where he came from and starts refusing to tell you where he's going; and I can't see *that* happening for a good few years yet! You carry on with those evening classes, *and* that gymnasium. You could do with losing a couple of stone. Really let yourself go since having those boys, you have!"

Realising that she was obviously pissing against the wind trying to deal with her mother tonight, she resigned herself to her cacophony, and agreed, "Yeah, sure, Mum, brain cells come and brain cells go, but fat cells last forever!"

* * *

As she stood in the warm evening air at the *FGV* waiting for the metro to arrive, Sinead pondered on the disappointment of Steven Randall. He'd seemed so promising until he'd taken pity on the divvy Charmaine.

"Still," she dragged on her cigarette, her face feeling slightly tight as it had tanned a shade darker this afternoon. She'd taken the day off to celebrate her impending short trip back to England. It had been a double whammy really, hearing her name announced for return to the UK plant and then seeing Charmaine's unveiled disappointment. She'd spent the afternoon siesta relaxing on her balcony after a morning at the *Plaza de la Reina* at Valencia's cathedral. She'd made the long climb to the roof and enjoyed the fantastic views over the city with its many blue-domed churches. So, feeling relaxed and contented, she waited as the metro arrived, hearing the gaggle of her colleagues as they alighted. They were set for a night out and were heading for the "in" places around the university region.

"The trendiest bars are on the *Avenida Blasco Ibáñez*."

"Yeah, that's what that gorgeous Steven Randall was telling me. *Picasso* and *Kubalitro* sound good."

"Wasn't he a dream?"

"Handsome, stylish *and* educated."

Sinead silently seethed at their admiration of him as they strode across the *Río Turia*.

* * *

Wednesday sped by in stiffened pain for Geri, rendering her a fleshy Tin-Man by the afternoon, in readiness for her next educational experience, Beginners' Spanish. Humbled by her expectations of Tim Heifer-nan and Dave Lomax she expected very little of Michael Fernandez, the Spanish tutor. Remembering only a little Spanish from her school days, she was anticipating a gaggle of th's, rrrr's and mispronounced accents. Imagine then, her surprise when, on entering the classroom she was faced with her last boyfriend before she'd married Kevin – John Dooleyson! His reasonably handsome, but slightly aged face, lit up immediately on recognising her!

"Hey, Geraldine Cumbers! Geri! What're you doing here?" Stupid question, she thought, but let him off, realising that she herself was the world's worst culprit for asking them. She held on to all temptations for smart-arsed retorts, and replied, "Beginners' Spanish. And you?"

I know, I know, I'm just as bloody bad!

"Same. God, well, you're looking good as ever, Geri!"

His eyesight has obviously diminished significantly along with his hairline.

"Thanks," she monotoned, on autopilot.

"Hey," he burst into expected life, "d'you remember that night we went to Sam Wenger's party?"

"Yeah," she gushed, caught up in the euphoria of

their irresponsible days, and memories, "and I wore those awful bloody shoes!"

"Stilettos," he corrected her instantly. She was a little taken back at his accurate recollection of it.

"Yes. Stilettos. God, they were high, weren't they? And I –"

"You nearly broke your ankle and I had to carry you home, piggyback!"

They laughed, totally uninhibited amongst the strangers listening to their conversation. It was only as Michael Fernandez entered the room that they settled, finding themselves seated next to each other.

As Michael Fernandez began his routine introductions, John whispered,

"Hey, we should do it again sometime."

"What?" she whispered, half listening to the tutor, half transfixed *by* the tutor.

"Go for a drink or something."

She took scant notice of him, being both unflattered and unfazed by his swift invitation and spontaneous attention. After all, she reasoned, it was *John Dooleyson!* It all happened a long time ago. Another lifetime really. She paid little attention to his interest.

"Yeah. That'd be nice. Sometime." Her tone politely dismissive, she craned to hear what Michael Fernandez was saying. Seemingly, still out of luck, John Dooleyson wanted to talk!

"Will you wear stilettos?"

"When?" she whispered hoarsely this time, only half concentrating.

"When we go out for our drink? Will you wear stilettos?"

"No, I go for comfort shoes these days."

"Not those squashy granny shoes?"

"Yep, and my waister knickers and industrial bra."

He laughed, "I bet you do too!"

"I do!"

Sidling up a little closer he teased, boyishly, "Bet that basque's at the bottom of your knicker-drawer these days?"

"You wouldn't recognise it! It's more wrinkled than Mother Theresa."

She ignored his chortle, too mesmerised by Michael Fernandez. Of all the tutors in all the classes in all the world, he had to walk into hers! Maybe her humbling experiences of evening classes were all in preparation for meeting Michael F. Whatever the reason, she knew he was tasty! Elegant and sophisticated, a tribute to George Clooney and all that he stood for. Within minutes of meeting Michael she knew that leaving him would be about as painful as a leg wax on period day. Her head floated three feet above everyone else's for the next hour. The cotton wool wedged between her ears was absorbing the sweetest nectar of Mediterranea as Mikey F enunciated, rolling his r's and poking out his shiny pink tongue teasingly as he pronounced the "th's" for the "c's".

"¿Qué es esto?" he questioned, holding aloof his fragrant leather jacket. Geri immediately envied the black silk lining.

"¿Qué es esto?" he continued, caressing his biro between his tanned, smooth hands. She was almost passing out by now.

By the time they took a break for a drink Geri was surprised to see tatty notes scrawled across her page, intermittently punctuated with love-hearts and arrows, and *GC 4 MF.* Feeling like a teenager, she clumsily closed her note-pad. As her legs wobbled beneath her as she headed for the door *He* stepped in front of her, blocking her exit. She was captivated by his gorgeous smell, even from her safe but not too protracted distance.

God, his eyes are so brown and twinkly, and what a perfect smile! Could those teeth be false, do you think? He's not a young man. God! He's opening his mouth! He's going to kiss me!

She snapped back to reality as Michael Fernandez smiled and said,

"Have you learnt Spanish before?"

Afraid to open her mouth for fear of being tongue-tied she nodded and smiled inanely.

"At school?" he continued, somewhat prying.

"You know, I've got two children at home. Boys. Two boys." She knew she was rambling again, getting more like her mother every bloody day! "My mum's looking after them. They're only young, you know. Boys they are. Two of them. Two boys. This is just a bit of free time for myself, you know. It gets boring all day with just kids to talk to. I've got two boys, you know. Two of them. I don't get much freedom you see. Too many responsibilities. What I really need is a nice quiet room on my own to do my own thing in. You know, learn my Spanish and play my piano and things. I shouldn't really be here at all. I was *never* any good at Spanish at school. Sorry to waste your time. You probably turned people away for this course too."

His politeness matched unnervingly by his charm he smiled as he steadily answered, in a voice to make love to, "Isn't it absurd that when we crave freedom we imagine a private room rather than an exposed open space. We yearn for an interior in which to indulge ourselves, our passions, our tastes and our fantasies."

She hated herself for answering in this way, but retorted, "Do *you* know a bus is a vehicle that runs twice as fast when you are after it then when you are in it!"

Brought back to earth with a thud, she reddened at her rambling, feeling alarmingly like her mother. She nodded, smiled and made her apologies, declaring war on her dry tongue. As she shimmied to the cold canteen her thoughts tumbled in her head. What was it he'd said? Passions and fantasies, passions and fantasies, fassions and pantasies.

Fifteen minutes later, on her return to the class, she sat next to Claudia, only knowing her name due to the infant-school-like name-plate that she'd scribed onto the folded cardboard slits that Michael Fernandez had distributed during the break. Geri watched in awe, as Claudia lifted the chair, brushing the seat with her papers before she lowered her arse to sit on it. She tutted and fidgeted, wriggling on the wooden chair, then stood and made for the front of the class, the offending chair in hand. Geri watched her bum as she walked, encased in a long white knitted skirt barely concealing a G-string through its fine weave.

A bad choice of underwear. The saggy cushions of her arse-cheeks look like two book-ends – heavy and thick at the bottom, and leaning in supportively toward the middle.

At the front of the room Claudia made known her distaste for the chair, and requested a replacement from charming Michael F. Unfazed by her snobbishness, he obliged graciously, even bringing the chair to their desk and holding it as she sat down. Claudia seemed contentedly settled in suburban domesticity and Geri imagined her to be one of those who watch the country programmes for people with nothing better to do than worry about how to make your own Christmas Cards and a matching centrepiece for the Christmas table.

Definitely the type who has nothing better to do than bake crusty scones all afternoon and make a Hansel & Gretel centrepiece of a log cabin entirely from biscuits and Angel Delight.

Intrigued by her, Geri watched as she rested her hands on the desk in concentration mode as she Maggie Thatchered at Michael Fernandez, patronisingly nodding and "mmm"ing at irrelevant junctures.

Her nail varnish matches her bloody outfit! Obviously the height of organisation, her mind is probably as tidy as her bank balance.

Geri's idea of tidy was only a *few* clothes at the end of the bed, a few *more* on the bannister, some unpaid bills on the stairs and a handful of crumbs on the kitchen floor!

Michael F's soporific, sedating tones lulled her into a hazy *ensueño*.

Spanish for daydream – only remembered because that's what my school Spanish teacher used to say all I was good for!

Geri was gazing blankly up into Claudia's face. Probably late forties, her distinct *lack* of wrinkles making Geri wonder whether she'd found the jet-set's antidote to ageing. The *ensueño* was suddenly disturbed by the sensuous baritone of Señor Fernandez, perilously close to her ear,

"Tu secreto se ha descubierto!"

Stunned back to reality, she unwittingly adopted pomegranate pallor and expression.

"Excuse me?" she muttered, all apathetic grins. Her brown eyes implored him to go easy on her.

At least until he knows me better! His smile demands instant melt-down as I feel a warm tingle in my 16/18 winter grey knickers. A sensation I last experienced well over a year ago when I'd had too many Martinis and had gotten drunk from the waist down..

"Do you know what that means, Señorita? I'll repeat it slowly – see if you can pick up any sounds you recognise."

A throb in the back of her throat threatened to drown out any ramblings.

"Tu secreto se ha descubierto!"

God! He sounds so damned sezy, I mean sexy!

Her inane grin masked the turmoil coursing through her head. Then, clear as Double Chocolate Pudding, her schooldays began to creep back to her. Braver because of his tempting closeness she ventured,

"*Tu* is you. Or your?" His nod encouraged her. "*Secreto*; could that mean secret?" Again, another confirmatory nod. "That's it, I don't recognise any more."

"Well done! Not bad for a first time. See, it's tucked away in there after all."

"Mmmm. Ha hee hee!" She shuffled on her seat, bumping her ample hip and thigh off Claudia's Prada jacket causing her to leap away as if electrocuted by her cheap jeans.

"Well!" He turned on the spot, clapping his hands together and walking back toward the front of the classroom. "What *that* actually meant was – your secret is out!"

God! What secret? What secret do I have that could possibly be out? That he could know about? Does he know me? Have I met him before? No! I'd definitely have remembered. He's just too gorgeous to forget.

Scrabbling her papers on the desk, listening to his instructions for homework and explaining what joys they could expect in next week's lesson, she watched him, almost onyx shining eyes, tall muscular frame, thick tanned forearms and great tight butt. Surprising her, he looked up into the busy bustling classroom, caught her eye, smiled and winked at her. As she reddened, his smile widened, and yes, he winked once again.

Chapter Nine

The clicking of the air conditioning as it cut in and then out wasn't the only irritation keeping Sinead from sleep. Feeling sticky as she lay on the warm cotton sheets, she listened to the intermittent buzz as yet another mosquito electrocuted itself in her mozzy-trap. She had been thankful when the phone had rung into the night. Despite her late night out she'd seemed to have hollow legs as the drink hadn't touched her.

"He *knows* something about me. I just know he does," Geri blazed down the telephone to a shaken and tired Sinead. Well, it *was* gone midnight, but she just *couldn't* sleep!

"How do you *know*?" Her voice was sluggish and irritable.

"I just know. He said to me, I can remember the exact words, he said, *tu secreto se ha descubierto!*"

"What? What did he say?" Her voice was disgruntled and agitated too.

"*Tu secreto se ha descubierto!* God. You don't know what it means, do you? And you *living* in Spain!" Her laugh carried a volume that had the power to warn Clinton that Monica Lewinsky had a penchant for gossip. Geri suspected that it only aggravated Sinead more.

"It means, your secret is out! Now. What does *that* tell you?"

"Gertie, darling please. It's three in the morning. I've got a plane to catch in the morning. *This morning!* What does it tell me?"

"You've got a plane to catch? Why? Where you going to?"

"England! I've got a flight leaving at ten thirty to Gatwick."

"You're coming home! You're coming back?" Her head reeled with excitement at the prospect of seeing Sinead, but her guts unhesitatingly reeled at the prospect of her being found out. How to conjure up her secret absent husband? Then her secret really *would* be out! She wondered at Señor Fernandez's psychic abilities.

"What time will you be arriving?" Geri changed the subject with a swiftness that hid her inner chaos.

"I've got to call into work first. I'm only back for a few days, but I'll ring you as soon as I get the chance. Probably sometime late in the afternoon or early evening. I'll call round. I can't wait to see Kevin and the boys. Have some Penguin bars ready. Oh, and some

Tetley tea bags. And proper English bread in a plastic wrapper, and Marmite and –"

"Yeah! OK, I get the message." She hadn't meant to cut her off short but couldn't bear her enthusiasm. There was no *way* Sinead could visit, only to see what domestic catastrophe she was living in. No way. NO WAY!

"Look Gert, it's late. Let's talk about your Spanish class later, eh? Face to face, over a nice cuppa tea. Proper *English* tea."

"Yeah. Right. You're right. Look, have a safe journey, and I'll see you sometime later."

"Righto. Take care."

"Yeah. And you. Bye."

"Bye."

Holding the *boo-oo*ing receiver mid-air, still in her hand, Geri began the mammoth task of contemplating how she was *ever* going to get around this one. She knew that Sinead would instantly smell a rat if she *didn't* let her visit. Geri had to think of something. And fast!

Her ascent to bed was interrupted by a quick look in the kitchen cupboards for something nice to take to bed, in the absence of anything not remotely appealing in human form. Including herself. As tins of sardines-in-brine and jars of pickled gherkins cascaded, avalanche-style on top of her, she loathed her obsession with the Buy 2 Get 1 Free scheme that Tesco were running. With her appetite immediately gone she clicked off the light, leaving a mountain of tinned morsels on the floor. Her mind whirred as she headed up the stairs. Her ritual began on the landing where she dimmed the hall light, but then tripped on the toy lorry left outside the bathroom door, causing it to ricochet down the stairs noisily. She just *had* to go into the boys' room and remove their dummies, pull up the blankets and check they hadn't wee'd their nappies – yet! As she tiptoed creakily into their room she took on Diane Fossey-like mannerisms as she'd congregated with the gorillas. Her heart was beating hard and fast in her chest and neck and she was almost afraid to look at them sleeping for fear of disturbing them. One creak, one toe out of place on the old wooden floor could send her peaceful home into the Good Ship Lollipop. She shuffled and crept, pulling at dummies and checking temperatures whilst at the same time keeping low, and trying to avoid eye contact. Then, she "Eerruuugh'd" in panic as Action Man's flexed foot caught the arch of hers, causing him to leap with the agility of the Man-With-The-Black-Magic-Box up and onto the end of Reece's bed.

Not a stir.

Content with her lucky escape, she made a dash for the door, leaving it only slightly ajar so that she could tune into their moanings and stirrings.

In the safe haven of her own room, she was faced with the unthankful task of undressing in front of the mirror. Not something that filled her with pride.

"Look at my chest!" she moaned. "I just can't see it in the same way since I squirted breastmilk into the midwife's eye." As she squodged and squeezed at her

162

flimsy, lifeless breasts she noticed the resemblance to the medieval-style oil painting proudly displayed on her bedroom wall. A romantic image of a pear-shaped poseur, amply stretched onto a chaise longue, shrouded by black velvet curtains, aesthetically balanced by a bowl laden with lush green grapes to her left, and a thick off-white cotton nightie left on the floor, to her right. *Bet she never got those hips eating bloody grapes! No wonder the bloody bowl is full! She probably stuffed her face with pigs' heads and trotters at every banquet invitation. All pasty white skin, ample hips and thighs and small boobs. Most definitely not Y2K+!*

"I'd probably have been a sex-symbol if I'd only been born about four hundred years ago!"

Recalling her ex-life, depressing memories flooded her head, recalling how, whilst her underwear was never quite Ann Summers, Kevin's expression had usually screamed, "Thanks, but I'd rather stick needles in my eyes!"

Four years of him in the sack would knock anyone's confidence! No wonder I'm a sexually incapable celibate! In fact my whole sexual life has gone from one inadequate disaster to another. In little over ten years of sexuality I've coped with premature ejaculation, retarded ejaculation, alcohol-induced-no-bloody-chance ejaculation, bend-to-the-left-syndrome and Will-You-Be-My-Mummy disorder. I've met Tripod, One-Ball, Percy, Mickey and Python.

"Is it any wonder I'm confused." she mumbled, staring down at the navy-blue chipped nail polish on her toes.

If I knew as a virgin what I know now, I'd have held out for a forty-year-old in a mid-life crisis. He'd be keen to impress, financially secure, the bearer of gifts and sexually shackled by his marriage.

Shame Mum never told me hymens are a girl's best friend!

Resignedly she pulled her cotton pyjamas up around her waist, her T-shirt over her head and climbed into bed. Reaching out for the first book to hand she viewed the title of the library book in the soft light of a peach-tinted bulb. Despite its flattering glow the bold red capital letters screamed out *Moulding Mini Males – WHY Boys and Girls are Different.* She placed the book back down onto the floor, unable to tackle the psychology of it, instead hoiking the duvet up and over her shoulder, and flicking the lamp off with a perfunctory *click*!

Four am and the lamp was back on again. Unable to sleep she tormented herself with the prospect that Sinead had found out that she'd been lying to her about Kevin being around, and was now laughing at her for being so pathetic!

In an act of sheer desperation she picked up the book again.

That'll surely send me off to sleep . . . .

* * *

Fresh-faced and looking every inch the career girl, Sinead occupied seat 14A and gazed out of the window at the morning sunshine. The plastic window cool, almost embalmed, glistened as the warming yellow rays washed over its scratched surface. The stewardesses scurried up, down and then up the aisle with drinks and perfumes. Since the abolition of duty free it seemed, to Sinead, that passengers weren't as desperate to purchase their cigarettes "in-flight". Ordering only coffee when asked, she closed her eyes, relaxing back into her seat with a longing for all things British. Marmite, proper tea, proper English sausages and bacon, rain and Gertie. Oh, and *proper* English bread in plastic-bag wrappings – all she could get in Spain was crusty cardboard squares appropriately named *"bimbo"*.

"If only my life was all it's cracked up to be," she whispered under her breath as she let out a deep sigh. This was to be her first trip back home since starting the assignment in Valencia and she felt a disturbing nervousness rising. She desperately wanted to go back and be "Sinead". The Sinead that left England. But she also felt that she had some kind of show to put on for them all, The-Sinead-They-*Expected*; the sun-tanned, happy-go-lucky, independent, world-at-her-fingertips Sinead. The Zorro Sinead who whipped and chopped her career into shape. The wealthy Sinead who had more disposable income than you could shake a stick at, and a social life to match. Quite an acting debût would be required for *this* performance. It was one thing putting on the style over the telephone. Friends and family always commented how she took so long to answer the phone and she blamed it on the distance between her pool and apartment, often cutting them off with a "Must go. My laptop's out in the sun. Won't do it any good." Or "My eyes have gone blind what with coming in from the brilliant sunshine to the dark apartment." The reality of it was she'd never been so miserable. The frequent bouts of retail therapy were the only positive factor in her life in Spain. She adored the continental style of clothes, spending more than half her salary on leather shoes and leather goods.

Smoothing down her exquisitely cut linen skirt she whispered to herself, consolingly, "At least I *look* the part."

With a string of dismally failed romances behind her, her career was little consolation for her emotional unfulfilment. "Enough of this," she scolded, opening her eyes only to see the dull grey clouds now masking the aerial view of France. Reaching into the pocket of the seat in front she grabbed the In Flight magazine, hoping for something mundane and anonymous to divert her thoughts. The first page proclaimed the benefits of a pension scheme, advising how to retire at 60 on *half* your current income. But you'd have to save 12% of your earnings now. She made a rough mental calculation and pulled her palm-computer from her jacket pocket, making a note to check her status in the company pension scheme. Her thoughts turned to Gertie, who, for now, was unemployed in the eyes of the government, but held down at least three full-time jobs in the eyes of mothers all over the world. Sinead reminded herself that with Kevin's good job Geri would be well looked after. As she rummaged to slot the palm back into her pocket she accidentally nudged the exuberantly perfumed sixteen-stone raisin next to her. She knew she was an emigrated Brit due to her sun-ravaged neck and mahogany face. The Raisin smiled widely, amazing Sinead at just how far Sheeny Pink lipstick could stretch.

"Sorry," Sinead said.

Watery blue eyes smiled at her. "Awright, luv, just 'aving a nap. Going 'ome, are ya?"

"Yeah, just for a few days. It's work though." Her disappointed tone was evident, opening the floodgates for The Raisin to begin a one-sided conversation as she dropped her 'h's and replaced her th's with 'f's and 'v's. Sinead couldn't help but be hypnotised by her rhino-arse skin, amazed at her obvious liking for more than her share of obsessive sun worship. She was clearly no stranger to casting aside the factor 30 for quick rub of baby oil and lashings of UV damage. Her trance was broken by a quick-fire question.

"Where d'ya come from? Originally, like."

"Oh, North London way. But originally? Originally from Ireland."

"Oooh, I luv Eyeland."

Sinead hated the way that people mispronounced Ireland, wishing they'd remember the -r-, but realised this was no time to mention it. Just as she thought things could get no worse, seat 14C, next to the raisin, rose from the dead. A man of retirement age himself, he had the most pungent garlic breath Sinead had ever come across, at close quarters anyway.

"Oh yes. I love Eyeland too. One of my great-great-grandfathers was Eye-rish."

Sinead couldn't conceal her contempt, made worse by her disgust at the garlic stink. "It seems everyone has Irish roots these days. It's fashionable at the moment, isn't it? To have Irish connections. Seems like the whole world wants something to do with Ireland right now."

Her annoyance lost on him, he continued, "Some people say they can still hear the lilt of it in my voice. When I try, anyway. Would you like to hear?" He continued regardless, "Well, oi'll be jiggered, oi'd say you'd loike a point o' the black stoff. Yer man's roight on toime, agan, and oi'll be wishing ye the top 'o the marning to ye."

This time, she shot from the hip, "You sound like a fucking leprechaun, you big idiot. Who the hell told ya you sounded Irish? A bloody Spaniard? You haven't a bloody clue."

A count of three: one . . . two . . . three . . .

"AND your breath absolutely *stinks*!"

The raisin involuntarily sprayed a G&T fountain across her food tray and onto the back of the seat in front of her. As she spluttered and coughed, Sinead could hear the beginnings of a raucous laugh emerging. And then, she unleashed it.

"*Haawww, heeee hawwww, heeee heeeee haaaawwwww!*"

She sounded like a frigging donkey.

"Jesus," Sinead turned her shoulder to the unruly pair, opting to gaze out at the looming clouds, "why did it have to be *me* sitting with these two?"

* * *

Moulding Mini Males proved to be disturbingly profound. Dr Discipline had gotten off to a shaky start by recognising how boys and girls are different, but steered on to highlight the potential problems. He'd clarified how boys lost their concentration easier than girls and explained how testosterone surges linked with aggression and sexuality enforced the crucial role of the father. "A childlike dad in the home is not good enough," he proclaimed. "Not *any* father will do!" he preached. Geri was left puzzled over breakfast as she wondered if that meant that an absent father is preferable to a present, childlike father! By ten-to-nine her thoughts turned to Sinead, suspecting that she had already landed at Gatwick.

"OK, lads," she said to the little boys, "today is your monthly visit to the barber. If you're going to see your godmother sometime in the next four days, then it at least warrants a haircut."

She found the barber's a horrific prospect. She felt she was offering her children up to Sweeney Todd. She noticed the barber's slight grimace as they bundled in through his doorway,

"Morning," his voice seemed guarded.

"Could you cut Cameron's hair, please?"

"Of course. Come and sit here, lad."

Sitting high on a leather chair, Cameron began pulling faces at himself in the mirror, enjoying the attention and finding himself totally hilarious. The barber switched on the trimmers.

"*Muuumeeee, ahhhh, noo!*" His high-pitched screams

were ignored as Geri cringed. With his face smeared with snot, as if tarred and feathered, half-inch hairs stuck everywhere. Then the coughing fit began bringing with it the threat of sickness, gagging and heaving as he stuck out his tongue, his eyes bulging until his face was scarlet.

Admirable really, the effort that goes into it.

As she frog-marched the half-shorn Cameron up the hill, pushing the buggy at the same time she tried her best not to moan at him, "Really excelled yourself this time, didn't you?"

"Mummy," he whimpered, "no cross, Mummy. Me no like."

Catching their reflection in a shop window, she thought he resembled something out of a Max Wall sketch. The top of his head shorn to within an inch of its life, the back and sides a good four inches longer, and hanging flatteringly over his ears. A kind of short back and sides in negative.

"I'll have to finish that at home, you know," she told him.

Even if I have to turn into a Kiwi sheepshearer, head-locking him in a half-nelson, I'll do it. I'll drive those clippers across his cranium with a swiftness that a NZ lamb would be impressed with.

* * *

Sinead sat composed in the back of the taxi, en route to Head Office. As they queued in the rush-hour traffic she watched the executive nose-pickers seated in their valeted, oversized mobile offices, stopped in the traffic on their way to work, unaware of the not-so-tinted windows all around them and revealing them rooting their fingers up in their noses.

"God," Sinead said, "I'm surprised it doesn't come out of his eye in a minute!"

"Sorry, love?" he grinned at her in the rear-view mirror.

"Oh," she'd forgotten he was there, "nothing."

Her recollection of England was disenchanting. She'd remembered the air to be cleaner, the people friendlier, the fields greener and the traffic faster.

"Been on 'oliday?" He insisted on trying for conversation, ogling her tan.

"No, I work in Spain."

"Really? What, barmaid or something?"

She felt resentful at his supposition,

"No. I'm on foreign assignment."

"Oooh, 'scuse me, missus," he teased. "Model then, are ya?"

Aware of her own snobbishness she decided to chat with him. What harm would it do anyway?

"You know," she confessed, "it's just not how I remembered it here. I suppose I've built it up in my head too much. A bit like that post-millennium depression that everyone suffered a couple of years ago."

"Yeah, I know what you mean – the big build-up, the big bang. You know loads of money was spent on that New Year's Eve."

"I'd say so, and tons of drink drunk. All that

anticipation and for what? A week later everything was the bloody same! Nothing had changed."

He cackled, his smoker's cough breaking through, "A bit like getting married really, eh?"

"Dunno."

The journey continued in silence and she was soon grappling in her bag for some sterling coinage to pay the taxi driver. She'd planned to call into Gertie for lunch. Surprise her! She'd reincarnate her memories and love of England. But first she focused, smoothing her clothes and straightening her hair. I'd better go and show my face to these stuffed shirts, this committee, this group of people who individually can do nothing, but as a group will debate that nothing can be done!

Chapter Ten

Sinead stood on Geri's familiar, yet strangely unfamiliar doorstep, fixing her hair and blotting her lips together in the hope that the micro-particles of colour advertised in her new lipstick would burst and give her a freshly applied look. She doubted it.

Pleasingly Geri hadn't changed, with coffee and chocolate biscuits at the ready and only ten minutes into their reunion they were sprawled on the sofas, stuffing their faces. Just like old times. Sinead had always struggled with her words when her mouth was spilling with Chocolate Mini-rolls, but Geri always seemed to manage competently.

"You know," Sinead stuffed, "you're so locky," she paused to tackle another, a whole-in-one. "You don't have to listen to their drap."

Geri knew she meant "crap" but was suffering from sponge-induced mispronunciation.

"What crap?" Geri's words were cut-glass perfect, despite her bulging cheeks and full mouth.

"You know," Sinead picked the remaining crumbs from her plate, carefully arranging them into mini-pyramids and then scooping them up with her adept tongue work, "that kind of office language they adopt."

"How does that make me lucky? What do you mean?"

Now content that there was no sponge or chocolate left Sinead crossed her legs, lit a cigarette and concentrated on their conversation,

"That bullshit they all talk." She exhaled the smoke and it floated up toward Geri's spotlit ceiling. "You don't have to listen to that any more. It must be great!"

"Remind me what you mean? I don't know!"

"Oh Gertie, you know when they say things like *"Oh yes, prioritisation is the key factor"* or *"Are you confident about the implementation techniques adopted?"* There's even a secretary in the London office who promises to "diarise you" if you try and schedule a meeting with her boss. Diarise you!"

Geri spat some of the moist sponge from her mouth,

"God, Sinead, do you *have* to?"

"Sorry, but you just don't realise how well off you are."

Nearly choking on the irony of the comment Geri kept the subject firmly distant from the subject of absent partners. "Oh you reckon, do you?" she teased as she stood and made her way to the kitchen. "Well, my day is punctuated by the garblings of a toddler and the squeaks of a baby. Think yourself lucky, at least you can understand *them*! Cameron nearly got me reported to Social Services in the caff last week just asking for a knife and fork!"

Sinead followed her and sat down. She giggled, resting her elbows on the familiar kitchen table and watched as she submerged two baby bottles into hot soapy water. She loved Gertie's kitchen as, unlike the hallway, stairs and lounge, it had remained unchanged since her last visit, a reminder of the old Gertie. The Just-Married Gertie, and not this new-styled one with the streamlined interiors, cool, classic chrome accessories and bleached beech floors. She moved in closer for her friend's amusing tale, "How?"

"He insists on asking for his fork and then his knife."

"So? What's the problem with that? Isn't it good he's asking for them?"

"Yeah, but you kind of say, well, could I have my knife and fork? You say it that way round, don't you?"

Remaining silent, Sinead nodded.

"He was demanding at the top of his voice, his most polite one, *I want my fork'n'knife! I want my fork'n' knife!*"

"Yeah?" Sinead still didn't get it.

"My fork'n' knife? It sounded like he was swearing at me! The looks we were getting from the oldies in there! God, was I starting to get embarrassed!"

The two women laughed, enjoying each other's company, both forgetting the slight misrepresentations they'd been feeding each other with for the last few months. As if transported back ten years, their conversation flowed, the chocolate appreciated and the cups of tea sunk. Sinead, not realising her luck that the fact Reece and Cameron were enjoying an extraordinarily long midday sleep was providing them with precious time for each other. Geri was bought back to life by the motherly break and the matey nostalgia.

"C'mon, lets go back in there – it's freezing out here." Sinead grabbed her mug and followed her back into the cosy lounge. "D'you remember your mate Linda?"

"Oooh," Sinead squeaked, "the divvy one."

"The boss-eyed one! She was rough, wasn't she?"

"Too right! Remember that night she knocked that bloke out?"

"The skinny guy with the diamante stud in his ear?"

"That's him! What did he say to her again?"

"He said, 'D'ya know darling, ya have the most gorgeous friendly eyes!'"

"That's it, and she didn't cop on to it, did she? The divvy cow said, 'Really?'"

They screeched at the memory.

"Yeah," reminded Sinead, "and then he said, 'Ah, sure, ya have, missus. They're so friendly they're looking at each *other!*"

"Do you think he was unconscious?"

"Probably. Did you ever see the size of her hands?"

"No. I was too busy being mesmerised by her eyes!"

Giggling, they tucked into more chocolate biscuits and Sinead relaxed into the sofa, looking around the room. She was immediately impressed with Gertie's clean and IKEA'd taste in interiors. She was also surprised that she'd managed to keep everything so tidy in the face of motherhood. She flopped down onto the sofa with the Swedish name printed in bold letters on a tab that was jutting from beneath the cushion. GIT IVÖR it deadpanned brazenly to anyone who cared to look its way.

"Jesus, that's a bit harsh on poor Ivör, isn't it?" Sinead gibed.

"What?" Geri was preoccupied with scooping up a handful of dried pasta that Cameron had been using as hay bales on his farm set, and had noticed an alarming lump of blackened banana plastered to the side of the armchair.

"GIT IVÖR – the name of your settee. Poor bloody Ivör."

"Yeah," Geri retorted only half concentrating as she scooped up the gunge bare-handed, "should really be called GIT KEVIN!"

Sinead was surprised; she'd never heard Gertie slagging off Kevin before.

"What's that supposed to mean?"

Geri felt as if she'd been slapped around the puss with a pair of wet boxer shorts.

"Oh, nothing. You know, these men. Know what side their bread's buttered and then they want to lie in it!" she muddled, scurrying to the kitchen. Fortunately for Geri, her clanging and cavorting in the kitchen woke both the boys, and the subject was swiftly changed.

Sinead spent over an hour blanketing her two godsons with the kind of attention that only a childless, independent person could bestow. That untiring, patient, ever-smiling play that renders them the eternal playmate and best friend in the face of the disciplinarian parent/teacher/football coach. Geri enjoyed watching them all playing and bonding with each other – almost literally at one point, when Cameron picked up the UHU and started to sweep the gluey wand over Sinead's forearms.

Shortly after, Sinead sighed, exhaustedly, "Well, I'd better be getting off soon. I've got to meet some crony from work at four, and then there's a meeting tonight too. You know what they say about all play and no work!"

"You don't know how lucky you are."

Sinead caught sight of Gertie's exasperated expression as she'd turned away, causing a sliver of concern to run fleetingly through her mind. A sliver of concern that was instantly brushed off as Gertie picked up her two sons, kissed them and told them to give Auntie Sinead a kiss goodbye, which they did repeatedly. Sinead grabbed her over-full leather bag and keys and kissed the children's sloppy lips and peachy soft skin.

"Bye darlings. Bye Gertie. Give Kevin a kiss for me, won't you. Tell him I'm sorry I didn't see him today, but I'll see him one evening, so I can catch him home from work. I'm *really* looking forward to seeing the old bastard! He never seems to answer the phone these days . . ."

Geri smiled, clenching her lips into a plastic grin,

willing them not to part and give away any unnecessary information to Sinead regarding the absent husband.

The time just wasn't right yet.

* * *

Saturday arrived and she bowled into the classroom for Beginners' Piano with Tim Heifer-nan, the Great Composers still hanging from the furry picture rail shrugging their starchy shoulders at her, their disdain made apparent by their expressions. Once again she was uncomfortable in her clothes although she was sure she had got more room in them. Having seen Sinead in her Mediterranean outfit she had decided on the luxury of a shopping trip after class, taking full advantage of Cynthia's offer to baby-sit.

It's time for me to shed my mumsy uniform for something a bit more up to the minute.

"God," she reprimanded herself, "even *that's* an old expression, isn't it? Up to the minute!" She was turning more into her mother every day! Her disappointment at the contents of her wardrobe had finally got to her, and having flicked through the magazine's fashion pages for inspiration she had decided to go for either the classic loose linen look or the urban chic image. In the shadow of stylish Sinead she felt she'd lost her identity. Easy to wear, easy to wash; her days of miniskirts were definitely *out* after her experiences with Adam.

Taking a seat at a desk comfortably midway

between the front and the back of the class she opened her notepad only to be faced with the notes she'd written on the first lesson: 'The Swan' from *The Carnival of the Animals*. She reminded herself to ask Four-foot, Five-foot for the notes to it, wondering whether he would write them down for her, rather than giving her the musical score. It'd take her the rest of her life to learn to *read* the music!

Sylvia's presence was obvious aurally prior to visually. With the smile of a saint but the voice of a sinner she would be hard to lose in a crowd.

"Yeah, and it's me burfdee!! Ooooh Mike," she squealed as Mike put his wide hairy forearm around her slight shoulders.

"Happy birthday, Sylv, twenty-one again, is it?"

Geri felt surprised at the pang of jealousy she experienced at the attention Saliva was already getting, before entering the room! Mike's arm was tanned and furry, and Geri could just imagine watching it working its way up and down her bare thighs languorously.

"Oh, you bugga! It's double that, mate! Comin' aaeert this weekend are ya, Mike? We're all gaaing aaeert for me burfdee on Satadeee. Come orn, we'll 'ava right larf all of us! Me son and 'is mates a comin' too!" Geri cringed as she waved at her on releasing herself, reluctantly, from Mike's embrace.

"Eey, Geri, you'll come, won't ya? Satadeee? Yeah, corse ya will, gal, young one like ya! Aaeert all the time, you young'uns, ain't ya?"

Feeling hideously embarrassed, especially as Mike

was leering at her from behind Saliva, and knowing that she in fact did quite fancy him, despite him being cornier than a box of breakfast cereals. Instantly the *Carnival of the Animals* seemed an appropriate description of the night out for Saliva's burfdee. The Tank Top came into the room and Geri's embarrassment evaporated, turning rapidly to a trembling, shuddering apprehension that poo-breath was heading in her direction.

"Hey, Sylv, come and sit over here with me. I've gotta talk to you about Satadee, I mean Saturday," Geri trilled, wondering what the hell this mismatched crowd were thinking of, wanting to learn to play the piano.

Saliva snuggled her chair up next to her, reminiscent of schooldays, and whispered in Geri's ear all chummy-like, "Oh, 'ere comes the toffs!"

She was referring to the quiet, unassuming few in the class who actually looked like they *wanted* to learn to play the piano. Quite unbelievably to Sylvia. Like a cocky class of teenagers the pre-teacher hubbub escalated to a sound that reminded Geri of a cattle market. As Saliva gabbled on the subject of the "Satadee night aaeert" Geri drifted into a semicomatose state, hearing only the punchy tones of Mike as he deep-throated somewhere at the back of the class to Tony (he of the wavy hair and hiking boots) and Joan, (the stuffy matronly grandmother of twelve, who insisted she had never been kissed).

"Hey, here comes Four-foot, Five-foot," announced Mike.

The volume slid down to zero as he made an entrance. Without speaking he made for the piano, lifting the wooden lid, resting it with a solid, echoey clonk. Scraping the stool out he sat astride it, his green corduroys baggy at the knees. A cough, a flick of his hair and he began, his fingers caressing the keys gently at first, the small padded hammers hitting off the strings within the wooden box of the piano. As a class they were mesmerised by the rich tone and presence of the music. Then quicker than you could say *Sergei Rachmaninoff* he was up and rattling off the keys like a deranged typist. His staid skin shed like a snake, the Little Richard persona he adopted was both convincing and exciting, although a little ridiculous for an evening class. Minutes later as his crescendo virtually finished him off, he swung around on his stool, red-faced and a little sweaty, with a "Don't-you-just-think-I'm-great!" expression plastered onto his grinning gob. They liked it. But not *that* much.

"That," he puffed, "was Little Richard's 'Good Golly, Miss Molly'. I'm sure most of you recognised it."

Four-foot, Five-foot stood and swanked along the width of the room, slowly and repeatedly, his thin shirt stuck to his moist back. "A six-inch-high pompadour topping a pancaked face was Little Richard. He named himself 'The Architect of Rock-and-roll'. Born Richard Wayne Penniman in nineteen thirty-five, he became one of the first black artists to cross over to the national white pop charts. Richard's banshee shrieks and propelling compelling rhythm stunned young white audiences who had never heard a gospel singer with the brakes off before."

"What about Chuck Berry?"

Geri might have guessed that Rupert would have something to say, great music genius that he was. Or thought he was.

"Chuck Berry was a guitarist, Rupert; although his distinctive style and witty lyrics certainly influenced Britain's pop renaissance."

Ha – she couldn't believe it! Rupert-the-Musical-Encyclopedia wasn't as hot as he'd thought. *Chuck Berry*! Even *she* knew that one!

Four-foot, Five-foot continued, "I want you all to understand and enjoy the piano as well as learning the techniques for playing it. I'll be encouraging you to appreciate the piano's music whilst we work our way through the course, but today's lesson will cover posture at the piano. Poor posture and poor hand positioning can result in ganglion cysts on your wrists and back problems. We'll also be starting to learn about musical notes and rhythm." Snatching the piece of chalk from his desk he turned to the blackboard, gesticulating wildly, and scribed a large white wiggle on the board.

"This," he indicated, "is a treble clef."

* * *

It seems that gone are the days when trousers were trousers. In my post-natal state I'm dazed to discover the numerous varieties on offer. It makes me wonder where I've been for the last five years. I know: Maternity Wear! I'd forgotten the traumas of deciding between high-waisted or hipsters; wide legs or slim cut. And then you have the sizes to contemplate! "Who is this woman who is 'standard' or 'one size'?"

she implored the blank-faced teenager behind the counter who held the black T-shirt aloft, looking as if she'd have no problem sliding into the tiny garment.

"Weird," spat the teenager, turning her back and walking away.

Geri's frustration grew as she struggled with the "One Size" wear. It didn't seem fair. It clearly wouldn't matter if you were a six-stone waif or a seventeen-stoner, your only choice remained: One Size. Whoever this One Size woman was, she was nothing like Geri. She thought back to the heady days of matrimony when she used to buy shirts for Kevin. She'd always thought it ridiculous that it went by the size of his neck. Totally unrelated to his severe lack of backbone, Kevin had a rather scrawny neck, but a beer-gut to die for. A fat git with a long skinny neck. The Mateus Bottle she had used to call him, all in fun of course.

When he had a sense of humour.

Years ago.

She finally decided, a little nervously, on a pair of designer combats and a black T-shirt with a Chinese slogan on the front, and stood behind the safety curtain of the changing-room. It had been years since she'd tried on anything that didn't have a Maternity label stuck to it somewhere, or was in a size range lower than 20. Buying clothes had been easy. Boring, predictable and mundane. But safe and easy. She'd just sift through for the brown and purple tags – size 18/20. She just looked for the brown and purple, wishing for the day that she'd be hunting out the orange – size 12. The irony was, before babies, if it didn't have YSL on it, she wouldn't have wanted it! She *knew* the difference between preppie chic outfits versus sexy and minimalistic. As she wriggled and struggled into the size 16 combats, resolving to stick with the gym, she realized that her resident cushion had gradually started moving out. The wobble factor seemed to have diminished slightly, but her dietary wrongs were still screaming at her. Staring at her red-faced reflection she felt like Mrs Merton in Meg Matthew's wardrobe and decided that she should look in the mirror from outside of her cubicle. Without a second thought, she whisked back the Dralon only to be faced with Jennifer Langley!

Jennifer Langley of the year above me in school! Jennifer Langley who we'd unmercifully teased, ridiculed, scribbled on her homework and padlocked her bags to the lockers! Oh so cocky in our teenage gangs as we had made her schooldays something to be dreaded. And now, fifteen years later and for the first time, we're confronted with each other. And here's me in khaki combats two sizes too small, a star tight on my crotch as the material isn't sure in which direction to pull first, and her – elegant, unwrinkled and trendy with an expression that says, "Don't you think I'm cute? Ordinary people feel unworthy standing next to me in all my elegance."

Awkwardly, Geri smiled, reddened further and reversed back into the safety of her cubicle. *She looks bloody great! They say good things come to those who wait! At least, my mum does! Well, at least I was good-looking as a teenager, even though I may be a frumpy tent-wearer now.*

She peeked furtively through a hole in the worn

curtain. *She looks twenty-bloody-one! And she's a year older than me! Older! Christ, I feel worse now than ever.*

Jennifer pulled off her clothes revealing sexy lingerie – Agent Provocateur, for sure! Burgundy, although she'd probably call it something like aubergine, pouting as she'd whisper it; lace bra, complete with underwires, uplift and push together, and matching high-cut knickers.

"Matching knickers? Who the bloody hell buys the matching knickers?" Geri whispered in amazement. "I thought it was only the women in the American horror films who investigate the strange noises in their haunted houses in their best undies." At second scrutiny she noticed the fake tan that had collected in the crevices between Jennifer's ample cleavage, her fingers and toes, her upper-arm gold twisted tourniquet reminiscent of Egyptian slavery, her slender form sliding into a fantastic and probably size 10 pair of cropped black trousers and matching black and powder blue T-shirt. Geri slid down the wall, slumped in despair at her current state of affairs. Despondent, dejected and virtually delirious she peeled the skin-tight combats from her, the origin of their name now evident, as "combat" is a word perilously close to how she feels the clothes are interracting with her. Her original intention to banish-the-black now a million miles away, she scrunched the clothes back onto their hangers.

They looked better on them than me anyway.

Geri thought nothing of walking home the back way, where the building works were going on – there wasn't as much as a whistle on passing a building site these days.

Shit, I'm not even worthy of a downward glance. Not even from the old fellas – the sweeper-uppers!

She trudged over rubble, cement powder and broken bricks on her way to her mum's and winced, reflecting on her sadness. She realised now that when you are trying on clothes you need a definitive portion of ICC – In-Clothes-Confidence – to prevent you looking like a poor imposter! *These trendy twenty-somethings clad in combats and chunky shoes don't just throw the look together. They carry it off with an excessive amount of ICC! That's the bloody secret!* As she kicked a boulder grumpily, expecting it to fly into the kerb, a pain shot through and up her leg. Limping as the boulder sat stubborn and immovable due to its weight, she hobbled and hopped round the corner to Cynthia's, already anticipating her remark, probably something consoling like, "Oh Geri love, you don't look half bad for someone twice your age!"

* * *

Ben worked to the sound of David Gray. He liked the harmonies and rhythm, finding the music let his mind wander creatively, juicing his ink onto the paper. His full-sized easel sat well in the corner of his living-room, and the banker's light shone approvingly onto his sketches, providing the only light in his open-plan lounge/dining room. A small lamp on the kitchen table shone a ray of light down onto the plastic laundry basket which was spilling with dirty linen. He'd decided to leave it until the morning. After a bellyful of Spag Bol and nearly a whole bottle of Chianti, he'd already left the encrusted pan soaking in the bubbly sink. Meals-for-one a regular thing these days, he was tiring of the humdrum routine of a sole existence.

He was delighted at his news. He had secured contracts with a major greetings-card company and also a small, new publisher of children's books. All he had to do now was come up with the goods. He scanned his many bookshelves, heavily laden with illustration and animation books, and sought inspiration from two much-thumbed sources, *How To Be A Successful Cartoonist* and *Drawing On The Comical Side Of The Brain*. The greetings-card work wasn't too taxing, just took a little imagination and quick wit, but the children's books? He'd never really had much contact with children, not for any length of time anyway. The series ran along the lines of a family of foxes who lived on a farm and the ups and downs of their lives. He'd already designed the main characters, so in theory it should be quite easy to illustrate the stories, right? Wrong! He'd learned all too swiftly that full-time posts for illustrators were not only highly specialised, but also as rare as a good-looking woman, with a fantastic personality and *no* emotional baggage! In this hugely competitive arena he was finding it difficult to maintain one strong, consistent style within his portfolio. Continuity was the key and Ben wasn't sure he'd be able to keep Felix looking friendly whilst also trying to scare off the dogs. Aimed at three to six-year-olds it had been stipulated that the characters had to retain a cartoony, soft look whilst still being realistic. He found little problem in sustaining their character through the narrative, more a difficulty in keeping their features life-like and convincing. Running his fingers through his hair, he tickled the paper with his pen, intermittently swapping to another, thicker or thinner-nibbed version. As he worked, his mind began to wander to Her. Her effect on him was mesmerising. His waking moments were starting to become confetti'd with thoughts of her, what she was doing, and who with. Ben felt mentally accosted by his mental image of Her. She seemed so down-to-earth, confident, contented yet sensual, intriguing and beguiling. He was well and truly hooked. It seemed ridiculous, having not even spoken to Her. He didn't even know her name! But each time Ben caught even the slightest glimpse of Geri, his feelings became more intense. His thoughts then led him to the conversation he'd had earlier that morning with his brother, Andy. Ben, in an attempt to get Andy out of his couch-potato existence, suggested that he start playing squash with him. Andy's answer had been, "I don't know."

"How can you not know?" Ben had cajoled.

"I don't know. I just don't."

"But you surely know if you fancy it or not?

"I just *don't*, all right!" Andy had barked.

Ben was ever hopeful when it came to his younger brother, the eternal pessimist, and never relinquished an opportunity to reinvent him, much to Andy's contempt.

"Come on, And," Ben jibed quirkily. "Turn the bloody telly off. Let's get out and get you into shape. You'll never find a woman if you don't get out."

"A woman! A bloody woman? Is that what you think it's all about? Bloody women?"

Andy's statement was as misplaced on Ben as a tiara on Kathy Burke: Ben rarely tormented himself about women; he knew the type he liked and had long given up relying on one-night stands to massage his ego. Andy, on the other hand, desperately wanted a relationship. Since the break-up (or break-down) of Andy's marriage two years ago Ben had watched the hideous transformation of Andy from gregarious, fun-loving and intelligent comedian to an overweight, insecure and resigned depressive. Determined not to give up on him Ben forced himself to remember Andy's good points. He used to have a great physique, a fantastic personality and he wasn't *bad*-looking. Ben had continued,

"It's all *you* used to think about! Every weekend you had a different bird on your arm! What's happened to you, Andy? When's it all gonna end? Come on, man, pull yourself together! Stephanie's not lounging around the house mourning for *you*, you can count on that! It's been over two years, Andy. Come on, mate!"

Andy's tone softened as he started to talk from the heart, a significant first in Ben's experience.

"What does the future hold for me, eh? It all starts with love-notes scratched into the tin foil around me sandwiches at work, and ends with a vigilante checking the itemised phone bill, rooting through me pockets and locking the door if I'm not in by eleven! What's the bloody point eh, Ben?" Andy shifted his vast bulk on the green crumpled settee, lifting his large legs up to rest also. Ben had hoped for the opposite effect.

"You're just a cynic, And! It doesn't have to be like that!"

"Huh, you're just a pissing romantic, you are!"

Ben was losing his attention and wanted to win his confidence back quickly. "Romantic, me?" He lifted Andy's thick ankles, pale and podgy atop vile green lace-effect socks, there were that many holes in them, and swung them down onto the floor. He sat on the settee with his brother.

"Look, mate. I haven't had a successful relationship for ages. There –"

"All them dolly birds after ya, what ya talking about? It's all right for you, going to the gym, pumping up your muscles, all suntanned and macho. You could have any girl you wanted, you could!" Andy interrupted bitterly. Jealousy had always been one of his stronger points.

"Yeah but, Andy, you don't get it! I don't *want* them dollies. Remember me at fifteen? Fifteen stone at fifteen? That's why I started going to the gym. That's why I take pride in my appearance. Doesn't make me any better than you. If I stopped bothering for a month, you'd soon see similarities between us! And there *is* a woman I really like." He'd said it before he'd realised.

Andy shuffled to sit upright, a mischievous grin

melting onto his face, a sliver of his former self glinting through, wickedly,

"Oh yeah?"

Annoyed at himself for letting it slip, Ben knew he'd made a mistake. Despite his depression, Andy was a relentless piss-taker. One of the few strong traits that remained with him whatever.

"What's her name then? Who is she?"

With little left to lose, and in the possibility that a heart-to-heart with Andy might help him to see his insecurities, Ben decided to reveal all.

"She lives down the road from me. I don't know her name. She's about thirty-ish, about five-five, slightly overweight but *not* fat. She's got shortish hair, and she's always laughing and smiling." Ben grinned inanely into mid-air.

Andy wasn't impressed, "Is that it? An overweight midget with a man's haircut and a clown's smile? What happened to the leggy blondes?"

"No! She's lovely. Oh, and she's got kids."

"Kids! Christ, I'm hearing it all now. She's got bloody kids! How many, half a bloody dozen? What you thinking of, Ben? All those gorgeous birds around you at work and that, and you want a middle-aged housewife with bloody kids! Need your bloody 'ead tested, you do!"

Ben didn't realise at this point how he'd already lost Andy's confidence, only to be replaced by his disgust. Andy flicked the remote control toward the telly, turning up the volume to a ridiculous pitch, breaking into Ben's daydream.

"What? What's the problem?" he asked, wide-eyed.

"Look at ya! Like a Cheshire bloody cat! Don't ask me, Ben. I don't wanna know about 'er. If *that's* what you're after, don't bother telling me!" And he went on mumbling and muttering ignorantly about tasty tarts and miniskirts and frumpy bucket-crotches.

Ben wished he'd never told him and left in silence.

* * *

Two hours later his eyes were forcing themselves shut and the music was doing nothing for him but keeping him awake. He checked his watch and his eyes blurred to focus on the hands.

"God, it's only half twelve," he groaned to himself, resting his head in his hands. He ruffled his short hair in a bid to waken himself up a bit, and rubbed his hands over his face vigorously. "Bloody BT!" he scowled as he stood up from his high stool and made for the kitchen. He'd called the operator the previous evening for a morning alarm call rather than change his watch to the correct time. He had incessantly woken through the night to convert the *wrong* time on his watch to the right time in his head, adding on the offending four hours and seventeen minutes to do so, worried that BT would forget to call him. By the time they had rung at quarter past seven, not long after him falling into something resembling sleep, he'd only had about fifteen minutes! Consequently he now had a bed fetish and a BT phobia.

Reprimanding himself for not being able to work

any longer, he stripped off his jeans and jumper, swapping them for the soft jersey fabric of his shorts and t-shirt. Padding across the wooden floor to his bedroom, he climbed onto his large double bed, switching on the side lamp as he did so. He snuggled down under the warm Moroccan-style plump duvet cover and into the wrought-iron double bed. As he viewed its solid black lines he was momentarily reminded of Chanelle. They'd been set to get married until she revealed herself as the precocious air-head she was destined to be. Years at Swiss finishing schools had only fermented her grotesquely inflated self-esteem and had now left him saddled with the mortgage on their flat. Ben now searched, fruitlessly, for a woman of substance. As the overweight streetwise woman had spat at him and his chubby friends in their teenage years as they'd ridiculed her, "I can lose weight, but you'll always be ignorant!", he now wanted a partner whom he appreciated more for her personality than her physical perfection. He now really believed that beauty was only skin-deep.

Once cosy and cosseted in his warm bed he reached for the paperwork that the estate agents had sent him. As he reached across to the mosaic bedside table, his eyes rested on the plaque that Andy had bought for his twenty-first birthday. A time when his family had been whole, his father had been alive and Andy and Ben had just left home to live together in their first flat. Everything had seemed promising, the future looked inviting and very welcoming. He smiled up at the psychedelic swirling writing that encouraged, *"Art is making something out of nothing, and selling it – Frank Zappa"*.

Andy had held such hopes for Ben, but also for himself. Shaking his head, feeling too tired for further analysis of Andy's dispirited attitude, he looked toward the wad of papers in his hand and wriggled his shoulders into his V-pillow.

"Now," he smiled, "Devon and Cornwall, what might you have to offer me?"

Chapter Eleven

Driving wasn't a term that Sinead could apply to her experience on the largest car park in Europe. As she inched along on the M25 in her hire car, the evening traffic congested, she watched the red tail-lights of the snaking cars as they followed the road, like molten lava sliding from a hot volcano, curving and dipping, finding its natural bend in the road.

"Well, what a novelty," she sighed, dragging on her Marlboro Light . "Makes a change from my usual journey – the road to ruin."

As she patiently slithered a path through to her required junction, she glanced at her reflection in the rear-view mirror. She loved feeling good in her clothes and today was no exception. Running her fingers through her sleek long hair she admired her bronzed reflection, finished with the red lipstick and jet-black mascara. The 'new' smell of her leather trousers wafted pleasingly up her nostrils reminding her how great she looked in her new Mediterranean wardrobe. Her self-admiration was interrupted by her mobile ringing. She grabbed it quickly,

"Hello?"

"Sinead, it's Mam. Did you arrive safely?"

"Course I did, Mam, and sorry I haven't rung you yet. It's been kinda busy."

"Sinead, now tell me, have you seen Geri yet? I'm just dying to know what she's at."

"I have, but I've got a strange feeling about her. In fact it hasn't stopped bothering me."

"What d'ya mean?"

"There's definitely something up with her, but I just can't put my finger on it."

"Maybe it's because you haven't seen her for a while. She's probably exhausted with the children."

"S'pose. She made a remark about Kevin though. Was a bit off for Gertie. She's *never* spoken badly about him, even in the early days when she was Miss Independent."

"Look, love, you're out of touch with her. Try and see a bit more of her while you're there. She probably misses you like mad."

As one of her favourite songs came onto the radio she switched her thoughts from Gertie and Kevin, keen to get off the phone to sing.

"You know, Mam, I probably have a romanticised view of relationships."

"Yeah, that's why you never had a successful one – you expect too much from them."

Irritated by her mother's analysis she quipped, "Aren't I the kind of girl known for saying things like, 'Ah sure, you know how it is: you're only as young as the *men* you feel!' and 'Hah, mention "commitment" and I *immediately* turn the page'?"

"Yes, Sinead, you're hardly known for wearing your heart on your sleeve. Never was."

"OK, Mam, have to go. Traffic-lights. Bye."

"Bye, love."

Sinead had learnt to conceal her lack of confidence from an early age. Unlike her sister, Bridie, she wasn't a natural swimmer. And Mum had insisted on reminding everyone, usually when she was drunk and desperate for attention – only when the room was bursting with an attentive, unsuspecting audience – "Well, even though Bridie works such long hours she still swims every day. But of course, you know, at only six weeks old we just threw her in; and she swam!"

"Shame!" Sinead always muttered, raising fewer laughs every time as she was now as predictable as Mum for saying it in the first place.

She concealed her insecurities famously, her inner turmoil a well-kept secret as she'd suffered a lifetime of plaguing herself with questions such as "Who *are* these child prodigies? Why can't they be 'normal'? Why can't *they* be flailing around in the shallow end, terrified and squealing because *they're* scared of the water? Why can't *they* be the ones without a note in their head, the one the choir throws out unless they *mime*!" All through her life Sinead's failings and disappointments stood in the front of the queue in her mind, whilst she made her many achievements and successes remain quietly and patiently at the back.

Her friendship with Gertie had been unexpected, but very rewarding. They'd mismatched themselves within two weeks of starting school, with Sinead as the new girl from Ireland and Geri so confident, when Sinead had rescued Geri from a shoplifting experience, displaying a competent blarney gift at a young age. They'd been virtually inseparable for the duration.

As the traffic crept slowly forward she reminisced back to their schooldays. The days of Shakatak, Kool & The Gang, Spandau Ballet, Shalamar and Adam Ant. Denim waistcoats, electric blue eyeliner and lip-gloss. She found it distressing to hear yet another cover version from the latest Boy Bland, only to find that she was word-perfect, remembering the original from twenty years ago. A smile spread across her face as she recalled her and Gertie and Caroline Pritchard singing at the top of their voices at the end-of-term disco, *"Ferret ears, ferret ears, what took us so lo-ong, to find each other, baby!"* to Shalamar's "There It Is" song, and everyone thinking they were dead funny. She suddenly had a mental block as she tried to recall the insipid gingered one that Caroline Pritchard had fancied. Realising she'd have had more success reciting the chapters of the New Testament, she enthusiastically picked up her mobile and rang Gertie. Only two rings and she answered, all whispery,

"Hello?"

"Hey, Gertie. It's me. Sinead."

"Oh hi. Where *are* you?"

"Stuck on the bloody M25. I tell you, the traffic isn't like *this* in Valencia! Listen I've got to ask you, Gertie – who was that singer Caroline Pritchard used to fancy at school?"

"Singer? At school?"

"He didn't *go* to our school! We were at school when he was in the charts. You remember that awful gingery bloke with the weaselly face. She was mad about him!"

"Oh, Rick Astley!"

"That's him! God! Rick Astley! Did he ever have any other records? I mean *where did he go?*"

They both laughed, Geri quieter than Sinead, not wanting to break the silence she'd created by setting Cameron up with his paints and colouring book and strapping Reece into his high-chair to discover how many different ways he could drop her car keys.

"When did you say you were going back?" Geri asked once she'd calmed down.

"Day after tomorrow," Sinead answered, a slight lilt in her voice.

Geri picked up on it immediately. "Are you looking forward to it?"

"You know, it sounds funny, but I am in a way. When I'm in Spain I yearn for all things English. Even the weather – 'inclement' my boss calls it. Some weeks I go for hours just wishing myself shopping in Oxford Street or walking through the wet park. Sometimes I even miss the Tube!"

"That's nothing new. You always missed it, even when you lived here. I can't remember a day when you weren't late for work."

"I don't mean I *miss* it! I miss seeing it, using it, looking at it, going down onto the dusty dirty platforms and hearing those 'Mind the gap' announcements. On a bad day I think I even miss the dried bogies wiped under the arms of the seats!"

"Oh Sinead, stop!"

"Only joking. But then, when I'm here, I start missing things about Spain. Do you think I'm mentally unstable or what?" She laughed.

"What do you miss?" Geri was intrigued – a visit to Valencia would be one of her dreams. Just a fortnight with Sinead. Just the two of them. She desperately wanted to reveal her abandonment to Sinead and request the chances of a cheap holiday, but her pride stood firm and solidly in the way.

"Well, obviously I miss the sunshine. Everyone's so much more relaxed and has time to enjoy their lives more. It's all so bloody mad and fast here. You're all moving so damned quick you can't see where you're going!"

"Oh, and tell me, how fast are you going at the moment, Sinead?" Geri teased, knowing her traffic-jam standstill.

"Yeah, well, you know what I mean. As I said, you'd never get a traffic jam like *this* in Valencia! It just wouldn't happen!"

"Go on, what do you miss?"

"I miss the clothes, the beautiful architecture, waking up to an indigo sky, the clothes, the culture and the cheap booze!" Sinead laughed, "Oh, and did I mention the clothes?"

Geri, warmed by her imagination of Valencia, wanted to know more,

"Tell me about Valencia. What's it like?" She thought about offering to ring Sinead back as she was obviously calling from a mobile, but thought better of it, on the assumption that her bill would be met by the company, and *she'd* be lucky if her own bill would be met at all!

"Well, there's a gorgeous museum, the *Museo de Bellas Artes*, with works by some of Valencia's most notable Renaissance painters. *And* it's one of the best outside of Madrid. Valencia hosts *Las Fallas de San José* which is one of the most important festivals in Spain. It costs around two-hundred million pesetas, don't *ask* me in euros, which goes up in smoke. It's in the week of 19 March – St Joseph's Day, or *San José*. During the year each neighbourhood builds a massive papier-mâché satirical figure which could be a politician or star or anyone really. They are set in the plazas of each neighbourhood at the beginning of March and are judged and awarded prizes. At midnight on March 19, the *Nit de Foci*, they are set alight. Each figure has a small model that is created by the children. The firework display is completely thunderous!"

"That sounds fantastic. What about Valencia's history? Do you know anything about that?" Geri was now completely engulfed by her dream of the Mediterranean.

"Course I do!" Sinead teased. "Valencia Cathedral is famous for its claim to possession of the Holy Grail which is supposed to be kept in a Gothic charterhouse!"

"Really? How do you know these things?" Geri was impressed.

"What do you think I do with myself when I'm not at work? I don't have men climbing the walls to get to me, you know! I have to fill my time somehow!"

Geri was a little surprised at Sinead's quick answer. She was under the impression that Sinead was out dating virtually every evening.

Sinead continued, "Oh Gertie, I'd love to take you up the *Miguelete Tower* of the cathedral – what a fantastic view. Talk about panoramic! There's a planetarium, an *IMAX* Cinema. The beach is only about three kilometres away from the town. The train station, the *Estación del Nord*, is beautifully tiled and there's the central square, the *Ayuntamiento*, oh, and the *Lonja de la Seda* is –"

"The what?" Geri interrupted, eager to soak up Sinead's pronunciation in preparation for her Spanish class in a few days' time.

"The *Lonja de la Seda*. The Silk Exchange is one of Spain's finest buildings. It has these fantastic Gothic doorways with carvings, and I can tell you, girl, some of *them* leave nothing to the imagination!"

"What do you mean?"

"Put it this way, erotic isn't the word for them. Actually," she pondered, "reminds me a bit of the stories you told me about you and Kevin!"

"God!" Geri whispered awestruck. That was something to think about when she went to bed that night.

* * *

Four hours later, Geri was still tingling at the prospect of the culture and coastline of Valencia. How she would adore a fortnight of people-watching, soaking up the sun into her tired skin and recharging her batteries ready for the abuse of the next thirty years. Kevin hadn't seen the point in holidays. They'd managed a week in Kos when Geri had been pregnant with Cameron. He'd spent the week sitting on the balcony with his head in a book, drinking bottles of cheap beer, whilst she'd lain on the bed groaning and complaining about the heat and her huge stomach. So now she sat on her bed with a crippling period pain and a fantastic painting of Valencia in her mind. Her imagination was running riot. She wanted to go there nearly as much as she wanted to play that song from the piano classes. As she slid open the drawer rummaging for a sanitary towel she came across a green envelope, containing a sample pantyliner claiming to smell like a summer's day.

"Christ," she threw it back into the drawer, "bloody scratch and sniff pantyliners now!"

Despite the *freedom* adverts she was a sucker for the cotton-wool pad that incongruously jutted out from behind her backside, even in the face of a potential groper being confronted with the brick in her drawers.

"Mind you, a fortnight swimming in the Valencian sun could well change my mind . . . "

* * *

Sinead arrived at her destination only an hour late. She'd arranged to meet up with Jonathon Morgan, her equivalent in the UK, for a few drinks and something to eat. She couldn't hide her amazement at seeing him still seated at the hotel bar.

"Oh," she flirted, "you waited." Her eyes scanned his handsome face, excitement leaping ecstatically in her stomach, lust nudge-nudge-winking at her insides and her nerve endings giggling and wriggling with anticipation.

"Of course. I figured you'd have trouble on the M25. I was right, wasn't I?" His grey-green eyes twinkled and smiled at her lustily.

He made her feel like a tourist; and she liked it.

He made her feel desirable; and she liked it.

He ordered her a vodka martini and Sinead loved the way he assumed she wanted it. The evening suddenly had potential. Realising that her lipstick had probably evaporated from her lips and her mascara had more than likely collected in unsightly black clumps in the corners of her eyes, she excused herself and made for the toilets.

As she leaned in towards the illuminated mirrored walls, her familiar hand adept at sweeping the mascara onto her lashes and pulling her fingers through her long auburn hair, she felt another familiar feeling. That disconcerting shift within her stomach. Standing bolt upright, placing her hand onto her abdomen, she winced as she felt the acidy pain again.

"God, no. Not tonight."

Then, as quickly as it arrived, it went. As she forced her make-up back into her bulging bag, Sinead scolded herself for not seeing the doctor before now; this nervous stomach was starting to become a problem. Surely something simple like charcoal or burnt toast or something could calm her digestive dalliances?

Jonathon was waiting for her at a dimly lit corner table, positioned cosily by the open fire which flickered and crackled warmly. She envisaged him with a cravat and a pipe as he sat contented in the high-backed chair, smiling at her as she approached him.

"Your drink," he offered, placing the chilled glass delicately on the table mat in front of her, the shiny wooden table gleaming and radiant, reflecting the fire's glow.

"Thank you," she flirted once again, forever the willing captive to such a charming species.

Twenty minutes later and she was sure sex was on the agenda. Jonathon Morgan was as handsome as he was charming, his sexiness matched only by his physique – he was *surely* married! His immaculate and extremely stylish suit jacket lay invitingly open revealing a gleaming white shirt, the merest hint of a hairy chest evident through the cotton, and a torso and wide shoulders to die for.

"Another drink!"

More of a statement than a question as he cupped her chin with one hand and lifted her glass with the other. Sinead found all she could do was nod, gormlessly. But as he brushed past her shoulder, leaving a waft of aftershave behind him, Sinead involuntarily broke wind. It shook and surprised her, seeming to come from absolutely nowhere! A deep volumeless rumble, whose silence belied its stench.

"Shit!" Sinead whispered, unaware of how appropriate the expression was to be. Typically untimely, Jonathon returned to the table, placing another large bubbly drink in front of Sinead, a large whisky in a cut crystal tumbler in front of himself and quietly lay a door key attached to a keyring (the size of a book), bound in leather and boasting the hotel's name and telephone number in embossed gold, on the middle of the table. As he stooped to sit in his chair he smiled at her knowingly, "If you'd like to –" his only whispered delectable words.

Sinead, holding her breath for fear he'd notice her recent malodorous addition to the atmosphere, sighed dreamily, and opened her mouth to utter her acceptance when she saw his expression shift. His face contorted from an "I'll-be-Your-Father-Christmas" expression to an horrific "Robert-De-Niro-in-Cape-Fear". Obviously, the cabbage-smell had made its way to his unsuspecting nostrils – his face now an ugly grimace.

"Christ! Someone's dropped their guts!"

"I know," she muttered, gulping her drink in an attempt to wash the smirk from her face. "It really is bad, isn't it?"

"Christ! It's making me feel sick!"

She coughed to conceal a laugh waiting to jump out from her throat. She didn't expect it to have this bad an effect on him!

"Come on. Drink up. Let's go upstairs," his voice now disappointingly ordinary and sharp.

Result! she thought to herself downing the drink in one. Please, God, don't let there be any more of them waiting to stand up and be counted! She clenched her bum cheeks together so tightly she was in real fear of knocking her teeth out this time.

Unfortunately she felt another bout of intestinal movement whilst in the sumptuous lift, as Jonathon was kissing her. He really was the most gorgeous kisser she'd ever come across. What was she going to do? Risk staying the night and stinking out the hotel room? Then he'd surely *know* it was her in the bar! Or hedge her bets, raincheck the whole affair, and make her polite exit. Why did these things have to happen at such inopportune moments? Just prior to the lift pinging at their floor he sucked on her tongue, and as he pulled away he whispered hoarsely,

"I want to be the last thing you put in your mouth tonight."

She saw her opportunity and took it, admirably, cooing thickly,

"The last thing I put in my mouth tonight will be what every good Catholic girl should put in their mouth last thing at night. A toothbrush." Although she knew it'd probably be a fag.

208

The lift doors glided open but Jonathon Morgan remained still, "What're you saying?"

Mustering up her chirpy, happy-go-lucky confidence from the pits of herself, she quipped, tracing her sultry painted fingernails down his smooth shirt front, "I'm saying, you sexy man, that tonight I will *not* be staying here with you. You've been lovely company, I'm very attracted to you, but unfortunately tonight I can't stay. Let's meet up tomorrow night, before I go back. Until then, here's something to remember me by . . ." She pressed button number thirty-four for the top floor, the doors slid closed, she got onto her knees and unzipped his trousers.

By the time the lift had reached the top floor Jonathon Morgan was slightly more relaxed than he had been. As the doors opened Sinead kissed him, whispered "Tomorrow" to his grinning face, exited the lift and when the doors had slid shut farted her way hot and stinkingly down the silent, carpeted corridor.

Chapter Twelve

"Morning, Geri. It's Mum!"

The early morning wake-up call reverberated through her sleeping brain as she held the telephone too close to her ear-hole.

"Mmm," she groaned into the cold plastic handpiece, discarding the toy banana she'd mistakenly picked up in her frenzy to quieten the household onto the *empty* side of the bed.

"I'm going to Boloing."

God, what the hell was she going on about now? What on earth is Boloing? And what's the time?

She looked at her wrist to read her watch only to realise that she wasn't wearing it. Now where had she left it?

"Where?" The exasperation in Geri's voice was more obvious than Paul Daniels' wig. "Boloing?"

I can't help but thinking how Mum sounds like Zebbedee

on acid, pronunciation being never one of her strong points, even in her own language. She tends to have her own language, you see. If someone says to Mum, "Tell me in your own words . . ." she literally can! She has a lexicon of her own words, their meanings a mystery to the listener, as she regales hours of virtually meaningless stories. In the name of posterity, I inhale deeply; one thing motherhood brings with it is an insurmountable tendency to take these frequently.

"Mum, *where* are you going? And *when*?"

"Oooh Geri, I'm so excited. Boloing in France. We're going for a day trip today with the WI. I got a last-minute ticket after the news last night. Auntie Glad rang and asked me."

"Don't you mean Boulogne?"

"Yeees, that's what I said. I'm a bit worried though, Geri. You know, will me feet be up to it? All that walking and all? Mind you, I s'pose the coach'll take us to the main spots, won't it?"

Her ailing feet were news to Geri; matched only by her mouth they seemed tireless, forever hitting the ground running.

"What's wrong with your feet, Mum?"

"Oh, I burnt 'em in the bloody bath last night. Got two bloody red socks now. When Auntie Glad burnt her feet in the bath I told her, 'If you get the red sock you get out!', shame I never took me own advice. I've got an undercarriage redder than Karl Marx's vest."

"Oh, Mum. You never sat down in it!"

"I did! Stupid idiot, eh? And you *know* what I always say about looking before you leap!"

"Mm, and I'd say that was some leap, Mum . . . " She had comical visions of her naked mum stepping into the bath, realising the water was too hot for her feet, and in typical Cynthia style leaping into a sitting position to relieve her feet, rather than leaping *out* of the offending hot water.

"Well, I thought I'd ring you before I go; tried you last night but couldn't get through."

Geri decided to ignore her disgruntled tone.

The silence spurred Cynthia on. "The coach is picking us up outside KCF at nine. I think the ferry goes about half-ten. I've heard there's a lovely hypermarket there and, Glad, she's been before, says you can get some smashing cream cakes and things for less than a euro! No tea though, not into tea the French, are they? It's all that coffee and cwasonts millarkey."

"Well, keep your bag with you, and don't go walking about with your purse in your hand, Mum. Keep it zipped up in your bag. You *always* do that, and you can't take any chances. Any would-be thief'd spot you a mile away."

"Kilometres, darling."

"Pardon?"

"It's kilometres in France, not miles."

"Ha, bloody ha. You *know* what I'm saying! Keep safe. You're a walking target the way you go about the place."

"Geri, please. You know what I always say, 'I might have been born yesterday, but I stayed up all night.'"

"I know, I know. But I'm not convinced."

"What's the racket?"

"Pardon?"

"The row, what's going on there?"

"Oh, that's Reece. He wakes in a bout of early morning tears – you'd think I'd been practising medieval torture on him, the way he wakes up so tormented." Taking her opportunity by the ears and kissing it forcefully on the lips, Geri excused herself, "Mum. Gotta go, he's bawling. Listen, have a great day. Take it easy eh? Don't go getting yourself into trouble and ring me when you get home tonight. Love you, take care."

As I sit snuggled up in my king-size bed next to Reece, his warm pudgy skin pushed cosily onto mine, a warm rush of love washes over me, warm, comforting and promising, a bit like your waters breaking really. I watch Reece's long-lashed eyelids droop heavily as he sucks and smacks his gums on his warm bottle, the teat dropping out of his mouth as sleep takes him.

She gently slid from the bed, and "ooh, aahh, ouched" her way barefoot across the plastic battalion on the carpet, as she went to open the curtains. She looked out at a pinky grey sky.

Salmon sky, Mum would call it and it reminds me of the first autumn I was married to Kevin. How we'd lie in bed after our mega love-making sessions and I'd lay my head on his warm chest, it rising and dropping with his contented post-coital snores. Amazing how I'd even loved the sounds of him snoring back then as I'd looked out at the October sky.

She shuddered, feeling a distinct chill in the air, stooping to turn up the radiator a little bit more.

Little was I to know that everything bridal really meant bridle, or that a few years and two kids later Kevin wouldn't even have been man enough to say "I've had an affair, you know". Why do I feel guilty? To blame? I desperately want to know if he was a serial adulterer and his feasting on variety packs only to be expected? Or did he just take an opportunity that came his way? I question whether or not I really did not know. I'm not sure that I can honestly look back and say I never ignored any vital signs that he was playing away from home. Or was I just turning a blind eye when my instincts screamed at me that he was being unfaithful?

Once again she wondered why everything couldn't be as easy as in the movies? Why couldn't the days prior to Kevin's infidelity have been as simple as defusing a bomb in the American films, the digital clock conveniently telling her how long she had left? Why couldn't he have told her face-on, and then as her emotions outnumbered her, they would have patiently danced around in a threatening manner until she was ready to take them on, one by one? Looking around the double bedroom that now housed only *her* belongings, the dim light shone onto her bad buys of yesterday as they hung promisingly in her wardrobe. Pulling a still-creased-from-being-in-the-bag Puffa jacket onto her pyjama-clad arms, its price tag poked her in the back of the neck, a clear reminder that it probably *should* be returned to the shop.

God! I look like a bloody hot-water bottle!

Flopping onto the end of the bed she excused her bad-buy as clearly a text-book example of PMS – Pre

Menstrual *Shopping*! Her wardrobe was full of these examples.

If the camera never lies then the mirrors in my bedroom should be arrested for fraud! With my stretched blancmanged stomach I'm more of a femme foetale. *The horror of my sagging neck makes me more of a manne*-chin *than a mannequin.*

Sickened at herself she decided to act as devil's advocate, stepping onto the digital scales. In for a penny, in for seven pounds. Virtually hearing them creak and groan as she stepped onto them, leaning all her weight forward onto her toes she sees the red numbers flick and flash as they rose up through the scales. Wishing they'd stop around the nine mark, she closed her eyes as the numbers kept going. When they finally stopped twelve pounds below what she'd expected her expression shifted from morose to something marginally happier. She stepped off, then on again, this time with a touch more vigour and confidence about her actions, and *without* leaning forward. She really took the plunge and remained *flat-footed* on the cool white plastic square. Once again, the red figures worked their way up, resting once again on the same spot.

"I've bloody-well lost twelve bloody pounds! Twelve bloody pounds!!"

Grinning inanely at herself she thought now that maybe her blancmangey tummy wasn't quite so wobbly, and, mmmm, yes, she thinks her thighs have reduced slightly. Still, the image in her mind's eye of how she wants to look is a far cry from the Geri she's looking at right now.

Feeling decidedly sylph-like, she strode towards the staircase determined to suck on a grapefruit for breakfast.

An hour later the boys are catapulting their Weetabix across to each other via their spoons and I've had three grapefruits that tasted like sucking goldfish soaked in vinegar. A bowl of Sugar Puffs and a Twix later I'm feeling more satisfied but am neck-deep in washing. As an excited and admittedly absent-minded expectant mum I'm sure I hadn't signed up for the additional lifestyles I seem to be receiving. Life in a bloody laundromat, a living breathing Widow Twanky – my life now a spin cycle of washing, washing and more washing. And then there's the drying! I mean, how do you even attempt to dry five loads a day between sticky fingers, sicky T-shirts, and shitty joggers. I'd always leant toward the Lynda Bellingham variety of "Mummy", believing I'd enrolled into the Oxo Mum School of Parenthood. The table sagging with the weight of hot food, grinning, ruddy-faced children expectantly waiting for "Mum" to sit down, a little harmless cheek and those saucy, fruity moments with hubby. Instead, it seems that I've traded off that guise and am now the Bella Emberg of Mommydom. Even though I've lost twelve pounds . . .

Spurred on by the first bit of good news in nearly six months she, Worzel-Gummidge-like, took off her depressed head and screwed on her industrious one. The boys gaped in bewilderment as she took on a Cinderella persona, the house a flurry of dust clouds, sweeping brushes, dusting cloths and black bin-liners. Not yet able to decide whether it's a belated spring-clean or an early one, she celebrated regardless. Either way, this was a job long overdue – just like her losing weight. Humming as she worked, she realised that she hadn't cleaned the house properly since before Kevin left.

Little did I realise how marriage would altar my life! I can literally feel the pounds dropping off of me. Maybe this was what I needed all along? Maybe if I'd have discovered the psychological benefits of housework a year ago my eye-colour wouldn't be diluted with tears.

"Maybe this is the first day of the rest of my life," she enthused. Suddenly thirty didn't seem too dreadful.

Without warning, the onus shifted from the trepidation of greying and thinning hair, liver spots and flabby muscles, wrinkles, jowls and the big print edition of her library books. Bending and stooping over the vacuum, she realised that her bra wasn't digging in as much around her back, her jeans weren't cutting into her waist as much either.

Right, well, back to the gym Tuesday night and I think I'll make more of an effort this week.

The shards of light bouncing from her kitchen tiles were dazzling. On cloud ninety-nine Geri looked at a floor surface unrecognisable to her as it almost welcomed her bare-footed presence – a shot from a Cif advert, her modest kitchen now wearing a zinging ring of confidence.

An intermittent ringing burst her bubble. She grabbed the telephone with her left hand as she wiped her sweaty forehead with her right. "Hello?" She didn't know why she was puffing into the phone, because she had actually finished working a good five minutes before. She suspected that she wanted the caller to realise that she'd been busy.

"Hey, Gertie? You all right?"

It was Sinead, obviously perturbed by her sounds of physical exertion.

"Hey . . . not interrupting anything, am I?" she teased, all cutesy and coy, the question heavily loaded, the irony of her own comment lost on her. Geri could feel the devil and the angel appear on her left and right shoulders coaxing,

"Go on tell her now. The longer you leave it the worse it'll be."

"Are you mad or what? Tell her? Let her believe her fantasies about you and your lifestyle! Don't you know she's envious of you? Don't let her down, girl!"

"She's your best friend!"

"A friend in need is a pain in the arse!"

"Don't be ridiculous . . . "

She let them continue their disagreement without her. She just *couldn't* tell Sinead now. Just couldn't. So she opted to ignore Sinead's remark – the easiest option,

"Noo, no, not at all. I'm just having a clean-up, that's all. Mopping and stuff, you know."

"God! Aren't you great! Don't think I've even got a mop. Anyway, the maid does all that for me while I'm at work."

"You've got a maid?" Geri can't believe what she's hearing. "I thought only duchesses and ladies or Wives-Of-Mafia-Bosses had maids."

"Babe, you're soooo out of touch!" the laugh in her voice evident. "She only comes in once a week, on a Friday usually, to sort out all my mess ready for the weekend. The company pays for it. Everyone on Foreign Assignment gets one."

"Blimey! A maid!" Geri is star-struck by the whole concept of the idea. Sinead laughs out loud at her, "Gertie! She's only in for a couple of hours a week! Don't think too much of it. I'm not Demi Moore, you know!"

"Yeah, I know *that!*" she retorts, sarcastically. "Anyway, what's up?"

"Shouldn't that be a question for Kevin?"

That's it – she knows. How the bloody hell does she know? My mind races. Paranoia hurtles through my veins again. Why would that be a question for Kevin?

Feeling herself start to sweat again and recognising the hot flush creeping its way uncomfortably up her neck, she retorts.

"What?" she managed to fluster.

"What's up? You saucy little minx! I bet you're all done up in your schoolgirl's outfit and those two little fellas are at your mum's. They're very quiet. Unusually quiet, in fact. They're not there, are they? Are they?"

As realisation hit Geri, Relief came rushing through the finishing line, breaking the ribbon with its jubilant chest, arms up embracing the air, smiling and exuberant. Paranoia ebbed away, disgruntled at such a short appearance.

"Ha!" Relief still gushed through Geri, ecstatic.

"Yeah, right! It's clear, Sinead, that you're living in a totally different world to me!"

"Mmm, waking up to eighty degrees, siesta from two till five, slow languorous pace of life, the gastronomical delights I sample every weekend, the free flowing local wines?"

"Don't rub it in! So, why are you ringing? What's wrong?"

"Nothing's wrong! I'm just ringing to say that I won't be able to see you tomorrow, I've got meetings all day. I wondered if you'd mind me calling round this evening for a couple of drinks, a bit of a chat and that? I'd get to see Kevin then too, wouldn't I?"

I doubt it. Heck, how am I going to get out of this one now? I just can't let her come round expecting to see Kevin and not tell her what's going on.

The seconds seemed to tick noisily as she groped silently for her answer. She just didn't know what to say to her!

"Gertie? Can I then?"

"Oh, sorry? What? Can you what?"

Geri could tell she was annoyed at the hesitancy.

"Can I come around this evening?"

"Mm, I er –"

Sinead interrupted her procrastinating. "I'll see you about seven then. You're not going out, are you?"

"No." She just couldn't stretch the realms of lying *that* far! Anyway, she might suggest meeting up somewhere, and then what would she do?

"Right, OK then. I'll be round between seven

and half past. Tell Kevin to get the Metz-on-ice ready."

"OK," was all Geri managed to mutter in response.

"Oh," Sinead tittered, " and remind me to tell you about last night. But not with Kevin there."

"What have you done now?"

"My stomach's at me again, that's all I can tell you."

"Right then! Look forward to it. See you later."

"Right, bye then."

"Bye."

As she replaced the humming receiver she noticed that Cameron had spent his time intently painting the newly mopped kitchen floor enough to make all her cleaning efforts a total waste of time. Having been brought into the world with a hotchpotch of dirty marks on the floor, it seemed he was unwilling to change his habits of a lifetime.

* * *

With only two hours to go before Sinead's arrival Geri decided to try and tire the children out so that she could get them settled in bed first. If she then decided to come clean about Kevin, at least she could confess in peace.

Only a parent can get away with lolling around the floor, arse up, head down, wailing "Errrghhhh" – elephant-style, the height of recklessness, only to realise the kids aren't in sight! Disappointed that her elephantine efforts had been wasted she clambered to her feet to look for them. Seconds later she found them ensconced amongst her minimal make-up collection.

I know it, a bath always does the trick. I don't know what they put into those bubbles but they have a terrific effect on their eyelids – it makes them close them a good hour earlier than usual.

"Come on lads, time for a bath!"

"Yippeeeee," Cameron burst into life, stampeding over Reece as he lay rolling on the floor, still struggling to find his feet. It seemed a bath was a good suggestion.

Forty-five minutes, three gallons of water and a bottle of Matey later, she pulled them from the sudsy tub – she fully clothed and wetter than they were.

"No, Mummy, no!" Cameron declined, opting instead for the slidey game he loved to play after his bath. Once she pulled the plug Cameron loved to slide around in the remaining bubbles, sliding on his tummy on the slimy wet enamel in a sky diving position. It took a lot of smiling, cajoling and bribery to get him out. Unfortunately it seemed the high jinks had only heightened their energy levels and Geri was now having serious doubts about getting them both to bed before Sinead was due to arrive in less than an hour.

"Come on, let's read a story."

"No!" He was taking on his father's arrogance before her very eyes,

She smiled, patiently, and tried again, "Come on, darling. Reece's ready, aren't you, love? Come on, Cameron, sit up here with us."

"Go 'way!" and then – she can't believe he does this – he spits at her.

"Cameron! Come here now. Do *not* spit. That makes

me very cross! Now, hold my hand and come over here, please."

"That's *my* hand!!

"I'll smack your bottom if you do that again!"

"That's *my* bottom!"

Feeling like she was getting nowhere, she continued nonetheless,

"I know that's your hand, but this is *my* hand, and you're going to hold it."

He looked at her like she was insane.

Maybe I am.

He skulked toward her, disappointed, as if the bounce had gone out of his bungee, and then declared, smiling, "I'm blowing off! I'm blowing off!"

Charming, boys, aren't they?

And, I believe, the charm only increases with adulthood.

Chapter Thirteen

For all of Geri's complaining about Quick Draw McGraw, she saved the evening once again. Back from Boloing early and unduly disappointed by the whole experience, she just turned up – disgruntled, tired and laden with French chocolates.

"Bloody boring place, that Boloing! No wonder the blooming ticket was free! All the blooming shops are shut on a blooming Sunday! Always a shifty oul' one that Auntie Glad of yours."

She's always my Auntie Glad when Mum's annoyed with her.

"Spent most of the time on the coach. Only good thing about it was Maurice . . . "

"Maurice!" Geri squeals.

"Ooooh, Geri, what a lovely, lovely man!"

She's taking off Dame Edna now, without realising it.

As she bumbled through the hallway she left a trail

of wet footprints behind her and a wet smearing from her mac on the wallpaper.

"Knows all his phobias too."

"How many has he got?"

"He hasn't *got* them all; he knows the *names* of them all – look."

She handed Geri a continental-looking A5 jotter pad. Maurice obviously found the day trip to France as boring as her mum did.

It seems he spent his entire time transcribing his book of phobias for Mum. I scan the page looking for interesting ones – if that's not a contradiction in itself.

"Mum, is this Maurice a doctor?"

"Why? How do you know?"

"His writing is as indecipherable as a prescription for haemorrhoid remedies."

She read the list aloud:

> "Arrhenophobia / Androphobia – fear of men
> Anuptaphobia – fear of staying single
> Arachibutyrophobia – fear of peanut butter sticking
> to roof of mouth
> Clinophobia – fear of going to bed
> Coitophobia – fear of coitus

Mum, how old is this Maurice?"

"Ooooh, I'd say about mid-fifties. What a lovely man! So chatty and intelligent."

"Mum, he sounds like a perv!"

"Geri! How could you be so rude about him? You've never even met him!"

"I don't think I need to. Just looking at these is enough to tell me. Fear of men, fear of staying single, fear of coitus! For God's sake, Mum, I've got all three of them right now, and I've just been deserted by my husband. What's a fifty-year-old man doing, interested in these? There's something wrong there if you ask me!"

"Not at all, Geri. I'm not having it. He's a very intelligent man. Knows all his Royals too. You know," she'd only just gotten round to taking off her wet mac, shaking its moisture all over Geri's despondent kitchen floor, and hanging it to dry on the door, "there's not a lot he doesn't know about the Queen and Prince Philip."

On hearing Cameron crying, Geri dashed into the living-room just in time to rewind the video. As she re-entered the kitchen Cynthia was still going on regardless.

"She's a lucky bugger doing that job. All them lovely clothes and free meals she gets. I'd do a better job than 'er. She gets paid for it too, you know! Maurice told me!"

"Who, Mum?"

"The Queen! I'd soon kick them kids of hers into touch too. And all them lovely dogs . . ."

"Yeah, Mum. Like, you *hate* dogs!"

"Maurice has got dogs. Three. Corgis too, you know. That Duke of Edinberg's a nice man too, in't he?"

"Mum, it's Edinburgh."

"Go'way. Edinbra. It's not BRA. Ha! Edinbra! Bet he'd like to get 'is 'ead in her bra! Ha! Bet that's just a distant memory for him!"

Geri's hair flapped onto her face as she shook her head, defeated, whilst washing the boys' dinner plates, at the same time wondering how she could possibly get her mum to baby-sit tonight so that she could go *out* with Sinead. She tuned back into Cynthia's ramblings.

"You know, I used to work with a woman called Edna. Edna Bucket we called her! Ha, ha, ha! Do ya get it? Edna Bucket? Ed-in-a-bucket? Ed-'n'-a-bucket?"

Geri chose to ignore her.

It's the best way when she's in this kind of mood. Verbose. Mindlessly verbose.

"She was a devil for taking them kids of hers out in taxis. Cost her 'usband a fortune! He bought a car in the end. Cheaper it was too. I used to say to her, I did – you know, Edna – kids in the back seats of cars cause accidents, but accidents in the back seats of cars cause kids! She used to laugh she did. Mind you, she had seven!"

Realising that there would be no juncture at which she could ask her favour, Geri decided to blast in with it now.

"Mum? Could you do me a favour tonight?" In spite of Cynthia's mismatched delivery and strange sense of humour she really was a natural with the children and they both adored her beyond belief. Literally.

"Oh, what, love? I'm dead on me feet."

"But you said you spent most of the time on the coach!"

"I know, but still it'd take it out of you all that travelling. And we walked around that boat a good few times too. You know, I couldn't help thinking how they must've felt on that *Titanic* when they hit them icebergs. Frightening stuff!"

Geri cut in. "Could you stay with the kids? I'm going out."

"Where're you going then, on a Sunday night?"

I just can't tell her about Sinead. If Quick Draw knows that she's back in the country she'll only want to see her.

Cynthia was very fond of Sinead, and would probably drop Geri right in it with the Kevin thing.

Once again she finds a lie is the best way out. "Oh, just out with some girls from the piano class. It's not important really, if you're too tired. If I can get them to bed then you can relax in front of the telly and eat your French chocolates." She realised an extra incentive was required at this stage. "I've got some Baileys in the cupboard too."

True to form, that does it. She's sold.

Ringing Sinead on her mobile Geri managed to persuade her not to come to the house and instead meet her at the Dog & Partridge at eight. Time enough to get the boys and Mum settled and then herself into something suitable to wear.

Her wardrobe contents became less and less attractive to her each and every day and so she settled for the safe and regulatory jeans and sweatshirt. Her PMS purchases were already re-bagged and ready for return to the shop.

After two quick Jack Daniels at the Dog & Partridge they eventually ended up breathing in the garlicky aroma of Pizza Hut. Bustling into a wooden seated booth Sinead slipped off her perfectly cut suede jacket, folding it inside out – expertly.

"So?" she said, smoothing her shining straight hair down over her shoulders, her complexion glowing beneath the tinted lights and piped music.

"So what?" Geri felt an uncomfortable pink tinge rise up her cheeks.

"So, tell me what's been happening in your exciting family life."

"Oh, nothing much. Not compared to you and your exciting existence. Makes mine seem so boring."

A carafe of house wine later and her blurring conversation was suddenly crystal clear as she noticed something she'd waited months to see. Three cubicles down, perilously close, she spotted Kevin talking very loud to her replacement.

To think all those years I'd wished he'd speak up. His wimpy whispering vocals of our marital years seem a long-lost memory. With his new-found confidence it seems he's found his voicebox.

She began to cringe every time he spoke for fear of Sinead hearing him. Thankfully Sinead was well oiled and Geri doubted her ability to hear her own voice clearly. A perfunctory nod at the right pauses kept her content as she hurtled through the story of the "office bike" in the Valencia office – Charmaine of the low necklines and high skirts seemed to incense her beyond belief.

By a pure stroke of luck, *She* was facing in Geri's direction, giving her full visual rights.

And, my God, she's awful! My mental picture of "her" for the past year has been inordinately complimentary! I'd imagined slimmer thighs, longer legs, bigger hair and probably a stubbornly tight fanny!

Despite being armed with insubstantial evidence, with absolutely no proof of vaginal intactness or lack thereof, she cringed at her backcombed straw-like hair and skin-tight lycra trousers.

She looks as far from virginal as Playboy of the Year. Little did I realise this would be an evening of adultural enlightenment.

As she scrutinised the back of Kevin's poorly cut and, she noticed, slightly greying hair, she just couldn't believe he was the same lover with whom she'd laughed and teased in those heady days in love.

Oh, the days of love and sexual gratification!

For the first time in over a year Geri began to feel her self-esteem making a guest appearance, her confidence proudly showing its face, and her mourning for the loss of Kevin leaving the building.

Chapter Fourteen

With Tuesday upon Geri again she greeted the day with a skip in her step and a smile, content that she hadn't felt as good in a long time. It seemed her new relaxed attitude was having a positive effect on the children too. They seemed to have been less turbulent lately.

"Yep," she smiled, "I can categorically say, I *like* being a Mum!"

With Sinead now back in Spain, Geri grinned into her washing-machine tub once again, recalling the drunken state that they'd been in and how she'd enjoyed her company. Still smiling gormlessly as she filled the machine, the Snickers struggled to stay in her mouth as she thought aloud, "Thank God she believed that Kevin was getting Cameron to bed. The problem is now," she mused, "that the lie is escalating. Every time I load more on top of it, it's getting harder and harder to break." Dribbling a clump of thick chocolate onto the floor and down her front she wiped her chin, and swallowed.

As she stood wrestling with a pair of jeans that just didn't want to go into the machine her confidence shook a little as her significantly reduced but still loose tummy jiggled as she moved. The communal catastrophe of getting changed after the work-out was getting slightly easier to cope with as the magnet buried in her muscles suddenly began to work at pulling the sagging flesh toward her bones. Only yesterday, in an act of confidence and in the name of a new start she decided to discard the baggy leggings and long T-shirt for an Adidas body-suit, despite Cynthia's hilarity on seeing it on her as she'd stopped off on the way back from her shopping trip.

"That's like what Big Daddy used to wear for his wrestling matches!" she'd guffawed.

"They're all the fashion now," Geri pleaded.

"Ha! Look at you in that get-up! Geri, you're not serious!"She left the room holding her sides for laughing. Compliments from her these days were about as rare as rocking-horse shit.

When Geri'd got home she'd tried it on again and was pleasantly surprised at what she saw in the mirror.

"Big Daddy! Huh!" she'd admonished as she leapt onto her crumpled bed, a vision of athletic acclaim in a lycra corset. Idiotically, she'd blushed as the phone rang, forgetting that the caller couldn't actually *see* what she was doing – thank God!

"Yeah?" she puffed, the bed still bouncing beneath her.

"Geraldine. It's Mum."

"What? Phoned to tell me what a bad mother I am? Or how repulsive I look in my clothes? Or could it be simply to let me know what a disappointment I've been to you?"

"Geraldine. I'm ... Well, it's like this, I'm ... "

"Can't even bear to apologise, can you? Sticking in your neck, isn't it?"

"No, Geraldine, it's not. I'm very sorry for upsetting you like that. I was just a bit surprised to see you in that get-up, you know. And after the way you came in last time when you wore those different clothes."

"When?"

"When you went to the night classes in that sheepdog bra."

"Oh. Look, Mum, I'm trying to find myself here. I don't really want to get into it right now, OK. I accept your apology, thanks. It really means a lot to know you've apologised. Really."

"OK, love. Take care doing them exercises tonight. You know how red your face goes when you get hot. Anyway love, drop the boys off when you're ready."

"Right, Mum. Bye. Thanks."

"Bye."

She's a good old stick really, harmless as they come. Just totally mad at the same time.

Geri sang at the top of her voice, *"The wheels on the bus go round and round, round and round, round and round ..."* as she flung towel, talc and deodorant into her worn sports bag not noticing Cameron at the bedroom door enthralled by the unexpected entertainment. Zipping it up with great gusto, she wondered if that sexy guy would be there again tonight? And she was curious as to what he'd think of her new get-up.

"*Although,*" she sang, "*if they can't take me as they find me these days, they'd better not take me at all . . .*"

* * *

Having looked forward, all week, to the possibility of seeing her at the gym on Tuesday night, Ben's week had culminated in a frenzy of anxiety. He'd pondered, wasting priceless hours trying to sketch the expression a cartoon fox would adopt on finding out that his best friend – the little red-breasted robin with only one wing – had caught his foot in barbed wire. His body was in dire need of the psychological cleansing of the work-out, more than ready for the energising session. Wriggling his toned, tanned and tasty legs into slightly too-tight shorts and throwing on an over-large T-shirt he whistled, carefree, into his deodorant-scented bedroom. In typical Ben style, he showered *before* he went to the gym as well as after. On arriving, half an hour earlier than usual, he began pounding the step machine with an extravagance long lost on him.

Twenty minutes later, time enough for him to work up a sufficient sheen of sweat; she walked in. She looked good in a new lycra training suit. A sexy thonged job, with the modesty of matching cycling shorts underneath. She'd lost weight too, and looked better for it. Somehow, a little like himself, she seemed more determined tonight.

I've got to make my move soon, he thought, as he upped his tempo on the stepper. He brusquely wiped sweat from his forehead, which was now stinging his eyes. 'I don't care what Andy thinks or says about her,' he thought. 'He's the sad bastard! What does he think he's doing anyway? Don't know why he doesn't come to gym with me, and lose some of the flab.'

He would have loved to find out her name, to talk to her. For the sake of just a couple of stone, she'd be his ideal woman. Fun-loving, sexy, down-to-earth, practical.

"Am I seeing her through rose-tinted specs or what?" he muttered aloud.

Mind you, he thought, despite her little bit of extra weight, she's still a lot more classy than some of them here what with their decaying, yellowing armpits of bras brazenly on display as they lift the weights up. I mightn't be Persil-white but at least I'm clean.

Regardless of his many girlfriends and dates, it seemed to Ben as if he'd subconsciously gone through a personality test to make sure that he was always assigned to the partner he was least likely to get on with. He realised that his teenage years of shagging his mature, experienced boss upstairs, whilst the office junior was waiting patiently downstairs, at the office party were long gone. Part of him was glad of that, much to Mark's disgust. Mark was the sound engineer at the theatre and made no secret of his life-long ambition: "I want a stunner, with a good job, her own place and her own car. Then, I can move in with her and she doesn't need *me* to keep her going. Only in the sack, like, eh?"

Despite Ben's fondness for Mark, a friendship sealed over numerous pints and chasers in the last six months, he just couldn't bring himself to *be* like him. They'd spent many an exuberant evening discussing the tactics involved in where and how to probe women's secret passion nodes. They'd discussed the differences between the G spot and the G-string, concluding that there was no relationship between the two. Since splitting up with Chanelle, Ben felt his singledom was a permanent state of temporariness, having attempted many relationships of varying length, with women of equally variable styles. Unfortunately, on hindsight, Ben had told Mark the gory details of every one, leaving it wide open for Mark to dexterously give each failure a title. Unsure whether the current production, Shakespeare's *Melting Pot*, had influenced Mark's choice of almost medieval-themed titles, but suspecting that it had, Ben now had to face the results of his sexual incompatibilities daily. As they'd sat in the pub only last week Ben had cringed as Mark recounted his failures to the pub footie team.

"Yeah, first there was The Scroll. He'd got her home and started to get her kit off. Found out she was wearing one of those bodies, so put 'is hand down to unpop them popper things. He said it was so bloody tight they'd disappeared right up into her crotch somewhere! Anyway, not wanting to let the side down, he pushed her down onto the bed and managed to unpop 'em. And, guess what 'appened? Quicker than a roller blind, the bloody thing curled up from her minge up to her chin and she literally spread on the bed! About fifteen stone 'e said she was!"

Their laughing had faded in Ben's mind as he'd sat choking himself on his pint, eager to make a swift exit. He'd not only heard it all before, he'd *lived* it! He knew all too well the repartee that the football team was to expect. Second there was The Knight – so named due to her impressive, but not-so-shining, armour of underwear. Mark would, no doubt, recall how disappointed Ben had been to find out that beneath her stylish clothing she wore every possible aid imaginable. First he'd had to contend with the tights that doubled up as thigh-slimmers, the stocking tops like bandages, and about two hundred denier thicker than the gossamer sheening knees, calves and ankles he'd ogled all night. Once discarded, and a little more sweaty, he'd had to contend with the corsetry of her knickers. 'Contraption pants' Mark called them; 'hips-gut-and-arse-squeezers' was another of his delightful terms. They'd seemed to hold *in* her stomach, define her buttocks and squash the flab that sat on her hips. They were over-elasticated beyond belief and Ben had struggled with the removal of them, and then wished he hadn't. The final blow to not merely diminish but totally extinguish his ardour had been the discovery of the Wonderbra. Not the Wonderbra *because* it had been a Wonderbra, but the horror he'd felt when two pink silicone pads had fallen from it onto the floor, wobbling gleefully on impact, like two raw spleens, as they'd smiled up at him from his wooden floor. He still had problems discerning the plastic chest from the real thing. He constantly tried to look for the swinging pendulous motion that occurred on running or even walking slightly too fast. Once in the sexual clinch, he found himself surreptitiously looking for their disappearance under her arms when horizontal. No loss of nipple sensation and no scars also proved to be a promising start. *Then* there'd been The Queen of Hearts. The one who'd sought romance with a capital R. Rosie had loved the idea of *being* in love and Ben had almost vomited with fright when he'd seen, inscribed on his toilet roll *Rosie 'n' Ben 2 Gever 4 Ever*. One-hundred-and-eighty sheets worth of it! She'd nearly killed him with kindness! Finally there'd been The Leper. She had been the most unfortunate of Ben's conquests as he'd met her at the end of a very long drinking session and a particularly rowdy day, the effects of over-consumption both distending his stomach and distorting his judgement. Calamitously he'd only really *seen* her the next day. When it had been too late. And Mark had arrived at his flat early on the Sunday morning to pick Ben up for the football match and seen her for himself. Her name, The Leper, was particularly befitting due to the unconcealable red welts pocked across her face from her freshly squeezed spots, giving her the allure and complexion of a fruit cake. Ben, being a 'new' man, and virtually obsessed by skincare for men, found The Leper to be the most disastrous of all these disasters. Depressing though it all was, Ben maintained his slight hope for the future by pointing out to Mark he yet had to meet The Princess. To which Mark laughed heartily, finding gross enjoyment in Ben's predicament, highlighting that he also was yet to meet The Jester, The Knave and The Executioner!

Despite his misdemeanours, Ben was determined not to be like his married friends, who on approaching thirty, had started to plan a suitable Midlife Crisis and had began to worry about hereditary hair-loss. They realised that this Midlife Crisis would probably not begin for a few years yet, but it was the sort of thing they'd felt they wanted to plan ahead for. They *still* refused to stop dreaming about showing up for their 'O' levels in their boxer shorts or of snogging Miss Garnett behind the cookery desks. They hadn't realised that if it hadn't yet happened, it was not likely to. Despite it being over half their lives ago, they still couldn't grasp the fact that school was far behind them.

The step machine flickered in red lights and beeped at him as he continued to pound the plastic steps, his mind wandering aimlessly. Little did he realise that Geri had been barely able to contain herself within her new Big Daddy outfit for fear of him catching her staring at his fine form as he'd pounded the invisible stairs . . .

* * *

Despite a two-day reprieve I still have Gluteus Maximus stiffer than the traditional British upper lip and my right arm is now on the verge of being dislocated. Cameron has spotted the Milky Bar Kid winking conspiratorially from the shelves laden with confectionery, and has now taken on Geoff Cape's determination in trying to pull me from the queue I'm standing in. It's one of the pre-modernised Post Offices where you can almost see the old wooden counter Mexican-waving as the wood-worm bustle beneath its surface – no red and green plastic surfaces sheening and gleaming in unwelcoming impersonal style. Instead the warm, worn wooden cubicle that probably saw the first issue of the penny black, and millions of pounds worth of giro cheques and mail destined for every country worldwide.

As the rickety framed door clanged open, momentarily the sound of wheels whooshing on wet roads roared into the shop. Turning to see how many were queuing behind her, she first noticed the blanket of condensation clinging to the shop front windows and then noticed, about three behind her, the tasty guy from the Gym.

Him.

I blink awkwardly with the grace of a wide-eyed frog with a wasp stuck in his eye and turn my head back round to face front once again. I'm sure the back of my neck must be giving off enough heat to warm everyone queueing behind me! I just hope he doesn't notice. About as much chance of that as me getting a full night's sleep! I try and divert my concentration onto something else, another reason why children can be a great accessory. Noticing that Reece is sleeping, cocooned by the plastic rain-cover over his buggy, I pick Cameron up and point to the small pictures hanging on the shop wall, the cheap prints and tacky frames unworthy of my intense explanations. "See those pictures up there?" I semi-whisper. "They're by a very famous artist from a long long time ago."

"Chocolate."

"Mmm." She turned full frontal to the wall. He had no choice but to look at the pictures. "They're by a man called Edgar Degas and he painted lots of ballerinas. They're ballerinas, those little girls with the big skirts on. They're called tutus."

"Choo-choos! I yike choo-choo's."

I'm now jutting from the queue, obvious as the hair sticking out from my chin. I hear a few titters and giggles – the women in the queue are awash with maternal hormones. The men seem to be ignoring me.

"Ha, no, love. Not choo-choo's."

My lips feeling startlingly similar to Mick Jagger's as I exaggerate the "ch", "Tu-tus. That's what ballerinas wear."

Cameron's attention, if I ever had it, is slipping desperately. Well, I've started so I'll finish. We move along to the second print.

"This one is called the 'Dance Class'. See those little girls on the stage. Look at the one at the front! Is she bowing?"

Fleetingly I'm aware of the beauty of these poorly reproduced prints and feel a great yearning to see the originals, my interest in art being severely repressed since motherhood. The Impressionists were something I'd always been interested in at school and I'd taken great delight in going to the galleries in the city, looking at the pictures, and also people-watching as their reactions and facial expressions conveyed their emotions toward the art. The only 'Impressionists' I'm familiar with today are the likes of Alastair MacGowan and Ronni Ancona! In the few years I was with Kevin, prior to the arrival of Reece and Cameron, we'd taken a great interest in art and the galleries. What a luxury it would be to have the time to myself to go to one now and see first-hand the crisp clarity of the meringue-whites of the netted full skirts, the dusty imitation of the stage, the elegance of the dancers.

"This next one is the 'The Ballet Rehearsal'. And look at the date, eighteen-seventy-five! Do you know that's over a hundred and twenty years ago!"

"Biooo," is Cameron's only comment.

I think he's referring to the azure shade of the ballerinas' tutus, but then again . . . anything's possible.

"D'ya want to move ahead, love?" *An elderly voice breaks our art appreciation as I realise the queue has moved ahead a couple, and I'm now holding up sufficient amounts of people to warrant half a dozen being forced to wait out in the rain.*

"Oh, sorry."

I put him down swiftly, grab the handles of the buggy and shuffle along a few feet.

"Chocolate!"

The diversion didn't last and Cameron's back on friendly terms with the Milky Bars! Resigned, this queue could be another half hour yet, I pick one up for him and unwrap it, keeping hold of the wrapper to pay for at the counter. As the slab of white chocolate disappears into his surprisingly big mouth my thoughts turn to the Spanish class tonight. Oh God, Michael Fernandez and my ongoing secret! Every week I worry I'll have to confront him to determine exactly how much he knows. Now, what was the homework from last week? I begin to mutter under my breath in an attempt to jog my ever-failing memory,

"¿Cómo se llama? What is your name? Me llamo Geri. My name is Geri." *My voice a hushed monotone, all traces of emotion totally extinguished as I concentrate to remember the last lesson.*

"¿Cuántos años tienes? How old are you?" *Now, how do I say I'm twenty– no! Thirty! Christ, I've even got to say it! What if they start asking it in class? Would it be obvious if I lied? Is that an option?*

My panic washes within me like a bad curry. My struggle to get to grips with my age just won't disappear. As I shuffle forward in the queue a little more I look down to see Cameron still devouring his treat, so attempt to continue with my practising – I whisper again,

"Manthanas – oranges. Or is it bananas? Mm, not too sure."

And then something terrible happens . . .

* * *

On his way to the station Ben had decided to call into the Post Office to pick up another forty-quids worth of stamps in preparation for the next big mailing project. Despite his new contract drawing the cutesy foxes that had started to give him nightmares, his ambition still lay with a larger project and the only way to be recognised was to be visible. He'd started to add to his already impressive portfolio and would soon be in a position to start posting out some more examples. The click of his front door as he'd closed it behind him seemed to alert the looming heavy clouds that it was now time to get active. Obediently the rain began. Shrugging up the collar of his leather jacket did little to prevent the sneaky damp drops from running down his neck and as the rain fell with more aplomb he gave up, as it washed into his ears, face and gathered on his short curly hair. As he rushed into the Post Office the make-shift bell connected by a cat's-cradle of string shook violently and the flimsy door-frame rattled in objection. He was surprised to see a queue already formed at only mid-morning, but decided to wait nonetheless. As he discreetly shook the rain from his jacket, trying desperately not to soak the newspapers stacked neatly on the floor, and wiped his moist face he noticed her, only a couple of people in front of him. She promptly turned around to face him. Her expression was void of recognition and he watched her smooth neck as she looked away, nonchalantly.

"Shit!" he thought. "She didn't even notice me!"

He watched her as she confidently stepped out of the queue to show her little boy the paintings on the wall. He admired the way she took the time to explain to her son the meaning behind the picture, and even seemed to know the names of them! He just *knew* there was more to her than met the eye. His heart began to quicken as she stepped back into the queue and he realised just how much he wanted to speak to her. It was then he heard her muttering to herself. Obvious that she didn't want to be heard, Ben stepped out of the queue and silently moved forward a little bit to catch what she was saying, under the pretence of looking at the note-pads and biros on the shelf beside her.

She was talking in Spanish! Ben was suitably impressed. As he strained to hear her, blind to the curious looks he was afforded from the pensioners lined up to collect their money, he heard her saying,

"*¿Cuántos años tienes?*"

Ben leaned back awkwardly to see if she was talking into a mobile or a dictaphone. Surely she wasn't speaking Spanish to the child? As he leant back, very Mr Bean-like, she suddenly spun to face him. He froze. A human version of the Leaning Tower of Pisa, his feet were parallel to hers, but his head was more in line with the suspicious gran behind her. Their eyes met, and it was uncertain who was more surprised, him or her.

Time to take the *toro* by the horns and act as romantic matador, Ben jumped in with both feet: "*Ha, hmm, nunca pensé ver el día en que nosotros hablar!*"

Her blank expression held fast. The light within her eyes clearly switched on – and very beautifully they twinkle, thought Ben – but her expression was zero.

He attempted another angle: "*¿Habla español?*"

Her response this second time much more marked, unfortunately not in Ben's favour. He watched the colour rise from somewhere beneath her fleecy blue jacket and keep on rising until it reached her hairline. With a bustle and a bundle, grabbing hold of the white-chocolated hand of her son and blundering her way through a three-hundred and sixty degree turn, she scurried out of the shop without a backward glance.

Ben stood, puzzled. The line of septuagenarians looked at him through bloodshot watery eyes and thick-rimmed glasses as he scratched his head, hating himself for trying to be smart, and hoping to God that he hadn't offended her.

Chapter Fifteen

By the time Sinead had brushed her teeth and rinsed her contacts in various solutions, settling them in their cages for the night, she finally got around to pulling back the duvet to see Steven Randall, disappointingly, snoring. Convinced she'd found her soul mate, she'd spent the three days since her return from England flirting outrageously with him within the confines of the office. The evenings had opened up their seductive vocabulary endlessly as they'd eaten at Valencia's best seafood restaurant *Civera* (and, to her delight, the most expensive) and explored each other's bodies with a passion she hadn't realised was possible. Queen of the One-Night-Stands, Sinead had always encountered the physical attraction, but rarely the emotional one too. A far cry from the silk-sheeted, candle-lit, pouting seductress's boudoir scene she'd imagined, this evening had culminated in a tequila competition between

Steven, Luis and Marco as they'd propped up the bar in the most expensive hotel in Valencia, the *Reina Victoria*. Situated centrally in the Calle de las Barcas 4, the *Reina Victoria* was a traditionally Spanish city hotel: noisy, busy and rather impersonal. Amid their drinking, slamming and sucking of lemon juice and salt Sinead had noticed the icy glares coming from the other side of the bar as their excitement increased in volume. Thus, she'd managed to drag Steven out of there and straight into a cab, hence the unanticipated snoring.

As she clambered into the cool cotton-clad bed next to his bulky form she complimented herself once again on such a fine catch. His firm strong torso naked and tanned atop the white sheets, his thick hairy chest and defined abdomen heaving up and down delectably as he breathed deeply. Feeling the stirrings in her lace underwear once again, she began to run her hand across his flat stomach, despite herself. How she adored his smooth muscular feel!

She'd started to have serious doubts about herself and her ability to maintain a relationship for longer than a day. She had even begun to suspect that she suffered from the same sex addiction that Warren Beatty and Michael Douglas had once admitted to. But she was sure now she'd just suffered from a Love/Like/Lust dilemma. The dilemma being that she'd had trouble in distinguishing between the three of them. Steven had cured all that in less than a week, and she loved, liked and lusted after him all at the same time. She wriggled her painted fingernails beneath the soft elastic of his boxer shorts until she felt the toasty warm firmness of his hipbones, the slight dip between them, and then running her hand slowly downwards, the encouraging firmness of himself. She slid her hand softly and expertly down his length and back up the other side, then shifted her grasp to his balls and cupped them with a firm but gentle squeeze. A light involuntary groan escaped from his lips, stimulating her to continue. With a feather-light touch she caressed the inside of his relaxed thighs, then back up and inside his boxer shorts again until she herself was desperate for him to satisfy her. Despite a sleepy grunt or two however, Steven continued to sleep; knocked out by a half-bottle of rum and a half-bottle of tequila.

Twenty minutes of caressing later, Sinead felt herself truly desperate for Steven, and whilst his encouraging firmness hadn't yet deflated, it was certainly true that it also hadn't stiffened. With a resigned sigh, feeling her head now starting to spin from the after-effects of the vodkas she'd drunk, she lay back onto the cool sheets listening to the whirr of the air-conditioning. Minutes later the sensations between her legs hadn't subsided, so looking to her left to check that Steven really was asleep, she slipped her deft fingers beneath her own lacy G-string and made them move to her own rhythm.

* * *

The following morning heralded itself as a Saturday, decreeing that neither Sinead nor Steven had to rush out of bed. A good thing, as they were both unable to anyway. Steven had woken in the early hours with a hard-on to rival the Eiffel Tower and had woken Sinead to give her an eye-ful as he'd slid on top of her, waking her from a tipsy slumber with a shower of intoxicating kisses and placing her hand expertly on his ready-to-play organ. They'd made exhaustive love for over two hours, Steven unable to reach his climax due to his over-exuberance with alcohol – but although his body wasn't willing, his mind wasn't giving in. Sinead, however, had the time of her life.

For the first half-hour anyway.

So determined was he to reach his own satisfaction he'd tried every possible angle and approach, so much so that Sinead's extensive carnal knowledge had been increased one-hundred fold. As dawn broke Steven had given up, debilitated and still unfulfilled, leaving Sinead to return to her sleep with an undercarriage so swollen and over-worked that she felt as if someone had pumped up her labia, and an aching tender pelvis. Fleetingly, as she'd curled into the comforting foetal position to return to sleep, the thought flashed through her mind that possibly Steven wasn't the most considerate of lovers. But only fleetingly.

Her doubts were forgotten on waking the second time. She'd woken hazily on hearing her bedroom door bang against the wall. As she'd lifted her fuzzy head from the pillow she'd had to squint to focus. A picture that only dreams were made of, Steven stood, tray in hand, at the end of her bed. Smiling.

"Your breakfast, darling?" He placed the tray on

the duvet, allowing her to view its wares. Toast, marmalade, fried eggs, sausages, beans. Eerrgh, her stomach somersaulted at the very thought of it.

"Mm. Lovely." She'd tried to sound interested, but couldn't muster enough enthusiasm.

"Something's wrong. What is it? Don't you like it?"

Sinead snuggled back down under the covers, unable for such an attentive partner so soon after waking – or more specifically, one carrying a tray full of fried food!

She answered him from beneath the duvet, her voice muffled,

"Don't you feel sick this morning, Steven?"

He shook his head, confused. "No. Why? Should I?"

She groaned at the memory. "Well, I just thought after all those tequilas last night . . . "

"Oh, yeah. I'd forgotten about that!" He sat on the end of the bed, his thoughts now back in the *Reina Victoria*. "*Who* was I doing that with now?"

"Marco and Luis," she responded, emotionless, the very recollection of the whole event churning her stomach even more.

Her queasy tone diverted his attention back to the morning and he turned to view the lump over which the duvet was mounded. He began to laugh and, putting the tray onto the floor, wriggled under the covers with her. Finding her in a ball in the middle of the bed, her face buried deep into the mattress as she held onto her head, he wrapped his arms around her waist and pulled her over to him.

"Aarrgh. My stomach! Don't squeeze it, please."

"Feel sick, do you?" he teased.

"Mmmm," she responded sleepily.

Steven Randall began to stroke her forehead and cuddled her. Sinead had never had it so good and despite her feelings of severe malaise, enjoyed every minute of it.

"I've got a great idea," he cooed into her clumped hair.

"What?" she whispered, unable to do anything more.

"How about today we take a stroll along to the *Jardines del Real* and *Jardín Botánico*. What d'ya reckon?" Her silence encouraged him to continue, "Of course it depends on your mood. If you like we can wait until tonight and see whether you feel *pijo* or *grunge*."

She just had to pull her head out from under the covers. She looked at him as he lay back resting on the pillows, quietly confident and smug.

"Excuse me?"

"*Pijo* or *grunge*. Posh or grungy."

Sinead laughed. "For a new guy you really know your stuff, don't you?"

"Yup! And then this evening we'll take a drive out to the villages nearer to us. West of Valencia, *Chiva*, *Siete Aguas*, *Alborache* and *Godelleta*."

"God. You're insatiable."

"Believe it."

She did.

Deciding to change the subject, she quipped, suddenly full of enthusiasm, "Right, who's for the shower first?"

"Don't chance it, babe," he sneered. "I've already

showered over an hour ago. These lightweights who can't take their drink. I don't know . . ."

"You've not!"

"I have! I showered and ate before I went to make this wasted lot for you. You know what they say, if you can't take the heat . . . "

"Just give me time, that's all. I'm not used to drinking as much as that. And you were rushing me too."

"Oh, no excuse. Anyway, I'll make a drinker of you yet. Now, go get ready."

Sliding out of bed and wrapping the white bed linen around her (she hoped seductively and very *Hollywood*), she shuffled toward the bathroom leaving Steven lounging on the crumpled bed picking at the toast and sausages.

Waiting for the lock to click on the bathroom door, he reached across to his briefcase, opening the lid with two snaps, and pulled the silver canister from it. Licking his lips as he unscrewed the shiny cap, raised it to his mouth, parted his lips and tipped back a hefty measure of neat brandy into himself. Smacking his stinging lips with an "aaah", he pulled the briefcase onto the bed, the open lid a safe screen for him to rummage behind in the event of Sinead returning unexpectedly. As he rummaged he pulled out the miniature black scales, empty plastic bags and ties and rested them on the bedside cabinet. Unzipping the top pocket of his jacket his hand emerged with a rotund bag filled with white powder. Steven Randall tipped a large quantity onto the wooden surface. Chopping and hacking at it with his works ID card he then proceeded to sniff a significant line up each nostril, and place the rest onto the scales. He'd gotten a good six bags made up before he heard Sinead switch off the shower. Time to put it all away again. For now. Wiping at his nostrils, smacking his lips and sniffing repeatedly, the Steven that greeted Sinead in the bedroom after her invigorating shower was a more confident, gregarious and potentially dangerous one than she'd left only twenty minutes beforehand. But, she never realised.

* * *

It had taken all of her resolve to fight him off so that she could get dressed. His sexual ardour flatteringly high, she had to struggle to pull on every single item of clothing that she was wearing. Her head spun with happiness as he'd grabbed her, kissed her, picked her up and showered her with compliments as they'd got themselves together in preparation for their exciting day, he like an over-zealous puppy. He'd even held the car door open for her, waiting, ever the gentleman, as she'd got in, and then closing it securely behind her.

The roof down, the music up, the sun out, her luck in, they sat laughing, chatting and singing as they approached Valencia, the warm breeze caressing their faces and hair in the scorching midday sunshine. Fifteen minutes into their journey and nearly there she asked him to turn the music down. Her mobile was ringing in her bag. Steven did as asked, and she fumbled for her trilling phone. She pressed "OK".

"Hello?"

"Sinead?"

She didn't recognise the voice immediately, "Hello?"

"Hi, it's me," the male voice confident and very English.

"Sorry, you've lost me?"

"Jonathon. Jonathon Morgan? We 'met' when you were in England last week?"

"Oh, Jonathon, yes. How are you?" She couldn't believe she was having this conversation with a man she'd given a blow-job to in a lift and then left with the stench of her upset stomach. Obviously he was either of a strong constitution or a nasally challenged family.

"I'm fine. Erm, I'm just ringing you, I hope you don't mind, to say I'm being sent over to Valencia next week. They'd like us to get together and discuss our work. See how we can streamline the whole affair. Em, I mean administration. They'd like me to spend a fortnight working with you. We have to try to adopt a specific routine to match our job specifications worldwide."

"Oh, great. God, it'd be great to see you, Jonathon. When are you arriving?"

"Monday. Monday morning. Ten forty, I think, I land."

"Great. I'll pick you up from the airport."

"Thanks. Right. Well. I'll, em, speak to you then."

"Right. Oh Jonathon, have they booked you in anywhere? You know, to stay for the fortnight?"

"Thanks, but yes, they've booked me in somewhere. Let me see now – the *Hotel Inglés*, *Marqués de Dos Aguas 6*. Where's that?"

"Valencia. It's opposite the Ceramics Museum in Valencia. Quite nice I've heard. Excellent tapas in the bar too. We'll have to try them one evening."

"Great! I'll look forward to it."

"Right, see you Monday then?

"Yeah, bye."

"Bye."

Sinead smiled as she pressed a series of buttons on her phone to divert her calls for the day, and unzipped her bag to place the phone within it. She hadn't noticed Steven's steely eyes and locked jaw as he drove increasingly faster.

But as the needle on the speedometer edged toward the 140km/h indicator she began to feel very uncomfortable, watching the rocky scenery flash past them.

"Steven," she placed her manicured hand on his thigh.

Without looking at her he growled, low, "Get your fucking hands off me . . . *now!*"

Surprised and startled she removed her hand swiftly, placing it in her lap with the other. A lump in her throat threatened to make her mute, but swallowing it down, she tried to find her voice.

"What's wrong? Have I done something?"

She didn't recognise his expression as he turned to look at her – his eyes full of hatred and sparkling dangerously. She had no time to think before he'd decreased their speed from 130 km/h to 20 in less than ten seconds. Her body lurched forward and she felt the restraint of the seatbelt across her chest.

As the tyres screeched to a halt and the car stopped haphazardly at the side of the scorching road, she felt confused at what was going on. Opening her mouth to question his actions she felt a blow to the side of the head. As her neck clicked and her head rolled to the side she got a mouthful of her own hair. Without time to recompose herself she managed just to catch sight of Steven's face before his fists showered down in rage as he scowled and verbally abused her until she lay virtually unconscious and bleeding in the passenger seat.

* * *

"Saturday night's all right! Saturday night's all right!" Geri sang as she washed-up, Cameron insisting on coming into the kitchen and trying to join in with her; although *"Saadaay ites arite,"* wasn't quite the correct translation. As he watched her devotedly, large innocent eyes gazing, windows into an untarnished soul, she marvelled at her love for her children.

Cynthia had agreed to baby-sit. They'd been as good as gold today, so they should be no problem, and Geri was now in a quandary as to what she should wear. Her complete embarrassment at the fracas in the Post Office had been buried deeply somewhere at the back of her head, it being just too hideous to recall. Now it re-emerged with a vengeance. She thought it just typical that it *had* to be that one guy, the only guy that she'd even looked at twice for years. And he could speak Spanish too!

"God, I've made a right twat out of myself now. He'll *never* want to know me now! Maybe I should give that Spanish class up. I've never been any good at it. I even struggled with it at school. There's no tasty men in it, except Michael Fernandez, and even *he* knows I'm crap at it," she scolded herself. Her thoughts wandered back to last night's lesson. Only lesson two and she was already in trouble! Despite her monotonous repetitions of "*¿Cómo se llama?* What is your name? *Me llamo Geri.* My name is Geri*," all week long, to the extent of humiliating herself in the Post Office, she *still* had made a complete fool of herself at Spanish class. The George Clooneyite, Michael Fernandez, had seemed disappointingly middle-aged this week, with a surreal quality about him, haloed by his freshly Grecian-two-thousanded thatch. They'd been, as a class, on the verge of requesting complimentary safety glasses as the orange glow that exuded from his barnet came close to blinding them. Again, she'd sat next to Claudia, the sophisticated woman in her late forties. Only this time they actually spoke. Geri had pigeonholed her as the type to make her own dinner-party centre-pieces, with an exorbitant amount of excess time and money, her sophisticated and cool image verging on icy – one of the consummate few who could quote, unerringly, "Tailored femininity sums up my style". They'd sat so close as to press their upper arms uncomfortably together and listened with concentration to Michael Fernandez.

As a class of English-speakers primarily, slaves to their mother tongue, a language which could virtually be spoken with the tip of your tongue pushed against the back of your bottom teeth, they'd waited patiently for Gloria to get her dentures around *"Tres manzanas, por favor. ¿Hay camareros?* and *en el aeropuerto"*. Spanish seemed to be a language which dictated persistent flick-flacking of the tongue and production of a pout that Sophia Loren might well have died for.

As they patiently witnessed Gloria's denture-induced predicament, Claudia had extended a slender manicured hand, heavy beneath the weight of Hatton Garden produce, and had drawled softly, "Evenink, dahhlink. I'm Cloud-eeahhh. Ant you are?" Geri had found herself beaming up into her welcoming face, probably a vision of myopic inadequacy, Claudia's charm being rather overwhelming.

"Geri. Geri Cumbers. I thought your name was Claudia," she grinned, shaking her hand over-zealously.

"Actually, dahhlink, it's pronounced Cloud-eeahhh. I'm Czech, you know."

Their mutual appreciation had been brought to a swift end as the Grecian-crowned one had thrown a question at them, interrupting their amicables. During the tea break Geri found herself leaning in toward the small table, almost meeting Cloud-eeahhh's nose across it as they'd sipped at their insipid, watery hot chocolate drinks. Within the twenty minutes Geri had managed to divulge the pugnacious tale of her domestics.

"Come on, dahhlink, this is hardly an exclusive! Dahhlink, I've been married fife times! Men! Can't live with them, can't live without them, heh?"

"Five times?"Her amazement was ill-concealed. "But you're gorgeous and look at your fantastic clothes! I bet men just fall at your feet!" Geri's admiration was as obvious as the consumption of British beef is dubious.

"Dahhlink, you're the original English pear!"

Geri's confused expression hung in the air.

"A bottom-heavy fruit, dahhlink! You know, that year two-tousand think – I must have thought it was the Meal-ennium – I put nearly a bloody stone on. In little under a blahhdy fortnight!"

"Well, you must have looked blaahdy, I mean bloody good *before* that too then," Geri groaned at her, jealousy almost taking over her whole body by now. "You know," she continued, totally devoid of any remaining scraps of self-respect, "I'm still carrying around the three stone I put on during my pregnancies!"

"Babies? Oh, no thank you, dahhlink. They're not usually house-trained. And they play absolute havoc with my Prada!"

"You don't have any then?" Geri smiled, warming to her despite her snobbishness. "Kids! Kids, I mean. Not Prada." She had no doubts as to the weight of the designer labels sitting proud in Claudia's wardrobe.

"Oh yess, dahhlink. I have a son. You know, dahhlink, he has more rings in his blaahdy nose and mouth than I possess! Cheap and nasty ones too! He's a total fascist, dahhlink. You should just *see* his clothes! Baggy, scruffy clothes and dirty spiky hair. You know, dahhlink, I'm sure he doesn't feel happy dressing that way. So lacking in style! So unlike my family! Yes, dahhlink, I suspect it's all a nasty plan to stop me from dragging him to the parties I attend so frequently!" She gulped a huge, and probably cold, mouthful of watery chocolate. "Well, I'll tell you what, dahhlink. I like you. You are so, so, British. So blaahdy paranoid!" She laughed at this point, much to Geri's disgust. She continued, "I'll tell you what. We'll go to an aerobics clahhss together. I really *must* lose that last fife pounds. My friends, dahhlink, they are so busy with their lives. Hortense keeps asking me to the studio to meet her personal trainer, but dahhlink, it's so difficult to find the time. Yes, I think we should go to a proper clahhhss. If I go with you, you will *make* me go! You like to do this? *Together,* dahhlink!"

Before Geri had the chance to consent, decline, or even open her surprised mouth, Claudia had latched onto her arm, pulling her up from the cold plastic seat and frogmarching her back to the classroom.

Back behind the confines of their desks, looking overtly geriatric, Michael Fernandez paced the front of class with the grace of a bull mastiff, spouting like a pompous old headmaster.

"Right!" he boomed.

No, I definitely don't fancy him!

"I asked you before, and now I'll ask you again: who has learned, or spoken any Spanish before?"

A few hands were raised, Geri's not amongst them. Fernandez immediately noticed and homed in on her quicker than a male heat-seeking missile toward a sauna full of Swedes.

"You! You have learnt Spanish before!"

Reddening at the accusation, especially as Cloud-eeahhh had turned to face her, her foundation-rendered face blurringly close. "You have?"

"No," Geri whispers.

He booms again, "I'll take that as *una negativa terminante*."

"A what?" she asks, her voice alien-like and despite the huge effort involved to project a sound from her throat, unrecognisably light and transparent.

"A flat denial."

"Oh," is all she's able to manage.

"Well, I said to you weeks ago that I knew what your secret was. And I do."

Geri's face now resembled an aubergine – it had gone *beyond* red.

"I can tell by your homework and your pronunciation that you are familiar with the Spanish language. It's nothing to be embarrassed about. You should feel proud that you've remembered so much." He looked around the classroom, seeking support, as he continued, "I'm sure most of you would relish the opportunity to feel confident with your pronunciation of the language." A low mumbling sound came across as their group agreement. Geri nearly kissed the carpet when he turned his attention to the Mr Bean-a-like sitting on the other side of the room,

"And you, Roland."

Roland is beaming, proud and expectant,

"You have learnt Spanish before too. I can tell by

your homework. Very, very good. Your grammar is excellent."

"Armitage!" Roland boomed. The class, *and* the thatched one stopped dead in their tracks.

Fernandez had to ask, "Excuse me?"!

"Armitage! Armitage Shanks! Thanks!"

"Right . . . "

"It's my own personal rhyming slang. You know what Armitage Shanks is, don't you? On the back of the toilet bowl? Armitage Shanks? Well, it rhymes with thanks!" He tittered, amused at himself, "I've always been good with words and grammar."

As a group they chose to ignore Roland, and whilst waiting for Fernandez to do the hand-out rounds, equipped with various sheets of homework, Geri looked around the warm room, the weather outside close to freezing; a sure sign of impending Yuletide, the chill seeping right into her bones. Daydreaming, the *ensueño* evident once again, she went back in her mind to a century ago when the turning of sixty probably meant cholera, typhoid, hip-replacements, hot flushes and cold sweats. These days it was more sex hormones in plastic bottles, head colds, chest colds, flu shots and pneumonia.

I'd always imagined fifty to mean forgetting the keys, the car, the kids. And seventy? I was sure that was a sure sign of hearing aids, walkers and adult nappies.

She dreamt on.

"Right, that's it, folks! *Ejercicios escritos cuatro, cinco, seis, siete, ocho y nueve. Hasta luego!*"

The chairs scraped collectively as they gathered

their things to leave. As they crossed the threshold into the cold painted corridor, Cloud-eeahhh linked her arm again, clutching the Next Directory in her knobbly fist.

"Dahhlink, I'f been thinking about you – I think eet's time for a little bit of male-order!"

* * *

True to form Geri was now wishing she'd addressed the matter of waist disposal earlier in the year. Christmas would soon be knocking loudly on the door and she was only an hour away from meeting Saliva & Co and she was shitting bricks! The small coloured dots of old nail varnish adorning the very middle of each of her fingernails hung on in there patiently, the raggedy red shade flaking off around it. It was months since she last used the nail polish remover and she knew she'd never find it now at the last minute. She decided to paint a darker colour over what was left on there, favouring that option over picking it all off and starting afresh. As she dipped the small nylon brush into the dark, chocolate-brown lacquer she began to worry about the extent of clothing she'd ordered from Cloud-eeahhh's Next Directory. Just being in her company fooled Geri into thinking she could *afford* to live like her. And then there'd be the embarrassment as every Size 16 would be too tight on her, and she'd have to return the lot to Cloud-eeahhh to send back! She regretted the whole thing! The classes, the social interaction, the embarrassment! Blowing onto her painted fingernails she viewed the contents of her wardrobe – they seemed to hang ashamed and embarrassed into silence as she visually sifted through each one discarding them without a backward glance. The last time she went out to a club shoulder-pads and neon lycra had been in fashion. What did they wear nowadays? If the mums she saw at the shops were anything to go by in their designer trainers and Reebok joggers or chunky boots and bootleg trousers she was in for a shock tonight. And there's all that Britney and Shakira thing going on – the hipster look with the tanned, toned midriff. And then there's the dancing thing! The last dance she had mastered had been the Birdie Song! Her mind went back to the early eighties when they'd just turned teenagers.

We'd stand in a circle singing along, "With a little bit of this, and a little bit of that, and shake your arse, la la la la!" *Well, it was funny at the time. Rather hideous now, though.*

She pulled a nondescript pair of black trousers from the back of the wardrobe, the hangers clanging in excitement. "Dress up tarty, you know," Sylvie had said. Tarty! She doubted she could look bloody tarty if she were filled with jam, covered in icing and baked for an hour!

"Anyway," she reasoned, straightening the pleasingly *loose* trousers,

"I'm thirty now. I've no reason to dress tarty. Take me or bloody leave me, although I've a clue which of the two it'll be, so don't bother answering, eh?" Thirty! She desperately hoped she wouldn't be too old for the place! As her tri-centenary once again hung over her like the Black Death she worried herself whether it was time to forget how to dance and throw away all of these old clothes?

Is it time yet to begin worrying about gum disease?

Is it time to correct my posture and go to bed early?

Almost ready now, her reflection betrayed her. The crotchety, hormone-deficient vision of herself is *not* the reasonably attractive, slightly overweight but smart image she is seeing. Call the police! This is a prime example of identity theft.

Where have "I" gone? I don't look too different from when I used to go out before having the children. Maybe a few slight lines around the eyes and a few extra pounds, but seeing myself dressed up for the evening brings it all back to me. My age, perhaps, is more of a mental state than a physical one. How old am "I" really?

She slid into a flatteringly tight black long-sleeved T-shirt and, deciding to keep it simple, put a thin choker around her neck. She was truly chuffed at the corset-like hold the T-shirt had on her, both enhancing her chest yet flattening her midriff, stomach and hips. As she stood with her back to the mirror, twisting to see her bum, she heard the doorbell.

"Nanaaaaa," she heard Cameron bellow, followed by the thudding of tiny feet as they run down the hallway to the front door. With only her berry-red lipstick applied she shuffled down the stairs like Baby Jane, all lips and poise.

"Geri! You look nice, love."

She was stunned and bowled over at the sound of a

compliment. Feeling like it had been a long, long time. Suddenly she realised that her time for mourning her loss of Kevin should be over.

Life goes on. Love goes on. Loss? Loss happens.

"Thanks, Mum."

Smiling feels nicer and warmer when you do it with lipstick on. I'm not sure whether it's the feel of the creamy silky coating on my lips, or the image I've got of my red-framed grin.

Right now, she didn't care. She felt nice for the first time in ages. Cynthia walked in and was immediately accosted by Cameron and his *Teletubbies* jigsaw.

"Nana, come help? Nana, help? Nana. Nana. Nana, help me. Nana, *help* me!"

"Allright, all right, love. Let me get my coat off. You only need to say it once, sweetheart." They trotted off into the lounge together to join Reece who was already in his pyjamas and almost asleep on the settee.

Geri followed. "They shouldn't be a problem tonight, Mum. They've been really good all day." Suddenly her feelings for them overwhelmed her. As she stood, feeling smart, glamorous and, yes, even attractive, her confidence at being a "person-in-my-own-right" radiated from her. She felt like she'd been eating bowls of self-esteem-boosting ReadyBrek, and now had the orange glow to prove it. Her love for the two boys that had come from within her magnificent body was irrepressible.

"Come here, you!" She crouched, her arms outstretched. Even her legs and bum felt thinner as she could feel the material still loose around them, despite her half-arsed position. Cameron ran to her, throwing himself into her arms; Reece's eyes began to flutter with tiredness. "I love you, darling. Be a good boy for Nana now, won't you. Mummy will see you in the morning."

"I love you too, Mummy. Mummy, where you goong?"

"I'm going out with some . . ." She hesitates, unsure as what to classify them as, she'd only known them a few weeks, and they were certainly not friends, ". . . em, some people I know from my classes."

"Mummy! We stay Nana's house anight?"

"Yes, darling. Nana has your little bed all ready for you."

"*Nooo!*" he screamed, the huge tears welling in his eyes. That's it. She knew it was the wrong thing to do.

By Christ, woman, they're only just babies. What the hell do you think you're doing? Done up like a bloody dog's dinner, face caked in make-up! Get up them stairs, take off those bloody clothes and pull yourself together!

Just as she got to her feet, her face resigned to cancelling her plans, Cameron continued, "No, no, no, nooo! I don't *want* to leep in my ittle bed. I want to leep in Nana's bed with Nana!"

"Oh, right." This was not what she was expecting at all. "Do you want to go to Nana's tonight? Or do you want to stay here with Mummy and we'll watch the Tweenies again."

"Noooo, no, no, nooo!" He started to cry again. "I

want to go to Nana's. Don't want to stay 'ere with Mummy!"

"Ok, ok, ok. Mum, are you ready to go now?"

Mum nodded, all ruddy cheeks, fleecy gloves and cold-faced. It was proving to be a particularly icy November.

"Right, then. Go get your coat and your *Thomas the Tank* bag." Cameron ran into the hallway excitedly.

"What do you want to do with Reece? I can put him into the pushchair with the Cozy-toes over him and his blankets. If we put the raincover on him too, then he'll be nice and warm in there. There's bottles and nappies and stuff in the bag underneath."

"We'll be all right, love. I've done it all before. Now you go and have a lovely time. You know, Geri –"

Geri sensed a Dame Edna coming on again as Cynthia tilted her head to the side and her eyes glazed over slightly.

"I've not seen you looking as lovely for a long, long time. Enjoy yourself, dear."

Warmed by her comments, suddenly the evening held great potential.

"I'll do my best to, Mum. It has been a long while, after all."

Cynthia's expression quickly shifted, her eyebrows coming down over her eyes and a deep frown set into her forehead, "Don't go smoking though. You don't need to do that. I don't know what comes over you when you go out sometimes. You *know* what I say about cigarettes, Geri, a pinch of tobacco, wrapped in paper, fire at one end, and fool at the other."

"Yeah, yeah. I know. Look, don't worry about me. I'll be fine. I'll have my mobile with me if you need to contact me."

"No, don't! I won't need to contact you! I'll see you in twelve hours' time! Just let me get these little darlings home, and you finish getting ready."

"Actually, Mum, I am finished."

"Oh. You're not wearing a coat or a jumper or anything? You'll bloody freeze out there tonight! Put some kind of woolly on you, love. It's very cold!"

Despite her feelings of being ancient, Geri felt like a teenager again. Only this time she was finding her mother's fussing amusing; she used to be incredibly embarrassed and irritated by it. She suspected that maturity probably gave her the ability to find humour in it now.

Hey, maybe this 'maturity' thing isn't so bad. . .

Ten minutes later she had said her guilty 'goodbyes' to her sons and was still putting the finishing touches to her make-up. She wasn't sure whether to plaster it on a little more, or go for the understated subtle look. As she brushed the bronzing powder lightly over her cheeks she realised the elasticity was going out of her skin faster than you could say alpha-hydroxy-acids. But still, one last look in the mirror and, she had to admit, she was looking pretty damned good. A last-minute change of mind as she struggled out of the T-shirt and slipped on a pea-green shirt, with a low wide-necked collar and elbow-length sleeves.

No, it's just not me. I feel like I'm just ready to do the washing up! Back on with the black T-shirt. *Yep. It looks even better this time!*

* * *

As she drove through the evening traffic with her car radio broken she heard the noisy engine chugging to keep the pace, noticing the temperature on the water-heater gauge was climbing.

The hum of the heater was sending her to sleep, and the traffic was snailing along at about three miles an hour.

And she was late.

And it was raining.

And one of the wipers wasn't working properly, and was jumping across the windscreen, leaving blobby lines across the glass.

She couldn't see out of it properly.

She passed a kebab shop and the smell of the chilli sauce, like old socks, was fanned into the car through the warm vents. It was Saturday evening and there was loads of traffic and because of the rain everyone was going really slow. Running fifteen minutes late, she finally reached her destination – *Skunk* – its name proud in blue neon lights.

Chapter Sixteen

As she approached the fake marble columns which marked the looming entrance to the club, Geri was relieved to see Saliva, flanked by two of her clones, chatting up the bouncers guarding the door. From a distance she noticed their animal-print mules, all three pairs virtually matching, and could hear Saliva's raucous cackle as she flirted madly. One of her friends bore an uncanny white resemblance to Tina Turner, although about three stone heavier and with only a fraction of her presence. Catching sight of her own reflection in the tinted mirrored doors, Geri felt relief and content that she'd pitched her outfit correctly, not too 'tarty', but still modern and, more importantly, not too revealing. She'd learnt her painful lesson on that score with Adam.

"Hey, Sylv," she called, her voice surprisingly light and pleasant. She silently congratulated it on the deception.

As Sylvia turned to face Geri, her over-made up face tinted blue from the flashing neon sign overhead, she smiled, revealing two front teeth smeared sloppily with thick red lipstick. Without being bitchy, Geri decided not to tell her.

"Geri? Oh, Geri babe, this is Francesca," Sylvia nodded towards the dark-haired woman, who smiled vacantly, "and this," nodding in the other direction, "is Summer."

One too many too, judging by the harsh wrinkles deep-set around her eyes and forehead.

"Ready to go in now then?" Saliva jittered, leading the way.

As they were stopped at the cloakroom for their coats, they were confronted by two American Diner waitresses, probably students needing to earn some extra cash and not particular about the choice of fancy dress involved, offering them a reduction on Christmas Eve tickets.

"Only twenty-five quid, and that includes your first two drinks!" the tallest one announced. With only a few weeks to go it seemed this was the beginning of the big build-up.

Geri declined politely, still reeling from the ten-pound entry fee. Sylvie took off her coat and handed it to the assistant, revealing herself as a zoologist's fantasy, top-to-toe in animal print. Before Geri's eyes had the opportunity to refocus, due to zebra-stripe-and-leopard-skin-blindness, the interior doors were opened, and they were shuffled through into the dark flashing, booming room. Needing time for her vision to settle in this flashing tardis, she wasn't prepared for the tutti-frutti of lipstick shades facing her. The place seemed to be awash with more fake-tanned skin and fake-tattoos than you could shake a shower-hose at. Geri watched the girls dancing, confidence oozing out of every amazingly unsweaty orifice, their navel rings dangling and glinting in glittering lights.

"Wanna drink?" Saliva broke her hypnotic state, her tinny tones a good three decibels higher than the thudding music.

"Yeah," she mumbled, following them to the bar.

It didn't take her long to form an opinion of the male population within the club. Basically a large crowd of pretentious pricks; all silk shirts, hoop earrings and thick leather belts. She waited at an uncomfortably waist-high table with Saliva's two chirpy friends, whilst Saliva queued four-deep at the bar.

Within only five minutes the Tina Turnerite is approached by a Barry White-a-like. All rolling eyes and dripping lip, he groaned, "I've got here in my pockets, the all-time thang that every woman's hips, thighs and buttocks have been waiting for . . . " undulating grotesquely.

"Oh, yeah?" She looked unimpressed. He was not to be put off,

"Yeah, babe. My *hands!*" He waggled them in front of her. The size of shovels, and just as dirty.

Geri realised that he was Jimmy-Savilled up to the knuckles.

"Piss off, mate," her friend barked.

Four Bacardi Breezers later Geri still couldn't seem to get into the mood. It could be the groups of drunk women singing karaoke. 'D.I.V.O.R.C.E' and 'I Will Survive' seemingly the only two tunes available, Geri wondered if this was what was meant by Girl Power?

Is this the solidarity between women of life-after-men? Is this what my foremothers burned their bloody bras for?

Saliva, now joined by another three women, significantly younger and much classier, continued to sing along and it was only when the announcement was made for the nine-o'clock slot, that Geri realised that the karaoke and drinking had been only a discouraging preamble to the main attraction – a male stripper.

Saliva screamed orgasmically as he writhed onto the stage, his ebony skin gleaming and shimmering under the spotlights, in fierce competition with his sequinned thong.

Saliva laughed, "God, he's not very hunky is he? I've seen bigger!"

Geri said nothing. She didn't think she could find the words.

Is this what I can expect for a social life now that I'm single again?

Without warning the stripper pulled Sylvia up onto the stage and, taking off his tie (purely an accessory to take off), he slid it between her legs, rubbing it to the crotch of her pvc zebra'd trousers. Her face was delirious. Seeing Saliva being true to her name as she spat and dribbled with glee, Geri just couldn't watch any more. She looked like she was about to self-combust and she didn't want to be witness to it. Disgust concealing her lack of confidence, she weaved her way through the pushing crowd as they squealed with delight at the stripper.

Finally, she made it to the bar. As she sat, stirring a Tia Maria – double – into a vodka, trying to escape the horrors of two hundred screaming lusting women, she realised that she was a sole female amongst a bored and waiting crowd of men.

Before you could say, "I've got to be home before the clock strikes twelve," a slick vision of silk slid toward her, grinning.

"Hey darlin'. Not watchin' the stripper then?"

She desperately wanted to say something smart like "What does it look like, prat?" But she didn't. The Oxo advert School of Motherhood hadn't brought her up that way. So, instead she smiled coyly, continued to stir her drink and said, "No. Not my scene really."

His eyes were concealed by dark-lens sunglasses and, as she watched his stubbly jaw wobble as he spoke, she could see her own reflection in his goggles. She scrutinised the frames, as he turned his head, for a hint of what lay underneath but all she was able to notice was a designer logo. She didn't recognise it as one of the famous ones. It actually looked like a snail peeping out from beneath its shell and a gold rainbow over its head. She found herself suddenly irritated.

"Why are you wearing sunglasses in a club?"

He was unfazed by her direct questioning. "They're cool."

"But it's dark in here!"

"Yeah," all sweaty and wet-lipped. "I've got a bit of a migraine."

"Then why don't you take Anadin like anybody else?"

"Oh sod off, babe. You wouldn't know class if it sat on your ugly face!"

Well, at least it got rid of him.

Soon after his departure she was approached by a fresh-faced Brad Pitt lookalike. Extremely attractive, but very young. She instantly warmed to him.

"Was he annoying you?" His voice was pleasantly open and calm.

"Oh, just an idiot."

"Oh, I'll tell him that. He's my brother."

"Oh, God, no! Sorry." Noticing the twinkle in his gorgeous blue eyes she realised she was being taken for a sucker.

"He's not, is he?"

"No. Please! Do I look like I'd have a brother like that? No, don't answer that one."

"What's your name?" she asked, feeling embarrassingly Victorian.

He didn't seem to mind. "Sam. And yours?"

"Geri."

"Nice."

"Thanks."

An awkward silence sat between them with its arms folded, as she looked up into his chiselled face, and he stood there –

Probably looking down the front of my top –

"Well, what'll we talk about? How about your underwear collection?

Definitely down the front of my top!

"Oh!" she heard herself guffawing nervously, "that won't take long. I'll have to get the smell of mothballs out of them first . . . "

"Well, maybe *I'd* better go shopping *for* you then . . ."

Without warning a lump stuck in her throat and her heart missed a couple of beats.

Or is that bloody indigestion again? I've never experienced this kind of swift approach.

He continued, thankfully, cos she couldn't think of what to say to him.

"I've got a good eye for underwear. I bet I could get you into a nice lacy little G-string. Not red. Men always assume that women would go for red but they don't, do they?"

She shook her head, wide-eyed.

I haven't a bloody clue!

"I think I'd put you in smoky grey. Classic, sophisticated, and very, very sexy. I'd get you a nice matching bra. Slightly padded and *very* uplifting. God, I can feel a stirring already."

He quite distastefully rearranged himself. She'd normally have been repulsed. She was too bewitched to let it bother her.

"I bet your skin's as soft as silk, and warm . . ." Then he murmured, "And I can tell you something else too." His face was dangerously close to hers and she could feel her heart beating in her ears, as he whispered, "Those trousers'd look better on my bedroom floor."

Willing her mind to think of a quick retort she was eternally grateful as Saliva appeared and screeched, "Sam*mmee*! You at it again?" She grabbed his chin between her finger and thumb and pulled at it playfully.

"You randy bugger, you are? And poor Geri! It's her first time 'ere! You could at least have broken her in gently!"

I know I'm smiling inanely, feeling conspicuous and ridiculous at the same time. And more than a little disappointed too.

"You know each other?" Geri had to ask, hating herself the second the words were out.

Saliva snuggled up to Sammy's chest, all roaming and fondling hands. He grinned down at her, affectionately.

"You've not been giving my mate 'ere that knickers 'n' bra chat, 'ave you?" she chided.

He shrugged his wide chiselled shoulders resignedly, and they both laughed.

Me? I'm still in the bloody dark!

"Geri? Meet Sammy. My son!"

Leaving Geri embarrassed, she turned to him,

"Did your mates come too?"

He nodded.

"Where are they then?"

"Over there, Mum. Billy and Zigger said they'd be over a bit later to give you a birthday kiss. I'd watch 'em if I were you though, Mum – they're a bit pissed!"

"Oh, go away, son! As if I 'aven't seen 'em pissed before. Saucy little sods they are too! Oh go and get 'em now."

Taking advantage of the diversion, Geri made her way to the toilets, despising herself for forgetting how to react to gross chat-up lines. In desperate need of a few minutes' quiet, she was not prepared for the stifling production line she walked into.

A row of bums stuck out pertly as two parallel lines of girls leant in toward mirrors, pouting, blinking and applying tons of colours to their already over-done faces. Bumping clumsily into their derrières, nudging lip liner and mascara over their grimacing faces, she left behind her a muttering of obscenities. As she finally reached the end of the line she was faced with a queue for the loos.

Standing behind a tall girl leaning against the tiled wall, Geri looked up at her platinum hair. A stick-insect in virtual underwear, she turned to face Geri, her eyes unfocussed and red, and smiled, revealing pink shiny lipstick and custard teeth.

"All right?" she slurred.

Geri smiled back distracted by her distaste for the place, "Yeah, thanks. Dying for wee."

"Mmm, nearly pissed meself back there I did. Brought me drink in with me." She held up a shot glass, spilling some of the brown liquid as she did.

"What's that?"

"Slippery Nipple!"

"What?"

"Slippery Nipple. It's lovely. Want a bit?" She held it to Geri's mouth, spilling more down onto her shoes.

Geri stepped back, unable to think of anything more repulsive than "a bit" of her Slippery Nipple!

"No, thanks. What's in it?"

"Sambuca and Baileys. It's lovely. The other night I had a Slippery Nipple, and then a pint of cider, Slippery Nipple, pint of cider, Slippery Nipple, Slippery Nipple, Slippery Nipple and then came in here, had two pints of cider and was pissed! It was great!"

"Right." Geri supposed she was meant to be impressed. She was far from it, feeling more amazed than anything. She was relieved when the cubicle at the end became vacant, and 'Slippery Nipple' shuffled her way down toward it.

As she stood waiting, Geri's mind suddenly zoomed back to the Post Office Experience. *He's really nice. I thought he was nice when I saw him at the gym – but confronted with him close up like that!*

Geri's feelings were surprising her. She found she really liked him a lot and she supposed she was just getting paranoid as she reached Middle Age-dom. Her mind wandered further as she realised that now she was officially thirty, she was robbed of her former pastime of mocking thirty-year-olds. She had now been cast into the unenviable role of the mocked rather than the mocker.

So what now for me? It seems my only option is to take the piss out of everyone under thirty and those over fifty. Oh, and Saliva. It seems my potential targets haven't disappeared, just changed their form. It also seems that the majority of the girls in the toilets are probably under thirty and are probably laughing at me!

A jabbing poke in her ribs indicated that the girl behind her had noticed there was a cubicle free and Geri hadn't staggered into it. Like the donkey and the carrot, she followed her nose into the unpleasant latrine. Decorated tastefully in various colours, the display of graffiti offered illuminating and educational reading.

I never knew you could do it in so many positions!

And the wet toilet-paper carpet sticks so nicely to the soles of my shoes!

As she headed back to Saliva and her ever-increasing crowd, Geri noticed that in her absence she had missed the arrival of Mike and a good half dozen of his friends. She squirmed as she realised that they all looked like ageing insurance men.

Joining the group as Saliva was trying to ponce a cigarette from a bevy of non-smokers, her irritation obvious, Geri couldn't believe her ears as Saliva squawked, "Ooooh, I'd give a donkey a blow-job for a fag right now!"

Mike's face beamed excitedly at exactly the same time as her stomach began to churn.

"Ooh, Mike! You couldn't go and get me twenty, could you, love? Oh, go on, be a dear," she instructed, rubbing herself lustily against his buttocks. Knowing which side his bread was buttered on, he did as he was told.

At one in the morning Geri felt drunk but unnaturally awake. She put it down to the vodka and Red Bull that Sam had started to buy for her. With *her* money. He just went to the bar for her and changed her drink. Her mind a stimulated and alert nerve-pad the words 'date rape' and *Rohypnol* swirled uncontrollably within it as she reprimanded herself for letting *anyone* hold her glass, never mind *get* her a drink! These weren't factors she was used to considering in her days of going out with friends. Rape was something totally different then and neither excused nor instigated by a drug in your drink. Feeling more than thirty, she suddenly felt overwhelming compassion and apprehension for young girls of today, having to cope with a lot more than she had only ten years before. She scanned the flashing room to see Saliva and Mike entwined on a settee, swapping spit, and her two muled cronies shuffling left foot to meet right, right foot to meet left on the dance floor. Glad for the opportunity to slide away unnoticed, she collected her coat and called a taxi from the reception. She waited under the marbled columns that had seemed so ominous only a few hours before, and now seemed plastic, fake and flimsy, watching the Barry-White-A-Like also waiting, his floor-length crombie smothering his huge form. A battered Rover Metro chugged into the car park, stopping in front of him. A woman, possibly his wife, got out of the driver's seat, and marched over to him.

Geri heard her voice, low and angry, as she slapped his thick arms.

"You said you were getting a taxi! Don't you know it's taken me all evening to get the kids to sleep! And now I've had to leave them in the house alone with JC! *And* he's drunk! Just like his father! Look at the state of you. Now, you'll have to come round to the driver's side and get in the back, I've got my box of Avon stuff on the front seat!" Obediently, he did as he was told. Geri's stomach bubbled with laughter as she saw him crow-barring his huge bulk into the back of the Metro, and cramming himself into the middle of the back seat, next to one baby-seat on the left, and *another* on the right!

Well, they say image is everything! It's obvious what his wife thinks of his "expert hands" he was so proudly telling us all about earlier!

As the taxi stopped at her gate she was relieved that the boys were staying at her mum's tonight. Although she wasn't really drunk, she was clearly a little tipsy.

The taxi drove away leaving her in a cloud of fumes as she rummaged in her bag under the orange street-light looking for her keys. Probably something else she shouldn't do these days, her mind nagged. Having found them, she was closing the gate behind her when she glanced up to see Him across the road! She hadn't noticed him around here before.

What is he doing here? Is he some kind of stalker?

Emboldened by the vodka and Red Bull, she called out to him, probably slurring, but what the hell!

"Hey, Española talker you! Come 'ere a minute."

Her smile was reciprocated as he crossed the street, heading towards her.

"You didn't appreciate it, did you?" he grinned, his voice smooth and friendly.

"I'm sorry. You caught me off-guard. You're very good, aren't you? I'm going to Spanish classes. I'm not doing too well though . . . in fact, I'm crap. I think I'm going to leave actually. It's worse 'cos there's a test at the end! A bloody test! I can't even pass an affluence test!" He laughed at her. She wasn't too sure if it was *at* her or *with* her. As she turned to her front door the words were out before she could even think about it,

"Coming in for a cuppa?"

Christ! I don't even know him! He could be an axe-murderer or something awful.

Geri wondered why she'd said it, reasoning that it could be because she didn't like the idea of being in the house alone, what with the kids at her mum's.

Oh well, here goes . . .

Ben was both amazed at his God-given opportunity, and surprised at her naivety. Overwhelmed but alarmed by her trusting nature, he felt a huge urge to protect her.

As he followed her in over the doorstep he had momentary second thoughts, as the scenario was just too perfect for him not to take advantage of her, and then tremendous guilt at the mere inkling of the idea.

She was unaware of this as she staggered into the kitchen, tottering, then holding onto the sideboard for balance, and began to make the tea.

He knew he liked the *look* of her already, but having

stepped inside her house, couldn't believe the similarities in taste they possessed.

"Don't come out here," she called from the un-modernised kitchen. "Sit down in the front room – I'll bring you in a drink."

Doing as he was told, Ben went into the clean but lived-in sitting-room. She called again, slurring her words and rattling delph as she did so,

"Kevin – the bollocks – said to wait till last to get the kitchen done. Got the whole house finished, except for the kitchen. So don't come out here, it's more of a kitsch-en!"

Sitting awkwardly on the sofa, he looked across to the large selection of children's videos. A catalogue, mainly courtesy of Walt Disney, his eyes scanned the various, and very familiar titles – *The Little Mermaid, Hercules, Mulan, 101 Dalmatians, The Jungle Book, The Lion King,* all characters that he'd studied in depth in his pursuit of a career as a cartoonist. His concentration was broken as she entered the room with two steaming mugs, a trail of drips being left behind her as she tilted both slightly.

"Do you take sugar?" she slurred at him, eyes smiling.

"Yeah. Four."

"Four! You *are* joking!"

Ben nodded, grinning, "Yeah, I am. Two. Please."

She came back into the room holding a dessertspoon egg-and-spoon style and deposited a mound of sugar into his mug.

"All the teaspoons are in the dishwasher. Sorry." Geri flopped down into the armchair and crossed her legs, Ben noticing every inch of movement. He found her amusing, her lack of ceremony endearing and comfortable. As a result of post-pub munchies she gorged on half a dozen choc-chip cookies and he watched and listened to her, fascinated by her, her humour and good personality.

Mouth full of biscuit crumbs, she declared, "You know my husband's left me. I am, *actually*, a single mum! Geri Cumbers, the reject!" She waited for his reaction. There was none. "Well? What do you think of that? Surprised? Disgusted? What?"

"I didn't even know you were married. I mean I've seen you about with your two children, but I never knew your personal circumstances."

"So. Now you know. What do you think?"

"I don't think anything. It doesn't matter. Who does it matter to?"

Geri, fuelled by the alcohol, but calmed by the tea and biscuits, was pushing for an argument.

"Of *course* it matters! I'm thirty, my husband's left me, I've got two little boys to bring up all on my own, a mortgage to pay, a life to get on with! Of *course* it bloody well matters. Hic."

Ben was sure she wanted him to feel uncomfortable and backed into a corner. Instead he felt amused and charmed by her spark and attitude. Deciding to humour her, he co-operated.

"It obviously matters to *you*."

"Yeah. So? What do you think?"

Feeling a stirring of affection for her, curled and snuggled in the chair, cupping her mug in her hands, Ben decided to jump in with both feet,

"Geri," his voice soft and low, "do you really want to know what I think?"

His tone quietened her, and she believed she was about to hear some straight talking, bracing herself for his opinion of her domestic disaster,

"Mm," words failed her, anticipation ticking loudly in her ears,

"I think . . . I think that your husband is probably the most idiotic, self-centred man that ever lived."

"You *know* him?" Her eyes were wide and amazed.

Ben was disappointed that she'd totally missed the point.

"No! I *don't* know him! I mean, he's walked out on an amazing woman, two gorgeous children, a lovely home and his family's future! Who in their right *mind* would do something like that?"

Slightly embarrassed by his declaration Ben fondled his empty mug, distractedly, and only on looking up did he see Geri with her head in her hands, blonde hair flopping down over her face, her shoulders wracked as she sobbed.

"Geri?" he whispered, putting her mug onto the floor and sitting on the arm of her chair. He was further surprised and taken aback as she buried her head into his chest and sobbed uncontrollably. Unsure of how to react he followed his instincts and put his arms around her shoulders, hugging her close to him. Like a small child the tears and pain escaped from her involuntarily as she blubbered, snivelled, howled and barked into his new suede jacket, leaving a snot trail and watermarks. Rocking and comforting her gently, he soon realised that the sounds had subsided. Geri lifted her head, wiping at her eyes, face and nose with *his* cuffs.

"Sorry," she whimpered, eyes swollen and red, black mascara panda'd around them.

Ben released his hug. "No need. What are you sorry for? Crying in your own home? Don't be ridiculous. No need to be sorry."

Composing herself, and sitting up straight in her chair Geri found her voice, and, taking a deep breath, attempted to smile, shakily,

"Well, I'm glad he's gone. At least now I don't have to listen about the way his mother cooked!"

"Yeah," Ben added, "*and* you don't have to smell his feet!"

They both laughed, and Ben settled back down on the settee once again.

"Sorry, Ben. Do you know, that's the first time I've really cried since it happened. I kept on thinking I had to put on a brave face. For the children, you know. I tried to keep going. I mean, life goes on, doesn't it?"

"Look, don't apologise. It's probably been very hard for you. But I meant what I said. He must be an idiot. You're a lovely woman. Don't let it knock your confidence."

Geri felt the tears well in her eyes once again so

Ben added quickly, "Do you mind if I use your toilet?"

She shook her head, her eyes looking to the floor.

"Em, where is it?"

Still avoiding his gaze, her eyes now blurry and wet she answered, "Top of stairs, straight ahead of you."

"Ta."

Minutes later Ben re-entered the room to find Geri collapsed in the armchair, her face wet with tears, snoring. Once again removing the half-full mug from her hand, he pulled up the second armchair to face her, stretching her legs out onto it. Propping her up with cushions and resting one beneath her head he slipped off her shoes, pulled the light blanket from the back of the settee and rested it over her. He kissed Geri lightly on the forehead and wiped her face dry. Smoothing her frowning expression with the palm of his hand, he turned and dimmed the lights. With one final check that she'd turned off the electrics in the kitchen, he switched off the other lights, and closing the front door behind him, left her to sleep.

Unbeknown to Geri, she had just been confronted with the man of her dreams; unfortunately she was a little too drunk to realise.

Skipping down the road to his house, Ben, however, is wondering how he can make her for life, and not *just* for Christmas . . .

Chapter Seventeen

After the lonely Christmas and New Year period, the reliably mild weather was beginning to intensify annoyingly, thought Sinead. The spring-like balminess that had greeted her daily seemed suddenly to heat up in a bid to be noticed. Along with this amplified warmth came the irritating beginnings of the tourists, evident initially only from the odd knotted handkerchief or neon-lime padded bikini top, but followed by a swarm of clones. Sinead knew they were the beginnings of the impending *Las Fallas*.

And as the temperature rose, Sinead's depression deepened. Three months after her first introduction to the "real" Steven Randall, she'd finally managed to wrench herself free from his emotionally unstable demands. The twelve weeks had passed more slowly than any she ever remembered. He'd had a way of distorting the sequences of events disturbingly, leaving

Sinead both confused and afraid as she listened to his warped account.

After the incident in the car, when she'd been knocked unconscious by his vicious lashings in what was to be a regular display of temper, she'd finally woken along the coast-road of Valencia to the sounds of him whistling jollily.

As her eyes fluttered painfully open and she tried to refocus through swollen bruised slits, he'd rested his large hand on her knee and chirped, "Oh, decided to wake up, have we, honey?"

Her thoughts had trudged through her mind as if restrained by balls and chains – desperate to move quickly and be alert, but shackled and disorientated through her headache. She recalled how he'd swiftly shown concern for her bruises, dabbing and cleaning the marks from her swollen face as he explained how an enormous bee had flown into his face as he drove, and how allergic he was to bee stings. His flailing and fisticuffs had been only aimed at the offending bee, whose sting could probably have killed him. How caring he'd been as he comforted and cuddled her, apologising for the damage he'd unintentionally done to her, and warning thickly how foolish she'd be to walk away from their relationship just because of this incident.

So, Sinead spent three months on the biggest emotional rollercoaster of her life. Just as her confidence would emerge, proud and bold as the trumpet on a daffodil at first, but weak and cautious nearer to the end of their relationship, Steven would be sure to beat her back down into her place.

As she lay now, suffocated by the airless heat circulating in her unkempt apartment, she felt as if the syrupy warmth was pushing down on her bruised naked body as it lay painfully on her bed. Her mind ticked through the barbaric emotional and physical abuse she'd suffered at Steven's hands.

She recalled how, only weeks after the incident in the car, Steven had invited her to his apartment for a meal. He'd offered to cook her an authentic English meal, to toast everything they missed from home. She'd revelled in how alike they were, enjoying similar tastes in music, food and clothes. She'd yearned for the time when they would both be settled back in England, and dreamed of how she'd walk the length of Oxford Street, stopping to buy various items along the way, and then how she'd take them home to Steven and watch his face illuminate with delight as he viewed each garment approvingly – and how she'd view his solid, sexy frame as he willingly tried each one on, only to look fantastic in them all.

As she arrived at Steven's apartment that evening her mind had been washed of the dangerous events that had occurred less than a month before. Spirits were high and she was being treated like a princess. She'd been seated in Steven's favourite chrome and black chair and handed a chilled delicate glass filled with cool, sweet Spanish wine. They'd chatted and laughed as he'd put the finishing touches to the tomato soup, and beef stew and dumplings, and they'd guffawed and roared when he'd pulled out a spotted dick and custard in a "this is one I made earlier" style.

"Jesus, Steven! You're priceless!"

"Course I am. My mum always said 'Steven, you're priceless. I wouldn't have paid for you!'"

As they laughed and chortled at each other's wittiness while putting the finishing touches to the meal, Sinead had failed to notice the dusty remains of white powder left on the edge of the worktop and hadn't thought to question Steven's frequent disappearances to the bathroom. Then, just as they sat down for the meal, Steven – hot, flustered and red-faced – had loosened his collar, complaining that he felt too warm. As he strode, wild-eyed and irritated, towards the glass patio doors Sinead, a little tipsy from the generous glasses of wine, had giggled saying that it didn't help that his apartment was so small. His large hand rested on the handle of the patio door and he'd slowly swung it open, letting in the slightly less warm air; Sinead hadn't noticed his face contort.

"What did you say?" he'd questioned, his voice slow and frighteningly monotone.

Sinead dipped a warm buttered roll into her tomato soup and replied, without raising her gaze, "I said, it's probably so warm in here 'cos your apartment's so small." She'd continued with a titter, "You know, our home in Ireland – I'll always remember what Mum used to say," she raised the dunked roll to her mouth and took a bite, continuing with a mouth half full of tomato-red dough. "She said our house was so small we had to go outside to change our minds!"

"You fuckin' bitch!" he'd screamed, swiping at the table and knocking her bowl of soup into her lap, scalding her legs as it spilled.

"What!" Sinead had screamed as she jumped to her feet, holding the sodden hot cloth from her legs as the soup dripped from her skirt onto his wooden floor.

He'd made another swipe at the table, and continued to swipe at it until the entire meal was splattered up the walls, and trodden into the floor. Then he'd started swiping at Sinead. Her screams and protestations went unheard as he'd lashed and savaged until they both lay crying on the slippery soupy floor. Her whimpering and crying was muffled as she lay in the foetal position, her arms up over her head in a bid to protect her face, and her legs curled beneath her attempting to shield her stomach and ribs.

It was then Steven made his way over to her, on his knees, crying like a baby as he did so.

"Why did you have to say that? Why?" he sobbed, uncomfortably close to her.

Sinead had remained curled, fearing to speak for saying the wrong thing once again.

He began to shake her gently, imploring once again, "Why? Why did you have to say it? Why couldn't you just let us enjoy our meal? All that trouble I've been to too! You just had to spoil it, didn't you! Why couldn't you just enjoy it? Why do you have to be so ungrateful?"

Sinead lifted her bloody face, wet from the smatterings of soup, beef stew, blood and mainly tears, "Why did I have to say *what?* I don't understand." Her voice had broke into an uncontrollable sob. "I don't know what I said."

Once again he'd cuddled and comforted her, rocking her gently, and she cradled herself in his open strong arms as he'd cooed and stroked her hair, lovingly. Her mind, once again, was reeling. He'd allowed her the 'privilege' of taking a bath whilst he cleaned up the mess and when she emerged an hour later, weak, fragile and sufficiently suppressed, wrapped in his over-sized bathrobe, he handed her a mug of warm sweet tea, settling her down on the sofa.

"Can I just explain?" he said, softly.

Sinead could only manage a slight nod as she sipped at the welcome drink, her wounds stinging and face swollen.

"You hurt my feelings, darling. You know how much I put into this meal tonight? I could have taken you to any of the top restaurants in Valencia. You could have *chosen* where to eat tonight, but instead I tried to make you feel a little less homesick by making the effort to cook you an English meal. But, instead of being grateful for it, and thanking me, and appreciating the money and effort I'd put in, what do you do? The first bloody remark you have to make is how poxy and small my apartment is! Talk about being ungrateful! Where did you *learn* such ignorance, Sinead? Did your mother really bring you up to be so fucking *rude!*"

She hadn't seen it from that point of view, nor had she realised how sensitive Steven actually was, but while the tears fell effortlessly into her tea and the guilt overwhelmed her, still an unbudging irritating voice in the back of her head screamed at her that it hadn't been like that. She was being manipulated.

* * *

Now, as she lay on her rumpled bed, she wondered how, months later, she'd finally found the confidence and strength to tell Steven Randall that "they" no longer were.

It had become suddenly clear, when he'd begun to taunt her about her weight, how he flipped between being her best friend and her worst nightmare with absolutely no warning – with what she now saw as cocaine-induced schizophrenia.

She'd tried to laugh it off at first with quips like, "Oh yeah. Didn't I tell you? I'm on a thirty-day diet. So far, I've lost eighteen days!"

To which he'd laughed. At first.

She just hadn't noticed the shift from the first flush of the relationship when, despite his wild tantrums, her favourite outfit had been a duvet. And now, with her self-esteem in the gutter and pains in her torso that she never could have imagined she sobbed into her pillow, the whirr of the air-conditioning muffling her gasps.

Though slowly, the strands of Sinead's insecurities were beginning to unravel. From the vantage-point of a third party and with the priceless gift of hindsight, she was now able to watch the movie of her life, highlighting and pinpointing the mistakes she'd made. How when Steven had tripped her in the kitchen, causing her to bang her head on the sideboard, she'd woken up with his hand around her throat and his fist clenched ready to punch her. And how, when Miguel Correa had leaned in over the balcony to see if everything was all right, Steven's hand around her neck had slid lovingly round to the back of her head, cradling it caringly, and the clenched pre-punch fist opened like a flower, and came down gently to caress her cheek. How he'd made cooing and soothing noises about "Silly girl, slipping on the wet floor like that! Are you all right? You didn't half give your head a bang there!" And how he'd then muttered curses toward Miguel Correa.

His sexual inadequacies were frightening too. His peverse manner of sexual foreplay was one that, despite her many partners and one-night-stands, she'd never come across before. As his sexual inclinations became too much for him to bear, he'd push her down onto the bed, demanding a meeting in her Oval Office as he tugged doggedly at her knickers, brutally tearing them to shreds, her discomfort with his demands irrelevant.

She recalled how Jonathon Morgan's grey-green eyes had blinked at her as his rugged handsome jaw was forced to stretch wide into a smile. He was well-travelled and diplomatic enough to realise instantly that her facial discolouration had little to do with the "accident" she'd gone to great and descriptive lengths to explain to him. She had met him at the airport, as promised, but said nothing of the previously mentioned *tapas* meal she'd suggested on the telephone.

As she'd waited nervously for his ten-forty landing, her stomach had been queasy as she directly linked the sound of his voice to the last thing she heard before Steven's fists had rained down on her in the car that day. The Sinead Kelly that Jonathon Morgan had been faced with as he strode from 'Arrivals', was a completely different one from the farty one he'd left at the hotel in England less than a month before. Sinead had been cold and unwelcoming toward him and for the whole duration of his fortnightly stay she'd adopted a completely professional attitude towards him. Despite him barely concealing his strong chiselled shoulders and well-toned, although a little pasty, forearms, in his casual polo shirt, Sinead seemed oblivious to his allure. And the trail of swooning females he left behind him. Jonathon, the consummate gentleman, had managed, within the first three hours, to apologise to Sinead for his presumptuous nature at their meeting in England, and revealed his respect for her polite but extremely pleasurable knock-back. His praise fell on deaf ears as Sinead, still tremendously scarred both physically and emotionally from the abuse she'd suffered, felt a totally different person from the confident young woman who had part-seduced him in the lift and then expertly farted her way down the sumptuous corridor! He realised that her confidence was dangerously bashed, so was kind enough to treat her with kid gloves. Taking the onus from her and onto himself, he explained how he had been going through a bad patch with his girlfriend. Sinead was grateful for the distraction. She knew he had suspicions about her bruises but was afraid to be too accommodating to him under the wrath of Steven and his erratic temper and jealousy, fearing for her own safety and Jonathon's also. He had charmingly managed to whisk her away for a 'working lunch' which she had tremendously enjoyed, and as they'd sat at the table, she'd shown the first promising signs of opening up to him and revealing the horror she'd been through. Reading between the lines, he promised her that he'd keep in contact, under the pretence of streamlining their jobs but, more purposefully, to make sure that she was all right.

So, for the past thirteen weeks, Jonathon Morgan had rung Sinead at least three times a week from England, and had proved to be more of a friend than any of her work colleagues who had accepted her story of the 'accident'. Jonathon Morgan had become very fond of Sinead, seeing through the very small crack in her tough exterior a warm, attractive woman who was extremely vulnerable and somewhat insecure.

To the untrained eye Steven Randall's mood swings and non-stop talking, his incessant chatter virtually melting the ears off anyone unfortunate enough to be listening, could be passed off as his gregarious nature. Sinead though was now able to recognise at twenty paces the tell-tale signs of cocaine-induced behaviour.

His jaw clenching and grinding just after sniffing the white powder, the continual thumbing of his nose and sniffing. The volume of his voice getting louder and louder as his raucous and uncaged opinions were broadcast, often drowned in immense humour, rendering his audience hysterical. And then the part that caused the majority of "their" problems – the coming down. The paranoia, the nausea, the nosebleeds. Sinead couldn't even begin to count the amount of times he'd barricaded the front door for fear of "people" trying to kill him. It was horrendous at the time; now it seemed absolutely ridiculous. Despite his mistreatment of Sinead she'd always been there for him when he'd been coming down. She remembered with particular emotion one night when in the early hours she'd found him locked in the bathroom, whispering mouse-like at her because "they" were waiting for him outside the window – and they had guns. Sinead had taken an hour-and-a-half to cajole him from the confines of the bathroom, promising that "they'd" gone away now, and everything was all right. When he'd finally appeared, white-faced and ashen, he'd broken down in tears in her arms. As she'd struggled to hold him, they'd shuffled toward his chair, and she'd sat next to him, cradling his head in her arms as he'd sobbed. Temporarily forgetting his brutal behaviour toward her, she'd rocked him like a child and stroked his smooth hair, kissing his head with small pecks as she'd questioned, "Steven, oh Steven . . . why do you do it?"

His voice wracked with emotion he'd spluttered, angrily, "Because it's there!"

Sinead knew, though, that it wasn't just "there". Steven often went to great lengths to secure a deal, sometimes travelling miles to meet with "somebody", often spending the equivalent of £100 a day, and seemed to need cocaine to get out of the front door. On a good day he'd be able to joke about it with her, his ebullience brimming, still reeling from the effects of the two grams he'd taken earlier, "Right, I'm off out to meet my mate Charlie!" He'd roar with laughter, leaving Sinead afraid for what the next twenty-four hours would bring, but grateful that he'd actually left the house for a time.

What had started out as social horseplay was cantering, fast approaching a gallop toward the hurdle of addiction. If that wasn't bad enough for him, his cash flow had failed to flow and when he'd stopped at his increasingly unreliable and uncharitable supplier only hours beforehand, he had laughed at his request for further credit. Steven was never in a good mood any more. He'd made excuses to go to the toilet and once in there had rummaged in his pocket for any small remains that he might have mislaid. Once he'd eventually located the paltry dust he'd scurry awkwardly to the vacant cubicle. Experience had taught him to run his hand across the lid of the cistern before laying the precious flour in a neat line. Many of the more trendy venues had taken to smearing the lids with Vaseline to inhibit the practice. He'd learnt that lesson quickly and expensively. Once up his nose, he felt almost immediately better, and had taken to giving himself a severe talking to as to how he'd get Sinead back into his life.

Chapter Eighteen

A few days after Geri's pre-Christmas crying scene she
and Ben had sealed an alliance. He'd knocked on her
door with a smile to melt butter and asked, "Would you
like me to help you with your Spanish?"

Not sure whether to be flattered or offended, she'd
just grinned pathetically and asked him in for a coffee.

Ecstatic at the presence of a visitor, Cameron had
discarded his empty *Petit Filou* carton, proferring his
yogurt goatie for a kiss and extending his yogurt gloves
for a hug. Ben had deftly ducked and darted to avoid
the contact with his crisp laundered combats.

"Do you take sugar in your coffee?" Geri had asked,
sniggering at Ben's swift dodges away from the yoggie-
fiend.

"Well, em – have you any beers?"

Surprised, Geri had responded, a little embarrassed,

"No. They wouldn't be top of my list of priorities these days."

Ben shrugged it off easily, rubbing his hands over a jumper that Geri supposed concealed a near-perfect washboard stomach, "Oh well, no harm. Beer guts run in my family anyway."

Yeah – right!

That afternoon had been one of the most pleasurable for a long, long time. Cameron had relished the male company, demanding more attention with his road rollers and building-site toys, and Ben had obliged, charmingly. He'd enlightened Geri on his struggle with his illustration work and had offered to do some pictures for the boys, asking in return for some feedback from Cameron with regard to his family of foxes. She'd accepted immediately, enlivened at the prospect of a conversation where she had extensive knowledge: that involving *Thomas the Tank*, *Winnie the Pooh* and various other kindergarten friends. Then Geri'd dug out the Monopoly. She wasn't too sure how it came around to that, but it did.

And me, a convicted and charged Monopoly cheat – I was delighted for the opportunity.

For Geri, cheating made the game so much more enjoyable. She was forever sneaking money from the bank, wishing it could be as easy in real life. She'd been suitably impressed at Ben's dedication to the game, and had listened, amused, as he'd advised her never to buy hotels, the rent on three houses was just as good, and how important it was to pay attention in the early stages of the game – the property acquisiton wrangle. Before they knew it, it was time for the boys to go to bed, and, surprisingly, Ben had cuddled up to Reece in front of the *Postman Pat* video whilst Geri tended to Cameron upstairs.

"Christ," Geri had thought as she ascended the dimly lit stairs with Cameron in her arms, "it's almost like having a husband. But a helpful one! There's a novelty." When she'd finally came down to see Reece snuggled down onto the settee, snoring lightly, she'd been amazed at the calmness of the house. To top it, Ben had greeted her with a steaming mug of coffee and two digestives. *Biscuits too!*

It had all looked so promising back then, as if her emotional outburst could be forgotten and she could be taken seriously for once by this new friend. On this cool February night, however, Geri concluded that what had started with her, red-faced and embarrassed, was set to continue along the same lines. She was now red-faced, once again, due to Ben. (Despite their friendship, she still didn't know him well enough *not* to go red, especially when he ridiculed her about her recent dates with Tony, which he had taken more than a healthy interest in.)

On this occasion, she'd been about to settle herself snugly in front of the telly, knackered, but content that she finally had a small bit of peace and quiet, when she decided that a little pampering was the order of the day – taking favour over calculating how to pay the phone bill *and* the mortgage that month. Blowing the clouds of dust off the Foot Spa, she ran the hot tap in the kitchen. Having filled the Spa with warm water she added a generous amount of drops of lavender oil, carried it back to the living-room and slouched in the armchair. Attired in her teddy-bear print pyjamas which were rolled up to reveal pale, stubbly calves, she plunged her feet into vibratory heaven.

Engrossed, she was watching Alan Titchmarsh (who, alarmingly, she was beginning to find cute and endearing) transform the weed-filled shoe-box into an astro-turfed be-planted extravaganza, when she heard the doorbell ring. Assuming that it'd be the Body-Shop-at-Home rep calling for her eleven ninety-five, she'd hobbled and hopped to the door, webbed feet splattering on the carpet as she'd done so. To her dismay she'd been faced with Ben, guffawing at her paddling-pool get-up. She turned in embarrassment and he followed her into the lounge. He was a frequent visitor lately, but she hadn't expected him at this time of night.

And he's still soooo fanciable!

"Oh great, I love these things," he'd declared as Geri had blushed, re-seating herself and plunging her wrinkly feet back into the warmth.

As she'd sat, highly embarrassed at being caught indulging, he suddenly pulled off his shoes and socks and immersed his humungous hairy feet into the water also. Disconcerted at this and seeing the water level rise precariously high, spilling over the sides, Geri had awkwardly complained, "Ben, em, you know, do you think you could, em, take your feet out! Please?"

Unperturbed by her discomfort, he'd obliged. Then he'd eyed her teddy-bear-print pyjamas and hadn't been able to prevent himself from remarking, "Geri. Why are you wearing your ten-year-old sister's pyjamas?" And then he'd begun to laugh, not realising her sensitivity toward the situation. "God, you'd be an alluring sleep-partner, I have to say. Geri! You really shouldn't wear those when people are coming round though, you know. You're positively temptation on a plate. So where's the teddy bears' picnic?"

Enraged and frustrated, she'd lashed out, "I didn't *know* 'people' were coming round; I didn't invite you here. I sleep alone in an over-sized bed, and if I choose to wear teddy-fucking-print pyjamas then it's no bloody business of yours! Now please, put your socks back on and get out!"

"Geri," he'd whispered, shocked at her outburst, "look, I was only joking. God, you can wear what you want! Don't be offended, please."

But it was too late. Geri was humiliated and wanted to be alone to recover.

However, on the whole, as she had got to know Ben, she realised how much she missed having a man around.

He was so good at those unsavoury tasks so unsuited to me such as fuse-changing, rubbish-bagging-and-removal and hedge-trimming. I also realised how good Ben was with the children. Only a short while ago we'd been at Ben's house and Cameron had been violently sick, fuelled mainly by an over-consumption of chocolate and cola. The coagulated mix had projected itself up his white muslin curtains, baked beans lodging themselves between his varnished wooden floorboards. And I must say I'd been impressed by Ben's reaction; he'd been so endearing and admirable as he rushed to the kitchen for a bowl of warm soapy water and proceeded to clean up without so much as a complaint, leaving me to do the maternal (and easy) bit which involved plenty of ooohs, aaahhs and it'll-be-all-right's.

As post-marital disappointments hurled themselves at her faster than moths at full-beam headlamps, it was refreshing to have a friend like Ben, who was unashamedly in touch with his feminine side, whilst still ninety-nine per cent in touch with his masculine side too.

And he was still soooo fanciable . . .

However, knowing that he was much too fanciable to ever fancy her, Geri had turned her attention to Tony.

Cynthia had begun to urge her on in the date stakes, insisting on reminding her in her usual unhelpful style, "Geri, God creates a worm for every bird – but He does not throw it in the nest!"

"I know, I know. Why d'you think I started the evening classes? I'd never have met Tony if not for them! That piano class has been the best value for money so far."

Geri knew she was jumping the gun but was going to the doctor that afternoon, thinking that perhaps the time had come to go back on the pill. *Ridiculous maybe, ambitious possibly, but still, you never know. As nervous as I've been about re-engaging my nether regions in nocturnal entanglements I reckon it's similar to having a car crash – the sooner you get back behind the wheel the easier it will be.*

She and Tony had already consummated their relationship, after their third date. But it had been an accident. Having sat in relative darkness for three hours at the pictures, with Tony's hand roaming further and further up beneath her skirt along her bare thighs, Geri had hobbled to his car with excruciating cramp in her calves. This was mainly due to sitting poised throughout the film, with her toes stretched on tiptoe, to raise her legs from the seat, therefore making them appear sleeker, rather than squadged and ungainly against the rough velvety chair.

On arriving back at Geri's house the cramp had worsened, and confident that the children were at her mother's, she'd taken Tony up on his invitation to help her in over the doorstep. Minutes later, after he'd assisted her in lying on the settee to "rest her poor sore legs", she'd found herself squashed beneath him, his slobbery kisses sliding across her face. Despite the vulgarity of it all she'd gotten caught up in the sex of it, and ten minutes later found herself skirt, bra and knickerless, feeling ridiculous and unsatisfied. Tony was lying on the floor next to her, red-faced and panting. Amidst her familiar homely surroundings she felt dirty and guilty at indulging in unsatisfying sex on the same settee where Cameron and Reece ate their Smarties and had their afternoon naps! Promising herself that she wouldn't lower herself again to one-sided copulation she realised that she had to take the pressure off contraception-wise. Maybe if Tony was more relaxed about her not getting pregnant it would be better than that!

She concluded that swallowing birth-control hormones on a monthly basis would relax the whole sexual situation. The next morning, she set out for the doctor's.

Sitting in the crammed waiting-room, amongst people pathetically sniffing and nursing their spring colds, Geri attempted to draw her attention from the gorgeous beefcake sitting opposite her, by immersing herself in an old magazine she plucked from the small table. With Reece in his pushchair and Cameron leaning on her, slouching into her legs, she attempted to flick through the pages with a light air of indifference.

As she turned one of the pages an advert for deodorant faced her. Cameron sprang into life, excitedly,

"Mummy oooses 'at!" he declared, proudly.

Delighted at his recognition of it, and proud as she watched some of the elderly ladies nodding approvingly Geri responded, smiling, "Yes, darling. Good boy." Nodding and proud of his product recognition, Geri continued to flick the pages noisily. A few pages on and Cameron spotted an advert for washing-up liquid, and again, declared, "Mummy ooses at! Mummy ooooos aaat!"

Nearly bowled over by his intelligence, she reddened a little, and a little louder encouraged, "Yes, very good boy!" whilst patting him on the head. She noticed the grans in the waiting-room cooing at each other, smiling and nodding.

Hey, pretty soon we'll be entertaining the whole waiting-room; they'll be in raptures at my attentive child.

Ridiculously impressed, Geri continued with her page-turning until, a couple of more pages on, there sat an advert. For sanitary towels. Cameron burst into life once again, "Mummy ooos –"

"Right, darling. Now let's put this back, now!"

Feeling the ailing congregation shuffling awkwardly in their seats, Geri's gaze raced around the busy room, only to find no-one willing to make eye contact with her. Various strains of smirks and smiles were directed toward the unseeing notice-board, the slightly ajar window, the dusty curtains and even the chipped paint door. Geri felt disgruntled and impatient.

God, why do these doctors make you wait so long?

Geri, Reece and Cameron finally left the doctor's eighty minutes later. Having to wait for old Mrs Braithwaite to come down the stairs had taken a good fifteen minutes, what with her wooden leg and walking-stick, and Dr Broughton had wanted to do a thorough check on Geri, given the trauma of her post-natal pelvis.

She'd started to date Tony, from the piano class, just after Christmas. He had been the one that she'd noticed wearing the Field & Trek clothing, with the wavy hair and tousled look, and Cynthia was delighted that she'd "met someone" quipping, "Let's face it, we know we aren't going to fix Rome in a day!"

* * *

Tony arrived at Geri's house promptly at eight o'clock, virtually ignoring Reece and Cameron as they played in the hallway, eager to see who the caller was at such an untimely hour.

"Ready then?" he deadpanned.

Feeling a pang at his bluntness, and wondering why he couldn't be a little more friendly toward her family, she said, "Yeah. Just got to say goodnight to the boys". She bent to kiss them both, their little faces smiling up at her full of wonderment. "Bye, Mum," she called behind her as she grabbed her coat from the bannister, and closed the door firmly behind her.

"Where're we going?" Her voice sounded crisp in the cool evening air.

"Back to my place."

"What?"

"Back to my place."

"D'you mean you're not taking me out anywhere?" She was confused at his choice of venue.

What I meant was, do you mean I've got all dressed up for nothing!

"No, I thought we'd watch a video and have some wine and nibbles and stuff back at my place."

Most certainly wasn't what she'd had in mind, but she thought what the hell, and climbed into his car obediently.

"What video have you got?" she'd enthused, anticipating something with Joseph Fiennes or Ewan McGregor.

"Well, I've got this ace one about the kids' programmes of the seventies."

Geri's face contorted into the Benny Hill look-of-surprise, "Oh right. Well, I must be honest, I did used to love that one . . . what was it called now?"

"Bod?"

Thick with sarcasm, you understand.

"Oh yeah, Bod! I loved that. No, but I didn't mean him. That other one – Ludwig."

"And Crystal Tipps & Alistair."

"And Rhubarb & Custard."

"And Mary, Mungo and Midge."

Really thick now . . .

"Oh brilliant, I'm glad you like them too. Looks like we're gonna have some fun watching them tonight."

On arriving at Tony's house she was suitably un-impressed with the decomposing foodstuffs and crinkled, discarded beer cans that seem to adorn every bachelor's home.

OK, so screwed-up scraps of loo-roll dotted with post-spot-squeeze blood aren't everyone's cup of tea; but hey, things could be a lot worse. And at least they're on the floor and not the table!

The smell of pepperoni and melted cheese filled the air and Geri felt her gastric juices kick into action. Fleetingly her mind juggled with the disappointment at his inability to do the same with her sexual juices, but she pushed it sternly away.

"Fancy a beer?" he asked, pleasantly, forcing an ice-cold can of Foster's into her hand.

"Oh, yeah. Right. Thanks." She wasn't sure whether he was going to offer a glass, so deciding to go along with the cool, I-always-drink-my-beer-from-cans routine, she wrenched open the ring-pull and poured a dubious amount into her mouth. Tony appeared at the doorway just in time to see the fizzy beer dribble down her chin and jacket as she cuffed her foaming mouth.

"Oh!" His faced dropped, surprised at her hastiness. "Don't you *want* a glass?"

His outstretched hand offered a zinging clean pint glass, emblazoned with the words "Show me yours, and I'll show you mine". Angry at herself for pre-empting the situation, and hence making a fool of herself, she sheepishly took the glass, turning to conceal her red face as she poured the beer.

He probably thinks I'm a geezer bird now. Shit! Why couldn't I have just waited. Always too quick off the mark!

Tony entered the room, smiling and clutching his pint of lager. As he brushed past her he deliberately ran his hand lightly across her breasts, her nipples jutting out promptly and embarrassingly obedient. He smiled on seeing their reaction, chuckling as he deftly switched and flicked buttons on his *Bose* stereo system.

"State of the art, you know," he said with his back still turned to her.

She presumed he meant the hi-fi.

"Oh right." She knew nothing of such equipment, content only with hearing the sounds of the music, rather than the apparatus that fired it. "I don't get the chance to listen to music much any more, what with the kids and that."

He stood up, turning toward her, "Why, what do you mean?"

313

"Well, you know, they're always watching the videos or playing with toys or something. If I put the music on they're both so keen on pressing all the brightly coloured buttons and flashing lights and that. It doesn't seem worth the aggravation."

He clearly wasn't impressed. "Why can't you listen to music when they're in bed?"

"I suppose I could, but I'm just so tired I can't be bothered really." She hated herself as she dug herself a hole deeper and deeper, marking herself clearer each time she opened her mouth as a 'mum'. She desperately wanted to turn the conversation around; this *wasn't* the way she wanted to feel right now.

Tony seemed totally unimpressed with Geri's explanation, settling himself on the sofa and picking up the remote control, directing it toward the telly. "Kids, eh? Can't bea –" As the blank screen burst into life, his face lit up on seeing the documentary programme. "Great! I'll have to watch this first before we watch the video. Hope you don't mind."

Grateful for the reprieve, Geri chirpped, "Not at all. It looks interesting. What's it actually about?"

"The flight patterns and mating techniques of the cormorant and the muscovy duck."

"Great," Geri smiled vacantly, slumping down into the armchair resignedly.

While sex hadn't been at the forefront of Geri's mind, her indignation at Tony's subsequent lack of interest in her seemed to fuel her need for it. Having sat for nearly two hours gawking at the muscovy duck, and worse still at Tony chucking enormous slices of pizza into his huge mouth, she wondered why she'd bothered in the first place. Determined to make the move from doormat to dominatrix, she focused on seducing him.

Despite the tomato and bechamel sauce dried around his mouth.

Sidling up to him on the settee, she flicked the remote-control button to switch off David Attenborough's dulcet tones.

"Hey, what you doing?"

Taking a deep breath before she began, wondering whether she could pull this off or not she breathed huskily, "Come on, Tony. Why'd you bring me here tonight? Not to watch the bird programme, surely." She ran her hand up his leg and further, until it rested just below his belly button, and began to tug at his T-shirt which was tucked into his jeans.

A nod being as good as a wink for Tony, Geri found herself ten minutes later naked on his rumpled and slightly malodorous bed. She couldn't quite determine the musty smell, assuming that it was probably a 'man thing' and nothing to be too concerned about. The distinct lack of mildew she took to be a good thing. Tony was kissing her wobbling stomach, although she felt good that her hipbones were evident, due mainly to gravity pulling the loose flesh down toward her hips, she hoped burying it into the duvet. Unfortunately the same had happened to her boobs, as what was left of them seemed to be hiding shyly beneath her armpits.

Despite her limited sexual history she felt slightly uneasy with Tony's quietness. Like a conductor at the helm of the orchestra he said nothing, and like the child being forced to take medicine from a spoon he clamped his eyes tightly shut. Feeling the pressure of his swollen pistol as he jabbed it toward her, she gasped, not quite ready for the impact. Starting tentatively and slow Geri relaxed, wondering as Tony began to find a rhythm whether he was the fast, strong or the slow, langorous strain. He'd stayed at a nondescript rhythm and, despite her raising her hips to meet him, she felt almost in limbo. She looked up into his face to see his eyes still clammed tight, causing embedded crow's feet around his eyes.

"Tony," she whispered.

He continued, not hearing her.

"Tony!"

Continuing with the concentrated look on his face, his eyes sprang open, struggling to focus in the dark room. She smiled, waiting for him to relax and kiss her. Instead he balanced himself on one arm, raising the other to hold his hand tightly across her eyes,

"Close your eyes," he instructed. "Don't look at me!"

"What?" She wriggled to push his hand from her face.

Wobbling, he rested back on both arms, continuing with the monotonous rhythm.

"Tony! What do you mean don't look at you! Tony!"

Once again he opened his eyes momentarily, slowing his pace slightly, and hissed,"Don't look at me! Please! Close your eyes!"

Anger surged within her, and she pushed him off, surprised at her own strength.

"Whaddya mean 'don't look at you'? What's going on?"

They sat on the bed, both naked, Tony's surprised missile glistening in the half-light – wondering who'd turned the heating off and pulled that lovely wet blanket from around him.

"Look, don't be offended. It's just –"

"Don't bother!" she snapped, suddenly losing all her inhibitions regarding her body and pulling on her clothes, doggedly.

"Geri!" he pleaded from the bedside.

"Hah!"

Slamming the door behind her Geri wondered where the nearest phone box was. She desperately needed a taxi.

She instructed the cab driver to take her straight round to Cynthia's, suitably convinced that her mascara had been wiped from beneath her eyes and the sexual flush had diminished from her cheeks. As her mum opened the door she heard Cameron and Reece still up.

"Love! It's not even eleven o'clock. I thought you weren't coming back for them till the morning?"

"Oh Mum, just get the kettle on, will you? Please?"

Once again Geri found herself drinking tea in her mum's kitchen, slightly agitated that the boys were still up, but too distracted by the events with Tony. To Cynthia's stringent questioning Geri only revealed that she suspected Tony was not quite what she expected for her first relationship after Kevin, painting a picture of how selfish Tony was.

True to form Quick Draw McGraw had a response, "A true friend is someone who dances with you in the sunlight and walks beside you in the shadows."

"Yeah but, Mum, I want one who can dance with me in the shadows too!"

"Oh, Geri! You know sex isn't the answer to everything! And you should be careful too, after having two children you'd be at your most futile now!"

Frustrated by Cynthia's continual incorrect answers, she grabbed another *Go Ahead* chocolate mallow and put it in whole, childishly opening her mouth to show her mum the mashed chocolate, strawberry jam and mallow.

Cynthia raised her eyes upward and shook her head.

Chapter Nineteen

As the kettle boils, churning foggy clouds up onto my desperately-in-need-of-retiling wall I wonder when and how I'll ever speak to Ben again, after the humiliation of the Foot Spa scenario. Just as I have the opportunity to re-invent myself to a new friend, I'm caught in the dismal act of immersing my stinking swollen feet into hot water. Despite getting off to an unfortunate start we've really gotten on well together, and he's been an invaluable help with my Spanish lessons.

Now, a stone and a half lighter but substantially more confused about the male species, Geri pondered the situation as she sterilised Reece's bottles.

Then the doorbell rang.

It was Ben. Seeing her bubbly hands and wet arms, he smiled cheekily,

"Busy?" he grinned.

Geri scowled at him, but with a hint of affection.

He took his opportunity quickly. "You're not still mad at me about the foot-bath thing are you? You know I didn't mean to offend you. I was just messing, that's all. Anyway, I've got a joke for you. Did you hear about the dyslexic who choked to death on his own Vimto?"

She snarled, turning her back on him, but leaving the door wide open, his entrance inevitable anyway.

Settling himself on her sofa, he called through to the kitchen, "Eeeh, gym lad!"

"What?" As she struggled with the hot steriliser she fumbled awkwardly and dropped the pristine gleaming bottles onto the floor. "Shit!"

"Iiit, iit, iiit," Reece parroted, much to Ben's mirth.

She stood bedraggled at the entrance to the kitchen, looking in at Ben, the disarray of bottles in her arms, "What did you say?"

"Eehh, gym lad!"

"Well, what's that mean then?"

"*Gym* lad. Or laddette. You haven't been this week. Why not?"

"Oh." Wishing she hadn't pushed the conversation, she went back into the kitchen.

"Well?" he persisted, raising himself from the settee and following her, stepping over an arrangement of cars as he did so.

"Oh, you know. Well, I'll tell you. You pissed me off and embarassed me. I didn't want to see you there, gloating and laughing at me."

Surprisingly tender, Ben took her face in his hands, lifting it slowly until her gaze met his.

"Look. I am so sorry. I've already told you. The last thing you need right now is me knocking your confidence. What can I do to make it up to you?"

"Well . . . ." she teased.

"I know. Take your socks off."

"What?"

"Take your socks off." He grabbed the bottles from her and placed them neatly on the worktop. Pushing her into the lounge he repeated, "Take them off."

As she was did as she was told, Cameron and Reece come closer to see what this nice man was doing to their mummy. Geri began to laugh. Ben swung her legs up onto the settee and sat at the other end from her, placing her feet on his lap.

"Now, my dear, you are going to experience the best foot massage you've ever had."

"I've never had one."

"See! Told you!"

"Don't tickle me though."

"As if! Now let's see what that Foot Spa's done for your toes."

As he manipulated and probed Geri's soft feet she eergghed and aahhhhed involuntarily. Nestling down into the sofa, closing her eyes and stretching her legs out so that he can reach every part of her feet, she didn't even hear Reece and Cameron chuckling and giggling at Ben as he pulled grimaces and funny faces at their mummy's feet.

Unlike any massage she would have received in a salon, Ben even made her a coffee afterwards, due to her declarations of not being able to stand, her feet feeling so light and marshmallowy. Sipping the warm liquid and trying to ignore Noddy squeaking out from the television to Reece and Cameron, her relaxed mind helped her to lose inhibitions.

"So, Ben. Tell me, why aren't you married?"

"What? And spoil my great sex life?"

"Go on! I'm serious, why?"

"Oh, just lucky, I guess."

"You don't mean that, do you?" Geri was concerned at his cynical view of matrimony, despite her own disaster. Ben was a very attractive guy, and although they were just friends, some woman out there was going to be extremely lucky when he picked her as his wife.

"No. Not really. It's just I seem to attract such girlies. You know, my friend Mark has even started giving them titles!"

"What do you mean, 'titles'?" She slurped at her coffee.

"The Knight, The Scroll, blah, blah. I won't elaborate further for fear of embarrassing myself."

Geri laughed, dying to know more, but decided to bring it up at a later date.

"So what's wrong with the girlie types then?" Geri knew her own opinions on such types but wasn't about to reveal any lack of solidarity between women, especially in the light of what Kevin had done to her. She didn't want to seem bitter.

Although I am.

"Oh, I don't know, Geri. You know, I just can't be myself. They're all so into themselves. It's all the image and the material things. I feel like I'm just an appendage – the final piece of their pathetic jigsaw."

"God, you sound disheartened!"

"No! I'm not! I'm just being realistic. One of the girls I dated actually wanted me to contribute half my wages to pay for her flat and bills, and I only stayed there at the weekends with her! It seems that to my mates marriage is just an expensive way of getting their laundry done for free."

"That's terrible!"

"I know. That's why I'm in no hurry. I don't want it to be like that!"

Geri stared at the dust particles floating towards the lamp in the corner of the room, transfixed as she gathered her thoughts about her own marital disappointment. "Yeah. You're right." Sipping at her coffee, her gaze remained unbroken, rendering her almost boss-eyed. Her trance was broken as she grabbed her cheek in pain. "Ow! I'm wearing out before my time! Even the bloody tea's hurting my teeth now."

"Oh no," he replied, smiling, "you *know* you're getting old when you get your annual dental check-up in a Jiffy bag."

"What?"

"In a Jiffy bag. No need to visit the dentist? Pop your falsies in the post, and he'll send 'em back to you?"

"Oh, yeah. Right." Embarrassed at her slowness and

horrified at the thought of false teeth, she continued, "You know, I absolutely dreaded turning thirty."

"Why?"

"Do you really need to ask that! How old are you, Ben?"

They'd never really discussed age, it being a subject Geri shied away from.

"How old d'ya reckon?" he'd grinned.

"Oh, I don't know – twenty-seven?"

"Ha, yeah – try again! Although I'll take that as a compliment."

"I don't know, tell me."

"Thirty-three."

"Get off! You're never thirty-three!"

"'Course I am! Why, did you think I'd lie about it? I don't care if I'm 'in the thirties'. Doesn't make up for anything you haven't got, nor make anything better if you're unhappy – it's just a number."

She envied his reasoning. "Yeah, but I'm not just single, like you. I'm soon-to-be divorced and *still* overweight – and you can guarantee that once you turn thirty you're destined to just pile it on. How much do you reckon could go on in the first couple of years of being thirty?"

"You're being ridiculous. You're paranoid!"

"I wish! Look, like it or not, thirty is the time to grow up. Time to read literary classics in bed. Time to buy a grave plot! And then there's the diseases! Skin cancer, breast cancer, colon cancer and lung cancer. Clogged arteries, high blood pressure, strokes and cardiac arrests.

They're all a sure thing now, you know – it's just a matter of time."

Ben shook his head in disbelief. "It's all a state of mind! Thirty's nothing worse than being twenty-nine. Or thirty-one! You just have to come to terms with your own mortality. But Jesus, Geri, you've got at *least* another fifty years in you yet. Fifty years! Christ, get over it, girl. Pull yourself together." His reprimands falling on oblivious ears, he continued, "Geri. You're a lovely person. Whether you're twenty-six or seventy-six, you'll still be a beautiful person. It's what's inside that counts."

"Yeah, I always thought that and look what happened!"

"What?"

"Kevin left me! Here was me thinking we were the complete family unit. He'd watched my facial contortions and groans and gasps as he'd got me pregnant, spectated throughout each nine months of pregnancy, and finally watched me give birth – twice! I thought a few extra pounds and a make-up-free face wouldn't even be noticed. And there you go, what was 'inside' was the same Geri – a bit more tired all right, but still the same. And it wasn't enough for him! He had to go for the image too! I mean what chance did I have? I don't believe it when men say that – it's *not* the personality that counts! Men don't have the sincerity in them to believe that one!"

"Geri, you're wrong. You've just met the wrong guys."

She was, by now, red-faced and blotchy across her neck and upper chest, due to the stress levels involved in declaring her hand so vociferously. She rerouted the conversation swiftly, "Yeah, I've met the wrong guys. But now I may have met Mr Right." She knew she was talking bullshit, that Tony couldn't be further from Mr Right, what with his selfish nature and blinkered opinions, but she wasn't about to admit that to Ben – who had already indicated a dislike for him.

"Mr Right! Tony? You *are* joking, Geri?"

"No. Why? What's wrong with him?"

"Ha! Now you're asking! Well, if you don't mind me saying, he sounds like a loser."

"How can you say that? Anyway, he can't be a loser. He's interested in learning to play the piano, isn't he? More than *you* can say!"

"OK, OK, don't jump down my neck. I'm just questioning your reasons for liking him, that's all."

"Well, I happen to think that the fact that Tony can remember the *original* Wombles – Crystal Tipps & Alistair, Bod, Grange Hill, Ludwig, Mary Mungo & Midge – is an exceptionally good start to our relationship. Kevin never remembered *any* of them. I don't think they even *had* a telly in his house!"

I just know I'm talking crap.

"Yeah, but Geri – that's no reason to like Tony!"

"'Course it is!"

Ben then proceeded, it seemed to Geri, to just go *blah, blah, blah*, voicing his reasons for disliking Tony – none of which Geri felt carried any weight whatsoever.

"All right then, Ben, about that day last week when he turned up here unexpected?"

"What about it?"

"When he said I'm not leaving here until I've made love to you at least three times?"

As soon as she'd admitted it she wished she hadn't. The proposition had held so much promise. His choice of words alone had been enough to send her dizzy.

Made love! Made love? The novelty value is absolutely priceless. And three times! Kevin would have never dared say that – he'd have had to have rung in sick from work for six weeks, just to muster the enthusiasm.

"Yeah, and did he?" Ben grinned wickedly, knowing that Geri was backing herself into a corner, digging herself an extremely large hole.

"What?" She reddened. "No. Well, not exactly."

"He either did or he didn't."

"Well," she looked sheepishly toward the suddenly immensely interesting pile in the rug, "no. No, not three times."

"How many then?" Ben's grin threatened to split his face in half.

"Once," she whispered.

"How many?" he teased.

"Once. One. One time. OK? Only one."

"Why? After such promises?"

Geri's face saddened. "He said that his ex-girlfriend's mum only lives around the corner and if she saw his car here she'd start spying on him again."

"You *are* joking me?"

"No."

"Well. There you go then. His *ex*-girlfriend's mum! That was some pile of shit he told you, you know."

"Look. I don't want to talk about it, all right? He's a nice bloke. I can't expect a relationship with someone without a history at thirty, now can I? Beggars can't be choosers, all right?"

"Yeah, sounds like déjà moo to me."

"Like *what?*" She was now irritated that the conversation was still running.

"Déjà moo. I've heard this bull before."

"Ha ha."

Geri stood up abruptly, causing Ben to smirk as he noticed that her skirt was tucked into the back of her knickers as she walked cockily out of the room, her mug in her hand.

She called back from the kitchen, "At least *he* doesn't consider lasagne a finger food, unlike some people!"

Ben wriggled down into the armchair, chortling, delighted at his ability to rouse her.

Chapter Twenty

Geri sat in her piano class the following morning, glad that Tony wasn't sitting near her, and still brittle from the truths that Ben had voiced last night, that she half suspected were correct. She watched Four-foot, Five-foot writing a musical score on the whiteboard at the front of the class. His verbose murmurings were disturbed by one of "The Snobs".

"Tim! With the homework, page fifty-two, question nineteen, – em, could you come over here, please?"

He placed the marker on the desk and slid over to her. She primly pointed out whatever it was in her book that was distressing her.

"If I did this in the exam, would I be wrong?"

"Oh, no. No . . . "

The volume of his mutterings diminished below an audible level, much to Geri's contentment – she wasn't interested in the class this morning. Seeing Tony smiling at her from the other side of the classroom was only irritating her. She wondered how he could look so ordinary to the outsider, but be so irksome in the sack.

"Right," Four-foot, Five-foot bellowed. "Now we're going to play the piece on page twenty-seven. Sylvia? Would you like to start us off today?"

"Not really, but someone 'as to, eh?" she cackled, scraping her chair and tottering toward the piano. Her "piece" was accompanied by intermittent curses as she "shit" and "bollocks"d her way through her mistakes. Geri laughed to herself as she watched the limping Four-foot, Five-foot cringe each and every time. To Geri it verged on slow torture. Months of this – waiting for each of the remaining twelve members of the class to sit on the dog-eared stool and churn their way through the same piece of music. It meant so much to the person actually playing the piece, but was unimaginably boring for the rest of the class. By repetition number eight the class had begun to get fidgety whilst waiting and the usual percussion of squelching cartoned drinks being sucked, and shuffling feet on the nylon carpet got louder. The ladies opposite started to relax their legs, letting their knees fall slightly apart beneath the desk, affording a view up the tunnel of their thighs, revealing be-tighted knickers, or unruly bikini lines. Mike loved it and deliberately sat in the same seat every week – opposite Sylvia and possibly Geri too, given a chance. Geri had to laugh at his spirit.

Four-foot, Five-foot interrupted her hypnotised state, "The slur, the slur! Don't forget the slur!" He was instructing Saliva, who hadn't noticed the curved line across the top of the series of notes, indicating that all the notes beneath it must be played smoothly. She gritted her teeth as she struggled with the piece.

And to think, this time last year I'd have thought a slur was a way of getting your opinion across after an evening on the drink!

"Here, let me remind you," Heffernan suggested, nudging Saliva's pert bum along the stool, sidling in next to her. It was an almost audible relief to hear the confidence of Four-foot, Five-foot as he struck the keys authoritatively, their resonance positive and intimidating.

Geri was no sooner over the doorstep after the tedious piano class than her mum's voice rattled through her head, the scraping of metal on metal, "Take your coat off, love, or you won't feel the benefit!"

Programmed-obedience led Geri to slide her jacket from her arms, hanging it on the bannister in a hunched mass. It was one of the recurring expressions that Cynthia had used since Geri was a child and consequently one that she'd absolutely grown to hate. Another of her favourites was accompanied by an expression of mock surprise and demanded that she roll her eyes upwards on chanting it.

It brought Geri back to her late teens/early twenties when she'd still lived at home with her mum and hadn't crawled out of her bed until the afternoon following a hefty night on the sauce. As Geri would pad down the stairs, usually just in time for the omnibus edition of *EastEnders*, Cynthia'd squeal, "Oh the resurrection!"

There were some things from her pre-pregnancy days that Geri definitely did *not* miss.

* * *

Geri's adult-edu class routine was now running extremely smoothly. As she sat in the Internet class, still squatting in one of the children's seats, she realised that she found it a lot easier to fit her rump on the seat these days. She daydreamed about how she'd managed to make friends in both the Spanish and Piano classes, but none really in the Internet class. She supposed that it was due to the fact that they never had to really work together, them all being glued to their screens. She'd probably gained the most valuable information from the "Internet with Dave Lomax", but could categorically state that she'd met no-one whom she'd be adding to the minimal entries in her address book.

On seeing Ben the next day at the gym they made fun, lightheartedly, as she complained about the awful men in her evening classes. She felt more confident at being single these days but secretly harboured sheer nervousness at the prospect of the straightforwardness of sex these days – no "courting" as her mum would say. If she were inclined to take any dark strangers up on their offers, would they be expecting her to have a bedroom full of sexual hardware?

Ben found her very humorous, seeing through her cocky exterior to a warm and lovable nature.

Suddenly a thought came into his head, "Tell you what! What are you doing tomorrow night?"

"Nothing. Why?"

"Right. You're coming out with me."

"Out with you! Where?"

"I, Ben Robbins, will take you out on a pretend date. A pretend date with a purpose. I will show you what you should be getting from a 'relationship' with Tony, and will show you how he *should* be treating you."

"Oh, I'm not sure, Ben. Why?"

"Because, Geraldeeene, you need to see how important it is that you're treated nicely. Just because you've had a bad experience with a couple of guys doesn't mean you have to settle for second best. Life's too bloody short. So. I'll pick you up at seven-thirty – and dress for dinner."

"But . . . " But 'what the hell', she thought, for the fun of it.

* * *

Geri was surprised at the butterflies doing bungee jumps from her ribcage down to the pits of her stomach as she got ready to go out. She'd already forsaken her black dress for her leather trousers, and then those again for her suede skirt. She really was in turmoil.

Dress for dinner! Am I equipped?

Finally, encased in her bootlegs, black ruffle-fronted shirt and suede jacket, she tugged on her spike-heeled boots – eternally grateful that she'd managed to lose the majority of her excess weight. Expecting to hear the ignorant blast of the car hooter, *Tony's* way of indicating his presence, she was taken by surprise to hear Ben ringing on the doorbell. Flicking her hair into shape with some glossing wax, and smearing on her lipstick, she trotted downstairs. On opening the door she was nose deep in the heady aroma of roses, as Ben thrust a full bouquet into her face.

"Beeeennn!" Cameron squealed with excitement as he ran for the door. Ben squatted, his arms outstretched as he grabbed Cameron and swung him up high, the little fellow giggling with delight.

"I'm taking your mummy out tonight, so you be a good boy for Nana now, won't you?"

"Yeeeesssss!" and Cameron ran into the lounge.

* * *

Ben nipped through the alleys and sidestreets of London, neon flashes of Picadilly Circus and Leicester Square flashing by Geri's window as they slalomed across the City. Before she knew it they were faced with Covent Garden. Pulling his car onto the cobbles, Ben let the engine run as he pulled up the handbrake.

He turned to her.

"I won't be a minute. I'll just get the key for this chain and we'll park right here."

"What, *here*? In Covent Garden?"

"Yeah. Stay there."

Geri watched him stride past the street performers and the crowd they'd attracted, feeling proud that she was his "date" for the evening.

As she people-watched, Ben dashed into the small craft shop, charmed the key out of his friend, and promptly returned to the warm running car. Geri watched as he bent and fiddled with the padlocked chain barricading the few parking spaces there. Lowering the chain he came back to the car, parking it neatly within the confines of the white lines.

"How come we can park here?" she'd asked, suitably impressed.

"Oh, a friend of mine's a partner over there. He always lets me have a parking space." He pulled the handbrake and switched off the ignition,

"Right, grab your jacket – we're going for dinner."

Seated in the half-lit restaurant Geri stared at the menu, feeling stupid. She couldn't even understand it, never mind know what to order!

Ben could see her struggling.

"Don't know what to have?"

"No," she smiled, "I've never had Hungarian before."

"No problem," he'd smiled reassuringly.

Before she knew it the waiter had arrived and had taken her jacket politely. She'd pretended not to notice Ben's appreciative glance at her chest as her semi-chiffon black shirt gaped as she bent to be seated.

Ben took control of the situation instantly. "Would you arrange a selection of different dishes for us to try, please?"

The waiter smiled and nodded knowingly. It seemed to be no problem. Geri felt so safe and confident in Ben's company. He seemed to take everything in his stride.

Ben proved to be excellent and stimulating company throughout the evening. She really enjoyed herself and felt a pang of jealousy toward the female who would secure Ben as their life-partner, and an ache of disappointment at her own game of relationship roulette.

Ben began to joke about his lonely single life.

"You know, as a single guy, life outside is very distracting. I just settle down for an evening of illustrating when the phone'll ring. Mark's forever dangling invitations to parties under my nose. It's just so easy to be lured out when they know you're single. They think it's like a competition to see who can pull a bird."

"What about your brother? Do you ever go out with him?"

"Ha. No, he's always too busy in front of the telly."

"He doesn't go to the gym like you then?"

"No. I think he's a founder of the Beer-swillers Work-out. The most I ever convinced him to do as he vegged out on the sofa watching *EastEnders* was ten-star jumps every time Bianca called '*Rickaaaaaay!*'."

Geri laughed. He was fun to be with.

As she finished their second bottle of exquisite Hungarian wine, feeling the flush to her cheeks and the haze around her eyes, Ben leaned in toward the table, the candlelight enhancing his dancing eyes, and said, "Right. When d'you want me to start with the chat-up lines?"

Geri felt disappointed, bought back to earth with a

bump as she was reminded that it was only a *pretend* date. She was surprised at her disappointment but felt a strong yearning, wishing that she could be the one that Ben held close to his heart, wanting more of the same, and on a regular basis. She managed to muster up a cheeky smile, pulling herself together to go along with the charade.

"OK. Give it your best shot."

"Right. You'd better start giving me mouth to mouth, because you just took my breath away!"

"Ohh," she groaned, laughing.

"All right then: you must be tired, because you've been running through my mind all day!"

"Uh-huh," she shook her head, smiling.

"Do you believe in love at first sight or should I drive by again?"

"I think it's time to go home, Ben."

"Mm, I think you might be right. Waiter? The bill, please."

Geri was disappointed at having to go home, but felt pleased that Ben had agreed to go in for coffee, thus relieving Cynthia of her duties, the two boys long since tucked up in their beds and sleeping.

Once Cynthia had called for a taxi home, Geri suggested, "Fancy a game of Operation?"

"What?" Ben laughed, not sure what she meant.

"Operation. You know, that buzzy red-nosed game where you have to remove the body parts without hitting the metal bits."

"God, you're not a Hannibal Lecter lover, are you?"

"Yeah, and you're a champion wanker! Come on. You put the kettle on. I'll go and get it."

Up for anything once, Ben agreed, "All right then."

* * *

Ben rubbed his eyes, the crusty formations in the corners grating against his eyeballs. Pushing the duvet away reluctantly his eyes chased around the room for indications of daylight. They weren't to be disappointed.

"Shit! Quarter to ten!" he exclaimed, looking at his Tag.

Now, where *was* he? He soon recognised his surroundings to be Geri's living-room. And he was on the sofa. All six foot two of him. Groaning as he stood, realigning his spine to something resembling vertical, he remembered how he'd ended up there. It had been gone three in the morning when they'd finished "operating" on the buzzy cartoon character. And the screams they'd had. Fuelled by the dusty bottle of ancient Ginger Wine that Geri'd found in the cupboard under her sink, they'd sat up squawking and screeching in fun as they'd both got carried away with the electronic tweezers.

But now the house was quiet. Ben padded into the chintzy kitchen. All was quiet. He noticed that their coats had gone from the hallway, and the pushchair too. He assumed she'd gone out with the children. The musty bummy smell of a lounge that had been slept in, after an evening of fine food and drink, hit his nostrils as he re-entered the room, climbing over the slumped duvet on the floor, opening the curtains and opening the top windows slightly. The watery sun glared at him through the nets. His mobile trilled.

It was Mark sending a text message.

It read "HOPE YOU HAD A GOOD NIGHT – WHY AREN'T YOU IN WORK?? RING ME. :->"

Folding the duvet into a neat(ish) square and leaving it on the sofa, he found his boots and coat and left the house, clicking the front door closed behind him.

Back at his house he was confronted with heaps of screaming laundry, begging to be washed. He decided to take the day off work, knowing he'd be in big trouble, but his heart just wasn't in it any more. He slid over to his easel, checking his family of foxes. Just on seeing them he felt the adrenalin rush in his stomach and the almost unbearable urge to pick up his pens and continue with the illustrating.

"No," he told them, "I'll take off these dirty clothes, have a shower and then put the washing on. Let's get things straight here."

Having removed his slept-in clothes and thrown them into the already overloaded laundry basket he roamed around in the nude, comfortable with the temperature of the room and enjoying the freedom. He'd changed his mind about the shower, deciding instead to run a bath. As he waited for the tub to fill he picked up the phone and dialled. No answer. Geri's answerphone cut in, her voice friendly and warm. He decided to leave a message.

"Hi, Nurse Cumbers. Only me. You could have woke me. It was nearly ten when I got up! Where are you? Hope you enjoyed your pretend date. Now you've got something to measure that cheapskate Tony by. See you soon. Take care. Oh, and hi, boys!"

As he lifted the pile of 'darks' to put into the washing machine a shower of screwed-up bits of paper, receipts and pennies fell from his pockets onto the commissioned rubber kitchen floor. Not bothering about them, he threw in two Persil tabs and switched the machine on, heading for the bathroom. Passing the seven dwarfs in their circular world of water they seemed to smirk up at him, almost contented and pleased with themselves, despite the fact that their water needed changing and he hadn't fed them yet.

As he lay in the steaming water, his feet sticking out the end, resting on the taps, he submerged his head, running his hands across his wet face and hair. He emerged, blowing orca-like, feeling a pleasant mix of calm and contentment. He'd really enjoyed last night and Geri's company was adorable. He couldn't understand her husband leaving her. What a damned fool! He really didn't know what he had. Ben lay back trying to plan another way to get Geri out for an evening, without frightening her off. His mind set to work, cunningly. Disturbing his plotting, his mobile rang again. Stretching across the sink, he grabbed his phone, swooshing back into the bath as he answered it. It was Mark,

"Hey geeze, where were *you* last night?"

"Out." Ben divulged nothing. At least not to Mark, for fear he'd entitle Geri with some awful moniker.

"Come on! No need to be cagey, you old git. Who were you shagging last night? You *never* don't come into work, unless you've been screwing!"

Ben ignored him. "Out for a beer later?"

"Yeah. How about meeting me in the Squiffy Bird at three?"

"Right. See you then."

Ben had barely pressed the OFF button when a text message appeared from Mark. He answered it again. It read,

"NICE (.) (.)??"

Ben's laugh echoed off the bathroom tiles as he flicked the OFF button once again, sinking his head back beneath the foamy water.

* * *

Mark and Ben sat in the pub full of old men, as was usual at three o'clock in the afternoon. The regulars huddled around the *Racing Post* arguing over the form for the three-thirty at Kempton Park, their caps and tobacco tins strewn across the worn chipped table. Mark and Ben were oblivious to their denture-rapping analysis.

Taking down a good half pint in one go Mark smacked his parched lips together in appreciation and, wiping the foam from his upper lip, placed the pint glass down and looked up into Ben's face. "Well? You gonna tell, or not?"

"Tell what?"

"Don't be a prat, Ben. It's obvious you were with a tart! Look at that expression on your face! It's *obvious!*"

"OK, OK, I *was* out with a woman. But she's *not* a tart. And," his voice quietened as he raised his pint glass to his mouth, "it wasn't a proper date."

"Waddya mean, not a proper date? What was it then? No! First, *who* was it?"

"I took Geri for dinner in Covent Garden."

"Geri! The one you've had your eye on for months?"

Ben nodded, swilling beer his primary concern.

Mark slapped his thigh, and drawled in his best Aussie accent, "Fair dinkum, mate!"

Ben had serious doubts whether any Australian actually did say 'fair dinkum', supposing that it was only the likes of Alf Roberts from *Home & Away* that did, but said nothing to the verbally dexterous Mark. He waited for Mark's elation to subside, and then explained how it hadn't been a proper date as he'd only been showing Geri *how* to expect to be treated by her current boyfriend, Tony. Mark listened patiently as Ben danced around the subject, telling him only the irrelevant pieces that he thought were sufficient to silence him. He was wrong.

"Well, here was me thinking you were looking for The Princess, and you've totally ruined my poetry! It seems you're shifting themes now and going for the Brendan O'Carroll characters!"

"What the hell are you talking about, Mark?" Ben stood, his empty glass in his hand, pausing for an answer before going to the bar for a refill.

"Ben! You're chasing after *The Mammy*!"

"Fuck off! 'Nother beer?"

"Mmm."

When Ben returned to the table Mark had been joined by three of the lads from the pub footie team. They were discussing their weekend plans for nights out in Laan-dan, their conversation led primarily by women, drink and first division teams. As Ben sat to join them Adrian, the only married one of the group, said, "Hey, Mark's been telling us about your pretend date last night. Glutton for punishment or what, mate! Looking forward to a lifetime of shitty nappies? If we'd known that's what you were after you could have baby-sat for me & the wife at the weekends!"

"Yeah," Gary quipped, "looks like we'll have to start calling you Pampers!"

They all laughed at Ben's expense, he too, amused at their banter. It was at this point Ben noticed the crate of beer underneath the table.

"Who's that belong to?"

"Me," answered Adrian.

"What you doing coming into a pub in the middle of the afternoon if you've got a crate of beer with you? Hey up, looks like it's all round to Adrian's for the afters!"

They all cheered.

"No," Adrian protested, still laughing, "I've got a crate of beer for the wife!"

"Good swap!" Ben retorted, his quick wit causing a

roar of laughter.

Adrian flicked him round the ear, playfully, "You bastard!"

* * *

Geri had arrived home from shopping to see the red light flashing on the answerphone. Without knowing why, her stomach jittered as she pulled the laden carrier bags from the handles and basket of the pushchair. As she fumbled and muddled with Cameron and Reece's coats, zips, shoes and socks her mind raced as to who might have left the message. She hadn't been to aerobics with Cloud-eeahhh this week, and hoped that it wasn't her, ringing to lecture her once again on how "the instructor eees great, dahhlink! Sarch a tight arse! You really don't know whaat you meeesed, dahhlink!" Or it could be Cynthia, calling to see how her night out with Ben had gone; or Tony ringing to cancel their date tonight. Unable to wait any longer, she shooshed the children into the living-room with two huge boxes of toys and, on the promise of lemonade and biscuits, managed to keep them quiet for long enough for her to listen to the new message. On pressing the button, the phone beeeped. Then she heard Ben's familiar tones. She rang him back straight away on his mobile. It had been gone half-nine when she'd left the house that morning, and he'd still been snoring on her sofa; she was sure he hadn't gone into work, especially now, knowing how tedious he found it all. He answered after three rings, the sounds of music playing faintly in the background, and men chortling and shouting. It sounded like he was in a pub.

"Ben?"

"Hey, Geri. How are you?"

She paused before responding, listening to the *"whoooooaaaarrr"* of his company in the distance.

"What's that noise?" She could hear the shwooshing of the phone against his stubbly jaw as he struggled from his stool, and the noises of his companions got fainter still.

"Oh, it's just the lads. I've moved away from them now. I'm standing in the lobby."

"Where are you?"

"In the boozer."

"Carrying on from last night, eh?" She relaxed. "I've really got to thank you for last night. I really, really enjoyed it. Tony falls short by quite a bit, you know."

"Course I know! That's why I took you! To make you realise how he *should* be treating you."

Geri was flattered that someone as good-looking and genuine as Ben had such an interest in her welfare. She secretly wished that the *'wwhoooaarr'* she'd heard his friends calling as he'd said her name meant that they knew he was interested in her, but cast it to the back of her mind as a fantasy. She'd only ever be lucky enough to have somebody as gorgeous as Ben as a friend, and that was how she intended to keep him.

She checked the chicken pie in the oven, and began to mash the potatoes and carrots for the boys' dinner, humming distractedly, a spring in her step and a knot in her stomach.

Why can't Bony be just a little bit more like Ten?

I mean, why can't Tony be just a little bit more like Ben?

It was quite a while now since she'd starting seeing Tony, and his charm, if it was ever there, was beginning to dissipate and his true boring colours were being revealed.

As they usually do!

The original pipe-and-slippers man, Tony seemed only to want a girl on his arm, a chef in his kitchen and a corpse in his bed! Unlike Ben, he displayed no interest in her children at all, nor in her home-life.

The telephone began to ring. She darted into the dining-room, placing the warm dinners in front of the children, and then grabbed the wall-phone on her way back to the kitchen.

"Hello," she puffed into the mouthpiece.

"What've you been doing?" His voice was condescending and almost humiliating.

Or is he just rubbing me up the wrong way today, after having such fun with Ben last night?

She decides to ignore his patronising tone.

"I've just put the kids' dinner on the table. We were just about to eat."

"Oh." He sounded so uninterested it was almost painful. "We going out tonight?"

"Yeah. OK. Where d'you want to go?"

"The pub, of course! Where else is there to go around here?"

Serves you right, Geri, for even asking the question. You should have known he'd say that.

"OK then. What time will you pick me up?"

"Seven?"

"Right. I'll ask Mum to come over for the evening."

"All right then." He didn't seem to care one way or the other.

"Fine. See you then."

"Bye."

She replaced the receiver feeling more than a little discontented. Only seconds after hearing his voice and she was already dreading the evening ahead of her.

"Muuuum," Cameron called, "Reece is putting his dinner up his nose!"

No time to worry about a small fry like Tony now. I've got enough to get on with!

* * *

By seven o' clock Geri was waiting for the usual toot that Tony used to indicate his presence. Knowing they were only going to the local, she didn't even bother changing her clothes – just threw her trainers and fleece on over her jeans and white shirt. Kissing her mum and the boys goodbye, she whispered to Cynthia that she doubted she'd be very long and would probably be in by ten-thirty.

Tony was waiting in the car for her playing a classical music cassette, intent on studying classical pieces featuring the piano for their evening class. She was chuffed that she could recognise Beethoven's "Moonlight Sonata", and then Liszt's "Consolation", Grieg's "Nocturne" and as they pulled into the car park, Debussy's

"Sarabande". She remarked excitedly that she would *never* have been able to name them six months before. Tony just grunted ignorantly at her.

Christ! I feel like I've been married to him for years. It wasn't even this bad with Kevin!

By eight-thirty she was back home.

Chapter Twenty-one

Sinead felt fragile and emotionally drained. Feeling low always brought with it feelings of homesickness. In a bid for all things English she decided to venture into the Marks & Spencer's in Valencia city centre after work for some typical, though simple, English foods.

As she drove back to Buñol in her Merc SLK, the warm breeze rearranging her hair haphazardly, she thought about the impending *Las Fallas*. She'd loved it so much the last couple of years and was more excited at Jonathon Morgan's interest in it, remembering the lusty electricity between them during her brief visit home, late last year. His sincere concern for her over the past few months had stopped her from crashing into a downward spiral of depression. He'd been on the phone doggedly, week in week out, to check on her, and raise her spirits. It had been only last month he'd shown an interest in *Las Fallas*.

"*When* is it then?"

"St Joseph's Day. 19th of March."

"So tell me, what actually happens? I know it's the fires festival but what do they do? Set light to each other?"

"No!" she giggled at him. "It's a week-long celebration where every village, town and city street in the province of Valencia builds a papier-mâché statue. Then lots of dancing and celebration takes place around this statue until the final day, when the statues are burnt. The heat given off is tremendous, with people standing only feet away. Then, spectacular fireworks displays are held every night in the dry river-bed that surrounds part of Valencia city. And every day during *Fallas*, at around midday, the *Mascaleta* takes place in the *Plaza Ayuntamiento*. *Before* you ask – that's a firecracker display. The traffic comes to a standstill and the whole city races to the central square for ten minutes of aerial bombs and percussion grenades. Some are so loud you can actually feel the percussion waves impacting on your chest, depending how close you are!"

"It sounds brilliant! Well, I think we'd definitely need to meet up again around the second week in March. I don't know about you, but I'm sure these end-of-year figures will need some realigning before the start of the next tax year?"

"Oh definitely!" Sinead had mocked, a wide grin appearing on her face. The first in many weeks.

But now, as she turned the key in her front door and stepped over the doorstep armed with carrier bags, she was again aware of the tension in her stomach – a reminder that she still had the nasty situation with Steven to contend with.

Most of the guys at work responded to his entertaining personality, thinking him the life and soul of the party. Sinead's recent coolness toward him had obviously been seen by them as her being put out about their recent, caustic splitting up. She suspected they didn't yet realise his addiction, brandishing *her* as the bad guy. In the face of their allegiance to Steven, she had to struggle at work to keep a brave face despite the harassment and her low self-esteem. Successfully managing to keep the act up entailed making sure she had an off-the-cuff remark for Steven when he approached her.

Only this morning, in full view of his audience, he had rested his bum on the edge of her desk, and leant over her. Sinead felt herself cringe inside, as he'd drawled, distastefully, "*Sinead*, Sinead, Sinead. You look about as happy as pig in *shite!*"

She'd heard the titters from around the room. As she'd used every muscle in her body to force her exterior to be cool, calm and collected, she'd looked up into his familiar face, the sight of his huge dilated pupils and red-rimmed nose a painful reminder. She just knew he was on a downward slope.

She'd taken a deep breath, composing herself before she'd responded, "Steven, charming as ever. Now, what can I do for you?"

"Oh Sinead. What can *you* do for *me?* Ha! Right, you

whore, I'd like you to do *this*." He'd begun fumbling with his fly, coarsely rearranging himself as if he was too much to hold with one hand. "You see, I've got this dick problem," his face had been virtually Cheshire-Cat-like as he reeled. "It's –"

"Steven. It would be my utmost pleasure." She'd risen from her seat, elegantly taking him by the arm and steering him gently away from her desk. Her actions had been so unexpected by him that he'd co-operated.

"Right, Steven, I'd love to help you *out*. Now. Which way *did* you come in?"

The guys seated at the desks around them had chuckled. It wasn't often someone got one over on Steven Randall. He had been humiliated and Sinead felt a twang of worry as she'd noticed his wild-eyed and red-faced expression as he exited the office, looking back over his shoulder at her, causing her to spend the remainder of the day with nervous butterflies in her stomach. She just *knew* she was going to pay for that little performance this morning. She had tried to ring Gertie – it was so much cheaper calling from work. Her phone rang four times before the answerphone picked it up. She relaxed at the sound of Gertie's friendly warm voice.

"Hello. We can't get to the phone at the moment. Please leave a message after the tone and we'll call you back. Thanks. Byeee."

Sinead took a deep breath before leaving her message, sounding exasperated and desperate. She wished Gertie'd been there to speak to, she always managed to get things in perspective for her.

Now, on arriving home, her stomach still in knots of anxiety, she opened the fridge door and took out a bottle of corked wine, pouring herself a huge glass and taking a substantial swig from the bottle before replacing the cork.

"Right," she took control of herself, "I'll go and have a shower, change my clothes, have a cigarette, ring Gertie and then I think I'll go to Chiva."

Chiva was a town about an hour's drive from Valencia which was renowned for its wine production. As she stood under the deliciously cool shower she imagined her evening in the Bodega – the wine cellar where she planned to buy gallons of good quality wine at ridiculously low prices.

She emerged from her bedroom forty minutes later, looking fresh and rejuvenated in a khaki knee-length skirt and her deeply v-necked Morgan vest, her tanned limbs elegantly on display and her hair still wet and loose around her shoulders. She flopped onto the chair, stretching her tanned legs out, reaching for a cigarette with her left hand and the telephone with her right. She dialled the numbers easily, the formula imprinted onto her brain. This time it rang only twice before Gertie picked it up.

"Hey Gertie!"

"Sinead! How are you?"

"Oh fine, fine. And you?"

"Not so bad at all . . . "

"Hey, is that a hint of mischief I detect in your voice?"

"No. You *always* say that about me."

"Yeah, I do, don't I! Must be something you're not telling me."

"Look, I'm going to change the subject – we always seem to get back around to this one. What are you doing? How's Valencia? How's your love life?"

"Valencia's busy and hot. I'm going to a place called Chiva tonight. It's a town not far from here with a wine cellar. I'm hoping to stock up a bit."

"Oh, I'm so jealous. You know my life consists of children's television, jigsaws, crayons, plastic toys, Early Learning Centre and Sainsburys?"

"Well, I've told you before, co-ordinate that husband of yours and get yourselves over here for a fortnight. We'd have a great time!"

Geri held her breath, the yearning in her chest almost unbearable. She was desperate to reveal to her what a cheating bastard Kevin really was, and then tell her all about Ben – *and* Tony! She composed herself, bracing herself for the undisputed lie she was about to tell her.

"Yeah, we'll have to sort ourselves out."

She felt this wasn't actually a *lie*, more a statement which was very true. They did have to sort themselves out. She still hadn't organised any financial assistance from Kevin, nor heard from him since just before Christmas – that was three months ago!

"And I bet it's already hot, isn't it?" Geri daydreamt.

"Yeah, it's quite warm all right."

"God, the temperature here's positively nipple-crippling!"

"D'ya know though, sometimes I yearn for a bit of frost or snow."

"Shuttup!"

"I do really. Those days when the air-con's not working properly, right in the middle of the season – July and August times – you'd just give anything for a bit of reprieve."

"Sicko!"

"Anyway, how's those classes of yours coming along?"

Geri resisted the urge to reveal all about the likes of Adam and Tony, but, being very selective about which parts she picked, regaled Sinead with the likes of Saliva and Cloud-eeahhh, Joan of Nark – the irritable pensioner on the piano course, tank-topped Rupert, Four-foot, Five-foot and Dave Lomax.

"You know, Saliva and Cloud-eeahhh are really lovely people. I'd *never* have dreamt I would have made friends with two women so far away from my own lifestyle. But they're really decent women. Saliva's really a spit-'n'-sawdust gal, and Cloud-eeahhh's more Logoland than Legoland! She's decked virtually from head to toe in Prada, D&G, Gucci, Fendi. You name it, she's got it!"

"She sounds manic."

"She is! But she's really nice too. I'd started going to aerobics with her, but I can't keep it up."

"Why not? You should."

"Oh yeah, could you imagine, her a vision in co-ordinated lycra and me! Forget it!"

"You're daft."

"I don't care."

"So, what about Saliva? What's she like?"

"She's mad! She's right cockney and doesn't stop talking. She's like Zippy on *Rainbow*."

Sinead chuckled at the mental similarity she'd sketched in her mind.

"But what's she like? Is she married?"

"Divorced. Probably about five times, I'd say. But she really seems to enjoy life. I'd love to be more like her in a way."

"I bet she's got fellas queueing up for her too? Women like that always do."

"She has! She's a right old spring chicken, I tell you."

"Mmm, I bet she could teach me a thing or two about men." Sinead's tone of voice dropped, being dangerously close to confessing her abuse at the hands of Steven.

"You? You must be joking," Geri was still in convivial mood. "Crickey, Sinead, you surely don't need any lessons when it comes to men."

"Gertie, I've been conned by my emotions more times than British pensioners with timeshare offers."

She was desperate to tell her about Steven, her battered emotional self, and hideously low self-esteem, but drew back just in time.

"Go on. I bet you give as good as you get. You always did!"

"Yeah . . . You're right, I probably do . . ."

"'Course you do."

"Look, I'm gonna have to go now. You know, I want to get a headstart on the evening before the tourists start pouring into Chiva."

"Oh. Oh, yeah. Right. Right, OK then. Listen, Sinead, thanks for ringing me. You really cheer me up. I don't half miss you, you know. I can't wait for you to come home again."

"Yeah, I was thinking about that. I think the next time I get a bit of vacation time I might go Home-Home for a fortnight."

"What you mean to Ireland?"

"Yeah."

"That'll be nice. Any reason why?"

"No, just missing the folks, that's all. You know how it is."

"Yeah. Well, I won't pretend I'm not disappointed, but I do understand. I'll speak to you before that though, won't I?"

"Yeah. Course. I'll ring you in a couple of weeks, OK?"

"Fine. Take care."

"And you. Bye."

"Bye."

As Sinead replaced the receiver, feeling slightly lifted by the chat, she stood, searching for her cigarettes and lighter, ready to throw them into her bag, and head for the car. As she turned she saw a face at the patio doors. Her stomach leapt and hit her in the throat, her heart thudding, reverberating throughout her whole body in a heavy judder. She felt her cheeks redden as she gasped for air. It was Steven. He was smiling through the glass at her, and before she could grab anything, he'd reached for the handle and slid the door open.

"Evening. Going somewhere? You're looking extremely sexy tonight, Sinead? Who is he?"

She felt her throat turn to carpet, but opened her mouth to speak anyway. She was surprised to hear a sound which was similar to her voice, but much raspier. She even managed a forced smile as she answered,

"Oh, just going for a drive, that's all. I'm not meeting anyone. Thought I'd just go out for a bit." She noticed his pupils hideously dilated once again. Fear ran through her body like electricity.

"A bit of what, you dirty old tart?" He was still smiling, inanely.

She strained to remain calm. "Don't be like that. I've told you. I'm just off out for a while."

She was surprised as he sat down, very relaxed, and said, totally rationally, "Look. Let's get back together. I'm sorry for the way I treated you. I really, really am. It's that powder! Once you get to like it, that's it. No-one *ever* does coke only once. No-one. It's too nice. It makes you feel like you're the life and soul of the party. You get more addicted to the person you *are* on coke – not the actual stuff itself."

"Look, Steven. I've told you. I don't care any more. You destroyed my life for months. No more. If you want to continue destroying your own, that's up to you. But don't involve me in it."

She watched as he stood slowly, his eyes glazed with anger once more,

"What are you saying to me, you whore?" he was suddenly bellowing, his loud booming voice making her flinch with every word.

She felt the tears well in her eyes but was determined to blink them down again.

He repeated, "You fucking whore!!" He poked her in the shoulder between every word as he said, "Who – the – fuck – do – you – think – you're – talking – to ?"

Her mind raced with despair. She'd so often been irritated by the sounds from the small bar below her apartment as the local men played cards and drank, seeming to frequent it all afternoon and night – but now, she begged that someone from below would hear the tone in Steven's voice and call up to check on her.

She couldn't rely on that alone.

"Leave, Steven. Or I'll call the police."

"Ha!" He mimicked her voice, "Leave, Steven, or I'll call the police! Yeah, I can just imagine you on the phone," he mimicked her again, this time in a tiny mock-Irish accent, "Hulloooo, is tat the *policía*?" Fleetingly, and absurdly, the image of Mrs Doyle from *Father Ted* rushed through her mind. If she hadn't been so afraid, she might have laughed. Instead, she stood expressionless, watching. Listening.

He continued, "You stupid cow! Do you realise what a prat you made me look in work today? And do you realise I *made* you? I turned you from a dirty old cow, who'd shag anything that moved, into a respectable, clean woman. Do you realise what a dirty bitch you are? You've turned back to that cheap slag you were before I started going out with you. Eh?"

"Well, Steven," she was surprised at her own calm, "what do you want me to say?"

She really wanted to pulverise him, but knew she wouldn't stand a chance.

"What do I want you to say? Well, for starters, how about thanks?"

Without warning the rage welled in Sinead, and suddenly everything was crystal clear. Just as Jonathon had kept on telling her, the longer she was a victim to this, the longer it would go on. Suddenly and irrationally she was unafraid of Steven Randall. She pushed him backward towards the patio doors, and once over the threshold she whispered, close to his face,

"How about thanks? How about bollocks!" and slammed the sliding door closed, and locked it. As she watched his face drop, surprise overwhelming him, she anticipated a repercussion.

There was none.

Without a backward glance Steven Randall walked away from Sinead's balcony and nothing further was said.

She couldn't believe how amazingly simple it had been.

Chapter Twenty-two

Even spring; the first buds and cool but very blue sky, couldn't make Elephant & Castle look pretty. It looked interesting, as usual, but definitely not *pretty*. But Geri was pleased she lived so close to this epicentre of Southwark Borough. With its predominance of red and pink architecture, and its hotchpotch of blocks of flats and ethnic groups, Geri always found it a great leveller. She'd have hated to live in a neat and orderly place such as Maida Vale or some mews in a more trendy part of the city, for fear that its perfect alignment and its inhabitants' orderly lives would have made her feel decidedly more confused. She felt she blended well with Elephant & Castle, its disarray and busyness overriding her tumultuous lifestyle, almost making her feel "normal".

As she pushed the double buggy along the New Kent Road, approaching the pink-lettered *Elephant*

Shopping Centre she ran through her shopping list in her mind. Top of the list, as expected, were nappies and milk – she'd decided on the turn of Reece's first birthday that she'd move him onto ordinary full-fat; pleased at the monetary saving. As she strode, her cheeks tinged pink – wondering if she blended with the reddy tones abundant around her – she recited her Spanish.

"*Son las nueve de la mañana de un lunes* – It's nine o'clock on Monday morning. *Café con leche y panecillos con mantequilla* – coffee with milk and rolls with butter. *El pobre hombre debe estar pasándolo mal* – The poor man must be having a bad time. *¡Por supuesto que no!* – Of course not!

She ignored Cameron and Reece craning their small, supple necks to look backwards and upwards at her, wondering what her jabbering was all about. She just knew she'd gone ahead in leaps and bounds since Ben had started helping her with her Spanish – the extra few hours a week he was volunteering to spend with her were totally priceless, and his suggestion of repetition to herself an excellent tip.

Nearly an hour later and she was putting the key into her front door, still reciting her sentences. The boys had, by now, fallen asleep, probably due to boredom. Sucking the melted chocolate from the dips in her back teeth she wondered whether eating three packets of Chocolate Buttons negated her diet. And she *still* didn't have anything for the boys' "treat" when they woke up! She should have bought some Wildlife Bars too! As she stepped in over the doorstep the telephone rang. She dashed to answer it not wanting to waken the children. Yet.

"Hello?" Her voice was whispery and puffed.

"Geri?"

"Ben!"

"Why are you whispering? They're not asleep at this time of day, are they?"

"Yeah, only a nap. They're in the double buggy. We've just been to the shops."

"Oh, right. Get anything nice?"

She laughed at his interest in her shopping expedition,

"No. Milk, nappies, blah, blah."

"Great!"

"Ben, why are you ringing me?"

"Well, you see," he teased, "it goes back to my days with Chanelle. Toward the end of our relationship I was so much happier talking to her on the phone. Her horrendous halitosis was just too much to bear, you see. Her diet of fags, tomatoes and coffee didn't do much to endear her to me. She said it worked wonders for maintaining her figure though. What good *that* was to her though, I don't know. She looked great from a distance but was unbearable on the nostrils within close quarters."

Geri laughed. He was an awful piss-taker.

"Ben," she managed to compose herself slightly, "why are you ringing?"

"Eeeh, gym lad?"

"Tonight?"

"Could do. What about you, up for it?"

"OK. I'll ring Mum and see if she can come over and sit with the boys for a couple of hours."

"Great, call for you at seven then?"

"Fine."

"Oh, and Nurse Cumbers?"

"Yes."

"Tell Mr Ogadwadu we have some good news and some bad news for him, please."

"What?"

"Now, Nurse Cumbers, please, put your mind to the task in hand. Tell him that we're terribly sorry but we have to amputate both of his legs."

"Oh yeah?" She supposed there was a punchline looming.

"Yes, please. *Try* and be compassionate, Nurse Cumbers. Breaking into hysterical laughter isn't considered polite by many cultures."

"Right, OK then. And the good news . . ."

"The good news is that Mr Smith, in the opposite bed, would just *love* to buy his slippers."

Geri replaced the receiver, smiling to herself as she did so.

Having organised for Cynthia to baby-sit for a short while, she turned the fish-fingers under the grill, whilst singing cheerfully, "*Tommy Thumb, Tommy Thumb, where are you? Here I am, here I am, how do you do . . .* " to two ecstatic children as they danced around her legs. Her mind, however, was on other things. She was a little concerned about Sinead; she didn't sound herself on the phone. Grabbing the biro from the kitchen worktop she scrawled in large capital letters on the wall calendar: RING SINEAD – COME CLEAN ABOUT KEVIN – SORRY!! And then in smaller letters as an afterthought: REALLY MISS AND LOVE LOTS. Crunching through the fish-fingers with the blunt knife, popping small fragments into her mouth as they fell to the wayside of the baked beans and mash, she was interrupted by the telephone once again. Expecting it to be either Ben or her mum she continued to dish up the boys' dinner, wedging the phone in the crook of her neck.

"Hmm?"

"Geri. It's Tony."

The phone sprang from beneath her chin and crashed onto the floor, bouncing on its coiled bungee strap wildly, something loose now rattling in the handpiece as she shook it. She took her opportunity to dash into the dining-room with the boys' fish-finger and beans dinner, picking up the abandoned phone from the kitchen floor on her return.

"Hi. God, sorry about that, Tony. I dropped the phone."

"You don't say!" His voice was thick was sarcasm, but not of a humorous nature.

"Yeah, right. What's up?"

"Fancy going out tonight?"

"Oh, well I *was* going to the gym tonight."

"Right, see ya then."

"Oh don't be like that, Tony." She knew she was going to hate herself for this, but continued regardless, "Look, it's no big deal. I don't *have* to go tonight."

"Don't force yourself."

"No. Look, I've said I'd like it. Where shall we go?" She was trying desperately to sound enthusiastic, provoked purely by her slight feelings of guilt at not giving it one hundred per cent with Tony. He wasn't making it particularly easy for her.

"Dunno, just one of the local pubs eh? We could stay in Elephant and Castle if you like. Into the Charlie Chaplin. Or the Crown and Anchor?"

Geri sighed, resigned to another exciting evening in the Lambeth Walk Public House, where, no doubt, he'd regale her, once again, with his boring story of how he only wanted to learn the piano to enhance his minimal understanding of music. Despite this, she decided to give him another chance, having suspected by now that she'd misread his surf-boy, casual style and thrown-together look for uncomplicated and laid-back. She now realised it meant plain scruffy and lazily unclean. As she had progressively reduced her body mass over the past few months, her confidence had grown, making her realise that what had appeared vaguely attractive six months ago, now only highlighted her post-natal desperation.

Putting down the phone she craned her head around the door checking that the boys were tucking into their dinners as expected. She melted a little as she watched them, Reece now well able to use his plastic fork and spoon, sitting up in his highchair, his pudgy little legs swinging as he smeared beans across his face.

I really don't want to ring Ben and cancel. I just know he'll be mad. Still, seize the moment.

"Hullo?"

"Ben."

"Hi. What's wrong?"

"I'll have to cancel tonight. Sorry."

"Tony?"

"No! Why d'you say that?"

"Come on, Geri, he's only got to click his dirty fingers and you drop everything."

Looks like I've been rumbled. Proven guilty before I've even explained!

"Sorry Ben."

I am, really!

"Don't worry about it. I'll call round later and see you, all right?"

"OK, ta."

"Hey. Boys all right?"

"Yes," *he's such a cutie, he never fails to ask for them,* "they're eating their dinner. Thanks, Ben."

"No problems. Bye."

"Bye."

The afternoon plodded on slowly. An unexpected surge of energy rushed through her about two o'clock and she rounded the boys up, zipping up their spring coats for a trip to Regent's Park. They waited patiently at the front door, while she struggled with the pushchair, turning round only just in time to see Reece picking her prized geraniums from the terracotta pots outside.

"Reece. No!"

He turned to her, a mouth full of petals, looking disconcertingly like Ermintrude.

"Come on now. To the car."

Surprisingly obedient, they stood by Geri's "trusty-but-rusty" as she unlocked the door and they clambered in. Clunk-clicking Reece into the baby-seat and Cameron into the booster seat she settled herself in the driving position and turned the key. A few coughs and blasts later, they were off.

Cameron chattered incessantly, overwhelmed by the anticipation of seeing the ducks and playing on the grass. Her mind, however, was elsewhere as she wondered why the car was spluttering and jerking. Five minutes later and they were being thrust forward and back in their seats, causing great mirth to some onlookers.

We probably look like the Three-fucking-Degrees doing a dance routine! Fortunately she spotted a garage up the road.

Great. I must pull in. This could be serious.

Before she got the opportunity, the situation was taken from her hands. Without any further barking, the car stopped.

Dead.

* * *

Two hours later she was sulking in her armchair, stuffing her face with Quavers and gazing at the chocolate éclair waiting patiently for her on the plate, wondering when things just *might* start going right for her! Humiliation didn't come purer than this.

Watching Cameron and Reece fighting over a red plastic tractor, she's disappointed they never made it to the park, but embarrassed beyond belief that she'd had to ask McLoughlin's Building Contractors to push her to the garage. But it hadn't ended there! The four lumberjack-shirted, dusty-booted beefcakes had cracked jokes and bellowed loudly for the whole duration of the pushing saga, while she had to sit amidst them, Buddha-like, merely steering the wheels in the right direction.

So now, fifty-three quid poorer and two hundred per cent humbled, we're back home, having achieved nothing but degradation and expense!

A knocking at the door forced her to climb out of her slumped sulk and make for the hallway. She almost enjoyed scowling as she reached for the handle.

"Hey, what's up?"

Shit, why'd it have to be Him? And me in such a bad mood!

She attempted a smile, feeling it quaking at the corners of her mouth.

"Oh, the bloody car! I only wanted to go –"

"Got any more of them? I'd love some, thanks," Ben interrupted, glancing down toward the half-eaten bag of Quavers in her crumby hand,

"Yeah. Come in."

As he hovered behind her in the kitchen he

rummaged elbow-deep in the multi-pack and asked, "So what happened to your car?"

"We were heading for Regent's Park. I only got a few miles up the road and it just conked out. I had to be pushed, *pushed*, to a garage!"

"Did they fix it?"

Why are men so to-the-point and practical? My humiliation is obviously lost on him.

"Yeah. Cost me fifty quid though."

"So?"

"So what?"

"So what was wrong with it?" he asked through a mouth crammed with Quavers.

"Crap in the carburettor."

"No!"

He's grinning!

"How often do you have to do that then?" he asked.

Shit-head! He always makes me laugh!

Ben had stayed until six o' clock, chatting to Geri as she'd got the boys' overnight things ready to go to her Mum's.

Cynthia was so looking forward to having them there – complaining how it had seemed an "eternity" since they'd stayed over.

Geri and Ben giggled at how Cynthia had reacted to Geri's misdemeanour with her car. "Don't feel embarrassed, Geri. Never forget that you are unique – just like everybody else."

And at how, when Geri had expressed her gratitude to her for taking the children off her hands that evening, she'd supported her with, "You *know* I'd always give you an anchor to keep you afloat during the storm."

As Geri had finished getting the boys ready for the trek to Cynthia's, Ben grabbed his jacket, aware that she was almost ready to go.

"Have you thought of a holiday this year?" he asked.

Geri turned in amazement, "Are you serious? I can't even begin to think of it." Noticing the expression on his face, she prompted, "Why, have you?"

"Yeah, well, Mark's been talking about a blokes' holiday."

"Right."

Why do I feel jealous?

"What – Magaluf or Ibiza?" she asked.

"Get outtof it," he looked disgusted. "We were thinking of sandboarding in Namibia."

"Blimey. Can you do that?"

"Yeah, not brilliant, but you know what they say about practice."

Her voice dropped slightly, "You know, I doubt we'll be in a position to take a holiday at all. Probably for the next five years."

"Well," he followed her to the kitchen, "nothing's been planned. I'll have to speak to Mark."

Turning her back to him temporarily she went to the wall calendar in the kitchen and wrote herself a note to ring Kevin to sort out his maintenance payments to them. As she pivoted round, throwing the pen onto the kitchen worktop, she noticed Ben squinting at her scrawl on the calendar.

"All right?" she asked him.

"Yeah, yeah. Sorry."

"Look, I don't mean to be rude, but Mum'll be here in half an hour to get the boys and I have to finish sorting them out. Spend a few minutes with them, you know? Could I catch up with you tomorrow?"

"Yeah, fine. Have a nice evening with boring-Tony. What's he doing – tooting for you half-a-mile down the road at half seven?"

"No! He's picking me up."

"Yeah, but he won't raise his fat arse out of the driving seat, will he? Don't forget now, Geri, keep the music down, or you might not hear him and his poxy hooter!"

"Shuttup, Ben. Don't be mean. I'm going to give it my best shot tonight."

"Yeah, yeah. Take care." He leant toward her, kissing her on the cheek amicably.

She felt electric shocks shoot across her face and down her neck, raising goose-pimples across her chest and arms.

Shaken, but *not* stirred, she replied, "Yes. See you tomorrow."

* * *

Having decided to make an enormous effort, Geri tugged her black lacy bra and a black lacy knickers from the depths of her knicker drawer. It looked like a set though it wasn't.

She reflected while showering how Tony had started to act decidedly awkward in class. She'd recently taken to watching Saliva and Mike flirting outrageously – how they always seemed to be laughing. By stark contrast Tony was the consummate bore. As awful as Saliva and Mike were, Geri never thought she'd see the day that she'd be slightly envious of them! Not that Saliva was anything but vocal regarding Geri's choice of man.

"'New Man, New Me' you told me you'd said!" Saliva continually chastised Geri for her relationship with the boring selfish Tony.

Despite trying to laugh it all off, appreciative of Saliva's concern but not so keen to act upon it, she felt more neglected now than she *ever* did with Kevin – at least she'd been ignorant of *his* complacency.

True to form Tony had "tooted" at eight. And they'd spent an unhealthy ten minutes in the car squabbling over where to go, then driving to Tony's choice of pub, in silence. So now, squatting on the wobbly wooden stool she was, despite her lacy underwear, finding it increasingly difficult to feel anything remotely similar to sensual. She felt almost dirty as she looked around at the swirly, velvet green wallpaper of the Lambeth Kitty pub, its smoky glass windows engraved with *Snug* and *Lounge*, the "night-in-an-ashtray" air-freshener and the pungent fumes of stale beer sodden into the carpet. She looked at the capped pensioners at the bar arguing over "the form" as usual, and when the barmaid – something *straight* out of *Heartbeat* – turned on the juke-box Geri had serious doubts as to whether she'd stepped into a time warp – was this *really* the twenty-first century?

"Right," she commanded, "come on. Let's go!"

"What?"

Only then she noticed Tony was actually tapping his foot to Cliff Richard's 'Summer Holiday', and, as everything seemed to go in slow motion, she noticed the barmaid's bleached beehive wobbling on her head to the rhythm.

"Come on. We're going back to my place. Now."

"Aw, come on!"

"Now. I've got a treat for you." She gave her best *Debbie-Does-Dallas* pout and stuck out her chest weakly.

Downing the remains of his frothy pint in one, Tony grabbed his coat, and skulked out behind her.

Back home, she poured Tony a whisky on ice – she wasn't sure what the appropriate drink was – and put some light music on while she went upstairs. She didn't know *what* she was going up *for* – just to calm her nerves really. She hadn't played seductress very often and felt a little rusty.

Meanwhile, as Tony stepped over the discarded toys that she hadn't time to clear up, he harumphed under his breath, "Kids – you can't beat 'em . . ."

Upstairs, like a teenager Geri giggled and skipped around her bedroom, as she nervously wondered whether she'd be able to complete the sexy task without collapsing into gales of laughter. As she haphazardly tidied her room and squirted perfume in obscure places she heard the stereo outlandishly loud downstairs. Recognising the *Gipsy Kings* as they sang "Sin Ella" she looked at her watch, amazed. *It's nearly eleven o' clock – what the hell is he doing?* She trotted down the stairs, irritated at his abuse of her favourite CD since Sinead went to Spain. Geri and *The Gipsy Kings* had spent many an evening relaxing together as she pondered over the modest comparisons between her and Sinead's lifestyles.

She put her head around the lounge door, sticking on her most sheepish grin. "Em, could you turn it down a bit?"

He's playing my CD's on my CD player – at volume thirty-two! It's nearly eleven o' clock at night!

"Oh, do I have to?" he pouted, adopting the increasingly familiar sulky teenager stance again.

He's like something out of a Kevin & Perry video.

"Well," *I am still sheepish and he is definitely Kevin,* "Andy and Angela next door work shifts. They're probably asleep by now . . ."

Tony grunted and slid the volume down to twelve.

And it's still too loud. And I think he's probably more Perry.

Deciding to move the activities swiftly upstairs now for fear of losing the moment, she managed to drag him away from her ex-husband's dusty Pink Floyd LP's, enticing him up the stairs.

As they stood, facing each other in the half-lit room, she took a deep breath, and began to unbutton her jacket, revealing her *pièce de la résistance* – the lacy *La Perla*.

For the first time that night – or at least since "Summer Holiday" – Tony's eyes lit up. He grabbed her awkwardly, tugging her jacket off her arms and groping at her boobs through the lace. Roughly and inexpertly he then flopped her breasts over the delicate cups of her bra.

No! No! Hold it right *there . . . You're supposed to caress my collar bone and shoulders, kiss my neck, slide the straps down my arms sensually and then as you rub your hands up and down my back, masterfully unclip my bra. And then you're –*

Too late. Minutes later she lay beneath him, his moisture on her bare thighs, her knickers still resident around her knees, him breathing his beery breath into the side of her face, sweating. She hadn't even worked up a pulse, never mind an orgasm! She pushed him off, and he "eerrghed" as he rolled beside her.

OK, don't let it put you off, girl – you can still take control.

She jumped astride him, pinning his arms down playfully.

"Come on then. Let's go again. *Properly* this time."

"Already?" His voice was already sleepy. He wiggled beneath her, causing her to fall to the side, and turned his arse to her.

"Hey – Tony. What're you doing?"

He sat up in *her* bed and lit a cigarette. Blowing out the smoke he broke wind loosely, cocking his right cheek to aid its escape.

"Hey, did I tell you the joke I heard in the pub last night?"

"No, tell me now." She liked post-coital chit-chat. In the absence of a loving relationship or even a cuddle it was better than nothing.

"OK. How do you make your girlfriend cry during sex?"

"Dunno."

After what I've just experienced I suppose he has the full ability to make his girlfriend cry before, during and after sex.

"Ring her up and tell her! Ha, what d'you reckon?"

"Not a lot."

Then he started. Inhaling the cigarette deeply, and blowing smoke-rings up into her bedroom ceiling, Tony started on Geri about her weight,

"You know, ordinarily I like to be able to define between a bird's tits, stomach, hips, arse and legs. But Geri, it's sometimes a problem to do that with you."

I know I'm not perfect, but I'm worth more than this poxy parody!

And she wasn't getting electric shocks the way she did when Ben's arm brushed against hers, or how she tingled when he pulled her hair from within her jacket collar, or rubbed her feet at the end of a long day.

"On the contrary, you ignorant bastard," Geri had seen the light – finally – and the worm wasn't just turning, he was reversing at full speed down a four-laned motorway, squealing and whooping as the 100mph wind blew in his excited face. "I am *losing* weight, not putting it on. Not that you'd notice, you inch-dick, but I'm almost two stone lighter than I was four months ago, you cretin! Tony, you scruffy dirty bastard, you're just talking out of your arse! Piss off outta my home!"

* * *

Having soaked off all physical traces of him in the bath, she was now sitting wrapped tightly in her comfort dressing-gown, curled up in her armchair, left only with the mental disgust of him. Dunking her sixth Penguin into a mug of tea, she chastised herself for even attempting to seduce Tony.

What the hell was I thinking of? Sinead. I want to talk to Sinead. But how can I? Sinead still thinks I'm happily married to Kevin. She probably imagines me at this very minute trying for a third child with my committed husband!

Instead she'd just thrown Tony's clothes at him, screamed – (*Sod Andy and Angela!*) – screamed at him to leave, and laughed callously as he'd tripped over Cameron's mini-rocking-horse in the hallway.

I must admit though, I'm still shaking after he turned, finally finishing the sentence that he'd been trying to finish for weeks:

"Kids – you can't beat 'em . . . fuckin' pity!"

But really, I hadn't meant to kick him up the arse so hard! It was just a reflex action – I couldn't help it!

The melted chocolate from the Penguins swilling around her mouth, drowning her sorrows in liquid heaven she stared at her Spanish course-notes on the floor. She'd been trying for weeks to perfect her accent, much to Ben's glee. She just couldn't get it right, and he was so good at it. A small part of her wanted to practise the "th" and the "rr" right now, but she felt too low to be bothered. A stillness only evident in the middle of the night hummed around her and as she blinked she could actually hear her eyelids scraping across her eyes. She suspected they were swollen and red from her tiredness and tears.

More angry with myself than with Tony. I should have known better. Hey, join the club for low self-esteem, admission through the side door . . .

With a sigh she rested her head forward into her hands, rubbing her forehead despairingly, willing herself to be positive. A light tapping at the front door jerked her from her trance. Her heart quickened and she blushed deeply as she felt the adrenalin coursing through her body instantly. Her eyes automatically read the clock – twelve forty-one.

Who the hell would be at my door at this time of night?

She dimmed the lights in the lounge and tiptoed over to the curtain, pulling back the swag slightly.

It's Ben! What's he doing here at this time of night? Something must be wrong!

She shuffled to the front door, swaddled in her comfort-robe, traces of Penguin still decorating the edges of her mouth. No sooner was the door open than he was inside!

He's pissed. If I wasn't feeling so fragile I might even laugh – but not tonight. I've been through enough, and to cap it all I've got a bruised and swollen undercarriage thanks to Tony's incessant pounding!

"Heeeyyyy," Ben slurred, his handsome face slightly distorted due to over-consumption of alcohol.

"So, where have *you* been? Not to the gym, obviously." She turned her back promptly, attempting to appear as if nothing is awry.

"Nooo, the lads from work were invited to the first-night party of the new production at the Aldwych. Oh Geri, it was a right laugh!"

She stood back, watching him swagger and sway his way through to the lounge.

You know, when men are drunk they forget how they walked when they were sober.

She found humour in his stance, the way he lurched forward, his arms hanging at his side.

Following him in, she watched as he swung his head from side to side, then crouched on the floor and looked underneath the sofa,

"Hey! Where's Tony?"

"Gone."

As he stood up, the blood rushed from his face and he literally drained before her eyes.

"Gone? Gone where? Now, you little minx, what have you done with him?"

"Ben. Please. Not tonight. He's horrible. I don't want to talk about it."

But a man with too much drink in him isn't a man to reason with. He continued, regardless.

"Noo, but I told you, didn't I? He's a loser! What happened? Come on tell Dr Robbins. Come and sit on my knee, Nurse, and explain it all."

Geri wasn't in the mood to have the piss taken out of her twice in one night.

"Ben, please. I want to go to bed. Please. Go home, and I'll see you tomorrow."

"Ooh, do you know, you're lovely when you're a bit

cross." His eyes wandered across her comfort robe, pulled tightly around her.

"What you got on under that robey thing?" He sat down, swung his legs up onto the arm of the chair and slumped back, taking in the vision of her in her glory.

"What?" He'd never made any sexual innuendos before and it threw her off-guard a little.

"You heard. What you got on under that?" He poked his finger, pointing toward her as he said "that".

"Nothing. Why?"

"Ha. You went to bed with him again, didn't you?"

"Shuttup, Ben."

He's clearly enjoying this, not coherent enough to realise that I'm not!

He snuggled down into the chair further, his long legs extended to their fullest in her armchair and his shiny black boots jutting into her airspace.

"Do you know," he teased, "I could do a lovely drawing of you in that. If you sat over on the settee there. No, maybe kind of leaned down into it. And then opened that robe a little bit. I could do you as Kate Winslet in *Titanic*! You know that one where she takes it all off in front of the fire and Leonardo DiCacksoff pretends to draw her. You'd look *gorgeous*!"

"Bye, Ben." She walked past him, slapping his legs so that his feet fell to the floor with a thud.

"What?"

"Piss off, Ben. Night."

"You can't throw me out!"

"Watch me – I'm learning!"

She pushed and prodded and shuffled him to the front door, finally managing to shove him over the doorstep – a feat he couldn't protest against too strongly, being too drunk to put up much of a fight. "Night, Ben."

"Aahhh, you! *Me estás dando la lata! And* you're a liar!" His voice got louder as he seemed to get angrier. "Here you are stringing Tony along, *and* every other man you set your eyes on! You're not even woman enough to be honest with everyone! Never mind Kevin, how about coming clean about Lover Boy?"

Geri was confused at both his angle and his apparent anger. Surprised at the smallness of her voice, she asked, her breath making miniature clouds into the cold dark night, "Lover boy? Who is Lover Boy? What do you mean?"

"Don't give me that!" He was now very angry and began to turn quite nasty, "You could at least be decent enough to admit to it! At least to *me!*"

"What, Ben? What? Who is Lover Boy?"

"*Sinbad!*"

* * *

For the second time that night, Geri was left alone in the house, totally confused, emotionally wiped out and physically exhausted . . .

Chapter Twenty-three

Sinead sat at her desk in the open-plan office, in her Spanish equivalent of the power-suit. The knee-length suede skirt and black body hugged her figure in all the right places, and the matching jacket hung fluidly on the back of her chair. Her arms, now deeply bronzed, were relaxed, her hands resting on her lap as she read the paperwork on her desk intently. She heard the irritating titter of Charmaine rattle through the air. Her concentration lost, she squinted to peek through the gap in the screens behind her workstation. She was talking to Steven. Charmaine's wide grin and huge eyes danced as Steven leant across her desk, ominously close to her. Charmaine didn't even flinch. Sinead watched Steven, once so familiar, but now strangely remote, as he casually glanced down at his watch. Charmaine tittered in her chair, wriggling as if she had a fly in her knickers. Steven confidently stretched his arm across her, thrusting his watch in her face. She pouted.

"Charmaine," he drooled, "this is a state-of-the-art watch."

"Oh, lovely! So, what does it do then?"

"Well, it uses alpha waves to telepathically talk to me," he explained.

"Oh, so what's it telling you now?"

"It's telling me, you little tease you, that you aren't wearing any panties."

Charmaine tittered once again, threatening to self-combust any minute,

"Well, Steven, it must be broken then because I *am* wearing panties!"

"Shit!" Steven began tapping at the face of his very ordinary watch. "Damn thing must be an hour fast!"

His innuendo was lost on Charmaine. She proceeded to instruct him how to claim a refund for faulty goods. "Well, a watch like that can't have been cheap. It shouldn't be running fast already. When did you buy it?"

"Charmaine. Hellloo!" He lightly knocked on her head. "Anyone home? I was joking. Get it? Must be an hour fast – no panties?"

The peseta finally dropped.

"Oh, you cheeky bugger, you! Oh, Steven, I'm all in a flap now! Ohh!"

She gesticulated and fussed with herself.

Having seen enough, Sinead turned back to reading the work on her desk. Steven Randall and Charmaine were welcome to each other. She wasn't two paragraphs further when her telephone began to ring. Still preoccupied with her work, she slowly stretched out her slender arm to reach for it. Before she could speak, she heard Jonathon Morgan's voice.

"Sinead! Guess what!"

"What?" She continued to read, unfazed by his enthusiasm.

"I've booked my flight for *Las Fallas!*"

"Oh great!" Her face lit up. She was excited about seeing him again. He'd been a rock to her over the past few months and she was keen to put right all the wrongs from when he'd visited before.

"Staying at my place?" she volunteered.

"If that's OK. You don't mind, do you?"

"No. You haven't got any absurd, distasteful habits, have you?"

He laughed, "Not that I know of anyway."

"We'll see."

"You know, what's the weather like? I don't know what kind of stuff to bring with me?"

"It's warm. But pack a few light jumpers for the evenings. It can start to get a little chilly then when the heat goes out of the sun."

"Great! D'you know, I can't wait to get out of this godforsaken cold country. It's so cold in my flat at night that I've been tempted to piss on myself to keep warm!"

"Yuk, Jon!"

He laughed at her disgust. "Only joking! But I've

already started to buy some new clothes to bring with me."

She was amazed that he was going to the bother.

"Jon, don't go mad spending money – you're only coming for a few days."

"Yeah, but I just had to get some new boxers before I came. I can hardly prance around your place in my faded grey pants now, can I?"

She laughed at the mental picture of him prancing in stringy grey Y-fronts.

He continued, "But do you realise how *embarrassing* it is for men to buy underwear in a female-dominated shop? It's that handing your pants over on a plastic mini-hanger that does it!"

"Go on, you're not embarrassed by that, are you?"

"Too bloody right I am!"

"Crikey, if you're that bad, you'd better not be prancing around my apartment in them then. I'm not exactly renowned for being able to keep a straight face when confronted with hilarity."

He changed the subject, "And I bought new socks too."

"Socks! What you buying socks for? You're coming to Valencia not bloody Vauxhall!"

"I know, but I'm always conscious that my smeet might fell in my shoes."

"Your smeet might fell!" She roared at his mistake.

"I'm sounding paranoid, aren't I?"

Through her laughter she answered, "Yes!"

"I'm putting you off of me, aren't I?"

"Yes!" she chortled.

"Right. I'll leave it there then. Could you meet me at the airport on the fifth at eleven twenty-five?"

"Course."

"Right then. I'm going now before I put my foot in it further."

She still chuckled. "OK, I'll let you go before you open your fouth wider only to stick your moot in it!"

* * *

Before she'd left for her piano class Geri had desperately wanted to ring Sinead. She realised that she had no regrets at seeing Tony's hairy arse walking out of her gate, only feeling disgust that she actually "did it" with him. Only now was she beginning to recover, the feeling of soreness and bruising subsiding. The quandary she battled with now was the *Sinbad* thing. She'd give him some time to settle, then she'd decided she'd ring him tomorrow.

Sinbad? Sinbad-the-fucking sailor?

Well, it's taught me a lesson anyway. I won't be getting close to anyone any more. Just as I've got used to seeing him around, enjoying his company and security, he goes and does this to me. I miss the afternoons he spent at home with us, the short but frequent calls at irregular times of the day and night. Even the children seem to be missing him! As if it isn't bad enough that their father has walked out on them before they're even properly talking, now even Mummy's 'friend' won't be coming around!

She rang Sinead, but without the intimacy of being

able to confess to her marital abandonment, she was forced to chatter about the children and the housework, resigning herself to listening to Sinead's recount of *Las Fallas* and climatic conditions. She knew Sinead would be horrified by the news of Kevin's behaviour and would probably drop everything in order to ensure Geri and the boys were all right. Geri had no doubt that Sinead would *know* how she felt about the situation and, without words, would tune in to her worries and concerns.

Saliva and Cloud-eeeahhh, however, had an extremely different perception of it all and voiced it loudly as Cloud-eeahhh met Geri outside the piano class ready to whisk her off to the gruelling aerobics.

"I've said before, dahhlink," drawled Claudia, "time is a great healer, but it's also a lousy beautician."

"Yeaah," agreed Sylvia, "you wanna get yourself annuver bloke, and sharpish."

"But, Seeelveeaahh, she mahst take control of her life, her bodty, her mindt!"

"Naww, gerraway wiv all that! Tell you what you need, gal – a good ould seeing-to!"

"Budt she mahst stop havingk sex weeth Tony!"

"Yeah, I'll make you right there, Clordya!"

Cloud-eeahhh winced.

Geri felt like a spectator at Wimbledon as she looked from Sylvia to Claudia to Sylvia . . . . And this advice coming from the viewpoint of two mature ladies who'd had more men than Lean Cuisines.

Cloud-eeahhh continued, "Do you know I saw a

voman in Tesco todtay weeth a full-grown moustache!"

Saliva collapsed into hysterical laughter.

"Seriously, she looked like Tom-Fuckeeng-Selleck – honest to Godt!"

As the three women stood in the gaudily painted corridors outside the empty classroom, Sylvia dressed in an obscenely short leather skirt and cheap sandals, Claudia decked head to toe in Nicole Farhi and Geri covered humbly courtesy of Hennes and C&A, they laughed together, their social status immaterial.

"I tell you, haf you ever thought aboudt eyelash permingk?"

Both Geri and Sylvia were astounded.

"I *swear* by it, darlingks! Only half an hour and you haf eyelashes like two fans! Andt all for only fifty queed! It's a fuckeeng godsend!"

Geri mentally rolled her eyes to the heavens. At this rate she'd be better off asking advice from Quick Draw McGraw, who'd already coined her own quote of, "Geri – believe your beliefs and doubt your doubts."

* * *

By way of convalescence Sinead had thrown herself into the Spanish culture surrounding her. She'd spent most of her spare time recently visiting more of the Valencian tourist attractions. With only a few days until Jonathon arrived, she'd decided to take a break from work, with the idea of seeking out some nice places to take him to during his short stay. He would be, she was shocked to realise, her first visitor from home.

One of the main attractions was the *Mercado Central*, with its modernist architecture, where she found all kinds of fresh Mediterranean food. She visited the Ceramics Museum, the *Gonzalez Marti*, which displayed the typical Valencian colours of blue, green and orange, and viewed the water jugs, vases, basins and jars, decorated with floral patterns, birds and animals. The colours were intensified as they were dotted against the backdrop of whitewashed walls. The simplicity of the lacy shadow of an olive tree cast onto a white-washed bungalow, its smoky blue door and window frames punctuating it, was reproduced endlessly on the many postcards depicting the area.

It took Sinead around twenty minutes to cross the old town on foot, and en route she really soaked in, for the first time, the beauty of the large terracotta square tiles, the most widespread form of residential external flooring. The mosaic or floral patterns of the ceramic tiles decorating the stairs leading to front doors and porches, whilst very different in design, were almost identical in colour. As she meandered along, she gazed up at the late nineteenth-century apartment blocks, now able to recognise the strong Baroque influence: they were adorned with ornate balconies, balustrades, scale-like shutters and long windows, the glass reflecting as lilac from the blue skies above.

Another day she'd visited the Palace of the *Marqués de Dos Aguas*, with its extravagant theatrical decorative effects. She stood before the portal, carved from alabaster, and spent a good ten minutes just gazing at it. It was flanked by two smoothly carved naked slaves, both male, standing on jars and spilling water signifying the two rivers – *dos aguas*. Above the door stood a Madonna and child surrounded by angels and streams of light. As she scrutinised the sculpture she was intrigued by the great detail in the slaves' muscle tone, their hands, feet and even the textiles, but the surprisingly minimal detail on their faces. It took her breath away – it was awesome. She stepped toward the ornate door which led her, in contrast to the bright sun on the alabaster frontage, into a black shadowed porch with dark carved ironwork inside.

During her meanderings, she admired the exquisite hand-painted fans – or *abanicos* – with ribs made of ivory, exotic wood and other material from the small workshops in Valencia and Aldaya. She breathed in the atmosphere as she sat outside the open-air bars on *Canovas Square* and the romantic dance halls with stage performances around *La Malvarrosa*. Everywhere, there were barbecues and glamorous little restaurants, discotheques, night-clubs, cafés-cum-theatres, flamenco shows and cabarets. The one place she'd decided to wait for Jonathon's arrival to visit was the *Casino Monte Picayo*.

On the Saturday she'd done the real 'tourist' thing and enjoyed the Aquapark. It had truly been a week of relaxation, as she'd recharged her batteries and felt rejuvenated. She had honestly enjoyed her own company for the first time – in *years*.

* * *

To complete her self-esteem-boosting week Sinead was

thrilled when Geri rang her on the Monday evening. Geri had been both captivated and envious as Sinead verbally animated her week of cultural enlightenment, pushing to the back of her mind the torment she felt about the one-sided argument with Ben. At least she *thought* it was an argument, only it seemed rather strange with only *him* squawking and shouting, and her gobsmacked and shocked on the doorstep.

As Sinead described in unnecessary detail the Valencian paella she'd had earlier that afternoon, Geri couldn't help but once again mentally compare their lives, as she'd spent most of the afternoon clearing up Reece's odorous nappies and contending with Cameron who was beginning to seek the independence of wiping his own bottom.

Really, the Andrex puppy has nothing on him!

Geri asked her, wondering why she wasn't mentioning the male of the species in this week of exploration, "Why were you off work? What's happened? Did you get the week off sick?"

"No. It's quite hard to get signed off sick. The last time I was off sick they sent Charmaine round to see how I was!"

"You're lucky. At least *someone's* worrying about you."

"Don't count on it! If it wasn't for you, me mam and Jonathon I don't think anyone would really give a shit!"

"Jonathon? Who's *Jonathon?*"

Geri appreciated the opportunity to tease Sinead for once.

She replied, her voice indicative of her wide relaxed grin, "Oh he's my counterpart in England. You know, I told you about him before. He came over for a fortnight's work just when I'd started to get serious with Steven . . ." her voice trailed off, realising what she'd just gotten into.

"Steven? So you're definitely *not* with him any more then?"

"No."

"Why not? He sounded lovely, Sinead. And didn't you have some good laughs with him? Oh, come on, you're always on to me to divulge my sexy secrets! Now let's hear some of yours."

Sinead cringed with every word Geri spoke, desperate to end the conversation. She even viewed the telephone handpiece conspiratorially as she decided whether to hang up, pretending that the lines to England were very problematic at the moment.

Out of the blue came a sliver of humour, and Sinead hung on to that one small piece, it being her lifeline, "Hey, do you know what I did yesterday? A *real*, embarrassing indication that I've passed the thirty mark?" Sinead knew it was a subject close to Gertie's heart and that she wouldn't query the change of subject.

"What?" She couldn't wait to hear.

"I was actually excited when I got to the Aquapark that there were parking facilities! And that they were free! Talk about a bloody tight-wad! Now if I was in my twenties that wouldn't have bothered me! What's happened to me?"

Geri laughed, familiar with the sentiment. "Well, how about this one? I don't get funny looks any more when I'm shopping alone and buying Walt Disney videos – the shop assistants always assume they're for my children! Do you remember how we used to be in love with those Farley's Rusks and –"

"And we used to buy them on the way home from school and eat them!"

"Yeah, *and* we used to buy them after work and sit on the bus eating them! I suppose we looked young then. I tell you what, we don't now."

"Speak for yourself, wrinkly!"

"Hey, you'll be the wrinkly one, out in all that sunshine."

"Ha! Think again. I'm 'factor forty-five queen' me. And as well as my new-found bi-lingual skills, I'm as bronzed and beautiful as one of the locals. Anyway, how about this one? I was actually sitting outside an open-air café last night, and found myself *envious* at their hanging baskets and flower arrangements. And then – even worse – started to be curious as to the names of the bloody flowers!"

"Christ, that's bad. You really do sound like your mother!"

"Never!"

Geri laughed at Sinead's vehement reaction. "You do!"

"I don't! Shuttup!"

"Well, I've got one. I actually found myself saying to Cameron the other day – we were watching *The Tweenies* –"

"The whaties?"

"*The Tweenies*. It's a children's programmy-thing – I actually *said* the words, *"They don't make them like they used to!"*"

"No! You didn't!"

"I did! And it gets worse. I then said, *"I remember when there were only three channels – BBC1, BBC2 and ITV!"*"

"God, we're getting ancient! And I used to think Mam was talking about hundreds of years ago when she used to say how in her day they never *had* a television!"

"I know."

"Hey, I think we've just come across the replacement to our WaWaYeRB game!"

"What is it?"

"Em, I think we'll call it Hiddykit."

"Hiddykit! What's that supposed to mean then?"

"It's my elongation of the initials HDYKYT."

"Yeah, so?"

"How Do You Know You're Thirty?"

They laughed raucously, delighted at their new invention.

"Well, I tell you what," said Geri, "I was *really* depressed at the prospect of turning thirty, but now, a few months down the line, it's not proving to be quite as bad as I'd anticipated."

"No, me neither. Still, I'd like to be a little more settled."

"Would you? God, I'm so envious of your life, Sinead!"

Sinead snorted. "Don't be. It's not all it's cracked up to be."

"Well, if only my clothes were getting baggy as quickly as my bloody eyelids I'd be halfway pleased! And the only Aromatherapy I experience is loaded nappies!"

"It can't be that bad. You've got a lovely life. You're the cliché of the traditional family. You're very lucky, you know, Gertie."

Geri knew different, but just couldn't find the words. She deftly changed the subject again, "So tell me, what're the bad bits about living in Spain?"

"The slow postal system, the cockroaches and the humidity – especially at night, it can be unbearable! It's that sticky warm heat that you can feel almost boiling your insides. Without air conditioning, you're like the rabbit in *Fatal Attraction!*"

"I can't wait to come out and see you. Do you think it'll be too hot for the boys?"

"No. But hey, *hay más días que langanizas!*"

"What's *that* supposed to mean, show-off?"

"There's plenty of time, of course." Sinead enjoyed flaunting her Spanish. She continued, "You could come over here and *a cuerpo de rey*."

"Yeah . . . go on . . . "

"Live like a king!"

"I doubt it. Although I still think there's plenty of Spanish nudist beaches for me to sample!"

"Hey, you're just *la jevez, viruelas* – before you ask, that's an old person behaving like a youngster!"

"Don't push it now!"

They both laughed, each of them feeling a little brighter, thanks to each other's company.

Chapter Twenty-four

Geri sat, yearning for warmer climes, enthralling her mum with Sinead's Mediterranean adventures. Ever since the trip to Boulogne Cynthia had been leafing through coach-holiday brochures boasting on-board mini-bars, on-board toilet facilities, tea and coffee machines, air conditioning and reclining chairs. It seemed she'd now realised that the world was only as far away as the bus station. She'd also taken to dabbling with her linguistic talents. Every time Geri paused for breath, she nodded patronisingly and whispered "Si".

Bloody crackpot! Why couldn't I have one of those mums who like to share your clothes and give you hints and tips on make-up and soufflés? One of the mums that seem to be forever screeching about on Jerry Springer? No, not the ones who come on stage decked in fishnet and leather, but the sophisticated fifty-somethings whom the audience and the camera warm to instantly.

Geri was just in the middle of explaining about *Las Fallas* when the phone rang. She paid little attention to it, expecting it to be a salesperson, reading from a customer services sheet, as he tried to sell her double-glazing.

Cynthia pulled a bag of sweets out for the boys and they rushed to her, excitedly. Geri mentally rolled her eyes heavenward – more sugar – as she answered the phone.

"Hello?"

"I'm sorry."

Startled by the male voice, for a split second Geri couldn't figure who it was. Kevin? Tony? Ben? Her mind raced as she tried to put a face to the voice.

Before she could manage to, he spoke again. "Are you still there?"

Casual tone.

"'Course."

Who is it?

"My favourite nurse, and I've been so rude to you."

It's Ben. I'm delighted. Out of the three possible choices, Ben was the only one that I wanted desperately.

"Hi. Have you recovered?"

I'm still trying to sound breezy. "What do you think?"

"Yes," he sounded weary, "I'm *so* sorry, Geri. What must you think of me?"

"Do you really want to know?"

"No. Thanks. Just let my imagination run riot."

"Ben, what *was* wrong with you? I know you'd had a few too many, but I've never seen you so angry before?"

"Sorry, I was a bit drunk."

"I know that! What I don't know is why you turned so bloody nasty!"

She stretched the coiled telephone lead around the doorframe so that she could speak to Ben in relative privacy, as she could see the back of her mum's head as she leant toward her, pretending to be reading a magazine, but ear-wigging for all it was worth.

"Geri, I don't really remember much. I do remember you looked lovely in your dressing-gown though."

He's trying to win me round! How can anyone think I look lovely in my comfort-robe! It's huge, hideous and hairy!

"My comfort-robe, actually."

"Oh. You were comforting yourself, were you?"

"Yes, I was actually. I presume you can't remember that I told you I'd thrown Tony out."

"I remember bits. That's all."

He has no tone to his voice – it's almost deathly.

"Look, what's wrong?" she said. "Have I done something to upset you?"

I really hope I haven't. I'd hate to think after becoming such good friends with him, that I've blown it – again! Seems to be the story of my life. His silence in response to my question indicates that I, in fact, have done something to upset him. What?

"Ben. Look I'd rather you tell me. I can hardly apologise or put it right until I know, can I?"

Still, I can only hear his heavy breathing at the other end of the line. It's quite bloody sexy actually. I can feel my heartbeat quickening.

"Ben? Look, tell me – I'm useless at taking hints!"

"I need to talk to you."

"Yeah. I think you do."

Ohmigod!

"What are you doing tonight?"

"No, sorry, can't –"

"Saturday then?"

"OK. What have you in mind?"

"I think dinner's the best thing really. But I do seriously need to talk to you."

"I know you do."

Silence again.

"And . . . is there any chance you can tell me what *dando la lata* or whatever it was you said, means?"

"Yes."

"Well?"

"I'll tell you Saturday night. At the restaurant."

"*And* who the bloody hell you think Lover Boy is?"

"*Sin*bad." He sounded exasperated.

"Yeah. Who *is* Sinbad? I don't know anyone called Sinbad."

"Liar."

"Look, we'll talk at the weekend. Are you picking me up or shall I meet you there?"

"Don't be like that. You *know* I'll pick you up. Eight OK?"

"Fine."

"Fine."

As she walked back into the room to replace the receiver Cynthia was gaping, wide-eyed, at her in anticipation.

"Well?" she asked.

Geri couldn't be bothered with the lengthy explanation. It would mean telling her about Tony and everything else too. She opted for the easy route.

"Oh, nothing. Ben's got a few problems – we're going out on Saturday night to talk about them."

Cynthia 'Les Dawsoned' at Geri, pushing up the boob with her crossed forearm and virtually gurning.

"Nice boy, that Benjamin."

"Mum!"

"Right, right, sorry."

She grabbed some insert to the magazine she was reading and Geri was despairing to see that it was another gadgetry catalogue. She sat on the arm of Geri's chair and opened the pages excitedly.

"Look here! I've just *got* to order these."

Geri feigned interest, by way of changing the subject, as Cynthia delighted in showing her the large plastic paper-clip-like invention that you shoved between your nostrils to prevent snoring.

"And *this* one is a definite purchase!"

She pointed to the Swiss Army knife of garden gadgetry. It looked, to a proud amateur like Geri, like a pair of oversized hedge clippers, concealing in its handles a fold-out mini-spade, shovel, fork, hoe and weeder. She was ecstatic that it's 'only' £49.95!

"Mum –" *I'm sorry, I just* have *to say something* – "Mum, you don't even like gardening!"

"I know, I know, but that's all set to change, Geri. And with *this* fantastic piece of equipment who could go wrong? You know what I say about gardening, Geri!"

I don't actually. She always hated anything remotely to do with mud, soil or shrubbery, so I'm interested to hear this new angle.

"I say it's never too late to get green-fingered."

Mmm, makes a change from light-fingered!

"Pull up those weeds, get turning that soil, and start planting. Not a more rewarding hobby going. So, Geri, I'm going to weed 'em and reap!"

* * *

Courtesy of Four-foot, Five-foot, along with the repetitive encouragement of Saliva, Mike and Rupert, Geri had memorised those punchy little ditties that help you to read music.

As they sat in the classroom she gazed out of the window, preoccupied, still chanting along with the others,

"Every Good Boy Does Fine Always – E-G-B-D-F-A"

"Right," boomed Four-foot.

She looked back at him.

He's standing on his left leg.

"I know you know how the spaces in treble clef spell F-A-C-E, so we'll move onto the lines of the bass clef." Moronically, they kicked into action, Geri's mind anticipating her night out with Ben.

"Great Big Dreams For America – G-B-D-F-A."

"And the spaces?"

"All Cows Eat Grass – A-C-E-G."

Despite motherhood depriving Geri of substantial amounts of sleep, she found it simple to remember these rhymes – they were engrained into her memory now, enabling her to recite them unthinkingly as she dreamt about Ben. As the summer months loomed ominously near, her time in "Piano" marked, she now recognised 3/4 as a time signature, and no longer a fraction. She was easily familiar with the term *adagio*, and could reel off the formula dictating that where a Quaver used to be a Walker's cheesy snack, it now meant two semi-quavers, a crotchet stood for four semi-quavers, a minim – eight semis, and a semibreve – now this was getting complicated – sixteen semi-quavers *or* four crotchets!

"Great!" boomed Five-foot.

Right leg this time.

"Now for your homework."

The room was filled with the rustling of papers being shimmied out of the confines of briefcases and, for the likes of Rupert, carrier bags.

"Who wants to kick off?"

Rupert put his hand up. Not only his hand, but his arm and shoulder too, risking the possible de-eyeballing of Mike due to his ribs sticking out so sharply beneath his light spring-coloured pastel tank top.

"OK, Rupert. What films did you find that used classical music?"

Rupert squeaked. Every time he opened his mouth, his high-pitched voice and foul-smelling breath made virtually everyone grimace. He continued, either oblivious or accepting of his physical handicap, *"The Titanic."* His voice was a pompous monotone. Four-foot, Five-foot was almost orgasmic with delight.

"Well *done*, Rupert! Well done!" Clasping his hands together, he surveyed the room for the next volunteer. After Rupert's performance there was unlikely to be any. Asserting his authority he focused on Joan, who was sitting grim-faced and tight-lipped.

"Joan, did you find any films?"

"Yes, I did! I found *Anna Karenina*, which has *Piano Sonata Number Two*, by Rachmaninov, and the film *Babe*, which has Tchaikovsky's *Swan Lake.*"

Geri enjoyed listening to the class's findings – it amazing her how some of the films didn't seem to match the people choosing them. For example, she would have put money on Mike coming up with *GI Jane*, featuring Mozart's *Adagio and Fugue*, purely for the Demi Moore connection, but would never have thought he'd have mentioned *Eine Kleine Nachtmusik* from the same film. She chuckled to herself as Sylvia, ever the romantic, chose *The Prince of Tides' Symphony Number 104* by Haydn and cringed as Tony stood up to reel off his feeble attempt with Orff's *Carmina Burana* in the film *The Doors*, it being only apparent at the beginning. But the real icing on the cake was when Joan-of-Nark stood up again to declare that she'd noticed Bizet's *'Habanera'*, from *Carmen* in the film *Trainspotting*!

"Well. Brilliant work, everyone," Four-foot boomed, clapping his hands together and limping across the room to the front. "It seems the left side of the class managed to choose a wider variety of pieces, but still, well done all."

Four-foot, Five-foot had turned to the blackboard, scribing the homework instructions for the week.

Mike leant in toward Geri, pushing his chunky shoulder onto hers, making it feel decidedly slender. He whispered hoarsely in her ear, "Don't worry, gal. The class is always keener on the 'uvver side!"

* * *

Geri felt an uncomfortable feeling of excitement at seeing Ben, anticipating another enthralling night like the 'date' they'd had, but still, nervous as to what she could have possibly done to upset him. With every second to countdown she'd agonised as to what she'd wear. It was that stupid situation where you know that they've seen you looking your worst – *heck, he's even seen me in the comfort-robe* – but still you want to make an impression, hoping they'll notice that you've lost another three pounds and chosen a new colour lipstick. Not sure how to pitch her outfit, wanting a comfortable mix between casual but smart, and serious but not austere, she finally decided on her new white linen shirt, black bootlegs and denim jacket.

When Ben knocked on her front door at exactly eight o' clock that night, he rolled his eyes and quietly wolf-whistled at her.

"You look great, Geri," he said, his eyes roaming from her toes to her neck and then down again.

Slightly uncomfortable with the compliment – *even at thirty I still can't quite manage to take a compliment graciously* – she grabbed her bag boyishly and retorted, "Thanks. But you said that about my comfort-robe!"

The polluted Elephant & Castle air was permeated with their laughter as she closed the front door behind them.

Two hours later they sat, virtually nose-to-nose, as Geri completed the hideous tale of Tony. It was obvious to her that Ben was digusted by Tony's antics, but not as much as when she then went on to recount his selfish opinions regarding her weight.

"Geri! I can't believe you let him talk to you like that!"

"I didn't! I threw him out, remember?"

"Do you realise, that there are three billion women who don't look like supermodels and only a few hundred who do! Don't let his ignorance upset you, Geri. You've lost a lot of weight. You're looking great."

Her nerve endings sparked as he unexpectedly reached out and clasped her hand tightly, his dark sexy eyes smiling at her across the candlelit table, his tanned, downy hand caressing hers.

Then she noticed a sadness sweep across them as he loosened his grip on her.

"What's wrong?" she asked, concerned at his sudden change of heart, secretly panicking that he'd noticed the fine hair on her upper lip or the spot forming riotously on her chin.

Composing himself once again, his voice was a mere

whisper to its former tones. "Chanelle was one of the most paranoid women I've ever known. She was beautiful, slim and stylish –"

Cheers, make me feel better, why don't you?

"But she only ever cared about herself. Her constant need for compliments and reassurance was draining and emotionally taxing. She had more modelling assignments coming in by the week, but still, she saw herself as the ugly duckling that she said she'd been at fourteen."

"Lucky bitch! I still see myself as the ugly duckling I was at twenty-nine!"

Her stab at humour was lost on Ben.

"That's what I like about you, Geri. You're so confident and at ease with yourself. You've got a great sense of humour. Nothing fazes you."

Can you see my eyebrows raised in amazement? Look closer, can you see?

"The unfortunate thing is, Geri, that men really need women."

I'm interested. I'm interested. Carry on.

"They help us to replace our bad habits with nicer ones."

"Like what, for instance?"

I know I'm pushing it but you don't get the opportunity for such candidness often, at least not from the species themselves!

He obliged. "Like kindness, patience and dental flossing!"

"No, no. The bad habits. What are the bad habits?"

"Oh," he seemed uninterested now, "like saying we're popping out for a quick pint, and staggering in four hours later with lager breath and a kebab. Like letting down our mates at the last minute. Like never cleaning the bath out afterwards." He seemed to suddenly come back to life, "Like treating women like shit, like having selfish sex."

Geri blushed. She knew what he was getting at. Tony.

"You were so wrong to put up with it."

"I know." *God, I feel awful now.* "But I think after Kevin going like he did, I kind of thought I had to put up with *some* kind of crap. I mean, at thirty, everyone's got baggage, haven't they?"

"Yeah!"

God, he's angry again now,

"But baggage doesn't mean self-centredness and ignorance!"

"I know, I know. Look, if it's any bonus, I *have* learnt my lesson. My self-esteem's right back up there again now. Do you know, I'd rather be alone now than with a man who didn't treat me right. And it took both Kevin *and* Tony to make me realise that."

"Mmm, so some good's come out of it then, anyway."

I'm glad now. At least I've made a positive note of the whole disaster. It doesn't sit so badly with me now. I'm not such a shallow failure.

The waiter came over to the table and, to Geri's surprise, Ben ordered another bottle of Chianti. Already smattered with alcohol rash across her chest and neck, and her knees beginning to feel decidedly jelly-like, she suspected that she'd probably had just about enough to drink. That's if she was going to keep her wits about her.

Ben, on a roll now, emptied his half-full (or half-empty) glass, swallowed, and rested his elbow on the table.

"You know, you're a fantastic mum, Geri."

The Chianti must be affecting his judgement as well.

"You devote all of your time to those boys. And before you think it, that's not the only reason I have such strong feelings for you."

Oh God, he has strong feelings for me!!

"Well, as far as Kevin's concerned, looking back on it now he was never really the fatherly type. And the boys haven't seen him for months! Out of sight and out of mind all right!"

"But surely he was *pleased* when you became pregnant?"

"Yeah, kind of. But I always remember when I declared a remote interest in a water-birth."

"What happened?"

"He'd laughed at me and said, 'Water-birth! Fuckit, Geri, you can barely fit *in* the bath without room for your splayed legs, the midwife's forearms *and* a baby!'"

"Mean bastard! What did you say to that?"

"Well, I was pissed off really. I think I said something about only having a *remote* interest and thanking him for his support!"

"Well," Ben raised his glass, "bums up!"

"Bums up!"

They clinked their glasses and grinned at each other.

* * *

Geri hadn't been into Ben's place much. She still felt that awkward middle-ground of knowing where things were located, but not familiar enough to make use of them. Ben had shouted at her to put the kettle on, as she heard him pissing from a height in his toilet. She poked around the kitchen stealthily, opening the fridge door. The interior light shone off the numerous tins of beers and tomatoes. She lifted out the small bit of milk remaining in the carton, sniffing it to check. You could never tell with men. His place bore all the hallmarks of a bachelor pad: the beers in the fridge, the abundance of hi-fi equipment and accessories and the over-full bin, stuffed to the brim with ready-meal cartons and empty crisp packets. She couldn't help but think of how she could wave her magic wand and inject a little of the woman's touch. She'd have diet Coke and nail varnish in the fridge, All-Bran in the cupboard and cotton-wool balls in the bathroom. The roar of the kettle approaching boiling point muffled the sounds of his footsteps padding behind her on the wooden kitchen floor. She gasped for breath as she felt his strong hands grab her waist and spin her round to face him. Still composing herself, strands of hair flicked across her face, and stuck to her eyelashes, she raised a hand to brush them away. He got there before her. As his eyes met hers, his firm but gentle grasp around her waist pulling her in toward him securely, she could feel his hot breath on her face.

Ohmigod – he's going to kiss me! He's going to kiss . . . .

He just kissed me. Wowee, I'm a little light-headed. Excuse me if I pass out!

"Geri?"

I can't speak. My tongue has turned to marshmallow. It's obviously OK, cos he's carrying on regardless.

"Geri! You must be honest with me."

I nod, like an idiot. Unable to do anything else.

"Come with me."

Not the bedroom, no! I'm wearing my greying knickers with the small peg-induced holes around the bum cheek area, and my bikini line's not fit for exposure. Help!

Ben led her to the settee, where he gently guided her to sit next to him. He took both of her hands in his and, facing her, asked slowly and very seriously, "Please. Now, be honest with me?"

"I will, Ben. What's the question? You're making me nervous."

"Sorry. I don't mean to. But I feel very strongly that you must tell me the truth."

"I always do, Ben. Now what the hell is wrong?"

"Geri? Forget Tony. Are you seeing anyone else?"

"No."

"Are you sure?"

"'Course I'm sure. I'd know, wouldn't I?"

He looks unconvinced. She probes a little more, wondering where he'd got the idea from. She was more than a little confused.

"Ben? What gives you the idea that I'm seeing *anyone*?"

411

"I don't mean to be nosy, but whenever I'm around your place you've got notes all over the place about Sinbad."

"*Sinbad!*" she screeched, not believing his refusal to let go of this.

"You said you wouldn't lie."

"You mentioned this on the phone the other night. This Sinbad is supposed to be 'Lover Boy', isn't he?"

"Yep. So, who is he?"

Geri began to giggle, purely due to nerves – she really didn't have a clue what Ben was talking about. Her tittering proved only to annoy him, so she strained the corners of her mouth into a more linear position as she concentrated, trying to make some sense out of this farce.

"Where did you see these "love" notes?"

"Well, on the worktop, and on your calendar in the kitchen for starters."

"Is it my writing?"

"Yes."

"What did the note say?" The penny still hadn't dropped. She'd never connected the two names, despite the minimal spelling difference.

"It said something like, "Must ring Sinbad. Love lots"."

Geri began to giggle, but her giggle soon became an out-of-control roar of laughter. She tried to get her words out, but sight of the confused Ben staring at her open guffawing mouth only made her laugh even more.

"Sinead! It's Sinead! Not Sinbad! I wrote it in capital letters, didn't I?"

He nodded, confused at what point she was trying to make.

"You must have read my capital E for a B! You dick!"

Guess who feels sheepish now . . .

Chapter Twenty-five

Despite Geri's hilarity and gargoyle-like expressions as she'd snorted and hooted at Ben's misunderstanding of the Sinbad thing, he still did the predestined thing.

He kissed her. Again.

And again and again.

Stopped dead in her tracks (*it not being very easy to cackle with laughter when a perfectly formed pair of lips is being pushed against yours*), she tingled as she felt his square and slightly stubbly jaw grazing against her face, his mouth licking and caressing hers.

But this is Ben. Ben! OK, I know I've been mad about him for ages, but he's not supposed to feel the same way! They never do! It's a known fact that the ones you fancy never reciprocate! What's going on? Who's changed the rules? Still, in for a penny . . .

After an initial freezing period (*about three seconds*) where she'd perched on the edge of his settee, her mind racing madly to keep up with the sequence of events, she soon melted into his firm hold. He'd expertly, yet gently, shimmied her back on the leather settee until she was resting against the soft cushions, whilst continuously nibbling and passionately moving his mouth on hers. She couldn't quite grasp what was happening. Was he drunk? She half expected the gormless face of Jeremy Beadle to spring from behind Ben's spotlit easel which stood, seeing all but saying nothing, in the corner of the room. What seemed like hours later, Ben finally came up for air, leaving Geri collapsed into the sofa, her hair bedraggled and her mouth and chin red. She blinked three or four times, trying to refocus on everything further than two inches away from her eyeballs. He smelt gorgeous, and she reached to him, grabbing him by the forearms, pulling him back down on top of her, surprisingly overwhelmed by the passion she'd signed off as dormant. As he nuzzled into the side of her neck she breathed his scent in deeply. She couldn't identify the fragrance, supposing it was one of the modern ones. She'd have been an expert on Yardley's Gold, or Kouros, even, those being the ones she'd bought year-in year-out for Kevin.

Kevin? Who the hell's Kevin?

Ben leaned up on his elbows, smoothing her scruffed hair away from her face.

"God," he moaned, it sounding as if it had originated straight from his groin. "I – think – I – love – you."

Red alert, red alert!! Sirens squealing, lights flashing, emergency services screaming to the scene of the crime! He said the "L" word, he said the "L" word! Sure! Now we're definitely doomed. Everyone knows that as soon as you mention the "L" word you may as well draw a line under the whole thing, and start again! Everybody knows that!

I look up into his handsome face, his warm eyes and relaxed expression and don't recognise the beefcake I'd seen on that first hideous trip to the gym. I can now see what I think Ben wants people to see. Not the exterior (although it's pretty damn gorgeous!) but his character, his affection and yes – even his failings. Ben. I look into his eyes and I see Ben. Shit, I think I'm in love. But even more, shit, he's just told me he's in love with me!

Unlike Tony, or Adam, or any of them before now, he doesn't move his hands any further south than my shoulders.

"Geri."

Hey, my voice has even got deeper in the wild panic that's spinning around my head!

"Geri."

Oops. It's Ben's voice – not mine. Sorry for the confusion.

"Spend the night with me."

Oh My God! I expect my voice to come out a squeak, but it doesn't let me down. Not yet anyway.

"Ben. Don't rush me. Not after the Tony thing."

He smiled at her, caressing her face and neck and, saying nothing, places his full mouth on hers once again. Five minutes later he responded verbally.

"Whenever you're ready. I'll wait for you, Geri."

As I look up into his warm, delightful face, I just know that he won't be waiting long. Post-Tony, however, my sexual confidence doesn't lead me to think that the best things come to those that wait. Whatever will Ben think of me in bed? It's a strange combination of undiluted lust, but nervous pre-coital butterflies.

"I'm sorry, Ben. I really feel a lot for you."

"Don't worry about it. It's OK. Really."

"Ben?"

"Mmmm."

"Can I ask you something?"

He's nuzzling into my neck again!

"Mmmm."

"Can you get off me so I can go to the toilet?"

He reluctantly sat up, squeezing her bum as she stood and smoothed her clothes.

The linen shirt's virtually in tatters – looks like a tie-dye.

She came back into the room to see him lounging in his armchair, listening to his Craig David CD and singing quietly.

God, he's gorgeous.

"Ben," she whispered, "I really must go. You know. I've got to pick the boys up early in the morning, and that."

He leapt to his feet, smiling.

He's so understanding!

"Ah, I was going to ask you about that?"

"What?"

"Is there any chance you could ring your mum in the morning and ask her to have them for the whole day?"

"Ben. I'm *not* staying tonight."

"No, no. Not for that reason. Do you think she'd keep them there until about six?"

"Dunno. Why?"

"I want to take you somewhere."

"Where?"

"To our special place."

She couldn't believe what she was hearing? 'Their' special place? The only place they'd really been together was on the pretend date and the gym.

"What do you mean? Where?"

"Look. It's a bit of a mystery. But Geri, you'll love it. Believe me."

In typical female style the first problem Geri could foresee had absolutely nothing to do with her children, her financial situation, what the weather forecast was for the next day or even which mode of transport they were going to use. It was her clothes!

"What should I wear?"

Ben laughed at her classic reaction and replied, "Something comfortable. Put it this way, don't get too *over-dressed*."

"God, Ben! What does *that* mean?"

"Look. I'll leave it like that for now. Hold on a minute – I'll get my jacket and walk you home.

"You don't have to do that. It's only up the road a bit."

"I do. Just wait . . . I'm ready now."

As they walked hand-in-hand in the cold early-morning air, the street lit only by the orange streetlights and the occasional passing car, the sounds of their shoes on the pavement were the only percussion to their conversation. As they reached Geri's house, he stepped in over the doorstep only to melt her with another lengthy and passionate kiss and to remind her that he'd ring at nine in the morning to see if she could go with him.

Having closed the door and literally floated up the stairs, she sank into her bed, contented , relaxed and on cloud ninety-nine . . .

* * *

Ben was home again within minutes, jogging at triple speed. The music was still mumbling in his toasty-warm lounge as he slid his arms from his jacket and threw it onto the back of the chair. He didn't bother switching on the kitchen light as he went in and opened the fridge door, taking out a cold can of beer and cracking open the ring pull. Holding the frothy liquid to his mouth he gulped down a good five or six swallows before "aahing" and sweeping his wet mouth with his sleeve. He noticed that Doc, Sneezy et al were still, suspended in the murky water, despite their goggle eyes being wide open, and he wondered if they slept at all. He switched on his telly, pressed the buttons on his remote and channel-hopped, not really seeing the images before him – more looking forward to the day ahead of him. Bored with the late-night tits-and-bums on the box, he got up and walked over to his large easel, displaying his cartoonery of the family of foxes.

As he rested his perfect left bum-cheek on the high stool, he wondered when and how he'd tell Geri about his planned move south-west. Picking up the sealed envelope from the easel, his writing in black ink scrawled across the front, he stroked the white paper distractedly. His resignation letter. It wouldn't be fair not to tell her. He'd have to bring up the subject of Devon and Cornwall first, let her know how his opportunities would be so much more lucrative there, how despondent and mundane the theatre had become for him. He knew he just couldn't have told her earlier. His feelings stood in stark contrast to those of a few days ago, when he'd fancied Geri madly but, as yet, had nothing to show for it. Whereas now, she hadn't screamed at him to leave her alone and they'd sealed their affection. So how would he break the news he was handing in his resignation letter? He now knew for sure that he was in love with her, his feelings so strong that he felt the stirrings of second thoughts rising inside of him. Perhaps he *could* stay in London? Perhaps, if Geri was involved in his life, he *could* stick it out in the Shaftesbury? No, he just wasn't too sure any more.

* * *

"Come on, come on," Sinead chided into the telephone, willing her mother to answer it. Despite having had the telephone for at least ten years now, it still didn't seem to have the desired effect on her family. Sinead believed an 'ordinary' family would, on hearing the phone ring, rush to answer it. But oh no. Not the Kellys. It didn't bother them that the ringing was a slight indication that someone might want to talk to them about something, or that it just *might* be an emergency. "Aah, ya take it all too serious, Sinead, ya do. It's only a fuck'n' pho-an!"

Abruptly her sister answered. Sinead was surprised – she hadn't spoken to her for months.

"Hey Bridie! How are you?"

"Sinead! Jeesus, I'd forgotten what your voice sounded like! How'r ya?"

"Grand! And yourself?"

"Ah sure, ya know yourself."

"Still happily married then?" Sinead quipped.

"Hah, lazy bastard! You know, he'd lay in that bloody bed all fuck'n' day'f I let'm. Sure, all I say now if anyone asks for him is: sometimes I wake up grumpy – other times I let him sleep."

Sinead laughed and Bridie joined in, enjoying the camaraderie of sisterhood, despite the miles between them.

"How the kids?"

"Ah, you know yerself, they're half-killing each other in the yard at the moment."

"No changes there then?"

"No, little feckers! Sinead, I really miss you. We can't wait to see you again."

"I know. I feel the same. It won't be long now."

"Are you looking for Mam?"

"Yeah, is she there?"

"I'll just get her for you. Take care. Lots of love."

"Bye."

Sinead heard Bridie calling *"Maaaam!"* at the top of her voice, and listened to her mother's mumblings and cursing as she approached the telephone.

She picked up the phone.

"Sinead?"

"Mam, how are ya?"

"Fine, fine. Got yourself a nice fella yet then?"

"Mam! I've told you I'm looking for the right guy."

"Ha, you'll end up a lonely auld spinster like your Auntie Eithne. Maybe that's what you want?"

"Mam, don't overreact! No-one wants to be a spinster, surely. Apart from anything else it's the most awful word."

"Well –"

Sinead could imagine her mam with crossed arms and a set jaw as she spoke.

"That's how you're heading. You're the eldest and the only one still single!"

"Mam, I'm just waiting for a guy with his feet on the ground, that's all."

"Sinead! Show me a man with both feet on the ground, and I'll show you a man who can't put on his pants."

Sinead felt herself tense, about to burst with anger, and then she saw the funny side, and began to giggle at her mother.

"What's so funny?"

"Mam, you're nuts!"

"Me? Nuts? And you're the one out in a foreign land with no-one but yourself to try and look after you!"

"Well, if it's any consolation, I have got a friend coming over for a few days, from England. So I won't be so forlorn. At least for a week anyway."

"Now, don't be funny with me, Sinead. Who? Who's coming over, anyway? It's not Gertie and the kids, is it? Oh, Sinead, it'd be so lovely to see her again."

"No Mam, no. It's not Gertie. It's Jon."

"A chap?"

"Yeah, a chap. He's my friend from the London offices. He's coming over for a local festival."

"Oh yeah, and that's all?"

"Meaning?"

"He's coming for the festival. Nothing to do with seeing you. Just the festival."

"Mam!"

"There's nothing wrong is there? Why're you ringing now? Why's he coming over to you?" With the intuition that only mothers are gifted with, Mrs Kelly had sniffed out Sinead's lonely tone. Sinead had wondered how long she'd be able to keep it a secret.

"No, Mam. There's nothing wrong. I am a little bit lonely all right, but it's nothing that won't pass. I get like this every now and then. Just a bit homesick too. You know."

"I know, pet. I do think you're ever so clever getting that job out there and the way you handle it all and everything. I was only telling Mrs O'Flanagan the other day about how well you've done for yourself since leaving school."

Sinead felt about twelve years old again. But it was so hard to be angry at her mother for long, so instead she smiled, lit up a cigarette and listened to the lovable familiar voice as it rambled on. Mrs Kelly was oblivious to Sinead's reversion to switch-off mode. As she tuned in again she caught the last of a sentence –

". . . and I said to Mrs O'Leary, I said, well, I know how it is. With the kids an' all. You don't mind 'em taking from ya, but you don't want 'em *dragging* outta ya. After all, that Olivia's twenty-three now. She should be earning herself a decent living. Or be getting married."

It was almost an hour later that Sinead said her goodbyes and hung up the phone. An hour – and eight cigarettes – later. Pouring herself a large Metaxa, she scraped the metal chair across the tiles on her balcony, sat on it and rested her feet on the wall in front of her. As she watched the sun set over Valencia, the warmth draining from the day, and the high-pitched chirping of the crickets making whoopie in the greenery, her mind wandered back to her family and her childhood days in Ireland. Despite their financially comfortable existence her parents were God-fearing and popular members of the local community; her father renowned for his ability to come up trumps repeatedly on the poker nights and her mam sought after for her soda bread and scones. Her dad had a wicked sense of humour coupled with a severe inability to cope with anything remotely stressful. Hence Sinead's mam took over the authoritative role when he began to lose his cool, and himself, inside the whiskey bottle.

As she shifted in the metal seat, its hard frame digging into her back, she reached for the bottle and topped up her glass, the whoosh of the night-time traffic hanging in the warm night. Her mind went back further, to their family holidays. Where she and her sisters had dreamed of destinations such as these, Spain, Majorca, even France, Mr & Mrs Kelly had driven them the two-hour drive to Dublin Airport only to spend the day watching the various flights depart and arrive. They never actually *went* anywhere – just spectated as the straw-hatted and suntanned holidaymakers returned to the rainy Dublin weather, their faces lit with smiles on recognising their loved ones who'd probably driven miles to collect them. The plus points to these summer 'holidays', however, were that Sinead and Bridie, by the ages of fourteen, knew all of the major airports across the globe – how to spell them at least – the prefixes of flight numbers and how they corresponded to which airline, and the uniforms of each of the airlines' stewardesses, down to colour of their tights. Oh, and how many punts a polystyrene cup of hot chocolate from the airport vending machine cost. And then, at the end of a surprisingly enjoyable day, they'd drive home early evening, eating the packed lunch that Mam had prepared for them. On a real good day, if they were lucky, they also got a Club Milk from the airport shop too. Until the next morning, when they'd set off again. She supposed these experiences could have sown the seeds for her yearning to travel.

* * *

Geri woke to the sounds of her clock radio blasting the tinny sounds of Björk into her delicate ear-holes. After only five hours sleep she knew she should have felt heavy-headed, bleary-eyed and lethargic. But she felt none of these things. On the contrary, she leapt out of bed and winked at her reflection in the mirror.

Christ, I feel twenty-two! I've had more sleep than this on a bad night with the children and have felt like a pile of dirty laundry for the next twenty-four hours. I feel like I've taken some kind of elixir of youth – even Björk sounds nearly good today!

As she'd hopped around the room, her actions disturbingly reminiscent of clog-dancing, she flung open the wardrobe doors to see what she could possibly wear that might just reflect her youthful feel today.

The telephone ringing jollily on her bedside cabinet disturbed her rooting through the jangling hangers. She answered it with an effervescent,

"Hello?"

"Geri. God, you sound happy! Had a good night, did you?"

"Oh Mum. Mum, Mum, Mum. It was perfect!"

"Finally got together with him then?"

"What do you mean?"

"Oh Geri. With Ben. You two finally got around to it, obviously."

"Why do you say it like that?"

"Geri, it's obvious that he fancies you."

"Mum!"

"Stop all that now. I know you couldn't see it but, Geri, I spotted it a mile off. He's mad about you, that Ben."

The grin spread wide across Geri's face.

Cynthia continued, "Play your cards right, girl, and your days of kissing frogs'll be long gone!"

"Mum. Would you mind hanging on the children until later on today? Please?"

"Course I will. Why, where'ya going?"

"Ben's taking me out somewhere special today. Sorry, Mum, for the short notice and that but –"

"Go on now. I'm glad for you, Geri, after all you've had to cope with. Oh, here's Cameron wanting to say something."

The phone rattled as Geri imagined Cameron's small hand grabbing the phone from his Nana.

His little cut-glass voice spoke clearly, "Ey, Mummeee. We watched the *Ion Keeng* and Nana made popcorn and we *ooooohhhhhhh!*"

Geri smiled, her love for her two boys threatening to burst within her chest. She could picture Cameron's little face stretching as he yawned. He continued from where he left off, "Mummeee? Mummmeee!"

"Yes, darling?"

"I got the yawns. Nana give me coa-cola nexterday."

Geri could hear Cynthia chastising Cameron with a "sshh", knowing full well that she forbade her from letting the boys drink it.

"Look, darling, put me back on to Nana now, love. Mummy loves you very much. A big kiss. And one for Reece. I'll pick you up after dinner, darling."

"Bye, Mummeee. Ruv oooo too."

The turbulence of the phone in transit attacked Geri's ears once more as the handpiece was passed back to Nana.

"All right then, love. What time will you be picking them up then?"

"Oh, I don't really know. Say about six?"

"Lovely. And you don't know where he's taking you?"

"Nope."

"Well, have a great time. See you later, love. Bye."

"Bye."

* * *

It was years since Geri had walked through London early(ish) on a Sunday morning. She'd forgotten how invigorating it was. The shops were open; the tourists stood in groups scrutinising maps and leaflets; the homeless lay unmoving amidst their filth-ingrained and damp cardboard boxes and ripped sleeping bags as they sheltered in the doorways and protective corners of the city's architecture. Ben held onto Geri's hand firmly and she literally tingled from the tips of her split-ends to the chipped ends of her painted toenails, as they strolled along Regent's Street en route from Tottenham Court Road tube towards Trafalgar Square.

The droves of open-topped buses, like mobile flower-vases topped with colourful bouquets blooming sped past, buffeting gently their top-floor passengers as they took in the on-board commentary.

Taking it all in, soaking it up, her senses heightened as she felt the inexorable chemistry shooting along her arm as she made skin-contact with Ben, in this almost unbelievable turn of events. She was surprised further as he confidently crossed the road, leading her into Caffé Nero, an Italian coffee bar on Regent's Street.

"What's this? Is this 'our special place'?" she teased.

"No," Ben grinned, and kissed her forehead, "just a late breakfast. You sit down – outside if you like. I'll get you something nice."

I can't believe my luck! Not only has the gorgeous Ben, for some insane reason, decided that he's – wait for it – "in love with me", but he's also the most attentive and protective bloke I've ever had the good fortune to clap my rose-tinted pupils on! Something just has to go wrong here. I mean, it wouldn't be 'The Life of Geri Cumbers' otherwise, would it?

Would it?

After the delightfully European breakfast, Ben led her back across the busy road and surprised her by taking a drastic left turn into one of the huge gold-framed shop doors that swung open heavily and invitingly.

"Where are we? Is *this* 'our special place'?"

"Nope."

She scanned the shop floor for clues as to where he'd brought her. Apart from the massive Disney presentation stands boasting almost life-size Buzz Lightyears, Little Mermaids and Dalmatian Puppies there were no tell-tale signs.

"Where is this?"

"Hamley's, you div. Don't tell me you've never been in Hamley's before! It's the biggest toyshop in the world. Probably."

"So what are we doing in here?"

"What do you think we're doing in here?" Ben asked

429

mockingly while picking up a *Jungle Book* plastic keyring and then a Mowgli lunch-box. "We've come to buy a present to take back to Cameron and Reece."

God, do I feel selfish! I hadn't even thought of that! In all the years I was with Kevin he'd never dream of coming into the city on a weekend day. He said he'd had enough of it by Friday to last him. And then, to think of buying a present for the boys too? No chance! He'd say they didn't need anything.

"Great. What'll we get them then?"

Eventually, armed with their Hamley's bags – Ben had gone a little mad in the *Lilo & Stitch* section – they turned the corner and were faced with the throngs mingling amidst the pigeons in Trafalgar Square.

"Well, this is it. We're here."

"Trafalgar Square! This is where you're bringing me? This is 'our special place'?"

"No," he steered Geri's arm lightly to the left, and guided her through some dark wooden revolving doors. "I'm taking you *here.*"

As Geri stood in the huge reception area she viewed her surroundings with more than a little confusion. She hadn't a clue where she was. The high stone walls and floor exuded a tranquillity that she immediately loved. A handful of people speaking in hushed tones were climbing an extremely wide and high staircase to her right and a well-lit bookshop on her left showed promise.

Then she noticed the information desk to her right, cleverly spotlit and boasting large white letters above it: *The National Portrait Gallery.* She spun around to meet Ben's smiling eyes.

"The National Gallery?"

"Yeah," he linked her arm, and led her toward the echoey staircase behind them. "Let me enlighten you on the world of art."

They first approached the Sainsbury Wing which displayed portraits dating from 1260 to 1510.

"My God, Ben, these pictures are almost over five hundred years old! Are they the originals?"

He chuckled at her innocence. "'Course they are!"

The high, high ceilings gave the gallery a relaxed, light and airy feel. The wooden floors beneath her thudded hollowly as the meandering visitors strolled from one section to another, viewing the magnificent, and sometimes rather ugly, pictures hung in the ornate gold picture frames.

Geri stood before a picture that amazed her. The subject's hands were so delicately formed, the colour and transparency of her skin almost translucent, that she couldn't believe that someone, least of all five hundred years ago, could have mixed the paint to such perfection. She stepped back to the middle of the small section, seating herself on the highly polished wooden bench in the middle of the room as she listened to the hushed mumblings around her. Ben strode up beside her, sat with her and took her hand.

"Found one you like already?"

"Ben," she whispered, awe-struck, "just look at her hands! They're so realistic. It's almost creepy. I love it! I love the whole place!"

"I knew you would."

"Yeah?" She realised he was driving at something, but wasn't sure what. "You knew I would what?"

"Like it."

"How did you know?"

Ben smiled. "Remember the day in the Post Office?"

Her mind reeled.

Oh yes, yes. Of course I remember it. The day he spoke Spanish to me. Embarrassed the life out of me. I remember, I remember!

"Oh right. Yeah. The Post Office . . . What about it?"

"You were showing Cameron the dog-eared Degas prints. The ballerinas. I knew from that minute you're so much deeper than what people see. That's what I love about you, Geri."

His sincerity bought a lump to her throat.

"God, Ben. But you're only seeing the good side. What about when I first get out of bed with hair like Cyndi Lauper and when I'm screaming at the kids, or crying at them, or when I'm walking into the sea in my bikini, accompanying my cellulite to the waterside and you're lying on the sunbed pretending to be asleep and watching me through your dark-tinted sunglasses?"

It was out before she knew it! The insecurities of past relationships still haunting her.

He turned to her, surprised. "What?"

Shit shit shit! Now what'm I going to say to him? Get yourself outta this one, Geri! I know. I'll smile endearingly and cutesy at him, and try to get out of it. I'll put on my whispery girlie voice.

"Oh nothing. Nothing."

I'm hanging my head down too. I want him to feel sorry for me, and not to push the subject. Caring man that he's proved himself to be.

"No, come on. What was that about walking into the sea in your bikini?"

He's grinning! He thinks it's something saucy! Ohmigod! Now what am I going to say?

"Well . . . well, it goes back to my days with Kevin. We went on holiday, you see." *Don't ask me why I'm saying this! It's probably got something to do with the flattery factor – always turns up trumps at loosening the old tongue. Now I have to go on . . . here goes . . .* "It was our first holiday together. Well, our *only* one together and I was so hot I was desperate to go into the sea . . . "

Geri cringed as she told the story.

It's amazing how these high stone ceilings carry sound, you know. I think the echo of Ben's laughter could probably be heard all over the building. The resonance was so intense that many of the 'Virgin & Child' works probably turned their heads to see where it was coming from! Still – at least he laughed. And – much more importantly – he called Kevin a plonker! A plonker!

"Come on," Ben encouraged, "don't let something like that get you down. Look. Let's not get too serious today. I want you to enjoy it all. Come in here and see The Leonardo Cartoon."

"Cartoon? Leonardo da Vinci drew cartoons?"

Ben smirked. "Not cartoons like I draw. Not like the family of foxes and the little robin and all that. Come on in."

He led her into a small, darkened room with the main part of the back wall taken up with an enormous black and white sketch, surrounded by soft spotlighting.

"What's it of?" Geri whispered, as they stood among a few people wearing earphones, experiencing 'The Soundtrack Tour'.

Ben obliged. "It's a picture of the Virgin and Child with Saint John the Baptist and Saint Anne. It's black and white chalk on tinted paper and was a preparatory study for a painting which was never done, but has been preserved in its own right as a finished drawing."

"God, Ben. How do you know all of this?"

He pointed to a white plaque on the wall. "It says it all on there, look!"

Geri swiped him playfully and they bustled out past the irritated art appreciators. They made their way down the stairs and decided to walk to the original building of the National Gallery by the pavements outside rather than the internal corridors and walkways.

Outside, Geri sat on the top step and pulled Ben down beside her.

"Just stop a minute. I want to look."

The roar of the open-topped buses passing amidst the traffic, making their way around the huge roundabout of Trafalgar Square couldn't drown out the continuous splashing sounds of the water as it spilled over from the two large fountains. Geri watched the trillions of pigeons as they flitted amongst the crowds. Four statues of black lions flanked Nelson's Column and they watched the tourists climbing onto their shiny backs, posing for photos. Geri followed her gaze from the pit of Nelson's Column up, up and up until she could see him, standing proudly, a hundred feet or so in the air. Ben watched her as she held her head back and looked straight up. He whispered deeply in her ear,

"You know, if you stare at him long enough, it looks like he's falling over."

She snapped her head back down to eye level. "God. It does too. Yuk, I feel sick now. Come on, let's go into the main bit!"

Inside, Geri eventually began to tire of the many 'Virgin and Child' paintings. Then she came across a painting by Renoir that she couldn't stop looking at. It was of a 'well-rounded' naked girl lying on her side, her slightly sagging milky white stomach rather rotund and small breasts dominating the centre of the painting. Her face was painted with much more detail than her body, which had been coloured almost entirely in shades of white, yellow, blue and grey. Geri read the plaque on the wall quietly: "A Nymph by a Stream by Pierre Auguste Renoir. Oil on canvas. Renoir's model – Lisa Tréhot – depicted as a naked nymph, wearing only a wreath of leaves in her hair. The combination of classical motif with realist treatment of the figure may have been inspired by Courbet's paintings of nudes. Probably painted 1869 – 1870."

"Well?" Ben questioned, eager to hear her opinion.

"I like it! She hasn't got a perfect figure, or a beautiful face, but I like the way she holds herself. And let's face it, she was confident enough to lie there for him in the nod, *and* let him use her name afterwards. She's just an ordinary woman, with nothing to hide. I like her."

"Well, come and see if you like this then!" Ben led her by the elbow lightly until they reached a painting by Jan Steen, called *The Effects of Intemperance*, painted around 1663.

"Now," he stood behind her, his hands planted firmly on her shoulders, "tell me what you see."

Geri looked at the painting, its predominance of browny colours and shades overwhelming. On the face of it, it seemed harmless enough. She answered Ben, enjoying the game of it all.

"Well, I see a woman resting her head on her hands as she sits, a parrot on a perch and a scruffy woman on her knees feeding him. Two huge bunches of grapes on the floor. Three ugly children – one of them looks like that Chuckie doll from that horror film – who are holding a cat. They look poor and dirty."

"Right," Ben said authoritatively, "now look again. This was painted by Jan Steen – he's one of my favourites. He was a Dutch seventeenth-century painter who liked to portray people like ourselves behaving as they shouldn't. Even today a 'Jan Steen household' is what the Dutch call a boisterous and ramshackle family."

"That's me!" Geri interrupted.

"I don't think so. Now look again. The woman you said was resting her head is, in fact, the Dutch housewife and mother who is slumped in a drunken slumber. See the little boy behind her – her child – he's trying to pick her pocket. The trio to the right – the Chuckie one – are wasting a meat pie by feeding it to a cat. The scruffy woman feeding the parrot is, in fact, the maid, who is offering the parrot wine – as the perfect mimic of human behaviour, he is taking example from the mother. And look further into the picture. Right at the back there the man, possibly the father, is flirting with a big-chested woman. Basically it's a message, I think, trying to preach against the evils of intemperance."

"Intemperance? What's that mean?"

"Extremes, excess, extravagance. That kind of thing."

"Wow. That's really deep. You'd never think all of that from just looking at it quickly, would you? Anyway," she swung around to face him, pressing her nose on his, playfully, "how do you know so much about Jan Steen?"

"I studied his work at college for a term. I loved it. I've been looking for some prints of his work for a long time, but can't get the ones I want."

"Well," she kissed him hard, "we'll just have to look harder, won't we?"

"Come on," he kissed her on the nose and then the forehead, "enough of this culture for one day. Now to 'our special place'."

"What, you mean this wasn't it?"

He tutted, "How could *this* be it? What's special for us about *this* place? Come on, only a short walk around the corner and we're there."

Within five minutes Ben was leading Geri into Leicester Square where they watched the street performers as they spun on their backs, and even their heads, to the bebop music that had been all the rage when she was a teenager.

"OK, so where's 'our special place'?"

He smiled at her, waiting for her reaction as he said, "Behind us."

"Behind us?" She turned to look behind her, only seeing the trees in the middle of the Square.

"No. Behind *me!*"

Geri looked over Ben's shoulder to see the flashing neon lights above the entrance to the Empire, all yellow and blue.

"What, the Empire?"

"No! Next to it. The Ice Cream Parlour."

Without looking Geri clamped her gaze firmly onto Ben's eyes.

"The Ice Cream Parlour? How is that 'our special place'?"

"Geri. Look at it."

Geri glanced again at the small ice-cream scoop-shop next to the Empire with American-diner-dressed girls behind the counter serving a queue of people. And then, she looked up at the name. She squealed with delight.

"Ben & Jerry's! That's us!"

"Sure is. Now what's your favourite flavour? Let me guess . . . Mint Choc Chip."

"No! Why do you say that?"

"Women always love that one."

"No. Oh, let's go over and have a look. I can't decide till I see what they've got."

Five minutes later they were strolling, holding hands and licking their Butter Almond Toffee and Caramel Chew Chew ice creams in the spring sunshine, Geri feeling like a lovestruck teenager – all over again.

Chapter Twenty-six

Ben wrestled with the envelope, struggling to find a loose corner by which to peel it open, his slender fingers working overtime as he grappled with the white A5 jacket. Having ripped at the self-sealant tab, he pulled a letter out. Headed paper, folded in the classic three-flap style, its black-inked linear layout all too familiar. Another rejection. Recognising the logo and company name at the head of the letter as one of the publishing houses that he'd offered his services to as illustrator of children's books, his eyes scanned the text despondently. The rejection letters were all too similar: *"Thanks for thinking of us, sorry nothing at the moment, please keep trying, blah, blah."* His expression remained still as he read the signature at the bottom of the page, and then it hit him.

This *wasn't* a rejection letter.

Moving over to the large window, his socked feet

sliding on the wooden floor, he rested his bum on the back of the armchair, focussing on the text once again – this time concentrating on the offer. He had to read it three times before it really sank in, and when it had he threw the featherlight letter into the air, punching at it delightedly as it wafted down again.

"Yes! Yes! YES!"

Without thinking of the consequences, only jubilant at his news, he grabbed his mobile from the coffee table and punched a sequence of numbers.

A few seconds later Geri answered, "Hello? Cameron, *put that down!* Sorry, hello?"

"Guess what?"

"Ben. Hi." She felt a strange coyness as she spoke to him. It seemed that the fantastic day they'd had yesterday, and his use of the "L" word had turned things full circle, back to the days when she'd first seen him at the gym and fancied the pants off him. As her stomach flipped nervously, she closed the lounge door, leaving Cameron and Reece to battle over *Thomas the Tank*.

"You have to guess. What do you think I got in the post this morning?"

She felt as if the volume knob had been cranked up cruelly as the butterflies in her stomach intensified. She knew what he'd got. After all, he was extremely talented, and it was only a matter of time before somebody influential noticed. She leapt immediately into denial.

"Dunno, what? The gas bill? Shares in Ben & Jerry's Ice Cream?" She felt her attempt at light-heartedness thud to the ground, its transparency embarrassing.

"I got it, Geri! I've been offered a contract with Patchwork Publishers! They want me to illustrate their *Farmyard Fables* stories *and* the *Massey Tractor* tales. I've done it, Geri!"

She gulped, swallowing her misery, before forcing a smile onto her face and responding, "Well done, Ben! You bloody well deserve it! You've worked so hard on those illustrations and spent a small fortune on them. Congratulations!"

"It's such great news! Right! What're you doing tonight? No, don't answer – I'll be over at seven with a bottle of champagne and a Chinese for us, and some juice and Chocolate Buttons for the boys. We can't leave them out of the celebrations, can we?"

"Oh Ben, you don't want to spend your evening celebrating here with us! There's so many places you could go to. What about that new bar that's opened in the West End that you were telling me that you fancied?"

I just can't let him get any closer to us, especially now that I know he'll be going soon. It just doesn't seem fair. If I act 'the cool bitch', then he'll get the message and stay away. Won't he? I'll just have to keep fielding his calls and shying away from any contact. Typical of my disastrous life! I said the 'L' word was jinxed, didn't I? Didn't I!

Her voice was ominously shaky as she forced to maintain some kind of composure, "Surely you'd prefer to be out on the town, telling Mark and your mates from work and footie and that. You don't really want to spend it here with me and two small children, surely?"

442

"Geri, I can't think of anything I'd rather do. See you at seven?"

"OK, if you're sure."

I'm *not* . . .

"I'm sure. In fact, I'm sure of two things. That's one, and do you know what the other one is?"

"No." She held her breath for fear of him confirming her dread that he'd be moving away from Elephant & Castle now that he wasn't tied to his job in theatre.

"I'm sure that I'm in love with you."

Geri gasped, surprised that he hadn't forgotten amidst all the exciting news.

"Ben! Thank you! Thanks for thinking of me, of us. You really are so sweet. Thank you."

"Seven? Bye!"

"Bye."

* * *

There's no hiding it any more. I am, officially, 'in love' with Ben Robbins. So now what? Watch him love me and leave me? The best thing that's happened to me in years, and he's moving on to bigger and better things? I'll be a distant memory by the end of the month.

The slimmer, confident Geri that had emerged in the last six months, faltering at first but then poised, wearing her new purchases, was suddenly crash-landing into the depths of despair. Whereas the boys were almost a year older and seemed easier to cope with due to the benefits of more talk and less sign language, the picture immediately shifted. As she replaced the receiver, she heard them still squabbling. Some days seemed so much harder than others, especially when she had something troubling her. Uncharacteristically, she tipped a dribble of brandy into her mid-morning coffee, inducing images of the Jan Steen household. She dismissed them with bitterness. The sounds of the children's disagreement continued, unheard by Geri as she sat, despondent on the kitchen stool, sipping at the hot sweet drink. Without invitation the old fears come rushing back.

Loneliness, spinsterhood, liver spots, aching joints, arthritis, indigestion, incontinence. It'll be the grey pubes next.

Slumping in the chair, she could almost feel her hips spreading, enjoying the depression and taking the opportunity to make her feel worse. Her imagination ran riot as she imagined wodges of pasty skin bulging from beneath her hi-leg knickers. *Even my bloody drawers are defying me!*

Swiftly rising, the crying from the lounge now beyond ignoring, she put the still warm, but empty mug into the sink, and as she turned for the doorway, caught sight of herself in the small kitchen mirror. Her red-cheeked, over-heated and exhausted face stared back at her. Barely recognising herself, she stood to take in her reflective portrait. Staring deep into her own eyes, she noticed a glimmer in the darkness of her pupils, the light from stark bulb shining down on the crown of her unbrushed hair – and she saw something else.

I see my own determination and strength of character. I see the Geri Cumbers that has put up with shit for the last ten years and can still chuckle on telling the tale. I see the strong-willed, resolute and determined Geri who, despite repeated knock-backs, will, someday – make something happen for her!

Recalling Sinead's birthday wishes of nearly a year ago, she voiced the words softly to her reflection, "Passion, Attitude and Alcohol. Passion, Attitude and Alcohol."

Lifting her hands to her face, she smoothed the furrows on her forehead, wiped her hands over her cheeks, brushing her hair back and tucking it behind her ears.

"Geri. Take it on the chin, girl. Get up, dust yourself down, and carry on. You know what Mum would say? Something like, 'he'll be sorry', or 'he wasn't worth it anyway'. Possibly even, 'one lost ten found', or 'it is better to have loved and lost than never to have loved at all'."

The problem was that she didn't believe *any* of these clichés. She found comfort in the ones that displayed a little more humanity, such as 'it was a very interesting experience,' or 'love hurts'. She felt a particular liking for the one that Cynthia often coined when things went wrong: 'Maybe I am a loser, *but at least no-one knows.*'

* * *

Between the hours of eleven and noon of that day, Sinead, Geri and Ben all experienced, in varying extremes, events that would somehow change their lives. Ben, as predetermined, handed over his resignation letter with a terse few words and only the hint of a grin.

Geri decided that she would 'keep the best side out' – *God, I am turning into my mother* – and see Ben off with all the encouragement and congratulations he deserved. After all, she flowered up the situation in her mind, they had only really known each other for little over six months. She'd get over him. Some day.

And Sinead? Sinead, for the first time in her life, cried at work. In the toilets, so it wasn't quite as humiliating as it might have been if she'd been stationed at her desk, but still, Gabriella and Marisol – two of the Spanish secretaries – had seen her sobbing into a wad of toilet roll by the mirrors, and worse still, so had Charmaine. The pressure finally hit home. It was the first time she'd cried – really cried – over the abuse she'd suffered at the unmerciful hands of Steven, having spent most of her time since then wearing a fantastic, almost Jim-Carrey-like, grinning mask and volunteering to do any of the additional tasks that her work determined. She'd thrown herself headlong into a proposition – her own – for preparing and calculating the Annual Reports statistics, amongst many other smaller tasks, and now the straw that broke the camel's back was ominously close to also breaking Sinead's. She couldn't keep the pretence up any longer. She was struggling with juggling. Trying to keep a lid on her emotions was proving too difficult for her to maintain. Attempting to keep a smiling, professional disposition whilst battling internally with her feelings about the

Steven situation, her homesickness, her loneliness and her overpowering work pressures was finally threatening to break her. The fluid rasping noises she made as she blew her nose vehemently hid the sound of the external door to the toilets creaking open. It wasn't until she wiped at her running, soon to be blocked from over-crying, nose that she noticed Charmaine standing in front of her again.

Through a thick but high-pitched voice Sinead said, not lifting her gaze from the suddenly very interesting tiled floor, "Piss off, Charmaine."

Charmaine answered with an almost sympathetic tone to her irritating nasal twang, "No, I won't piss off, Sinead. Nor will I go away. I want to 'elp you."

"Ha, *you* want to help *me*? Now that's an interesting concept. What on earth did you have in mind? Dyeing my eyelashes, painting my nails!" Sinead continued to gawk at the floor, speaking in a monotone. Charmaine continued, squeaking softly, "Mr Moreno's looking for you too."

"Hm, probably got more work for me to do. Forget it."

"I don't fink so, Sinead. 'E said 'e had some good news for you."

"Yeah, right."

"I've got some good news for you too. Steven Randall's been sacked."

Sinead stopped blubbing and looked up at Charmaine for the first time, her swollen red eyes meeting Charmaine's twinkling over-made-up ones.

She was surprised to see that Charmaine was actually smiling.

"Why?"

"Drugs."

"How's that good news for *you* then?" Sinead questioned.

"Ooh, he's a proper bastard, Sinead. Now I realise what you meant when you warned me off of 'im. Talk about mood swings! You know," her volume dropped significantly as she leant in toward Sinead to whisper, "we only lasted free weeks. 'E said I irritated the life out of 'im, but I was quite glad really. 'E wasn't the man I thought 'e was, but I'm terribly bad at ending relationships. I'm sure 'e done me a favour really."

For the first time Sinead felt a twinge of compassion for the bimbo facing her. A strange solidarity rose in her and, despite her personal crisis, she suddenly felt rather protective toward the naive Charmaine.

"Yeah," Sinead's voice softened, "I'm bloody sure he's done you a favour." She put her hand on Charmaine's shoulder. "I'd say he may have done you the biggest favour of your life."

Charmaine tittered, not seeing the point, as usual, but realising that Sinead was coming from an angle far deeper than she'd probably ever understand. She put her hand on Sinead's and squeezed at it, as she whispered, in almost sing-song style, "Noow, come on wiv me. Let's see what Mr Moreno wants eh? I wonder whose news'll be better, mine or 'is? Mind you, eh," she nudged playfully at Sinead, "what could be better than seeing the back of that moody Randall? Nuffin' that I can fink of anyway!"

Sinead mustered up a smile, realising that she hadn't cried for at least three minutes, and deciding it would be a serious step back to begin again. So wiping at her red face, and asking Charmaine to tell Moreno to give her five minutes, she set to work with the cold taps, damp loo roll and her make-up bag.

Five minutes later she sat opposite her Departmental Director, Mr Moreno, looking the consummate professional, and as composed as the Mona Lisa. Moreno suspected he saw a trace of bloodshot in her right eye, but couldn't be sure. He didn't want to stare at her too intently. He had good news for her, didn't want to make her nervous. Offering her a chilled bottle of local Valencian mineral water and a pristine gleaming glass, both on a silver tray, he told her to sit down and make herself comfortable. She knew this was an indication that she'd be here for a while, his generosity with his office space not an everyday habit.

"Sinead," he began, his Spanish accent thick and grinding, but his elocution perfectly English, "I have good news for you. Eet ees to do with the findings of Jonathon Morgan."

Sinead nearly choked on her water.

"Jonathon Morgan!" she exclaimed.

"Yes, and the work ee's been doing regarding your positions? Well, I won't make you wait unnecessarily, Sinead. It seems that your position 'as been undergraded. You 'af not been graded fairly, and eet seems that the

Head Office in London 'as requested that you be
promoted to the next grade. So from the first of the
month – this month – your salary will be increased to
that of Grade Feefty-five and you are, officially, Higher
Management. Congratulations, Sinead."

Extending his brown, perfectly manicured hand to
Sinead made her realise that she was expected to stand
up and shake it. The shock hadn't yet sunk in. As she
slowly lowered herself back into the chair, taking a
large gulp of the cool water, she shook her head slowly,
her eyes wide.

"Mr Moreno. Are you telling me that Jonathon
Morgan has found that I am doing the work of a Grade
D, in a Grade D position and he hasn't told me?"

"Yes, that ees what I'm saying to you, Sinead."

"But I speak to him nearly every day! He hasn't said
anything!"

Mr Moreno smiled and shrugged his shoulders.

"Sinead, more importantly I theenk you must realise
the added advantages you can now receive as a Higher
Manager."

"Yes," her mind raced – like what? "Like what?"

"OK, seet down there for just a few more meenutes
and I weell explain to you." He reached across to a
filing cabinet so small they're only ever seen in
Directors' offices, taking from the top a thick blue
binder. "OK, een line weeth UK policies you are now
officially a grade D, wheech means you instantly receive a
promotional salary increase of –" he tapped at his
calculator carefully, "ten thousand euro a year."

"Ten grand a year!" Sinead couldn't contain her amazement.

"Yes," Mr Moreno continued, oblivious to her excitement, "and you can now have your own office, eef you want one. You are allowed an additional two thousand euro a year for clothing allowance, and an extra two thousand for your entertainment's budget. Oh, and you are also allowed a secretary, and one administrator." He looked up from the blue binder, closing it in front of him, waiting for her response. There was none, yet. He continued, in a quieter tone, "I do theenk though, Sinead, that the extra work you have been taking on, while admirable, ees also a leettle too much for just one person. Eef you are wise, I theenk you will starting looking immediately for a secretary – that's eef you choose to continue weeth the extra work."

"Oh yes, Mr Moreno," Sinead suddenly burst into life, "with or without this promotion I have every intention of keeping up the extra work. I've got so involved I can't possibly stop now. I'll be honest with you, it had started to grind at me a bit. It is too much for just one person. But if you don't mind, I don't really want my own office. I prefer to be sitting out there with everybody else. I think it'll help me keep my finger on the pulse a bit more."

"Whatever you want, Sinead. Look, I'll let thees seenk een before we speak again. Feel free to go ahead and organise your new staff, check weeth Personnel first before you begeen any interviews, but the salary rise will be backdated effective the beginning of thees month."

She rose, this time extending her suntanned arm and firm hand for Mr Moreno to shake. "Thank you, Mr Moreno. Between you and Charmaine, you've *really* made my day!"

He smiled at her vacuously, not understanding how he could be linked with the blonde bombshell in any shape or form, and watched Sinead glide from his office, seeming at least six inches taller than when she'd skulked in.

Back at home that evening, she celebrated with a bottle of champagne. Krug was her current favourite and didn't come too cheap, but what the hell? She was getting an extra ten grand a year!

"Ha! Blow the expense!" She laughed into her drink as she lifted the fluted glass to her mouth, swallowing an obscene amount in one go. OK, so two out of three weren't bad, as the saying goes. Steven had finally been given the push and, so the gossip went, he was on the early morning flight to England. And whilst the work situation hadn't exactly been lightened, at least she was now getting more money for it, *and* was given the offer of assistance. A secretary *and* an administrator. She didn't know where to start looking! Grabbing her palm computer from her handbag, which still lay dumped at her feet as she curled on the settee and quaffed her bubbly, she turned it on and began to type in a list of things to do. The list involved mundane things like, checking with her old pal Eamon Lynch's office about the statistics for the Year-End Profits, and ordering some more staples for her desk stapler, to asking Personnel for a list of secretaries who were looking for a change or an opening into Finance, and names of administrators she might be able to interview. As a second thought she added a note to ask about local Employment Agencies who might have suitably qualified people on their books. After the third glass of champagne she began to relax, resting her contented head back into the sofa cushion and her mind began to wander. The only one thing from her troublesome three that hadn't been dealt with today was her homesickness. The trouble with homesickness is that it's completely unchoosy. It confuses the places you used to frequent regularly with those that you only went to once every five years. She found herself yearning for trips to Avoca, which had since her arrival in Valencia become the setting for *Ballykissangel*. She'd *never* gone to Avoca when she'd lived in Ireland! Likewise she really fancied the idea of a coffee in Bewley's Cafe. Now, Grafton Street on a hot August afternoon was Sinead's idea of heaven. Arriving at the end of the street, and entering St Stephen's Green with her twenty or so carrier-bags, emblazoned with the shop names across the fronts, was something that she really did use to love. How she and Gertie had loved their summers in Ireland! They'd shop for hours and then stop for the picnic lunch that her mam had made for them, before getting the bus home. They'd sit in St Stephen's Green watching, as if invisible, all the young students lying out on the grass, smoking. Probably dope, they'd imagined, excited by the illegal thrill of it, but frightened to touch it at the same time. She loved the atmosphere of Dublin. Even on rainy days there was an air of cheer and ambience. Or was that just the fumes hanging heavy on the sultry air, she wondered with maturity. As she and Gertie would relax amidst the cosmopolitan crowds enjoying the sunshine, they'd fantasise about their futures, the men they'd end up marrying and the fantastic jobs and children they'd have. Only, they were supposed to *both* do this. It seemed that, so far, Gertie was streets ahead of her, losing out only on the fantastic job. And when the boys were old enough she was sure to return to work. She had a gorgeous and supportive husband in Kevin, two beautiful children, an immaculate house in a great area of London and Sinead could just imagine her in three or four years' time, as one of those 'mommies' who drove the huge 4x4 off-road vehicles just to drop the kids off at school. The impeccably dressed, firmly toned mums, perched high on their pod, overlooking the roofs of the mere mortals' cars. Sinead giggled as she imagined Geri behind the wheel on the school or the gym-run. But Sinead? After a lot of work, and a near mental-breakdown, she'd bagged the Management position. But the husband, house and kids?

They seemed eternally out of reach.

* * *

Geri waited, embarrassingly anxious, for Ben's arrival.

She too had bought a celebratory drink, although her pockets weren't near as deep as Sinead's and so had settled for the bottle of Ernest & Julio Gallo that cost £5.49 in Sainsbury's. It too sat expectantly, on ice in the fridge. Cameron fidgeted in his chair as he finished off his Chicken Nuggets and Reece made a great effort at raising his Chicken Nugget-clenched hand to his mouth in co-ordination with the action of actually *opening* it. They really were coming along great guns.

I'm desperate for a slug of that wine, but I must keep it for when Ben arrives. I know he said he'd bring champagne and Chinese, and bits for the kids, but I'm so nervous I can't keep out of the toilet. It's not in my nature to be 'cool' and 'frosty', especially when I know I'm in love with the guy. And worse still, he's said he's in love with me! I've been to change my clothes three times – fashion and toddlers don't mix – and every time I look at my face in the mirror I'm spotting more and more defects. As if time is speeding up! My laughter lines are deepening into hideous witch-like wrinkles, my freckles are turning red, almost spot-like, and my lipstick's starting to bleed! As Mum always says, 'You never look as bad as you feel, nor as good as you think you do!'

In typical form, the doorbell and the phone rang simultaneously. Geri ran to the hallway, grabbing the phone first, it being the nearest, made a swift apology, laid the receiver down on the stairs and opened the front door.

"Evening!" Ben's wide grin made her virtually melt on the spot. His hands, hidden behind his back, were then outstretched, one clenching a massive bouquet of lilies, and the other supporting a carrier bag wafting deliciously of Chinese and with a bottle of champagne peeking out the top. Unlike Sinead, Geri didn't give a shit about the name on the bottle. It all tasted pretty awful anyway.

"Come in, Ben. I'm just on the phone. Go through. You know where stuff is."

Stepping over the doorstep, he craned his neck to kiss her, but she deftly dodged, as she reached down for the telephone once again.

One ear cocked to the kitchen as Ben greeted and played with the children, tipping their chocolate buttons into their plastic bowls, and the other cocked to the telephone, she said, "Hello! Sorry about that."

"Gertie. What's going on?"

"Sinead! Oh, nothing. Just Ben at the door, that's all."

"Ben? Who the hell's Ben?"

Oh shit, oh shit. I wasn't thinking.

"Oh, just a, em, a friend. A friend, em, of Kevin's!" Sinead laughed at her hesitancy, "You don't sound too sure about that."

"Oh sorry, you know, the kids are pulling at my trouser-legs. I can't concentrate properly. Right, OK. Well, how are you?"

See, another lie.

"Fine, fine. I got some good news today, I just had to ring and tell you."

"What?"

"I got promoted. To – wait for it – Higher Management!"

"Jesus! Well done! So, aren't we the successful businesswoman?"

"God, yeah. What d'ya reckon?"

"Well done! So you're celebrating tonight too then?"

"Are you celebrating something as well?"

"Well, not exactly me. It's Ben. He's just got a contract with a big publishing company, illustrating children's books."

"Blimey! He must be good."

"He is." The proud tone was evident in Geri's voice.

"So, who is he? A friend of Kevin's, you said?"

"Yeah. Hang on, let me get him to talk to you. He's really nice."

A mad move I know, but when faced with a difficult situation, sometimes madness is the best policy.

She ran into the kitchen and, grabbing Ben by the gorgeously chunky arm, led him to the phone.

"If she asks, you're one of Kevin's friends!" she whispered urgently, pressing the receiver against her breast so Sinead wouldn't hear.

"What?" He pulled away from her, his face confused.

"Please, Ben," she whispered, her best cajoling face plastered on, "if she asks just say you know Kevin from the boot sales."

"The boot sales! Geri, what is this?"

Geri held the phone away from her and raised her voice to ensure that Sinead could hear what she was saying. "Ben!" She gesticulated wildly. "This is Sinead on the phone. You know," she over-emphasised her words, "Sinead! *Aka Sinbad!*" She shoved the phone into his hand.

He scowled at her, and then beamed falsely down the phone. "Hey, Sinbad! Do you know I really thought Geri was having a secret affair with a guy called Sinbad! And all the time I'd mistaken her writing. She'd actually written down 'Sinead'! God, I'm an uneducated fool, aren't I?"

* * *

Sinead was suffering the ultimate in confusion for the next two hours after her conversation with Gertie and Ben. She'd really liked the sound of Ben. He seemed a really genuine bloke, with a great sense of humour, and she felt herself wishing that she could meet someone more like that. Kind of like Jonathon too, she supposed. What she couldn't figure was how someone as tuned-in and strait-laced as Kevin could ever be friendly with a guy like Ben. An illustrator! And how Gertie hadn't mentioned that Kevin was there, or even offered for her to speak to Kevin. And somehow Sinead had such an uneasy feeling about the whole situation that she hadn't even asked to speak to him. Had he been there at all?

Initially, it had been fun and laughs on the phone, Sinead getting in the opportunity to call tit-for-tat with Gertie and explain to Ben the history around *her* nickname. But then, the gut feeling that something was amiss had grown on Sinead. She hadn't confessed to Geri about her struggling at work and how she'd been finding it hard to cope. She hadn't mentioned how she'd taken on extra tasks to take her mind off of

Steven. She'd joked however, at her immediate promotion, but laughed it off with,

"I always try to go the extra mile at work, but my boss always finds me and brings me back. It must have finally paid off!"

This caused Gertie to roar with laughter, and she'd passed the phone to Ben, for Sinead to repeat it to him as well.

She'd got the full story of Ben's slow acceptance by the publishing company and how he'd decided to move to Cornwall in search of a new lifestyle to go with his new career. And she'd also picked up the disappointed tone in Gertie's voice as she'd reiterated the tale. Disappointed on Kevin's behalf?

In fact, Gertie had sounded totally different on the phone after Sinead had listened to Ben explaining how he'd actually handed in his resignation letter and how excited he was at the prospect of life as an illustrator. Yep, something was definitely not right.

Chapter Twenty-seven

"Why'd I have to say I was Kevin's poxy friend?" Ben demanded, his frown reminding her of the night when he'd screamed at her on the doorstep.

"Hey, that reminds me – *danda la lata!*"

"*What?*"

"That's what you said to me that night. In Spanish. You said something about *danda la lata*. You still haven't told me what it means."

"Well, what a golden opportunity! It means you're a bloody nuisance. How very apt! Now. Why the lie to Sinbad?"

"Sinead."

"She'll always be Sinbad to me. Why the lie? Stop wriggling out of it."

Geri struggled with the wire around the champagne cork, inadvertently knotting it tighter in a bid to appear distracted. He firmly but extremely carefully held Geri by the shoulders and twisted her around to face him. His voice was soft and reassuring. "Geri. I love you. I've told you I love you. So no secrets now, eh? Why did I have to tell Sinbad I was Kevin's friend? Please?"

"Ben," she relaxed her tense shoulders beneath his touch, "I'm so sorry to put you in that position, but . . . but, em, you're gonna think I'm really weird now. You know how Sinead's my best friend?"

He nodded encouragingly.

"Well, you're gonna think this is mad, but, I, em, I haven't told her about me and Kevin splitting up."

He held her at arm's length. "You *are* joking me, aren't you?"

"No. I'm sorry. I'm embarrassed and ashamed and every time I speak to Sinead it seems the worse it's getting. So now she doesn't know about Kevin, or the money worries, or the kids being without a proper father. Shit, she was even here a few months ago, and I still managed to keep it a secret. But not having told her about *that* has meant I haven't been able to tell her about Tony and all the hideous news there and, also, I haven't been able to tell her about you. I'm disgusted at myself. She's supposed to be my best friend, and I've just deceived her for nearly a year of our lives. What kind of a woman am I, Ben? No wonder everything goes arseways for me. I deserve it."

Burying her head in his chest her eyes filled with tears, but before the tears could drip weightedly from her eyelashes Ben took her face in his hands and turned it upwards toward him, wiping at her brimming eyes.

"Geri," he said softly and with conviction, "I'll tell you what kind of a woman it makes you. It makes you a proud one. It just underlines your strength of character, your pride, and your courage. It can't have been easy, holding all of that back from your best mate, just as it can't have been easy coping with the domestics of your lives all on your own, with no-one to lean on. Coping with pigs like Tony on your own, with no-one but your mum and me to talk to about it. Geri, you're only human, but maybe the time has come to be honest with Sinbad. I'll support you every way I can, you know that, but don't risk your friendship over a small thing like this. It wasn't officially a lie, was it? More a withholding of the truth. Don't punish yourself too much. Maybe tonight, maybe tomorrow, maybe next week – pick up that phone and ring Sinbad. It won't be easy, but you have to weigh up how much the friendship means to you."

"Everything." She was unhesitatingly frank. "And stop calling her Sinbad."

He grinned, kissing her cheek, "Sorry, no can do."

She hugged him, and buried her face in the warm velvetness of his neck, breathing in his manly scent.

"OK, I'll give you that one. But *you* can tell her you're calling her Sinbad, not me!"

"No problem. Now, are we gonna open up this champagne or not? We'll deal with Sinbad another day. Tonight, we are celebrating!"

He adeptly worked at the cork with his thumb, and prised it off with a loud bang, which caused both Reece and Cameron to start crying uncontrollably. Geri giggled at their frightened reactions and tried to reassure them, as Ben held the overspilling bottle on the worktop, trying to aim its bubbly into the cheap glasses. Geri lifted the boys down from the table, scurried with them into the lounge and tried to settle them with some toys and the remains of their chocolate. As she returned to the kitchen Ben handed her a glass of popping champagne, and held his up, indicating that she should copy him. She did so. As they held their celebratory glasses aloft, he stated,

"To Patchwork Publishers!"

"To Patchwork Publishers!" she replied.

"Right. Down in one."

"What?"

"Go on! Now!"

They raised their drinks to their mouths and grimaced as they swallowed them down in one go. Ben let out an unmerciful burp afterwards, and they both collapsed with laughter.

"Right. Another one?" he challenged.

"Go for it," she answered, holding out her glass to be filled. Expecting more of the same kind of routine, Geri stood poised for the "Go" and was surprised when Ben dragged her raised arm down, gently.

"No. I've got some things to say before we drink this one."

"Oh." She was surprised, and put her drink down on the worktop.

"No, pick it up. We might have something else to celebrate."

"OK." She was blind as to where this was leading, so followed his instructions obediently.

His voice softened as he stepped closer to her. She looked up at him, loving the way he made her feel so small and protected.

"Geri. I need to ask you something."

Her eyes widened and she let out a theatrical gasp.

"No," he smirked, "don't worry. It's not The Big One. You're all right on that count. What I have to ask you doesn't require an immediate answer. You'll probably need some time to think about it. I can give you a week."

"OK." She beamed excitedly, flushed in anticipation of this great question. He took a deep breath and began.

"Right. I'll be straight with you. I always have. You know my plans. You know from what I said to Sinbad that I handed in my notice today."

She nodded, wide-eyed, trying to hide the shudder of disappointment at his confirmation of that news.

He continued, "In two months' time I'm moving to Pendennis in Cornwall. I've already found a gorgeous cottage-style bungalow that I can afford to rent. It's got a lovely stone wall around the front and a small paddock out the back. Geri, you'd love it. So *un*-Elephant & Castle."

Her heart began to boom in her chest.

He continued. "You know how much I feel for the children?"

She nodded.

"You know what an upheaval it is to move — especially such a distance."

She didn't nod this time, just gawped at him with big eyes.

"Well, I need to ask a favour of you."

She nodded.

"Would you mind very much – erm, would you like to – no, would the *boys* like to –"

"Like to what for God's sake?" She wasn't sure she liked the sound of this.

"Would the boys like to look after The Seven Dwarfs for me? No, not mind them. *Keep* them!"

"What?"

"I know it's a cheek and I should take them with me really, but God, it'd be so awful for the poor little critters, being swilled and swoshed all the way down the west coast."

Disgusted, she plonked her full glass down on the worktop and walked out of the room and up the stairs, the tears heavy in her eyes once again.

"Geri. Geri!" Ben ran up after her, two at a time. He caught up with her in her bedroom. She sat on her bed, with her head in her hands.

"Geri. Don't be like that! It doesn't matter! I can take them with me. It's OK. Forget it."

He tried to hold her but she punched and pushed him away.

"Geri!"

"Is that it?" she screamed at him, part hurt, part infuriated. "Is *that* it? The bloody fish? Jesus, Ben, I knew you were daft, but that's ridiculous!"

"It's OK. Don't *worry* about it."

Geri stared at him, angrily. For a split second she thought she saw his bottom lip wobble. Her gaze shifted from his mouth to his eyes where she met the devilish glint of a man who'd just pulled a fast one.

"You lousy bastard!" she swiped at him.

He roared with laughter at her gullibility. "You div!" He threw his arms around her and pushed her onto the bed, where they rolled together, his strong arms cuddling and cherishing her as he laughed at her naivety.

"You didn't really think I'd ask you to do that, do you?"

"God, Ben, I never know with you!"

After suffering her slaps and swipes, he pinned her down on the bed and passionately kissed her. She melted into the duvet, all signs of anger disappearing.

"I love you, Gertie."

"Hey! That's what Sinead calls me."

"I know, I like it. Gertie."

"No."

"Gertie!"

"Stop."

"Come on," he jumped off the bed and straightened his T-shirt over his taut tanned six-pack, "let's get down to the boys. We can't leave them down there on their own too long, can we?"

"No, s'pose not." She stood and flattened her rumpled hair, tucking it behind her ears again, then grabbed his hand and let him lead her down the stairs.

They found Cameron and Reece throwing plastic toys at each other contentedly, and in the hour that followed Ben sat cuddling Reece while Geri took Cameron to bed. When she came back down the stairs she found Reece lightly snoring in Ben's arms. Again.

"Ben, they're so at home with you," she said as she gently lifted Reece. "It's really lovely."

"See?" he teased. "I'm a natural!"

"Yeah. Right – shame you're leaving."

"Don't be like that. We need to talk."

"Not tonight though, please."

"OK, not tonight." Then, as she climbed the stairs he called after her, "Hurry back down!"

They spent the first part of the evening finishing the champagne. And the second?

Well, I don't know if the champagne loosened my knicker elastic or what happened. But, guess what? Yep. You're right. I did it. I had sex with Ben. And do you know what? It was passion. Pure unadulterated passion. No! With a capital 'P'. Passion. That's it. Sinead would be proud of me. It's taken me nearly a year, but in just one night I've managed to achieve two of her birthday wishes: Passion and Alcohol. Both at the same time, and with the same person! I've only got the Attitude one to contend with now. Still – as they say – two out of three ain't bad! So, you want to know more, I suppose? All right, in the light of not being able to divulge all to Sinead – just yet – I'll tell you. It had started with an innocent kiss and cuddle. You know the situation. You, sprawled on the settee, him pushing his weight down on you and kissing. What more can I say? But then? Then he says . . .

"Geri, I want to make love to you so bad it hurts."

"Ben, no thanks! Are you a sadist or something?"

"What?" he leaned up on his elbows, surprised at her retort.

"You want to make love to me so bad it hurts! No thanky you!"

He laughed. "No. Not make love to you badly, nor to hurt you! I mean I just love you so much and want you to be ready."

Geri took a deep breath, her confidence strengthened by the champagne. She still couldn't believe her own ears when she stood up gracefully, turned to Ben and said:

"Wait here. I'll be back in a minute."

Dimming the lights as she left the room, she tiptoed up the stairs, careful to avoid any mislaid toys on the way, and having checked the boys were sleeping peacefully went into her bedroom, and rooted in her ancient sexy-knicker drawer.

Feeling an over-abundance of confidence, she shook the few creases from a lacy bra and suspender belt and laid them on the bed. She then dug silently through the drawer, looking for a lacy g-string she thought she once possessed. Just then she caught sight of her reflection as she bent over the open drawer, her bare white arse dimpled with small dots of cellulite smiling back at her.

What are you thinking of? And look at yourself. Tried that with Tony and what difference did it make?

She threw the redundant lingerie back into the dark drawer and slammed it shut. She shimmied to her wardrobe and pulled out a silk kimono-style robe. Squirting her naked body with a few sprays of perfume, she slid the smooth fabric onto her arms, and tied the belt in a knot at her waist.

As she padded down the stairs barefoot, she saw Ben fiddling with the CD player.

He caught sight of her from the corner of his eye as he pressed the PLAY button and music quietly filled the room. He groaned appreciatively as she approached him. Sliding his arms around her waist he pulled her toward him, kissing her face and neck with the smallest kisses she'd ever experienced. With a tug at the knotted silk belt, her kimono-robe fell open, and his large warm hands quickly found their way around her naked waist and slid up around her back.

She was surprised many times during the next two hours at the things that turned her on. Ben revealed erogenous zones that she never realised she had. At the selfish hands of Tony and Kevin who had purely used her as a vessel for their grindings, a sexual experience with Ben was definitely something to write home about. At thirty years old she, for the first time, felt she was crossing the bridge from being a girl to being a woman. Despite having had sexual partners in the past and hell, even giving birth, she still felt that she wasn't quite fulfilled as a woman. And now she'd met Ben. Caring, considerate, passionate Ben. Ben who spent ages kissing her toes and licking the inside of her naked thighs until she shuddered with anticipation. Ben who nuzzled the nape of her neck until the goose-pimples shot straight over her shoulders and down her chest, rendering her nipples rock-hard and over-sensitive.

Ben who was enjoying making love to *her*, in all her nakedness and entirety, and *loved* her. Not just fancied her, or "serviced" her out of some kind of perverse duty. He loved her. He told her so, repeatedly.

They didn't realise that the CD had played its whole sequence of songs already. Twice. As she lay in his arms, covered only by a loose cushion that had fallen from the sofa, she felt fantastic. Her body had almost shocked her with its reactions to his touch. She'd taken on roles and positions that she'd never dreamed she was capable of.

Now they lay, satiated and exhausted in the dimly lit room, her head resting on his chest and his naked downy arm protectively around her bare back.

* * *

The next morning Geri awoke in her bed, feeling slightly different "down there", and then recalled with a rush of affection the night she'd spent downstairs with Ben. They'd pulled themselves together at about three in the morning, and Ben had declined Geri's offer to stay the night, saying that he'd feel bad if the boys were to see them in bed together the next morning.

"There's time enough for that. Let's not rush them, eh?" he'd said.

Admiring him, she'd snuggled up into the warm spot he'd occupied in the bed, trying to hold on to the smell of his aftershave, watching him as he'd dressed and wishing he could stay for a night full of cuddles. He'd leant down to kiss her again and she heard him tiptoe down the stairs, fumbling in the kitchen for what seemed like ages. She must have fallen into a contented sleep as she never heard the front door click as he'd finally left.

Now, singing and whistling as she flitted down the stairs, she heard Cameron call for her in the way that only three-year-olds can, pronouncing her name as something like *"Maaa-meeee, maaaa-meeee, weeee-weeees"*. She turned around on the bottom step and leapt and skipped back up the stairs, helped him out of his bed and shuffled him into the toilet for his early morning piddle. Nothing would knock the stuffing out of her this morning. She was too happy with her life. She twisted the bath taps on, dropped in the plug, poured in extravagant amounts of bubble bath, then trotted back down the stairs with Reece in her arms and Cameron bumping down on his bum behind her. This *'hills are aliiive'* trotting-and-skipping scenario was bought screechingly to a halt, however, when she laid eyes on the kitchen table. A sick feeling of déja vû swept over her as her eyes focused on the envelope propped up by the salt and pepper pots.

Kevin?

Still staring at the blank white envelope she, zombie-like, took the boys' plastic bowls and filled them with Weetabix, milk and sugar and, plonking a spoon in each, rested them down on the table. In front of 'the envelope'.

Not again! But somehow it's worse this time. It's still so fresh and new and lovely. At least with Kevin, I now realise, we were probably incompatible from the start. Things had

471

started to get boring and mundane. He despised my figure and, obviously, my personality – otherwise he wouldn't have gone off with Her would he? But Ben? God, it's all so great and new.

She lifted the envelope between her thumb and index finger, almost afraid to touch it. Swallowing hard, she ripped it open as she slid down onto the pine chair at the table. Her eyes were unblinking as she took it in. It read:

Dear Geri,

I didn't really want to ask you to look after The Seven Dwarfs, but after we had such a laugh about it, I couldn't get my real question out. It, somehow, made it seem a joke. And, Geri, this is far from a joke.

I love you Geri, very much, and have done for a long time. You know how I feel toward the children and while it breaks my heart to think of moving to Cornwall, I just know that it's something I have to do.

Which is why I want to ask you this.

Geri, I know you've established a life for yourself here but would you at least think about it? Would you consider coming with me? Move to Pendennis with me, Geri. You and Cameron and Reece. We could start a new life there. I can't promise you that it'll be roses around the door, but I can assure you that I'll love you and cherish you and the boys with all my heart and soul. I want us to be together, and I know it's selfish of me, because I'm the one that's going, but I'd be the happiest man alive if you'd only say yes.

Say you'll move to Cornwall too. Just think, what have you got to lose? You've no job to worry about. No ties, no strings. *Cameron hasn't even started school yet. We could enrol him in a Nursery and Infants school there. It'd be great for the children. Imagine them, living in the country!*

They'd love it! And when you're ready, you could find work there. We'd have a better lifestyle. A better life!

I've always thought, Geri, that you can never answer the 'what if's' if you don't try them out. There's only one way to know and that's to say yes. Yes, you'll come with me. And I promise I'll continue to love and look after you for as long as I live.

Sorry to leave a note like this. Call me a coward, "Gertie"!

Lots of love and love and love,

Ben XXXXXXX

"Bastard!" she shouted as she slapped the note down onto the table. "Why couldn't he ask me to my face? 'What have you got to lose?' Why couldn't he tell me what a loser I was last night – *before* he conned me into sleeping with him!" She slammed and banged her way around the kitchen, causing Cameron and Reece to run to the door and ask her what was wrong. She answered, "Nothing, love," and forced a smile until they'd retreated back into the lounge, for their early morning blast of Teletubbies, when she'd continued cursing under her breath.

It seemed it was time for the third birthday wish, Attitude, to rear its ugly head.

Then, she picked up the telephone and screamed at Ben for a continuous fifteen minutes. He struggled and spluttered to make himself heard, but she blasted him out of the game every time with her accusations and insults. She felt hurt and betrayed that he thought so little of her.

"Oh yeah," she hollered angrily, "sure! I've got no job, no ties, no friends. I just stay at home with the kids all the time. You've got it all worked out, Ben. You could have discussed it with me first! It seems you've already got their schools organised, my job arranged! Jesus, Ben, don't you think I've got a mind of my own! Don't deny me my personality! I've managed with the boys on my own for nearly a year and we're doing *fine*, thank you! *And*, have you any idea what went through my mind when I saw that envelope on the table this morning? Have I ever *told* you about Kevin-The-Coward? Have I? The sneaky bastard of an ex-husband, who was so confidently having an affair behind my back, but didn't have the balls to tell me to my face! My ex-husband who ceremoniously left me and two very small children without so much as a *goodbye!*" She was almost out of control now, screaming and sobbing at the same time.

Ben tried to get a word in, "I'm so sorry . . . it didn't occur to me . . . I didn't think . . . sorry . . . I love you . . . don't, Geri . . . I should have said . . . please . . . please!"

"Fuck off, Ben Robbins! You conned me into the best sex of my life! You conned me into thinking you loved me and had my – no – *our* interests at heart! And all you were thinking of was yourself! You just wanted the security of a family of chaperones to go to Cornwall with you! I *never* want to hear from you again. Ever!"

She slammed down the phone.

She spent the rest of the whole day crying.

No, mourning.

* * *

By evening she'd managed to compose herself. If the truth be known, she'd cried herself dry – there was nothing left to sob. For the fourteenth time that day the telephone rang. She already knew who it was, but had to answer just to be sure.

"Hello," she whispered, her voice hoarse and small.

"Geri, just let me –"

She put the phone down. Ben. Again. He'd been knocking at her door resolutely for an hour earlier in the day, and it had broken her heart to watch him from behind the upstairs net curtains, begging and pleading to let him see her. It had been doubly painful to watch Cameron crying on her bed, begging and pleading to let them see him. God, she was stuck in the middle of a mess. She vowed *never* to let a man close to the three of them again. Never.

Shortly after the beginning of *Brookside* the phone rang, again. She answered it, despondently, knowing once again who it was.

"Leave me alone!" she barked.

"Gertie, what's wro–"

She hung up again. As she did, it hit her that it had beem a woman's voice. It rang again, immediately.

"Hello?" she said hesitantly.

"Gertie? Whatever's wrong?"

It was Sinead.

I don't want to think of her as Sinbad any more. The fun's gone out of it now, what with it just being a reminder of Ben. So it's back to Sinead again.

She began to cry at the friendly sound of a familiar voice. However, the scene backfired dismally as she finally confessed her domestic disasters of the year. She revealed to a silent, listening Sinead the turmoil of the disappearance of Kevin, her pain and the strange, misplaced guilt at being abandoned, the horror at the unveiling of Tony and finally, the joy and happiness she'd found with Ben, building up to a pitiful climax as she recounted the past twenty-four hours.

As she mopped her tears and sniffed, the voice at the end of the phone was ominously silent.

"Sinead?" she whispered, hoping that she was still there and she hadn't poured her heart out to an empty line. "Sinead? Are you still there?"

Then, amazed beyond belief, she listened to Sinead's booming and furious voice as she yelled, "*Am – I – still – here?* Are you joking me or what? Am I still here? You snidey bitch!"

"What?" Suddenly shocked back into the real world, Geri couldn't believe Sinead's cruel retort.

Has she been listening at all?

"You out-and-out bitch! You mean to say that every time we've spoken for the last *year* you've been lying and bullshitting to me? And what about that weekend I was there with you? All that shite about Kevin working late and being in bed! Total, utter lies? And I thought we were friends, Gertie? Ha! You deceitful cow! Forget it, Gertie! Stuff you and your 'friendship'! I never want to have anything to do with you again!"

And with that, Sinead slammed down the phone.

This has all gone horribly wrong. She was supposed to 'oooh' and 'ahh' in all the right places, and be sympathetic and friendly and kind. She was supposed to tell me how men are bastards and how we're better off without them and how sorry she felt for me and my predicament. She was supposed to say how she understood why I hadn't told her about Kevin and the rest of it, explaining how it reflected my pride and courage and strength of character. Just like Ben said! I should be Gertie the Victim, not Gertie the Accused.

It's all gone horribly wrong . . .

Chapter Twenty-eight

Sinead resented her own tears. The tears that were unprompted and unexpectedly spilling from her mascara'd eyes. On replacing the receiver, she paced angrily through the open patio doors and leant on her balcony, watching the local men quietly smoking and playing cards on battered sun-damaged tables outside the small bars. As hurt and pained as she felt at Gertie's inability to confide in her, Jonathon Morgan was arriving in the morning and there she'd be, once again, meeting him at the airport with a red, swollen face. But this time it was from tears rather than punches. Pacing around her apartment, dragging deeply on her Marlboro, she sucked in the smoky haze, held it for a few seconds, and then blew out its remains with a sigh. She was already recognising the preliminary twinges of guilt.

* * *

Ben sat astride a ministool, leaning on the shiny wooden table and staring into his full pint vacuously.

"Hey, mate, you get pissed quicker if you drink it!"

His trance was broken as Mark arrived, slapping him heartily on the back. But as he pulled out a stool from beneath the small table and plonked himself down on it, Ben returned to beer-gazing.

"Hey," Mark's tone was jovial, and he paused to take a large slug of his Kronenbourg, "what's up? Not sorry about leaving now, are you? Not too late you know. You can retract it."

Ben shook his head, irritated, "No, it's not that."

"Ah, I get it. Bird trouble. Yep, I can spot it a mile away. Here, listen to this one. You know I told you I'd started seeing that bird from Ladbroke Grove?"

Ben shook his head, not interested, continuing to avoid eye contact with Mark who continued, regardless.

"Well, snotty cow she turned out to be! Just 'cos I voiced my opinion to her snobby mates about the New Labour she's chucked me! Here, and this is the best of it, d'ya know what she called me? Really," he began to laugh as he took another large mouthful of beer, now leaving less than half a pint remaining, "it's hilarious really! There we were shouting and screaming at each other outside her front door, and it was going great, you know. I was calling her names and she was calling me names, and guess what she said?"

His question hung emptily in the air as Ben failed to respond. Mark wasn't going to be put off that easily. He nudged in him the ribs. "'Ay, mate. What d'ya reckon she said?"

"Dunno." Ben's tone was flat and indifferent.

"Snotty cow. She said, and I quote 'Mark, you're embarrassingly working-class, aggressive, ignorant and *petulant*'!"

Still no response from Ben. Mark nudged him again, this time harder, causing him to grimace.

"*Petulant!* Fucking petulant." He downed the remaining half-pint in one, then stood up, digging his hand deep into his jeans pocket. "Daft bitch," he muttered as he walked to the bar, "I don't even *like* animals!"

As Mark's murmuring voice faded, Ben took his opportunity to get out of there before he returned to aggravate him all the more. Grabbing his jacket from the torn velvet chair, he left the pub leaving behind him a full pint of lager and a bemused and confused Mark.

Back in his flat, he sat down, intent on writing another note to Geri. It was, in his mind, almost as if two wrongs would make a right, as if to explain his poor choice of communication by another poor choice would render him in the clear. He really wasn't thinking clearly, his desperation at making things right paramount in his mind. Half an hour and three-quarters of a note-pad later he still wasn't any closer to finding the words to redeem himself. Sheer wretchedness forced him to pick up the phone once more, ready to launch straight into an explanation rather than perform the routine hello-hello-phone-down scenario. He dialled her number sloppily and listened to the ringing tone. She picked it up after six rings.

"Hello?" her voice was harassed.

Right. Now!

"Itdoesn'thavetobeCornwall. I'msosorry!"

Four seconds. He estimated that was all she'd given him. Hardly worth it.

* * *

Geri sobbed, distressed and distraught. The desperation in Ben's voice was cutting her in pieces. She felt terribly cruel at refusing to speak to him so doggedly but she was, at least temporarily, unable to talk. To anyone. The only person she had wanted to speak to in the whole world was Sinead. And she had. And look what had happened. So now she was wallowing in mourning for the loss of *two* loved ones: Ben who with or without her was moving to Cornwall and Sinead, her best friend for over half her life who now, through her own stupidity and pride, wanted absolutely nothing to do with her.

"Maa-meeee, want anofer jiiink!" Cameron's request for another drink of milk broke her trance. Shifting immediately into autopilot, she sprang from the chair and marched into the kitchen where they were both playing on the cool tiled floor.

"Come on now, boys, no more drinks. It's bedtime. Now!"

"Nooo, nooo," they both chorused, Reece now more than able to mimic Cameron's speech.

God, where's Ben when you need him? I could just do with him here tonight. Reece'd sit with him and watch Jungle Book while I cajoled Cameron up the stairs and at least settled one of them down. More often than not Reece would fall asleep on Ben's lap anyway. Still. No point in tormenting myself any further. I wish I could just pick up the phone and turn the clock back three hours with Sinead. I'm so upset at her reaction. Why was she so angry? I know, really. I'd probably be the same in her shoes. She's so sorted and organised – her life so perfect. It seems we've drifted apart more than I'd realised. Maybe motherhood has alienated me from my pre-maternal buddies more than I'd cared to notice. She just doesn't understand what it feels like to know you're lying and deceiving your best friend. I suppose I started to lie because I didn't want her to judge me – my life. But now, I've made it worse. She's angry with me now – at least she wouldn't have been angry *if I'd just told her about Kevin in the first place. I just want to speak to her and Ben. My two closest people in the whole world, and they hate me. They really hate me . . .*

* * *

"I'm *not* going anywhere without her!" he shouted into the empty room, throwing the lid of the cardboard box across the bed. "I don't even *want* the job now. I wish I'd never handed in my notice!" Why couldn't I just be contented with what I had, he thought – a warm, loving woman, a decent flat, an acceptable lifestyle and a decent job? "But no, no," he continued out loud, "I have to try and grab too much from the situation!" Cornwall, or *wherever*, only holds an attraction if I've still got Geri in my life, he thought. Illustrating's great, something I've always wanted to do, but now, on my own? After finding what I'm looking for in a woman, I'm going to walk away from it, stubborn, just for a job as an illustrator? Shit, Ben, you're an idiot! You can be an illustrator anywhere! You don't have to be in Cornwall. You'll be working from 'home' – wherever the hell *that* may be, anyway, so what's the big deal with Cornwall? Swallow your pride, man, and go round to see her in the morning. Give her the evening to calm down and think about it all. Then go around tomorrow and tell her Cornwall's off *and try to get her back.*

He felt sick. So sick, in fact, he couldn't even go near the family of foxes. Everything was annoying him. Finding every chair uncomfortable, he marched over to his easel, sat on the high stool there and viewed his work so far. The family of foxes looked amateurish! He was finding it unbearable to even think about them at the moment, and so moved, once again, to the kitchen. As he illuminated the spotlit ceiling, he noticed the Seven Dwarfs flick their fin-tails in unison. Resting his elbows on the drainer he leaned in toward the fish bowl to watch them, often finding their fluid smooth movements relaxing. Even *they* couldn't make eye contact with him! And four out of the seven were excreting worm-like black fronds indignantly to his face.

"Sod you!" he yelled at the unsuspecting, and totally uncaring, fish and threw the tea towel over their bowl, shrouding them in darkness.

It seemed the walls were slowly closing in on him, the pale blue painted walls trying to suck him into their structure. He felt suffocated. Suffocated, sick and desperate. He had to get out. Even for a walk. Jabbing his arms into the sleeves of his jacket he looked down at the now adorable, dried, snotty patch that Geri had christened his once-new jacket with. He smoothed his fingers over the crusted swirls lovingly. What he'd give right now to have her wiping snot on his jacket. A wave of emotion overwhelmed him as he suddenly realised that if only he'd managed to find his words and *tell* Geri, rather than write that damn letter, things might still be fantastic. The dread that his actions had ruined everything forever washed over him again. He sat down, pulling off the same jacket again, and throwing it in a heap on the floor.

After a further hour of deliberation and anguish, he decided to try and temporarily put it all out of his mind by concentrating on what he might take away with him. As he walked into his dimly lit bedroom, intending to sort out some boxes of stuff that he'd never even gotten around to unpacking when he'd moved in years ago, anger rose over him again, and he stripped naked and got into his cool bed.

The pain in his chest was so bad as he lay in bed that night it kept him awake.

It was hours later and he was still discussing it with himself, in a deranged state of confusion.

"OK," he voiced into his pillow, "so I handled it badly. I hate myself for my cowardice. But is it really too late? Please, God – give me another chance with her!"

Finally, at four fifty-one he found sleep, having

turned the whole affair over in his mind all night. He'd finally concluded that, despite his obvious love for her, she couldn't see it. He'd suggested to himself that maybe she wasn't ready for a relationship yet. He'd reprimanded himself that maybe he should have tried harder, but followed up with encouragement that maybe it wasn't too late, just a prime case of bad timing.

He'd see her in the morning.

* * *

Sinead knew she'd been a little bit unfair on Gertie. She realised she had taken the opportunity to release all the pent-up anger left over from Steven Randall, coupled with her recent work pressures and even her homesickness. She suspected that Gertie must be horrified at her reaction. Try as she might, the guilt just wouldn't shift. It hung on in there with both hands, refusing to let her shake it off. She knew herself that the wrath of Sinead Kelly's tongue was not a nice thing to be subjected to. But still, she defended herself slightly, Gertie's actions were lamentable; after all, they'd been friends for years, and *never* had any secrets like that. Not major ones anyway. Surely Geri *knew* how lonely and homesick she felt? She couldn't find her usual solace in food, making her realise how severely this had upset her. She was renowned for bingeing in a crisis. Bad news? No problem – just pass me the chocolate biscuits *first!* But right now the last thing on Sinead's mind was food. Well, not exactly the last thing, because she kept going to her cupboards and opening the doors to see what she could pick at, but on seeing the huge shiny bags of *Fritos*, *Palitos de Papas* and *Solchitos* smiling back at her, she cringed, unable to bear the savoury flavour of crisps. She opened the fridge door expectantly only to feel sick on seeing the *Campo Frio* hot-dog sausages, three bars of *Milka* chocolate, *Bimbo* bread and a half-empty jar of *Nutella*. Food wasn't going to help her through this one. Moving back out to her balcony, she sat, bathed by the warm evening air as it smothered her bare arms and the back of her neck. Her hair, which had been so perfectly secured with the enormous clip was starting to drop, long tendrils now kissing the back of her neck and cheeks. She didn't care. Her appearance was irrelevant right now. Lifting an opened wine bottle from the plastic table she brought it to her lips, taking a swig of the slightly warmed juice. She felt so dispensable! 'Out of sight and out of mind' was a term that continued to run through her head. Had her absence pushed her to the back of Gertie's mind? Had it been *that* easy to be forgotten? Gertie obviously hadn't realised how close Sinead held her in her heart and mind. In a country of strangers and an unfamiliar culture, Sinead had clung on to the image of Gertie as something which reminded her of her roots. Her home. The confession of this huge, year-long lie had revealed that Gertie's life had moved on, quite significantly, and Sinead guessed that she probably had many new friends now. New, more exciting friends, who probably knew the ins-and-outs of Kevin's departure and all the related gossip. Feeling her depression worsen (she was on the brink of it anyway what with her disastrous relationship history and overpowering work commitments), she felt a strong sense of being 'in the right' at her anger at Gertie, but conversely a terrible feeling of loss.

She sobbed and sobbed into her alcohol-fumed flat, as she got slowly more and more pissed. Feeling despondent beyond belief, she grabbed the telephone again, hours after screaming at Gertie down the same line, and punched in the 00-353 code for Ireland.

Mam.

When in a crisis, always turn to Mam. True to form and as she expected, the phone rang a good seven or eight times before it was answered, giving her time to clear her throat and wipe her eyes.

Surprisingly her mam answers. "Hello?"

"Mam, it's me?"

"What's wrong? Ya sound awful. Are ya all right?"

"No, Mam," she begins to snuffle again, "I'm not all right."

"Whatever's wrong? What's after happening?"

"I've fallen out with Gertie."

"Gertie! What, is she there?"

Why do mums always have to pick up the wrong end of the stick?

"No! Over the phone. I've fallen out with Gertie on the telephone."

"Ah Sinead, youse are not at it again, are ya? You girls, I don't know, forever bloody fallin' out."

"Mam," Sinead's tone was surprisingly condescending,

considering she's the one looking for support, "we're not teenagers, you know. And we've not just 'fallen out' – I've screamed at her and told her I don't want to know her any more."

"Things must be bad. What's happened?"

Sinead spent the next hour explaining, between crying and sniffing and blowing her nose, how deceived and betrayed she felt. In typical Mam-form, Mrs Kelly merely 'mmmm'ed, for the most part, listening carefully to what Sinead was telling her. Only when she paused for breath, at the very end of the tale, did she voice anything resembling an opinion. As Sinead drew her breath in deeply, having lit the cigarette, Mrs Kelly remained silent.

Blowing the smoke into the air, Sinead spoke again, agitated at the silence, "Mam? Have you nothing to say about it?"

"I do, Sinead. I do."

"What? You're supposed to tell me what it is, not just confirm you've got an opinion! What do you think?"

"Right. I think, if I'm honest – which I always try to be – that you've jumped the gun a little with our Gertie."

Sinead exhaled dramatically. "How d'ya mean?"

"I mean," Mrs Kelly's tone was controlled and level, "that you're a hypocrite if you're sitting on that phone in Spain, telling me for the last hour, that you've never, and I do mean *never*, Sinead, told Gertie any lies."

"No, I haven't."

"Ah, now, Sinead! Just hold on to yerself there a minute. Take a few minutes now to just think about things. Are ya telling me that you haven't pretended, maybe even just a little bit, that you're having a fantastic time out there? Can you honestly hold your hand on your heart and say to me that you haven't just coloured in the whole picture a small bit? I'm not wanting an answer from ya, Sinead – it's for you to answer yerself, but I'm sure that, if you thought about it enough, you'd be able to point to a good few times you'd twisted the truth a little bit to your pals in England. Sure, even Bridie was telling me the other day that you sounded like you were having a great time. But, Sinead, I'm your mam. I *know* ya. I know that, sometimes, it's not all as great as you make it out to be."

The words washed over Sinead like a wave of cool, calm water. She knew that, once again, her mam was right. She herself had lied to Gertie and deceived her. Maybe not with such a serious sequence of events – well, she had deliberately kept the Steven tale from her, and the beatings and lies and her desperate homesickness. As her mam's words continued as staccato background percussion, Sinead's mind whizzed back to the weekend that she'd spent in England. The night they'd gone for the pizza when she had got drunk in an over-zealous attempt to prove what good fun she was these days, how she was used to going out drinking virtually every night, and how the Spanish guys were literally, *literally*, fighting over her. She could already feel the burden of a hangover looming, and so, thanking her mam profusely and replacing the receiver, she headed for the peaceful solace of bed – Jonathon Morgan's flight was due in a few hours' time.

* * *

Geri suffered a fitful evening. A vice-like grip inside her head squeezed out one of the most painful headaches she'd ever experienced.

Having finally got the boys to bed – it was nearly eleven before Reece settled – I'm now suffering with post-crying disfigurements. Huge, blocked, red swollen nose. Enormous puffy pink eyes and overwhelming tiredness but a resilient, overactive brain. Charming.

She'd sat bolt upright in bed several times, surprisingly *not* because she'd been woken by the boys but as her mind had catapulted between her anxieties about Ben to Sinead and then rebounded back to Ben again. She'd been tempted frequently through the evening to ring Quick Draw McGraw for a motivational quote, but chided herself for her two-facedness – usually she dreaded hearing them and now she was ringing up for them!

Pull yourself together, girl! She'd probably quote you something hideous like that shoe thing she goes on about, what is it now? Something like, "I thought I was bad because I had no shoes, and then I met a man with no feet!" Or, what's that other sicko one, "When the pony dies the ride is over"! All of a sudden Mum's dreadful quotes are swarming through my head haphazardly. I'm disturbed between the "A banker is someone who lends you an umbrella when the sun is shining, and who asks for it back when it starts to rain" and "A candle loses nothing by lighting another candle". Christ, I am confused.

But I'm also very depressed.

In less than twenty-four hours I've lost the best thing that's ever happened to me in the wrappings of a gorgeous male body, and the best thing that could ever happen to me in the shape of a lifelong friend who understands why I don't like tomato juice and vodka in the same glass!

The question is, can I cope without them? Or more importantly – do I want to?

A decision is definitely called for. I can't let these situations go untouched. It just feels that, after a year of finding my independence – no – being forced to find my independence, Ben has come along and swept me off my feet. Before I can even come to terms with the feelings we have for each other, before I've even showered to wash him away from last night – he's making decisions for me! He's assuming what I want for the future! OK, so I'll be honest – I did find his considerations for the boys' lifestyles quite endearing – you know, the way he'd mentioned the playschools and how they'd love living in the country. I'd be a liar if I didn't say that a part of that really appeals to me. But that's not the point! Is it!

Is it?

Am I being selfish? I think it was just the déja vu thing with the envelope! It bought all those insecurities back again. I suppose Ben got what Kevin deserved.

I'll just have to make some amends. If I don't hear from Ben by lunch-time, I think I'll ring him, and I'll have to wait *until the evening to try and explain things to Sinead a bit more. Something's got to be done. To think I'd dreaded telling her about Kevin going! Really, I've just revealed myself as the shallow, selfish bitch that Sinead sees me as. To think I've managed to keep it such a big guilty secret for the best part of a year and then I only decide to tell her when I want to cry on her shoulder. Just because I'm looking for sympathy! She's right – I have taken our friendship for granted and totally abused it. No wonder she doesn't want anything to do with me! She's probably got beachfuls of attractive, single friends who enjoy her company, don't just lie to her about their lives. I've probably, without realising it, been pushing Sinead away all year. Now I deserve to pay the consequences. I hate and despise myself. I feel older, fatter and sadder than when Kevin went. Christ – he did me a bloody favour!*

Chapter Twenty-nine

Despite her nocturnal promises as she'd finally managed to settle down, Geri woke in a different frame of mind. Casting aside her intentions to ring Ben and contact Sinead to explain herself, it seemed her confidence had been sapped from her overnight, almost Samson-and-Delilah-style. Running her hands through her hair – no, *it feels as if it's all still there* – she's just experienced that awful feeling when you wake up after an incident the night before, but don't recall it immediately. After a heavy night she awoke, initially feeling quite good, and then a slimy, niggling worm crawled through her mind, reminding her that 'something' had happened. For a minute she couldn't recall what it was, her stomach churning in anticipation. Then, it came to her: the feelings of despondency hanging around her neck like a ball and chain. Full sure that she didn't feel brave enough to call them now, she chose, instead, to toss it around in her head endlessly, feeling miserable and sorrowful. If the gorgeous euphoria of sex with Ben had been the calm before the storm, then this sickening guilt was the barren devastation afterwards.

And I suddenly imagine the tumbleweeds blustering through my hallway and bedroom, the ghostly whistle of the wind blowing through my, now empty and lonely, mind. Where I'd begun to feel good, I now feel shite! I feel fifty-four and fifteen stone today. Depression's an awful thing, isn't it? Or is this just thinly disguised guilt? All I know is that nothing quite looks or feels the same. I suppose I've tried to run screaming, away from anything that might turn me into my mother, but I can admit to you now that I even looked through Cynthia's gadget catalogue, and I'm slightly embarrassed to admit that I could even see the benefits of the plastic man for the car to deter would-be-thieves. Am I turning into my mother?

She finally dragged herself out of bed to respond to a determined and devastated Reece calling.

A full nappy with disappointingly leaking seams!

Geri stared at the Special K in the bowl, wondering whether its benefits were diminished by the four teaspoons of sugar she'd just heaped in on the top of it.

Life goes on, doesn't it? That's the new attitude I need to adopt. There's no point in wallowing in this. I'll have to keep myself busy, and if Sinead and Ben really think anything of me, they'll both be on the phone before ten o' clock to apologise. And then I'll make them realise how unreasonable they've been.

By seven fifty-three, however, Geri had the boys dressed and fed, and was hanging various bags and implements from the pushchair handles. As she tugged Cameron's cap onto his head, checking that the weather was promising to be sunny again, he looked up at her with large innocent eyes and asked, "Where we goin', Mummeee?"

Glancing at her watch, and realising that the shops weren't even open yet, she ad-libbed, "Oh, just to Nana's for a little while. How would you like to go and play at Nan's for a bit?"

"*Yeahhh!*" they both cheered.

Cynthia instantly knew something was askew. The sight of the three of them glistening in the early morning sunshine, and on her doorstep at quarter past eight in the morning! Unusually diplomatic, she invited them in, unquestioned.

It was, however, only a matter of minutes before curiosity got the better of her, compelling her to ask, "So, what's happened? It's not like you to be out so early?"

"Nothing!"

The intuitive expression on her mum's face was enough to instigate a lengthy, and somewhat emotional, spilling of the beans. Nearly two hours later Geri had enlightened Cynthia on the world of being a single parent, right down to the shitty-gritty of Tony, the powder-sniffing Adam, serial-student Sylvia and then, the breathtaking, beloved Ben. Surprisingly, Cynthia grasped the whole idea rather quickly, "Right, so you've come *out* to avoid the phone calls that you're desperate for!"

"Mum! You make me sound pathetic! God, you

must think I'm a right prat if that's how you see me!"

"Geraldine! You *are* a prat! Excuse my language. You sound paranoid. If you're waiting to speak to Ben and Sinead so much, then *why* have you come out?"

"Cos I'm scared that they won't ring."

"But how will you know?"

"Look, Mum, I'm sorry. Just leave me on this one. I just can't stand rejection second time around. It was bad enough to fall out with them in the first place, without waiting for a potential phone call only to find that they're not even bothered with me!"

Cynthia, like a dog with a bone, couldn't let go of this one. "Bet you've left the answerphone on though, haven't you?"

"Mum!"

"OK, OK."

* * *

Sinead had spent the morning preparing herself to collect Jonathon Morgan from the airport. She took only twenty minutes to clean her place up, disposing of chocolate wrappers and old wine bottles. If the poor devil had gone to the trouble of buying new underwear then she supposed she'd better make a slight effort too. Whilst her mind buzzed painfully with Geri's betrayal she forced herself to be jovial and hospitable to the charming Jonathon, and on meeting him at the airport was surprised at how her memory of him hadn't been as complimentary as the real thing.

As they sped along the road from the airport at

Manises back to Buñol, chatting and laughing easily, he asked her if she'd heard anything from Steven lately.

Intrigued by his question – they'd discussed it many times over the last few months and he *knew* that she had nothing more to do with Steven – she answered, "You know I don't. He's left anyway. Why do you ask me that?"

Refraining from making eye contact with her, busying himself with a speck of imaginary dirt beneath his finger-nail, he replied, "Oh, just that I can see you've been crying. I just can't help but compare this to the last time you met me at the airport."

"No. No, nothing like that." She dismissed, pulling down her shades over her red eyes.

"Well, what then?" He wasn't about to let it go that easily.

Sinead cursed under her breath. She'd only recently commended herself on her expert concealer application and excellent mascara'd eyelashes which, she thought, had hidden all signs of tears. Bloody Jonathon Morgan! Why couldn't he mind his own business anyway?

"Oh, I've had a row with my best mate in England."

"Oh," he over-dramatised his speech, "girlie stuff."

"No," she spun her head to face him, her expression angry, "*not* girlie stuff! Very serious stuff actually. *Don't* ask me about it! Please."

"Point taken," he replied, and swiftly changed the subject. "So, what're you gonna do with me for my few days in Valencia? Any plans? Other than *Las Fallas?*"

She was grateful for the diversion. "Yes, I have

actually. I spent a week recently exploring loads of the tourist spots, and there's just tons to show you."

"Great!" He sounded genuinely pleased at the prospect. "I've been reading up about Valencia and wondered if you've ever heard of the *Tomatina*?"

"Course I have!" she laughed. "How could you live *in* Buñol and *not* know about it?"

His face lit up a little, "Have you been to it?"

"Yeah. Last year."

"It sounds amazing! I want to come to it this year. It's in September, isn't it?"

"August. The last Wednesday of August."

"So, what's it like?"

"Mad!" she laughed, turning down the car stereo a fraction.

"Tell me!"

"Well, it's basically an opportunity to slug ripe tomatoes at people and enjoy it. It's been going for about sixty years I think and happens every year on the last Wednesday of August in Buñol."

"Why?"

"Just for the fun of it! It seems, though, there are some very loose rules. You can only use tomatoes, and you must squish them first, before throwing them. It's not only tomato-chucking though. It's a week-long celebratory festival with music, bands, fun and food. Last year there were loads of Spanish teenagers, but also quite a lot of Australians here."

"So tell me, how does it all start? What actually happens?"

"Well, last year we followed the crowds down the hill passing the stands that were selling T-shirts and drink. Loads of people are on the booze before it even starts. It's crazy. You'll see when we get there, but in Buñol the streets are quite narrow, and they close all the buildings up, their shutters and doors latched. They're smart enough to put plastic covers over anything lower than three storeys high. The people in the street sing and dance, chanting, '*Agua – Agua – Agua*,' – that means water."

"I know. Get on with it."

"Sorry. They chant '*Agua – Agua*' hoping that they'll be drowned by a bucketful of water thrown from the balconies above or from the fire hoses spouting from the shaky wooden stand in the middle of the chaos. But they needn't shout too loud. We were all soaked repeatedly with the freezing water. Soon the chanting turns into Spanish songs and everyone starts to squat and rise to the music. I didn't have a clue what they were singing about though; we just joined in for the fun of it. By about half eleven, the streets are packed shoulder to shoulder and everyone is really hyper, and then at midday the cannon fires."

"What's that for?"

"Stop interrupting me!" Sinead scolded, as she got lost in the antics of last August. "An enormous dump-truck starts to come down the blocked street. Everyone squashes themselves together to make room for it. We were all absolutely soaked to the skin already, and we kind of all stuck together as if we were in a mass wet T-shirt competition."

She saw Jonathon glance at her chest and then raise his eyebrows appreciatively. She continued, "In the back of the truck are about ten guys standing on top of tons of tomatoes. They start to throw them all out into the crowd and soon it seems like thousands of tomatoes fly out, pelting our helpless, exposed bodies. As the truck squeezes through, the entire contents are unloaded by the Spaniards in the back, and then the real battle starts. Tomatoes begin just whizzing through the air."

"Did you chuck any?"

"Course I did! It's kill or be killed out there, I tell you!" Sinead was grinning widely at the memory, her first sincere smile since collecting Jonathon. "I chucked a few into the crowd and then from another direction I got one in the face. They really sting when they hit you. Everyone goes tomato crazy. Kids hit adults, neighbours mush tomatoes in each other's faces. Do you wear contact lens?"

"Yeah!"

"You don't wanna wear 'em. It'd sting the eyes outta you. Swim-goggles are your best bet! Some of the guys from the office were there last year and when they finally found me they mushed tomatoes in my face and shoved loads of gunge down my T-shirt!"

"Did you get any photos?"

"No! I didn't get the chance. There were some people popping out their cameras, but not me! It seemed that the ones taking the photos were the ones that the Spaniards really went mad on targeting. I think they really don't want their festival polluted by tourists. This goes on for about an hour, and now and again another tomato-laden truck comes through the slippery crowd. The sludge on the street is about three inches deep afterwards – it smells awful! We then had to go and find some water to wash ourselves off with. It was great!"

"But *why* do they do it?"

"There's no meaningful reason. It's just for the good fun of it."

"They're mad, aren't they?"

Sinead laughed. "Yeah!"

"I'm coming over for it."

"Great!"

"When did you say?"

"August. Last Wednesday in."

"Book me in!"

"Done."

At this stage of the morning, Gertie couldn't have been further from Sinead's mind.

* * *

Ben spent four days breaking his neck to keep a low profile for fear of annoying Geri. As desperate as he was to speak to her and make some kind of peace, he found himself spending lots of time with Mark and the lads. Unsure whether or not he was doing the right thing, he assumed that if he *did* contact her she'd only tell him she needed time. Or, he wondered, was he just being arrogant? He couldn't figure it out and just couldn't do right for doing wrong! 'Confused' was a word that dominated his thoughts. In conjunction with beering it up with Mark and the footie lads, Ben also concentrated on nurturing his illustrious illustrating career, the most recent distraction of late being that he had an agent interested in representing him. Christopher Johnson rang Ben the day after his distressing indiscretion with Geri, requesting that they meet that day at two. He finally felt, despite the travesty of his relationship life, he was actually achieving something.

Facing the three-quarter length mirror in his bedroom, he panicked as he tried to pitch his clothing correctly for meeting a potential agent – it not being something that he'd had to consider much before now. Ordinarily a confident dresser, opting for smart but casual clothes in plain but complementary colours, he found himself struggling as he half-strangled himself with his tie. He cursed himself as he tried to knot the damn thing.

"Shit!" he blasted, as he looked down his nose, and slight double chin, his hands swapping over one another, holding onto the length of smooth navy silk. "If *only* Geri was talking to me! She'd know the right way to knot this! And she'd probably know the correct length. Is it supposed to cover all of my shirt buttons and hang over my waistband or should it sit above my belt? I don't know!" He was starting to lose his temper. He recalled the night they'd sat up laughing about the Gentlemen's Clubs in the City and how, over a bottle of Virgin Vodka, they'd made jokes about the different ways the gentlemen probably knotted their ties in that institutionalised, Masonic way, giving the knots themselves names: the Half Windsor and the Double Windsor. He was annoyed at himself for letting her sneak into his mind at this vulnerable stage of undress. He was due at the restaurant in Soho in forty minutes.

Arriving only five minutes late and looking extremely smart yet comfortable, Ben recognised the agent immediately, his unflattering 'mullet' hairstyle screaming. His mind, once again, flashed back to Geri and how they'd hated that 'style'. Despite introducing himself and shaking Ben's hand vigorously with his sweaty smooth one, Ben can think of no other handle for him now but 'The Mullet'. Ben was instantly put off and knew, before even sitting his bum in the shabby threadbare seat, that this wouldn't be an allegiance with a future. Full of nervous prattle, The Mullet started to pour the wine as he diversified, regaling Ben with the information that body-piercing was now so passé amongst body adorners that the new craze was for forked tongues, and how his girlfriend wanted him to have one!

Ben couldn't even imagine how he'd acquired a girlfriend. Not with *that* haircut anyway. However, he politely smiled and responded at the correct junctures, wondering when The Mullet would ever get around to discussing his illustrations. Despite Ben continually steering the conversation back to the purpose of their meeting, it seemed The Mullet's intent was on entertaining him.

As he spooned a piping hot soup-spoon of minestrone into his gaping mouth, The Mullet leant over the table and whispered, conspiratorially,

"Hey. A man goes to his doctor about his sore neck. The doctor looks worried and asks him to get up onto the couch so that he can look at it. The man obliges. Then, as the doctor scrutinises it, he says 'Hmmm. Sir, do you masturbate much?' This guy is, of course, slightly embarrassed but replies, 'Er, em. Well, yeah, I do, yes.' And do you know what the doctor says?"

Ben really didn't give a shit at this stage *what* the doctor said, but shook his head anyway.

The Mullet's face contorted into a grotesque over-smile as he punch-lined, "*Great*, isn't it!"

As The Mullet roars at his own hilarity, Ben feels the minestrone swilling in his nauseous stomach, the doctor and nurse thing only reminding him of Geri even more. Feeling an overwhelming urge to get away from this awful bloke, there being no *way* he'd give him fifteen per cent of his hard-earned and long-awaited earnings, he choked his way through the starter and, almost at the end of the main course, still hadn't managed to discuss his work, but at this stage didn't care.

* * *

Geri returned home to an irritatingly bright and *non-flashing* red light on her answerphone. In the hope that the flasher mechanism might be broken, she pressed the PLAY button anyway. It beeped at her loudly, confirming her fears. No messages. Neither Ben nor Sinead had even *tried* to contact her.

Right! That's it! Life goes on! I'll put them both out of my mind until they're ready to see sense! Bastards!

As she cooked the chicken-pie and baked-bean dinner for the children her mind rattled noisily in her head, planning the week ahead of her.

Take it in stages – one week at a time. I've messed up, big time – but it's time to move on. If I give myself small hurdles to get over, then before I know it months will have gone by. I'm lucky really that I've made some new-ish friends in Saliva and Mike at Piano and Cloud-eeahhh at Spanish. Imagine if I hadn't started the classes! I'd have no new pals to replace Sinead!

Although, in the back of her mind, she knew that her evening-class mates didn't come close to the relationships she'd had with both Sinead and Ben. As she chopped at the pies, wafts of steam rising from beneath her knife, she came to a conclusion, voicing it proudly to the unhearing pies,

"I'm leaving the Internet class! That's it – I'm going no more! I'm bored with it. I know the Net from the Web, and can even publish my own web pages. I'm au fait with Netiquette and can recognise an acronym from twenty paces."

She rested the knife and fork down, letting the dinner cool on its own.

I mean I haven't met any friends like on the other courses, she thought – only a few women who, months ago, didn't know difference between html and java, and are now bait for local office firms. I'm *not* going back!

Her positivity emboldened her, reiterating the lack of time in her life for wasting now, a new positive approach being what the doctor ordered.

New Man, New Job, New Me? Ha, just keep the order for the New Me, please! I've got a New Positive Attitude.

* * *

As the week dragged on, her panic to get out of the house so as to avoid any impending telephone calls decreased, the prospect of them now only a grim hope.

It hasn't, in fact, rung at all, except from Mum a couple of times. I even skipped my evening classes this week – for the first time! But, I must admit, I did ring Cloud-eeahhh last night. You know, for a bit of a heart-to-heart. Well! A girl needs some kind of support network!

Geri had dialled the familiar number that would connect her to Claudia's house. She both loved and hated ringing there. She loved it because there was always something totally manic going on in the background, making her own inner-city semi and its infantile inhabitants seem comfortably 'ordinary'. She hated it because she'd never know quite what mood Claudia would be in as she answered the phone, politeness and reserve not being top of her list of credentials. It seemed that tonight was one of those nights. The phone rang a few times and, knowing that she *needed* Claudia to be in a receptive mood so as to listen to her dilemma, her heartbeat pounded fiercely in her neck. Checking her watch, she saw it read nine seventeen. She hoped that Claudia's house was as peaceful and quiet as her own. She'd hoped wrongly.

"Andt faark you too, dahhlink! Sorry, Cloud-eeahhh here! Who is speeaking?" Claudia's opening gambit was, to say the least, captivating. Geri swallowed hard, contemplating replacing the receiver – she didn't think she'd get much sympathy from her tonight. Finding confidence from somewhere, she spoke.

"Cloud-eeahhh. It's Geri."

Claudia's tone altered immediately, her loud friendly voice booming down the line, "Geri, dahhlink! How vonderful to hear from you! Are we goingk out tonight, dahhlink? I can be readty in, ohh, an hour andt a harf! Oh, say two, at a push!"

Geri felt inadequate and guilty as she was about to burst Claudia's bubble,

"Em, no. I can't go out tonight, Cloud-eeahhh. I haven't got a baby-sitter. Sorry. I was actually ringing you for a chat?"

"Oh dahhlink, how lovely! Just vait a meenute, dahhlink." Geri listened as Claudia's voice became slightly muffled, as if she was addressing a third party in the room. She heard her call, "Sebastiaaan! Sebastiaaan, dahlink! Oh, dahlink, pass over my drink there, would you, love. There's a good boy now!" Then her voice tightened a little, as if annoyed, "Now, go on weeth you, please. Can't you see I'm on the phone!" The clanking of Claudia's arsenal of bangles rattled against the telephone, as she wiggled to find comfort with her vodka. She coughed loudly – ignorantly, Geri thought – into the phone and continued virtually where she'd left off. "My fucking son ees causing me nightmares." She slurped at her drink, "You know, Geri, he has just spent three hundred queed on a tattoo, some kind of friendship band around the top of his penis and now he wants the theeng pierced too! Christ, Geri! I'm getteen too oldt for all thees crap! Oh, I'm sorry, dahhlink, you wantedt to speak to me – what's wrong, dahhlink? Tell Cloud-eeahhh!"

It suddenly doesn't seem such a good idea. She's so wrapped up in herself and her materialistic life. I'd feel stupid telling her about Ben and Sinead.

As Geri skirted around the issue, she was very soon interrupted by Claudia once again.

"Oh dahhlink, haf I toldt you about Salivfa and Mike? Oh, you meesed the class thees week, too. They only havfe stood up in the class, and told everyone that they are now an 'item'. They toldt me after that they've just booked a holiday together een Jamaica – on some nudist beach or sometheeng. Ha, couldt you imagine those two weeth no fuckeen clothes on!" Claudia roared down the phone, still slurping on her drink, and judging by the amount of times she'd done it so far, Geri imagined that she had very little left in her glass by now. Making small talk with Claudia was relatively easy, you just wound her up, pointed her in the right direction and she'd rattle on for hours, so Geri was quite pleased when she finally found a pause long enough to say her goodbyes and make her excuses for hanging up. Claudia was thick-skinned, and probably thrived on it too, Geri suspected.

So, Saliva and Mike are an item. Maybe I'd get more sense from Saliva, especially now she's back in the relationship arena, what with Mike and that. I'll ring her. She'll have some advice for me.

Twenty-five minutes later, Geri had heard *the ins-and-outs of Saliva and Mike's their sex lives, their financial lives, their working lives and now their academic lives. It seemed that they were now serial-students in unison, having already earmarked the courses they'll enrol on in September – together. Wait for it, you won't believe what they've chosen! Firstly, I didn't have the heart to tell her that Fur, Feathers and Friends isn't a kinky dressing-up experience, but a painting and drawing class using animals and birds as their models. They're also interested in Feng Shui, them both hoping it will enhance their sexual selves purely by the repositioning of the candles and mirrors in the bedroom. And American Line Dancing. She was delighted that Mike already had some snakeskin cowboy boots from the seventies that he hadn't thrown out yet. I did get the chance to tell her a bit about Sinead and Ben, not too much though – I didn't want to jump in with both feet. She thinks I'm taking it all too nicely. She thinks I should be mad with them both for treating me like that in the first place. Maybe she's got a point there too . . .*

Almost overnight Geri's feelings of hopelessness mutated into a vicious wild anger.

* * *

As she stamped out of her bed at five o'clock the next morning, desperate for the loo, she realised that finally Anger had just turned up at her party.

Best friend? A stranger would have had more compassion than that! I don't need either of them. After all, what does Sinead know, snuggled into her financially secure life? Stuff her! Daddy sitting on the sidelines, cheque book and pen in hand! I've managed for the last year without her, so I can carry on quite well without her too. And Ben! Forget him! Men! Presumptuous and piss-taking. Men! They only think of themselves. The only reason he probably wants me to go with him is to cook his meals and be his 'Mummy'. He's probably terrified to go alone. Well, they can keep away from me! And my kids! I'm a lone ranger now, and proud of it! I've got a New Positive Attitude.

* * *

By the weekend Anger had dissipated into something a lot less venomous and, she could even admit, had transformed into the vein of the 'New Positive Attitude' she'd promised. The Saturday morning post had bought a lift, in the form of a letter inviting her for an interview on Monday morning. She'd applied for the position as part-time receptionist last Tuesday, two days after the row with Ben, in a bid to push her life forward and give her an importance in the scheme of things. No longer was she going to accept second-best. No longer would she be a scapegoat – a second-class citizen. The children were getting older and more independent every week, and whilst she'd called on her mum to baby-sit during evening classes, she was now going to do the same for a couple of days a week, when she'd hoped to go out to work and get her foot back firmly on the base rung of the career ladder. Cynthia, however, was enormously perplexed by this metamorphosis and made several remarks to Geri on her new-found arrogance, in a bid to get to the bottom of it and calm her down a little.

"There's no mad rush, Geraldine. One step at a time, love," or

"Darling, if you can't dazzle them with your brilliance, then just baffle them with your bullshit!"

Geri ignored every one of them, concluding vociferously to her mum that only the thick-skinned survive.

"Sure, Mum. I know it's unfortunate, but really, it's the way of the world now."

Cynthia skulked back into the confines of the lounge, muttering something about being disillusioned.

The promising news inviting Geri for the interview on Monday morning was enough to spur her on to attend her piano classes on Saturday morning. She strode into the bright, sunny classroom, supremely confident in the face of her week of disasters.

Rupert obviously wants to live life to the macs, sitting swaddled head to ankle in a nondescript raincoat. I still can't bear him, but find him quite entertaining – from a distance! They all seem strangely unfamiliar, exposing various parts of skin that has, up until now, been kept under winter clobber.

She accepted, with her new-found optimism and realism, she would never play The Swan, from the *Carnival of the Animals*, but is content that her enthusiasm has ebbed to an acceptable level so that she can now enjoy it without the need to play it. Breezing through the lesson, feeling at ease and comfortable, the week's horrors having knocked a good six pounds off her, enabling her to sit easily in her grey trousers and white blouse without them cutting welts into her waist, she can, when invited, confidently play the scales.

Whereas 'playing' the scales had, last year, only meant surreptitiously turning down the dial half-a-stone when Kevin wasn't watching in preparation for my weigh-ins.

As Four-foot, Five-foot prattled on about time signatures and beats-to-the-bar, she watched Saliva and Mike whispering and giggling at the back of the class, their romantic union excusing them from further participation. Watching the group, including the now unbearable Tony and Joan of Nark, it seemed strange, almost surreal, as the weather turned more summer-like.

It feels weird to lean back and rest my head on the ice-cold radiator, to hear the boom of the traffic speeding past the hot roads, leaving echoes from the warm tarmac to waft in through the open windows.

As she turned her concentration back on the class she heard Four-foot, Five-foot reminding them of the basics such as how a 'sharp' raises a note by a semitone, a 'flat' lowers a note by a semitone, these being the black keys which have no names of their own. "So, basically, class," he boomed, clapping his hands together for impact, "C sharp is the same as D flat. "

Well, whoopeeee!

Chapter Thirty

By the following Thursday – almost two weeks after the Screeching Geri – Ben had come to the conclusion that he had left her alone for long enough to stew, and decided to ring her. He had spent the previous week organising his new life in Cornwall, and liaising and meeting with his publishing company in the West End, discussing his contract and terms of what they required from him. The agent was, as suspected, a definite no-no, and Ben was organising things for himself, finalising his arrangements. Now, with only one and a half weeks to go before he left, he still desperately wanted Geri to go with him.

Deciding it was time to eat humble pie and to have one last stab at resurrecting the relationship, he braced himself while picking at his toast and strawberry jam, confirming that she was too good to let go. Having finally thrown on his navy fleecy joggers and cream sweat-shirt he turned up on her doorstep at nine o'clock that morning – he just couldn't wait any longer – not bad, as he'd been up since six. As he mentally repeated his speech over and over in his mind, he came to a halt, surprised to see Geri, fully made-up, her hair groomed gorgeously and dressed in a flattering linen suit, as she opened her front door.

They stood, aghast, and before they had the chance to say anything, Cynthia's head came poking around from the lounge doorway, craning to see who was at the door. On recognising Ben she smiled awkwardly, muttering to herself as she disappeared back into Geri's lounge. Geri raised her eyes heavenward, apologising for her mother quietly.

Ben was transfixed. She looked great.

"Where're you going?" he whispered, breathless.

"For an interview."

"For *what*?"

"A part-time receptionist."

I like this! He can't believe his eyes! What a stroke of luck him turning up this morning of all! It's just too good to be true. And I look great! I know I do!

"Where?" He wasn't suspecting this. She was not only getting on with her life, but, it seemed, in leaps and bounds! And in just over a week. It seemed to Ben that his actions had a greater reaction than he'd initially suspected.

"Hooden Walley Kinder." Her voice was controlled and pleasant without being too familiar.

"Where?"

She giggled, repeating the name.

He burst into laughter, all traces of their disagreement forgotten, temporarily.

"You're not serious! You won't be able to say *that* into the phone two hundred times a day, will you?" She laughed, shaking her head,

"Probably not!"

"Can I come in?"

He suddenly sounded and looked like the old Ben. The way his eyes wrinkled at the corners as he smiled, the deep, slightly vibratory voice and the way his Adam's Apple rose and fell fluidly as he spoke. Without a second thought she stepped back, inviting him in. They danced around each other awkwardly and then, unable to wait a second longer, he held her in his arms and the pain was so intense for her she began to cry. He shimmied her into the kitchen and he wiped her mascara-streaked eyes gently, reminding her of the interview, and asking what time she was supposed to be there.

"Ten," she replied, pulling herself together.

"Come on!" He took control, reaching for the kettle, filling it from the tap and plugging it in. "Just time for a quick cuppa and then I'll get the Tube with you. I'll wait for you if you like."

Her face lit up, "Oh, would you?"

"Course! Come on now, no more tears. We'll talk later."

They sit in the kitchen, taking full advantage of Cynthia being in situ to mind the kids for Geri's interview, and the next time they looked at the kitchen clock it was flashing ten twenty-three at them.

"Your interview!" Ben leapt from his seat, placing his empty mug in the sink.

Geri remained seated, calm and smiling. "Oh, don't worry about it. I didn't really want it anyway."

"But you said you did! You look fantastic too. Geri, I thought you *wanted* this for yourself?"

"What? A part-time receptionist job? No thanks." Clasping her hands in her lap she gazed down at them.

Ben noticed the spirit ebbing away from her again. He sat back down at the table with her.

"So why did you apply for it then?"

She still avoided looking at him, and her voice was small as she replied,

"I just wanted to change my life. I've messed it all up again, what with falling out with you *and* Sinead."

"Sinbad!"

Oh, it sounds so good to hear him call her that again.

"Why've you fallen out with Sinbad?"

Of course, he doesn't know, does he! How could he? Why would he? It all happened after he'd left me.

Geri slipped off her jacket and hung it on the back of the chair as she explained it all to Ben: the New Man, New Job, New Me, and the New Positive Attitude saga. She confessed how she hated herself for ruining it all, and how she really wished she hadn't been so quick at screaming at Ben.

"I suppose you'll be off next week, won't you?" she asked him.

"Yeah," he enthused, "next Friday, I think. I really can't wait, Geri. I've got a fantastic contract from Patchwork Publishers and they're more than all right about me working away from London. As long as I can courier the work to them by the deadlines, they don't mind at all."

"Have you got a picture of your cottage? You know, the one you were telling me about?"

"I have, yeah." He pulled a screwed-up piece of paper from his track-bottoms' pocket. "Funnily enough I put this in here last night to show Mark and the lads. They reckon they're all coming down to Glastonbury and to try the scrumpy. God, that'll rock the neighbourhood, that lot turning up for the weekend!"

They laughed at the image he painted.

Geri interrupted, "Glastonbury! That's not Pendennis, is it?"

"No, it's Somerset. But I suppose it's nearer to stay than London. Anyway, you know what they're like, anything for an excuse."

"Yeah," she replied, wistfully.

"Yeah," he confirmed.

Geri's stomach churned as she looked at the beautiful little cottage that Ben was going to be renting. She imagined, as Ben had described to her before, the boys playing in the paddock out the back, and her terracotta pots decorating the stone wall out the front. She yearned to still be a part of it all, sorry for all the mayhem she'd caused, but knowing it was now all too late. Ben had made up his friendship with her, but all she could do now was take it on the chin, and wish him all the best.

"Oh well." She stood, indicating that enough was enough. "Be in touch, won't you?"

He smiled at her, hugging her shoulders from a slight distance. "Course I'll be in touch. I'll write to you."

"Great."

"Great."

As they passed the lounge door Geri stuck her head in and said, "Ben's off now."

The boys jumped up, delighted to see him again. *"Bennnn, Bennnn, 'Ennnn!"*

They leapt up into his open arms and hugged him, remembering instantly the way they used to rub their noses into his cheek and playfully pinch at his nose. They all laughed together. Cynthia even rose from her chair.

"Bye, Ben," said Geri. "Good luck to you. Hope it all works well in Cornwall. Sorry to see you go though."

Her words hung heavily in the air as she choked on them, the reality speeding past all too quickly for her.

Ben charmingly kissed Cynthia on the cheek, and Geri watched him hug the children, kissing them lovingly and putting them back down. The boys settled themselves back down with their *Thomas the Tank* toys, and Geri escorted Ben to the front door, her stomach knotted and queasy.

This is it! This is the final goodbye. I think I'm gonna cry. God, let's get it over with. I feel sick.

"Well?" He said, turning on the doorstep.

"Well." Her voice was flat and unemotional as she looked down at the floor.

"Well?"

His overemphasis caused her to look up. He was standing in front of her, grinning, and dangling an old-fashioned key in front of her nose. As she tried to focus her eyes on it, its pendulum motion and close proximity to the end of her nose making it difficult, she grasped it lightly to stop it from swinging.

Ben let go of the key, letting it rest between her fingers. He repeated the question, "Well? 'Gertie'?"

"That's what Sinead calls me!"

"I know. I told you I liked it. It makes you sound old and cute and adorable."

She blushed. *I'm blushing!* "What do you mean 'well'?"

I think I might know what he means but my heart's beating so fast in my ears and I'm scared of looking a prat, so I'll just ask again to be sure.

"I mean," he spoke clearly and softly, "Gertie, will you *please* come with me to Pendennis? I respect you as an independent, and may I add extremely gorgeous, woman who will *not* be told what to do and how. I am so, so sorry for the way I asked you before. Please forgive me that. Please. But I love you and the boys very much and would like to think that we could, as a family, make a go of it in Pendennis. It's not forever. It's not set in concrete. Things go right; things go wrong. But let's give it a go, eh? Just for a year? A few months even? There's nothing to stop us from coming back here. *Not* that I'm telling you what to do, but I'm only renting my place out for an initial six months. It'll still be here if I want to come back. *If.*"

My mind is a whirl of emotions and before I realise it the tears are dropping from my eyelashes, huge and splashy on the doorstep. I finally manage to find some words.

"You mean you still want us to come with you? After the way I treated you?"

Of course the reality is that I've thought about nothing else for the whole fortnight! I know I'd love to go with him. Sure, it's what I've been convincing myself was just what we need. A new start. A new environment. But still, you know, a woman's prerogative and all that stuff . . .

"Oh Ben, I don't know. I'm just not sure. What about Hooden Whalley Kinder?"

"You said you weren't interested in them."

"Oh yeah. I did, didn't I?"

His expression dropped slightly, rattled by her lack of spontaneous response.

She spotted it instantly. "OK."

"What?"

"OK. I said OK. We'll come with you."

"You don't really want to, do you?"

"No."

His voice was despondent once again. "Please?"

She grinned widely, the teasing look twinkling in her eye once again,

"OK."

* * *

Sinead had spent the majority of her time with Jonathon Morgan exploring Valencia and discussing Geri. She had paid little attention to the hunt for her two new staff. Mr Moreno was all right with that, reiterating that it was her choice, and her back that was breaking under the pressure. On the morning of Jonathon's departure, as she stood under the cool shower, its needly shards spiking down onto her already wet hair, she decided that she would no longer be a victim to her emotions after the Steven situation. The time with Jonathon had culminated in bed and she felt totally at ease and comfortable with him, in a way that she'd *never* felt with a man before. They loved each other's company without suffocating each other. They enjoyed the same foods and drink, the same places, the same opinions even, without being competitive or boring. She was sad to be taking him back to the airport, but pleased that they'd found each other, and the most promising sex she'd had in years. And, after all, he'd be coming back within the next two months and then again in August for the Tomatina.

On the drive back to the airport Jonathon brought the subject up, once again, about Gertie, suggesting that she should try and address the situation with her.

"Well, you know," she admitted, her sun-streaked hair buffeting wildly in the open-topped breeze, "I really feel that I laid some ghosts to rest by letting it all out to Gertie."

"Well, that's a good thing for you. But for her? She really must be feeling horrible."

"I know. And do you know what the worst thing of all is? My mam made me realise, the first day after our argument, that I've been doing exactly the same thing to Gertie – by lying to her all along."

"How do you mean?" Jonathon was pleased that he had the opportunity to draw her out on this, their conversations regarding Gertie so far being mainly of the reminiscent variety.

"Well, Gertie must have a view of me as fun-loving in the sun with a whole village full of boyfriends. She'd *never* believe that I've been treated like shit for four months by an eejit like Steven Randall."

"Well, then. You know what to do. Time to be humble and pick up that phone. It's been nearly two weeks now, hasn't it?"

"Mmm." Sinead pondered as she turned, reluctantly, into the airport grounds.

Having kissed Jonathon goodbye, repeatedly, and promised to ring him the next morning from work, Sinead arrived back at her apartment just before lunch-time. She'd spent the whole journey back from the airport mulling over her approach to Gertie, realising that what Jonathon had suggested was right. It was time to salvage their friendship and sort things out.

She smoked three cigarettes and deviated wildly as she tried to busy herself with other tasks rather than address the issue in hand. She first stripped the bed, sad to wash away the scent of Jonathon but realising that it had to be done. She completed transcribing the phone numbers on the small Post-It notes in the bottom of her bag into her telephone and address book, and she washed up. Things must have been bad. Sinead wash up? Sure sign of a dilemma.

"OK," she exhaled deeply into the room, "no time like the present." As she plonked down onto her chair and dialled Geri's number she prepared to stuff her cheeks so full of humble pie that the crumbs would try and escape from the sides of her mouth, and her palate become so clogged and dry that she feared she'd never eat again.

* * *

Back in Geri's house they were celebrating. Cynthia, while sad to see her daughter and two adorable grandsons planning to leave the convenience of Elephant & Castle, was delighted that they were making a go of it with Ben – he was such a lovely man! She was excitedly writing down her order for Pizza Hut while consulting the mini-menu that had been posted through their door, as Ben and Geri had decided to order a take-away for lunch and were hugging each other excitedly in the kitchen.

"I can't believe you're really coming with me!"

"I can't believe you've actually asked me to!"

"We goeeen Dennis, we doeeen Denniss," Cameron chanted and Reece attempted to repeat, with a little difficulty.

Just as Cynthia brought her scribed request through to the kitchen, Geri excused herself for the loo, rushed upstairs, shouting on the way how she'd get her shoes while up there, and she'd be ready in two minutes.

As she reached the top stair the phone began to ring and in her over-exuberance she yelled down, "I'll get it. It's OK." Flinging herself wildly on her bed, bouncing with it as it ricocheted, she grabbed the phone, puffing into it happily. "Hello!"

"Gertie."

Fighting to catch her breath, the smile was instantly wiped from her face,

"Sinead?"

"Sorry."

"What?"

"I'm sorry." She sounded sincere, and meant it. She was truly sorry.

Geri was grateful that she'd answered the phone upstairs, away from the distractions and ear-wigging lugs of her mother, and also that she had not expected the call. It seems to help her find the right words. The words that she'd struggled with ten days ago, in the anticipation of Sinead ringing to apologise.

"I've no right to call you those names, Gertie. I've got to confess to you that I've lied to you just as much as you've lied to me."

"Don't be daft!"

"I have, Gertie. I've made you believe that I'm living the high life. I've led you think that I've got men fighting to get near me. It's not true, Gertie. I'm a fraud."

"Sinead! Don't say those things about yourself."

"It's true. I've crawled from one disastrous relationship to another, and ended up with a cocaine-addicted man who beat the shit out of me at least three times a week.

"*No!* Who was that?"

"Steven Randall."

"Steven? The Steven that you told me was mad about you?"

The pain of the confession was almost too awful to bear.

She almost whispered in response. "Make that the Steven that was mad *with* me. Constantly, and for no reason."

"God, Sinead, that's awful!"

"So, I've bed-hopped with more ugly ducklings than you could care to imagine."

Geri began to giggle, "Sounds like me!"

"Go 'way!"

"I'm telling you! I've been with a sexually-retarded coitophobic, a spare-tyre-squeezing coke-head, a –"

"You too!"

"What?"

"Coke-head!"

"Yep! I tell you what. We really should get together and compare notes."

"But what happened with Ben?"

"Oh, another long story. Well, I lost him, and then found him again. He's just come around and asked us to go to Cornwall with him."

"And are you going?" Sinead sounded excited.

"'Course we are. Anything to get away from this place."

"What about your classes?"

"They finish in June anyway. It's no problem. I've

got all I need from the Internet course, I can rattle off a few tunes for you on the piano, and can probably hold my own in a conversation with you in Spanish."

"Spanish?"

"Yeah, how about it?"

"Oh, yeah, I forgot you were doing Spanish."

"I was hoping to surprise you with it later in the year."

"Well, there's still your chance! So, why Cornwall?"

"No real reason really. I think that Ben just fancies a total change from the London scene. He wants to be somewhere where he can create and enjoy the colours and life around him. Somewhere other than the greys and pinks of Elephant & Castle."

"So, he's everything you're looking for in a man then?"

"Yes. He's perfect with the children. Patient and fun. Although it seems inherent in males for them to always wee down the side of the pan, but still, we can't have it all, can we?"

"Too many lies have gone on over the last year. I really would like to see you all, and to meet Ben. Is there any way youse could all get over here to see me in the next six weeks? It's just coming into the season now, and the weather'll be great."

"I can't afford it, Sinead. I'm not working, although I was supposed to go for an interview this afternoon for a part-time job. But until we're set up in Cornwall, and I start getting a small bit of money in, there's no way I could afford it."

"So how will you live in Cornwall then?"

"Ben got a good advance from the publishers and he's also got some money saved to cover the rent for the first two months. It'll be fine. He's a sensible guy. He's got it all calculated."

"Gertie. You're gonna hate me."

Geri's stomach churned again.

This is becoming a habit lately.

She dreaded what Sinead was about to say, for fear that she was about to confess some other awful thing that she'd just recalled. She proceeded with trepidation, "Why? What have you done?" Her tone is both cautious and nervous.

"Nothing. Yet. Gertie. Please say yes to this. You're gonna hate me chucking a spanner in the works, but please, please, please. It's just the perfect situation. I can't believe I haven't thought of it before."

"What?"

"Gertie. How would you and the boys and Ben fancy a year in Valencia? Here, with me?"

"What? Have you gone mad?"

"No! Hear me out. I'll arrange for your flights – call them my treat. Ben can create here like never before. Valencia is renowned for its colours and artwork. He'd have the sea and the sand and the sun. The relaxed pace of life would be fantastic for an artist to let his imagination wander."

"Yeah, and what about me and the kids? Where are we going to live. Where am *I* going to earn some money?"

"That, my little dirty Gertie, is exactly what I wanted you to say."

Sinead explained to her about her requirement for a secretary and administrator, and convinced Geri that she was the perfect candidate – she'd worked with Sinead before and understood what made her tick, also she had new-found Internet skills and conversational Spanish. What more could a partnership require?

"So you see, Gertie? It's just perfect!"

"God, Sinead. How exciting! I can't believe it! I've gone from so pissed off this morning, to delighted at seeing Ben and agreeing to go to Cornwall and now you're ringing and inviting us to go to Spain! God, you don't know how much I've wanted to go to all the places you've told me about on the phone for the last year! My heart's been breaking some nights as I've sat and listened to the drunks falling out of the Lambeth Walk pub or lain in bed listening to the cold rain rattling against my bedroom window with no-one to cuddle up to. What do I do now?"

"Well," Sinead laughed down the phone, "I think you'd better go and ask the boys and Ben."

"Yeah! I will. Wait there . . . " She dropped the phone on the bed, leaving Sinead to wait as she flew down the stairs, two at a time.

As she burst into the lounge she interrupted a family scene with Ben playing with the boys on the floor and Cynthia beginning to snore in the armchair. The three of them looked up at her – her wild eyes and excited expression startling them.

"What's up?" Ben asked, calm and contented as he fixed Thomas the Tank's funnel.

Geri puffed her words out in a babble, "Sinead's onthephone – Ben – standup – I needto talkto you!"

Ben led her into the kitchen. "Now, calm down. What's happened?"

She took a deep breath, composing herself, but with her mind still working overtime. "Right. Sinead is on the phone. I'll explain later, but it's all made up and OK. A misunderstanding really, more than anything. *Anyway,* I've got to ask *you* a 'well?' question now. Trust me on this one – it'll all be sorted for us."

"What's the question, Geri?"

"Right. Well, you know you said it didn't have to be Cornwall?"

He looked at her, slightly confused.

She expanded, "You know when we argued, how you tried to apologise and explain how it didn't actually *have* to be Cornwall?"

"Oh, right. Yes."

"Well, how do you fancy, instead of the cottage in Pendennis, an apartment in Valencia. For a year. At *least!*"

"What? How?"

Geri explained and Ben beamed a little, then more, and more again, and a little more, until his whole face was animated with a huge smile.

"Come on!" she yelled at him. "Sinead's waiting on the phone for our answer."

He followed her up the stairs as she leapt, three at a

time, and landed down on the bed with her, grappling for the phone.

"Sinead?" she puffed.

"Sinbad!" Ben interrupted.

"Oh you," Sinead yelled, "I heard that! You wait till I meet you!"

"Can't wait!" he laughed.

"Sinead, he said yes! *I said yes!* Yes! We'd love to come. We're so excited, yes!"

"Great! Gertie? Gertie? Gertie?"

Sinead wondered whether the lines *were* playing up as she couldn't hear any response from Geri. If she'd been able to see down the line she'd have realised that Ben had grabbed Geri by the face and was kissing her passionately on the bed, leaving Sinead hanging on the bungee-wire of the phone as they kissed.

"Gertie!" she yelled, disturbing their slobbering.

Geri picked up the phone again. "Sorry, Sinead. Look. I'll have to go and tell Mum and the boys. Let me sort out my head first, and I'll ring you tonight. We've got a lot of organising to do. When can we come out?"

"As soon as you want. I can organise a cheap place to stay through work, and you'll be on a good salary, even part-time. Don't worry about anything. Trust me, eh?"

"No problem. Sinead? Thank you, thank you, thank you!"

"Love you, Gertie."

"Love you, Sinead. Speak later, bye."

"No – *adios!*"

As they both collapsed back on the bed with a deep sigh they heard the light padding of small hands and feet as they crawled up the stairs after them, a sure sign that Nana was asleep. As Cameron and Reece's peachy faces appeared at the bedroom door Ben called them in, pulling them up onto the bed with him and Geri. The boys loved the opportunity for a bundle and immediately dived in on Ben's head.

As he was bombarded from a height, Geri tried to talk to him. "Ben. Thanks for saying you'll come. Look at me! A few hours ago you were thanking us for coming with you, and now the tables have turned! We're thanking you for coming with us!"

"Yeah," he tried to talk straight whilst being hammered on the head by small but solid arms and legs, "but what does it matter? At least we're all together. And at least we're trying something new. You know what I say about the 'what if's'!"

"Ben, I'll do my best for us, you know that. I promise that we won't become a 'Jan Steen household'."

Ben laughed out loud, wrestling the boys playfully to the floor, and hugged her.

"I can't ever see it happening, but if it does I have only one request."

"What's that?"

"Please, could I be the one that's pissed in the armchair?"

* * *

So, as I approach my thirty-first birthday the future looks decidedly bright. How I'd dreaded and loathed the turning of thirty! How I'd felt ancient, worn out and over the hill! I was overweight, overworked and underconfident. I was abandoned, desperate and unsure. And now? Now I say "roll on thirty-one!" I feel as if I've gone back ten years, and now look forward to my new life with a zest and enthusiasm that I thought had died long ago. I can even see myself having more children with Ben, pregnancy being something I would never have volunteered for again, a year ago. He's so great and natural with them, and such a devoted father-figure. God, don't go and get me all broody now! We're going to Valencia for a year – maybe two! I haven't got time for scans, and folic acid, morning sickness and antenatal classes. I lie in my bed, now cosy and comfortable with Ben beside me. I finally feel complete.

"But one thing . . . " *I snuggle into the side of his neck – it's so warm and velvety – as I whisper.*

"What?" he says.

"If we ever *did* have kids – I'd like them to take my name. What do you think? Do you mind?"

He holds me away from him, at arms' length, as he adopts a very serious expression.

"Well, no. Not if it's a girl. But if it's a boy I don't think I'd like him to be called Gertie!"

The End